Daisy Sale

Forever

By Catherine Dehdashti

Dehdashti, Catherine, 1969-

Daisy Sale Forever / Catherine Dehdashti—First American edition

Library of Congress Control Number: 2024913434

ISBN print book 978-0-9863686-0-8

ISBN ebook 978-0-9863686-1-5

www.catherinedehdashti.com

Causy Taylor Literary Publishing

For my mom, Leslie Dees Hakkola, who did her retail stint at Sakowitz department store in Houston, Texas.

"More than 350 have been with us for periods varying from ten to thirty-three years—they are in every deed 'part and parcel' of this institution; their very lives are interwoven into it; this is their store, 'our store.'"

— **A Message from George Draper Dayton,** *The Daytonews,* **January 1935**

"Denise était devenue toute rouge: entrer dans ce grand magasin, jamais elle n'oserait! et l'idée d'y être la comblait d'orgueil."

"Denise had turned very red; she would never dare to enter that great shop, and yet the idea of belonging to it filled her with pride."

— **Emile Zola,** *Au Bonheur des Dames* *(The Ladies Paradise)*

Prologue: January 2017, 700 Nicollet Ave., Minneapolis

Noelle Nichols and her cousin Mardi were not the only women photographing Macy's department store bathrooms that day. Even Mardi's brother, Bernard, in town for the weekend, let the women drag him into the ladies lounge on the twelfth floor for what could be his last chance to witness the vintage glamour.

All twelve floors might become offices if the redevelopers gutted the old brick building. This was a final farewell.

These members of the Petit retail family, originally of St. Paul, waxed nostalgic for this Minneapolis Macy's building. But it was forever Dayton's to them. That vintage glamour was all Dayton's, not Macy's. They had no such feelings for the Petit family business as they did about the flagship Dayton's store. Noelle and Mardi had belonged there at Dayton's, not at Petit's Party Central.

They'd moved on with their lives for the past ten years after Macy's, with its frightening red star, took over and let them go. Noelle, in particular, rarely let herself look back at her 17 years at 700 Nicollet Avenue.

Noelle's memories as a department store employee weren't like those she heard spilling out of the mouths of the other women funneling into the lounge on a preppy pilgrimage, reminiscing about coming downtown for lunch at the Oak Grill Room and taking a break so their grandmas could powder their noses and recapture their coiffures.

The large, round washroom was like the inside of a flying saucer. It sat between the lounging area, with its rounded sofas and nose-powdering stations, and the row of bathroom stalls. The toilet stalls were tucked off to the side of the washroom. A woman had purposes for being there above any bodily processes. More than a dozen washroom mirrors, one at each sink, reflected into each other at the vanity-in-the-round. A mother, daughter, and granddaughter could wash their hands and gaze back to the beginning of time in these mirrors together, as if to their first common female ancestor.

Or, in this case, a trio of aging cousins could stand there and take pictures in the kaleidoscopic mirrors with their cell phones like teenagers.

Bernard, satisfied with his peek into the women's lounge, left to join the line at the Oak Grill Room host desk. There hadn't been a line there in years, but news of Macy's selling the old Dayton's building brought out Twin Cities old-timers and the next two or three generations below them. He welcomed Mardi and Noelle to pay their final respects to the other vintage women's room, in the fourth-floor lingerie department, without him.

He would text Mardi when their name came up for a table.

This art deco bathroom was small, so it was a good thing nobody else was touring it at the moment. If the twelfth-floor lounge tucked away the toilets, the fourth-floor women's room put them on a pedestal. Mardi relieved herself in one of the "Free Toilets" advertised by *Gatsby*-esque lettering. The gold letters stood out against black lacquer trim separating the stalls, up one step, from the washing area.

Japanese waterlily tiles shone from the walls above heavy jade-green sinks. These sinks were not built into a vanity; rather they jutted out from two facing black and cream walls.

It was said that the new developers might preserve that bathroom. Noelle didn't care much. Unlike her cousins, she had never been brought here on shopping trips. She used the regular bathroom by the basement shoe repair counter when she worked there. Still, she aimed her iPhone at all of the elements she thought she should include in a photo composition.

It was a stretch to get the art deco "Free Toilets" lettering, the tilework, and at least one sink into frame. Noelle reclined farther in search of the wall she was sure was there to support her.

She misjudged.

The back of her skull thudded against a hefty block of jade porcelain before her whole body flopped sideways onto the floor.

"What do you mean, the wall moved?" Mardi asked before Noelle realized she had said it out loud. As Mardi crouched to help her roll to her hands and knees, Noelle looked down at the green floor tiles separating into yellows and blues in front of her eyes.

She cried out, "I have to get downstairs—I'm working the Daisy Sale. Fran will kill me if I'm late!"

"You haven't worked here for ten years," Mardi said. "And Fran Hart even longer. Let's get you to a doctor."

Noelle stood, her brain turning somersaults.

From that moment on, her head would pound every time she saw a freestanding vintage sink.

"I'll shake it off," Noelle insisted. "I know it's 2017, not 1992, and I'm not leaving until we have our last lunch at the Oak Grill Room."

Mardi's cell phone dinged. She squinted at Noelle to see if her pupils were dilating. "Our table's ready," she said. "But we're taking you to the doctor right after lunch."

They rode the elevator up and took their seats at a table near the Salisbury fireplace. Within minutes, warm buttery popovers appeared on white plates in front of them.

Next came the wide-rimmed bowls of wild rice soup. Mardi and her brother dipped big spoons into theirs, but Noelle only looked blankly ahead into the fire, her left pupil a black pool twice the circumference of the right, the last bite of her popover still between her lips.

"Uh-oh," Bernard Petit said, tilting his head toward his cousin. "Just how hard did she fall?"

Noelle planted her face into the soup.

The next thing she knew, her cousins and a friend rushed to her side in the Hennepin County Medical Center. Clearly, something had happened, but faith swelled among the group surrounding her. Noelle would recover.

"You're awake!" they cheered in unison.

All that Noelle had moved beyond, all that she had forgotten now that she was almost fifty years old, it all came back in one long stream.

She had been here before, and she remembered.

PART I. 1990-1994

1. Jubilee Sale, 1990

A self-adhering stocking began to slip from its perch on Noelle's juicy right thigh. She slid her fingers under the lace edge, yanked it back into place, and launched herself from the stock room onto the sales floor of Women's Shoes.

An onslaught of customers ("guests," as they were supposed to call them) rushed through the air door. Another flank entered through the Nicollet Avenue door and rounded the corner by the grand piano, gliding across the marble tile floor of the cosmetics department under crystal chandeliers, through clouds of perfume and face powder.

Noelle, a commissioned salesperson—or "Guest Consultant," as her name badge titled her—was in business.

It was her first big sale day—the Jubilee Sale, in fact—since she arrived at the downtown Minneapolis department store. Her assigned mentor, a third-generation Dayton's employee named Gary Gorman, assured her. "You can do it," Gary said. "All the Dayton boys had to start out just like..."

Noelle's stocking held its position. She was out on the floor before Gary could say, "everyone else."

The electric blue pumps Noelle needed sat on the highest shelf in the stock room, beyond reach of the special box-grabbing rod.

"Fuck," she said, sliding the rolling ladder into place.

Dean Ohlman, a salesman about her age, appeared. "Your customer is getting antsy," he said, averting his gaze.

If Noelle's yellow silk dress wasn't short enough already, the four-inch slit in the back guaranteed the dress wasn't made for climbing up a ladder. No one else could take the blame for her exposure since she had sewn the dress herself, bringing scandal upon her grandmother's sewing machine. She squinted to see the size printed on the box, then climbed slowly.

"These boxes are too high," she said, her caramel highlighted hair cascading further down her back as she gazed up. She reached for the size eight box just under the nine, which towered out of reach. As she jostled the size eight back and forth, up and down, she expected the size nine on top of it would slide into her waiting left hand.

The size nine started its descent, and then the top flew off as it took a nosedive.

Dean lurched forward to catch the lidless box, the two blue pumps, and a sheet of white tissue paper between his arms and his broad chest. Noelle glanced down at him in his suit.

All the salesmen had to wear suits, of course. This wasn't some mall kiosk—it was Dayton's flagship store, established in 1902.

But none of the other men looked like Dean, with whom women more beautiful than Noelle, like Allison from Women's Accessories, loved to flirt. It wasn't that he wore a suit so fine or a shirt so crisp, or how his garnet tie was only slightly darker than his burgundy lips, which now parted but made no sound. He stood there as if it had all landed in his arms from outer space, then stuffed the shoes and tissue back in the box.

"Thanks," she said, looking over her shoulder and grabbing the ladder sides with both hands, but she didn't hear a response.

Dean hadn't tried talking to Noelle much yet. He hadn't even mentioned that one tanning bed commercial for Petit's Party Central everyone had seen. Finally, he bent his neck back and peered up at her. The Dayton's employee dress code required pantyhose, but Noelle's ended on the way to the top of each thigh, where they defied gravity, as Dean could now see from his advantageous angle. He wouldn't have known about the science behind the magic.

The stockings stayed up thanks to grippy beads of silicone distributed along the inside of wide lacy bands that encircled her thighs. She'd discovered the miraculous invention in the hosiery department, but they'd been invented in 1967, the year of her birth.

Noelle turned herself around to face Dean, a precarious stance in her sling-back heels. His eyes swept over her, above him in her frothy lemon soufflé of a dress. He held the shoebox out and Noelle stepped down, both hands bent backward gripping the wooden ladder. On the next rung, her hemline reached eye level. She stayed for a moment on the next rung down, liking how Dean's head lined up with the spot on her body she was suddenly thinking about pressing him into.

Two more rungs and her full breasts met Dean's eyes, those eyes made bluer against his hair matching in walnut color and end-of-summer streaks the hair of the boy she'd loved from the third to the twelfth grade.

That boy was beside the point. A dead end for her. But Dean's round cheeks, too, brought back that feeling she had back then.

If she let go now, maybe she could fall back in time, back to the day she met that boy at the baseball diamond, and life could start over from there.

On the lowest step, their eyes met with split-second intensity. Dean leaned toward her with the shoebox. "Here," he sputtered. Hot steam spread up through Noelle's body, then dissipated across her cheeks.

"I owe you one," she said as she took the box and walked out to her customer, who asked for another style and another until she left Noelle knee-deep and commissionless in the pile of shoeboxes and tissue paper.

She got lucky with her next customer (Donna Karan boots, not even discounted for the Jubilee Sale) and won the praise of her department manager, Fran Hart. It wasn't easy to win Fran's praise, but the boots were nine hundred dollars and Fran was in a Jubilee competition with Handbags for a big prize from the first-floor manager. Noelle knew Fran didn't choose her. Human Resources did the hiring. The nine-hundred dollar boots seemed to ease Fran's doubts and she put one arm around Noelle's shoulder for a second before chastising her for not selling her some shoes, too.

"Hug them with one arm and punch them with the other," the manager in Handbags had advised Fran years ago.

At the end of the day, Noelle clocked out on an ancient Simplex machine, pleased at how the others were impressed by her thirty-five hundred dollars of sales. She'd sold more than almost anyone, including one style of Ferragamos in every color—black, red, and teal green—to a cereal company heiress.

Teal green shoes? Well, she'd bought a teal green dress, so of course. It was 1990. Fashions matched.

There were twenty-four employees in Women's Shoes. Other than a couple of managers, such as the thirty-something Fran who was too private to even make a guess about, the other staff craved to be paired up like the shoes they tried so hard to sell.

Most of the women felt hopelessly romantic toward a male theater student. Theater boy, in turn, felt drawn toward the male engineering student from Iran, who in turn worshipped an Amish maiden with an overbite, ne'er returned to Harmony, Minnesota, after her *Rumspringa*. She was in love with Kalmer, a graphic artist only working there until he could find a job in his field. Kalmer sported spiral curls and Minnesota Vikings tattoos of his own design covering one forearm. Kalmer was kind to everyone, so it was hard to know if he had any return interest in the Amish-country exile. That was okay; she also liked a twenty-six-year-old with one foot in the real estate market. He dated a forty-five-year-old temptress who wore brick-colored lipstick and kept her figure fresh by drinking gallons of water and smoothing her cellulite with a rolling pin.

Then there was the tall and graceful freelance display designer with long, golden hair. Every man was in love with Ralphina Beranek in one way or another. Watching her moves as she created the tableaux of shoes for each season was like being treated to a performance at the Ordway. Even Gary Gorman, ever devoted to his wife, called her Ralphina the Ballerina.

And with whom was Noelle Nichols hopelessly in love?

Nobody at the department store, not even the dashing Dean. A few mid-career men had tried talking to her—they were the ones who probably stayed up late in hope of catching that commercial with her sprawled out in a tanning bed in her hot-pink bikini. She'd sewn the bikini herself, holding it together more with string than seams.

Most likely, the men imagined tugging on those little string bows. Perhaps it was her appearances on those Petit's Party Central TV commercials that made Fran doubt Noelle's seriousness at Dayton's. A bikini might help her family sell tanning beds, but not women's shoes.

Gary, too much of a talker to pretend he hadn't seen Noelle in the commercials, asked her if she was a part of the Petit family. But he was a loyal enough friend to Fran to keep it to himself that Fran had a connection, although long-lost, to the Petits. Gary knew Fran wouldn't want him gabbing about that. He did mention knowing of Noelle's cousin, Mardi, up in the Dayton's business offices.

Noelle didn't know that Fran knew her cousins from out west of Minneapolis who had even less to do with Petit's Party Central than she did. She just assumed Fran didn't like her. Noelle didn't even like herself much since failing to get a "real job" after college. Her beauty, deepened by the potions sold only yards down the marble walkway from her own department, helped with her self-confidence.

Blisters stung the bottoms of Noelle's feet after the long day, but such was the life of a *shoe dog*. Like a hunter's bird dog finding and retrieving ducks from a marsh, shoe dogs ran all day to fetch shoes from the cavernous stock room. Noelle felt like a dog that should be shot and put out of its misery. Others admired her ability to wear such high heels at work, so she kept it secret that the concrete stock room floor bruised the balls of her feet, which bore the weight of her curves.

She said a silent prayer: *Dear God, please return me to the wealth of my ancestors so I don't ever have to run on concrete for a paycheck forever.*

A return to the wealth of her ancestors wouldn't happen here, not unless she parlayed the job into a successful search for a rich husband. (Maybe the men's shoe department would give her a chance, her mother, Annette, had suggested.) Still, she was getting something from this place: first crack at the merchandise, the glamour of walking under crystal chandeliers to the Lancôme counter when she forgot to toss a lipstick into her purse, the employee discount of twenty percent.

The Marketplace Deli, one short escalator ride below, sold Leeann Chin fried rice and cream cheese puffs. There were carob chips for the frozen yogurt and wall-to-wall glass cases filled with not only gummi bears and gummi strawberries, but with Noelle's deceased grandmother's favorite chocolate star nonpareils.

Yet, it wasn't only material delights. Noelle was good at something for once. People included her in their stock room conversations. Some didn't even connect her to Petit's Party Central and their stupid commercials.

Maybe it wouldn't hurt to settle in here for just a little while, she thought.

And so, like many others who at first told themselves Dayton's was just a way station at a crossroads in their lives, she stayed.

2. Bus Stop, 1990

Fran Hart rode the bus through South Minneapolis, taking in the view on her way to her evening shift as one of the managers of the women's shoe department. It had been a dry fall and the Van Dusen mansion's burning bush hedge glowed in the late afternoon sun, like flames creeping up the pink Sioux quartzite exterior. The home that had once belonged to a grain tycoon now sat empty after having long served as the Aveda beauty school where Fran got her glossy black hair cut. Her thoughts wandered until she reached her downtown stop at the Eighth Street side door of Dayton's.

She stood up, then paused.

Even in his long coat and hat, the man talking to Mardi Wirt was easy to recognize. He peered toward the oblong windows of the bus door that was about to fold open and eject Fran onto the sidewalk. At the same time, Noelle Nichols nearly clipped him as she ran along the sidewalk in ridiculous stilettos. They exclaimed something and hugged before he looked back toward the bus. Noelle recaptured his attention. The bus door opened. Fran sat, deciding to ride to the next stop.

Stupid Noelle wore no jacket—just some shiny blouse and skirt. She sported that fake bronze skin, absurd in autumn when every other white northerner molted their tan in exchange for a winter pallor.

Fran alighted from the bus after it passed Nicollet Avenue under the acanthus-leaf-edged round windows of the Dayton's building. Golden finials punctuated the ends of flag poles beaming out from their seats in the brick at regular intervals. Nobody noticed these ornamentations anymore since they all now entered the building through the parking ramp or skyways.

She entered Dayton's through the J.B. Hudson jewelry store, briskly walked to the employee door looking out onto the bus stop, and saw the man shake someone's hand. Mardi Wirt—formerly Mardi Petit—was suddenly standing a foot behind her.

"Don't worry. My brother wasn't here to find you," Mardi said, pugilistic in stance although a head shorter than Fran.

"I wouldn't think so," Fran said, although Mardi's brother—Fran's old high school sweetheart—had shown up there to try to talk to her a few times. Fran rarely had anything to say to Mardi, but she couldn't help asking, "What *was* he doing here? And..."

"He was visiting someone downtown about funding for the school where he teaches," Mardi said.

Fran didn't know anything about Bernard's life now. She repeated Mardi's words,"Where he teaches?"

It had been years since the day Mardi discovered her brother's old girlfriend working at Dayton's. She'd pressed her about why she hadn't shown up to meet Bernard at Pepperdine University in California, about why she ditched him when it was her dream to go there in the first place.

"I thought he looked right at me through the bus window," Fran said.

"If he saw you, he didn't say anything."

Fran gave a thankful roll of her head from shoulder to shoulder, although it was hard to be sure there wasn't a modicum of disappointment in her eyes.

"It's been fourteen years since my dad and I went out there to calm him down after he found out you weren't coming," Mardi said. "He wanted to drop out before school even started. He tried to call you so many times."

"I know, I know," Fran said, then sang a snippet of a Crosby, Stills & Nash song. "From a noisy bar in Avalon, I tried to call you..."

"You're weird as ever," Mardi said, turning away. But the song was the truth. Her brother had called Fran from that town on Catalina Island after he'd joined a sailing excursion there to try to forget about her.

"I see he still hasn't quit smoking," Fran said to Mardi's back. She'd noticed the lit cigarette he held low by his legs. She wondered if it was a Merit. Bernard never wanted to be the Marlboro Man. Maybe if the Marlboro Man rode a boat instead of a horse.

Mardi kept walking and Fran went to stash her St. Louis Cardinals tote bag in her stock room locker. Her parents had moved back to Missouri after years of making a family and a home in Minnesota, and she'd just come back from visiting them.

Gary Gorman limped lightly (high school hockey injury) alongside her, uncharacteristically quiet. He hardly ever shut up, and she regretted the slow nights on the sales floor when she let herself talk, too. She'd divulged too much and now he gave her advice about it all. She hoped he didn't launch into it again—how she'd told him Pepperdine had been her idea, how she said she preferred to shake up a conservative school than float along at one that already had a women's studies department. She didn't need Gary to remind her how she told her high school boyfriend that the name Pepperdine made her taste peppermint and ocean air and that she couldn't wait to go sailing there with him. It was all too long ago. It didn't matter anymore.

Finally, Gary said, "Noelle is a Petit. She's *his* cousin. Younger than him and Mardi both. Their dad's sister's kid." Fran turned away, annoyed they'd had those conversations.

The Petits were none of his business. He hardly knew Mardi. He'd only met Bernard when Bernard had come in to try to get to the truth with Fran. Gary, big butt-in-ski, somehow small-talked him until they'd landed on the topic of hockey, sealing their acquaintanceship.

It was hard enough to avoid Mardi, who worked in the Dayton's marketing and advertising units. Once, Fran had narrowly missed running into Bernard's mother, Irene, when Irene came to have lunch with Mardi in the Oak Grill Room. Irene booked through Women's Shoes, gripping tightly to her Louis Vuitton purse, a thick spackling of Lancôme covering her cotton candy pink face, her hair freshly frosted. That day, Fran wore a now-vintage Diane von Furstenberg wrap-around dress Irene gave her long ago. She supposed Irene intended for her to wear it when she accompanied Bernard to the Wayzata Country Club instead of showing up in her women's lib t-shirts. The melon-colored dress was still structurally sound; it was too good of a dress to give up.

(A necklace with a sailboat charm Bernard had once given Fran was also too pretty to give up, but she kept that stowed in her jewelry box.)

So, as if working in the same building with Mardi and nearly running into Bernard and Mardi's mother were not enough, now she had to supervise Bernard's bimbo cousin.

And, damn, she had those same hazel eyes to remind her of him, too.

3. The Infirmary, 1990

Mardi Wirt dug through cardboard boxes of theatrical costumes and props and pulled out a studded black leather jacket. No, it didn't have enough heft to be leather. Vinyl, then. Who knew what that was used for? It looked like something her ex-husband (the one who'd given Mardi Petit the name Wirt) would have worn for one of his punk rock concerts. She'd left him, having decided he wasn't much of a man, and Mardi was sure of one thing. She wanted to be married to a real man.

She put it back and kept digging.

Well, she was pretty sure, at least, about wanting to be married to a man. She did like men—solid and handsome men, not skinny little wisps jumping up and down on the stage like her ex. So, it would seem like the first person to catch Mardi's eye after the divorce would be some tall beefy guy with a strong jaw.

The person to catch Mardi's eye was indeed toned and tall, but it wasn't a beefy guy. It was the beautiful display designer, Ralphina Beranek. Ralphina the Ballerina. They called her that upstairs, too.

Ralphina was the reason Mardi was up on the abandoned tenth floor of Dayton's just now. She'd sent Mardi on an errand for some old backdrop for an ad related to the upcoming holiday exhibit in the eighth-floor auditorium. It was *Peter Pan* this year, and Ralphina had recalled the perfect iridescent fabric for Neverland up there in the heaps of old things.

The freelance display designer was probably five years older than Mardi, not that she knew her well enough to guess her age. She didn't, not at all. And she was one of those women whose age was hard to tell. She had golden hair, but her skin was the light ageless brown of a fresh acorn.

It wasn't the first time the freelancer had insubordinately demanded something of Mardi, and there was something about the way she knew exactly what she wanted and where it was that excited Mardi and made her want to go fetch. She looked forward to seeing what creation Ralphina would conjure. It was always something a little weird. Not just normal art deco, for example, but art deco sci-fi cowgirl pop.

Mardi admired Ralphina's freelance spirit, like how she didn't care about company benefits or stacking up within the hierarchy. Like how she always dressed in layers and stripped them off when she worked up a sweat creating the displays. Like how her displays never came off as being about selling the merchandise. Ralphina Beranek's displays let the merchandise live inside a story, little worlds of their own.

The tenth floor was a jumble and it smelled like decaying silk and old boxes. Good design materials and display pieces weren't kept there. It functioned as a forgotten attic for the old junk nobody needed until they suddenly had to have it.

The advertising and marketing department managers were always meaning to figure out what to do with the broken display cubes, the stacks of old drawings for ads promoting the dresses and fur coats of yesteryear, and the bolts of yellowed satin display-case linings rolling around in a dusty area that had long ago been an infirmary for sick employees and customers. Although it was nothing more than a nurse's station, a placard on the wall named it the "Hospital."

Mardi had first discovered the archeological relics of the tenth floor when looking for vintage Dayton's hatboxes to feature at an event for the company's eighty-fifth anniversary in 1987. These were the kinds of things she did as a marketing-advertising liaison, MAL for short. Mardi could have complained about the acronym, knowing *mal* meant "bad" or even "evil" in French, but she instead regarded her title with dark appreciation.

Dayton's had five separate elevators lined up in a row to make sure everyone had a ride to and from any of the accessible floors. The first five floors were retail. Six, seven, nine, and eleven were administrative. Eight was the auditorium for the festive walk-through holiday exhibits and the spring flower show put on in collaboration with Bachman's Floral. Twelve was the fancy Oak Grill Room and Sky Room, where everyone of any means (or who wanted to look it for a day) had dined with their family after a successful round of shopping.

The tenth floor wasn't accessible from those elevators now. A flat, round slug took the place of what should have been the numeral 10. Floor ten had to be accessed by the same employee freight elevator that also went to the subterranean loading dock. The escalator would only bring you to a locked door.

You could take the employee stairs to the tenth floor, which Mardi did more regularly than any of her colleagues would know, but not usually for backdrops and display props. She went to visit the relics of the old store hospital.

In a place like downtown Minneapolis, one had a variety of places to take a break. The city's center was connected by skyways, clear glass hamster halls for scurrying into any boutique, office building, or café without ever going outside.

Mardi liked to take her breaks in the infirmary instead. There was a bed in there.

She also happened to keep a special treat in the infirmary cabinet: a black glass bottle of Madeira, a brandy-fortified wine she'd developed a taste for during a college trip to France, Spain and Portugal. Mardi found the shimmery backdrop Ralphina wanted, then she opened a mint green metal cabinet and pulled out her bottle. She opened it and took three sips, savoring each one.

What could be wrong with that? Didn't there use to be a bar cart in every executive suite? Well, maybe not at Dayton's. They were Presbyterians.

The white metal patient bed beckoned her, but she resisted it this time. The mattress was some sort of ancient vinyl with no sheets on it. Next to the bed, on a small metal table, sat a nurse's cap from a bygone era.

Mardi picked it up and put it on. A small mirror on the door of another cabinet showed how she would have looked as a nurse in the olden days, with her geometrical brunette hair topped off by the efficient-looking cap.

"Smart," she pronounced to her reflection.

Maybe she should have gone to school for nursing instead of for teaching French, since that hadn't done her much good. Besides her work as a MAL, she picked up part-time substitute teaching gigs at her brother Bernard's school. This was her life now.

A drawer still held an old hot water bottle, made of rubber covered in plaid fabric, with a wide stopper. Mardi pulled open another drawer and found a clipboard and a yellowed patient log last signed by a nurse named Thora Moholt in 1957.

Mardi took one more sip of the rich wine. It was almost syrupy, like cough medicine. "Thanks, Nurse Moholt," she said, pushing the cork back into the bottle and returning it to the cabinet.

Mardi was sure she was not in love with Ralphina. It was just one of those "girl crushes" she'd heard of. She knew she didn't love her because she didn't want to kiss her. If kissing had been part of her dreams about Ralphina, as it had been about certain boys and men in her life, then she might have worried that she was gay. But, no, Mardi was sure that she had never thought about kissing Ralphina.

Of course not. She was a perfectly normal heterosexual woman who just happened to be imagining putting both her hands up a display artist's sleeveless turtleneck sweater to feel those firm buttons she'd seen poking out.

Mardi returned to the design studio with the Neverland backdrop, but Ralphina was gone.

"Where's the display freelancer?" she asked the only other person in the department.

"Some sort of family emergency," her teammate said. "She was supposed to be working late tonight, but there was a phone call and then someone came and got her."

Ralphina didn't return for several weeks. A death in the family, Mardi heard, but she never asked. By the time she came back, the 1990 holidays were in full swing, which meant it was practically time to start worrying about next year's project. The far-off 1991 holiday exhibit was to be *Pinocchio,* and when Ralphina returned to work, she was already on the hunt for Italian display items. Not just Italian, but the perfect Florentine village whimsy to bring Geppetto's wooden puppet to life.

4. *Dudley Briars, 1991*

Working in retail was like farming. It was all about the seasons. There was always planting season, and there was always prom. Ralphina Beranek traipsed toward the design studio, lugging a bolt of taffeta for the spring prom shoe display.

"There's a phone call holding for you," a receptionist called out.

The freelancer had only given the number to a few people. It had been several months since that horrible day when one of those people had called. Now, every time she received a call the ground froze beneath her feet.

"This is Ralphina Beranek," she said. She hoped it was the real estate agent. Or maybe the Zen Meditation Center on Lake Calhoun calling to say her name had risen to the top of the waiting list for the Saturday seminar.

"Hello, Ms. Beranek, this is the nurse from Dudley Briars Elementary. I'm sorry to call while you're working, but we're going to need you to come and pick up Owen as soon as possible. Please meet him in my office."

Ralphina dropped the taffeta. "Is he okay?"

"He's physically fine," the nurse said, "but otherwise in need. Please come right away."

Ralphina ran back to the studio to get her purse, then proceeded toward the employee exit next to Women's Shoes, where she was supposed to connect with Fran Hart, department manager, in another hour.

"I'm sorry," said an employee whose nametag read
Noelle, Guest Consultant. "Fran forgot to bring her lunch,
so she went down to the Marketplace Deli."

"I have to run," said the freelancer. "Can you please tell
Fran that my nephew is sick and I'm going to pick him up
from his school? It's not far though. I'll need to postpone
our two o'clock an hour or so."

Before Noelle could answer, Ralphina was out the door,
her long hair flying behind her, making her look more like
a teen superhero on TV than a freelancer born in 1956.
Within moments, she was in her boxy little car, spiraling
down five levels of the Dayton-Radisson parking ramp.

"Another reason why I had to move him to Dudley
Briars," she said out loud in the car. "So I can get there
quickly. Again." Dudley Briars was the best public
elementary school in Minneapolis, situated in Ralphina's
Kenwood neighborhood where she rented an apartment in
an old Victorian mansion.

"You can go right in," said the secretary, recognizing
Ralphina from the previous week's incidents. It was her
nephew's third week in the school.

The pang for her own mother she felt every time she'd
seen this nurse hit Ralphina's chest like a rubber bullet.
Vilda Beranek had also been a school nurse, at the private
Highcroft Elementary in Wayzata where Ralphina and her
sister went to school. She'd worn her candlelight-colored
hair in the same loose ringlets around her face as the
Dudley Briars nurse.

Owen sat in a chair, holding a rock that he always
kept with him. A magazine photo of a Minnesota loon
was decoupaged onto its smooth surface and shellacked
into place. He pocketed the loon rock and climbed onto
Ralphina's lap. The nurse called the teacher out of her
classroom and told Owen he needed to stay so his aunt and
teacher could talk.

Ralphina held Owen's hand while they waited for the teacher to find someone to watch her class. "Aunt Ralphy's got you. I'm sorry this is still so yucky for you. It's the pits, the absolute pits."

The acknowledgment was what he needed, and he snuggled into her. "I tried to tell the teacher not to make you leave work again," he said, biting the corner of his mouth. "I wasn't being bad. She just didn't like my picture of Mommy and Daddy."

The nurse came in to indicate Ralphina could meet with the teacher in a conference room now, and she got out a Candy Land game to play with Owen.

The teacher motioned her to sit down. "Owen is just so lost without his...mother," she said. It was obvious when people didn't know if they should mention Owen's father too, or not, since he had killed Owen's mother and then himself. Owen's mother, Catherine, had been Ralphina's older sister.

Ralphina's eyes were dry. She wanted the teacher to get on with it. "What happened today?"

"You know I'm not a psychologist," she said, clearly about to dispense psychological advice, "but I think he may need more help than he's currently getting."

"He's a six-year-old boy. He needs time. What happened?"

"He didn't shriek or cry much all week, so that was good. But during free time, he drew this." She pulled a piece of paper out of a yellow folder.

Owen had drawn the earth. High above it floated a man and woman. The woman's head lay limply on her shoulder, but she sat up. Next to her, blood spurted out of a hole in the man's head. Both smiled, dressed up as if at a ball. He'd drawn their hands clasped together. Animal-shaped clouds drifted under their feet, a loon's tremolo call echoing up to them in musical notation. The detail and perspective were beyond what kids twice his age could draw, but the horror was what the teacher noticed. The contrast of those smiling, loving faces against such violence.

"It's good work," said Ralphina. That much had to be said. "And he's processing."

"Yes, in front of the other children. I thought you took him out of his Wayzata school for a fresh start. He won't get that if he keeps sharing what happened."

Ralphina stared at the drawing. Owen had illustrated the incongruity of the violent act just as she'd felt it too. What on earth had made Andrew do it?

The teacher took a deep breath. "He told me, and his whole table of peers, that he wants to go live with his mom and dad in heaven. In my sixteen years of teaching, I've never heard a six-year-old talk about committing suicide. It's certainly not what Dudley Briars parents expect their kids to come home talking about."

"I don't think he meant he wanted to commit suicide. A six-year-old wanting to see his parents—that's normal. He wants to see them, and they are in heaven. That doesn't equate to suicide."

"That's not the way the other parents here at Dudley Briars are going to see it."

"Please drop this 'here at Dudley Briars' business," Ralphina insisted. "What happened is not normal anywhere, so don't tell me he doesn't belong *here at Dudley Briars*."

"I've talked to the principal. She's out at a workshop, but she will call you. I just wanted you to know that I understand it's hard for Owen."

"Damn right it's hard," Ralphina said. "He saw his father try to move his mother's strangled body and then give up and shoot himself in the head. Andrew told Owen he loved them, and then he kissed him on the cheek and shot his own brains out. The poor child tried to clean it up before he went to get the neighbor because his grandma always said you shouldn't have people come over when the house is messy."

The teacher swayed in her seat for half a minute. Ralphina slumped in her chair, refusing to fill the awkward silence.

"Good God, I'm sorry for all of you. I know it's not easy losing your sister and raising your nephew through this. Owen said he recently lost his grandma too. And his grandpa?"

"He lost my mother to an aneurysm shortly before he lost his own mother. His grandpa is alive but has Alzheimer's. It's a blessing my dad never understood what happened."

"And this all happened in the house where Owen and his parents lived?"

"Yes, my sister and her husband took over the house our dad had built for our mom. It was in our family since the 1940s, and so Owen lost that as well."

The pen made a scratching noise as the teacher jotted down a few notes, for what purpose Ralphina had no idea. Perhaps they weren't even about Owen. Maybe it was her grocery list.

Ralphina continued, "He also lost his other grandparents. After Andrew killed Catherine, Andrew's parents couldn't take the gossip and skipped town. They've never even called to see how he's doing. So you can see, it's been very hard for Owen to sustain any connections."

"And it's been hard for you, too," said the teacher, trying to sound more sympathetic. "I just think...*we think*...Dudley Briars isn't the right school for him. The principal will tell you. Owen needs resources we can't offer here."

"It's a public school. You can't kick him out after three weeks. You aren't allowed to do that." Ralphina stared at the teacher. "Owen needs to be in a school near where he lives now, near where I live and work. And where he can feel like nobody is giving up and kissing him goodbye again."

The teacher chose her words. "It is a public school, but in a lot of ways here at Dudley Briars we are more like a private school, and we just don't have the help they have at some of the public schools that are resourced for such *social issues*."

"You're not like a private school. You're like all public schools would be if they were resourced nearly as well as Dudley Briars. I'll be talking to the district about this."

The teacher waved her hands in front of her face and tried to smile. "Please don't misunderstand. I will let the principal handle it with you from here."

"I'll be home tonight for her call."

Ralphina slid back into the nurse's office just as Owen's plastic gingerbread pawn jumped to the next blue square matching the card he'd drawn. She waited, and in another minute, he called, "Candy Land!"

He didn't seem that depressed. He looked up at his aunt and asked for a piece of drawing paper. She told him he could draw later.

"Ralphy?" Owen studied his aunt, who looked so much like his mother. Owen looked more like his father, Andrew Hess. "Should we go over to my old house and see if it got sold yet?"

"It didn't, Owen. I would know because I'm in charge of it now."

"Okay, then are we going home now?"

"Nope, I need to go back to work. You know I get paid by the hour, and until the house sells, we need every penny." Kids weren't welcome visitors at the office, but it wasn't like she had a choice.

They drove from the Kenwood neighborhood, back along Hennepin Avenue by the Walker Art Center and St. Mary's Basilica, then pulled into the parking ramp. They took the stairs down to the main floor of the department store and then the elevator up to the design studio. Owen sat alone with paper and colored pencils while Ralphina headed back down to Women's Shoes.

"I'm back," Ralphina said to Noelle, the same young saleswoman who had been there before.

"Oh my God, I forgot to tell Fran," she said, clearly annoyed with herself for forgetting but not exactly apologizing either.

Ralphina made a face. *Forgot to tell her?*, her expression seemed to say. She summoned her Zen compassion by looking into Noelle's hazel eyes.

Noelle didn't notice any Zen compassion. "She didn't seem to be looking for anyone," she said, fiddling with her nametag and adjusting a satin bra strap.

"I came back from picking up my sick nephew just to meet with her about the prom shoe display," Ralphina said. "Is she still here?"

"She went home—it was a shorter shift for her today. She works nine to nine tomorrow," Noelle answered. Ralphina hung her head.

"How's the little guy?" asked Noelle, as if Ralphina had anything more to say to the irresponsible member of Fran's team. With Ralphina's hair hanging over her face Noelle couldn't see her expression, which was a wide roll of the eyes. Her hair fell in the same long waves as when she was twelve, but with the more layered cut of 1991.

"Fine. I was going to let him hang out up in the design studio while I met with Fran. But there's no point in him being here now," Ralphina said.

"But if he's sick, shouldn't he go home anyway?" Noelle asked.

"He's not actually sick," Ralphina said. Then for no reason besides just getting it off her chest to this utter moron, she added, "Just school problems. The staff has decided his new school isn't a good fit for him. Or he isn't a good fit for them because his artwork disturbs the tiny princes and princesses of Minneapolis."

Noelle paused. She was about to say something, but then closed her mouth and listened for more. It was something she'd learned in the Dayton's sales orientation. *Listen for their needs.*

Ralphina said, "Never mind. It was a mistake to bring it up. I mean, I'm not asking for your advice. It's not like you are likely to be the guardian of any traumatized kiddos."

Noelle wiped away a fallen mascara-coated eyelash. "No, but my cousin, Bernard Petit, is a teacher at Twin Cities Success School. It might be a good school for your nephew if he has trauma stuff. He wouldn't be unusual there. And he wouldn't freak anyone out."

Ralphina told Noelle the short version of how he had lost his parents, something she had not discussed with anyone at Dayton's. Noelle didn't seem too bright. But she had been nice enough to ask and offer an idea.

"Please tell me more," Noelle implored, a useful line from the Dayton's customer service training scripts. Ralphina responded about the gruesome picture Owen drew of his parents. Noelle refused to wince, instead recounting the benefits of the Twin Cities Success School.

"He's only in first grade and your cousin's school sounds like a rough place," Ralphina said. "He needs a place that will let him be creative. It's how he copes."

"Bernard told me the school is *strengths-based*. If they don't have an art teacher, they'll find ways to pull that out in him, and they'll let him draw whatever he wants." With that, Noelle turned toward an oncoming customer.

Ralphina returned to the design studio more relaxed. She let Owen come down and help her with the prom shoe display. They could tweak it later if Fran wanted something different. What they left in their wake that evening sparkled so magically that Fran, Noelle and all the other shoe dogs would wish they had a dance to attend that spring.

And, of course, Noelle couldn't resist trying on—and buying with her discount—the exact pair she would dance in all night if only she could do prom all over again.

5. Twin Cities Success, 1991

It was the fall of 1991, a year since Bernard Petit had seen Fran Hart through the bus window in downtown Minneapolis. He smoked behind the wheel of his car, his mind drifting from the upcoming hockey season to a time long ago. He inhaled on his Merit cigarette, then forgot to exhale as he remembered the rainbow-striped maillot Fran wore on his sailboat during the summer of 1976.

It was fifteen years ago, but he would never forget.

Fran wouldn't wear a bikini because they "objectified women," but once out on the waves, she pulled the one-piece down to her hips to let her skin drink in the sun. The gold sailboat pendant he'd given her shone between her breasts atop a hot little slick of lemony Jean Naté body oil.

The car several car lengths in front of Bernard halted. Bernard snapped back from his reverie, coughing up a cloud of Merit smoke that shone almost yellow in the morning light. He braked hard and the car behind slammed into him. All of his senses heightened, Bernard pulled over onto the shoulder. Surely there would be damage.

"You can't say that was my fault!" the man yelled at Bernard as he opened his door. "You can't stop like that in this kind of traffic."

Bernard waved at his hefty rubberized bumper. "I don't see any damage and I'm not hurt. Are you?"

"No, so let's just call this a meet-and-greet and be on our way," the man said. They both got back in their cars and continued on their routes.

As he continued his morning drive southward from his girlfriend's place in White Bear Lake, he chastised himself about his distracted driving. It had taken him years after Fran ditched him to get over her. Those memories of sailing with her had disappeared, until now.

When he'd seen her a year ago, he'd just run into his sister and their cousin, Noelle Nichols, and he'd only glimpsed

Fran for a split second. He could barely see her through the bus window, and she was covered in a fall overcoat, but he wanted her just as much as ever. He remembered the last time he'd visited her at Dayton's after Mardi had tipped him off that she worked there. She showed no interest in talking. He hadn't waited around for her that day. Anyway, he had someone.

He couldn't promise himself he wouldn't try to see her again, though. What had happened to Fran was the biggest mystery of Bernard's life. He couldn't let go of the desire to know why she'd ditched him.

Bernard and Fran had received their acceptance letters to Pepperdine University the same day. It was the late 1970s. Fran went with her mother to visit family in Missouri the summer before college was to start, but it was meant to be only a short time apart before meeting up on the southern California campus. So why didn't she show up, and why wouldn't she talk to him when he called her except to make their breakup official? And why, now fifteen years later, was she managing a shoe department instead of working on international women's rights and writing novels as she planned to do?

If his current girlfriend knew he was thinking about Fran, a topless memory no less, she'd be furious. If only he could wish the thoughts away. "Get with the program," he told himself. It was the same thing he said to his students.

Life at Twin Cities Success, where he taught economics and life skills to at-risk boys, demanded a mind and a half. He had no time here to reminisce about his teenage years. At this school, it was all hands on deck all the time.

Things had been even harder lately. It started with the whole Gulf War, in which one of his recent high school graduates was killed by so-called *friendly fire*. Then the recession hit the school's budget. Maybe his mother had been right to discourage him from becoming a teacher. Irene Petit had hoped he would become a real economist or finance expert, a college professor perhaps. Maybe get into public finance and politics like Bruce Dayton's son, Mark.

The day got off to a good start though, somehow. This economics lesson, showing how to chart the break-even point in pricing, was his favorite. The kids, used to so much more drama in their lives, picked up on Bernard's thrill as he made his standard graph with an erasable marker. They hung on his words as he drew an axis and marked price points and costs, connecting them with diagonal lines.

Just as he reached the finale of his performance— passionately marking the big X, he heard pounding on the frame of his open door.

Paj Yang, the school counselor, was a short young woman who had grown up carrying five-gallon buckets of water from a well at a Thai refugee camp. Her Hmong family lived in limbo there for years after the war her father had fought in for the Americans. Despite her stature, her presence was strong. So was her knocking.

"We have a situation. Nothing too urgent, but could you see if your sister could come in and sub for you for the afternoon?" she asked.

Bernard shook his head, then handed out worksheets to his class so they could solve four problems similar to the one he'd just demonstrated. Paj didn't leave.

Mardi only subbed for him with at least a week's notice. Just because she had a teaching license didn't mean she wanted to teach, and her job at Dayton's kept her plenty engaged. Occasionally, though, teaching sixteen traumatized and troubled boys, one of whom once stole her wallet, sounded better than being a marketing-advertising liaison in an upscale department store during a recession. Her team members were brilliant, but she would sometimes take a vacation day to do her brother the favor.

Lately, Bernard knew Mardi was immersed in a "marketing personas" project.

"How about you step in for me for a bit?" Bernard asked Paj.

"I could...," she said. "Gimme a few minutes."

Bernard's back, which he had been sure wasn't injured in the minor car crash, began to stiffen and ache. He popped two Tylenol pills and got back to his lesson. When he got really into teaching economics, the boys got into learning along with him. When he tipped off kilter, all hell could break loose. He was starting to feel off kilter.

He realized it was a good thing he was going to meet with the principal instead of staying in the classroom, but a principal visit wasn't ideal right now either. Home, in a warm bath with Epsom salts, now that sounded ideal.

Paj came back to the room with a prefab classroom activity in a box. Bernard, hand on his aching back, hobbled to the principal's office.

Since the school counselor had been the one to summon him, he assumed the crisis was related to one of the students. Perhaps the one who had been prostituted by his foster parents, or maybe the one who recently turned classroom furniture upside-down in anger when another student punched the buttons of his calculator too loudly during a math quiz. Paj, or Ms. Yang as the kids called her, had been trying to have that boy's mother in for a meeting all month but learned that she was in prison again. Bernard imagined this was the most likely kid to be in crisis right now.

But the crisis wasn't about the students this time. It was a run-of-the-mill problem—the school's financial mill.

"We won't make payroll the day after tomorrow if we don't make a deposit by the end of the business day today," the principal told Bernard. "We're four thousand dollars short." Bernard thought back to the graph he'd just been drawing. There was never to be any surplus here at Twin Cities Success. It was always about trying to break even.

But it was only the fall of the 1991-92 school year. How could they already be behind?

"Offering summer school for the most at-risk students," the principal reasoned, "while it was a good idea you had for those boys, didn't pan out financially."

Bernard got the drift. He had pushed hard for summer school, incentivizing it with free breakfast and lunch, knowing some of the boys spent their summers and holiday breaks getting into trouble or being preyed upon by pimps and drug dealers. Bernard was an economics teacher, but that didn't mean he had a firm handle on the day-to-day finances of running the school. Twin Cities Success was a charter school. It had a local college acting as guarantor, but it had to live within its budget or raise money from private donors.

Private donors often meant Bernard Petit, whom everyone knew had once made a fortuitous investment in some odd little invention that made it much more convenient to pop popcorn in a microwave.

This was how he managed to restore the crumbling Victorian house he'd inherited from grandparents in the Irvine Park neighborhood and the houseboat, too. Irene was scandalized that her son had gone from a good upbringing in Plymouth—it wasn't Wayzata, but it was walking distance to that town on Lake Minnetonka—to living in the popish capital city and owning a river shack on the Mississippi. Never mind that Irene herself had married a St. Paul Catholic. She'd turned him around so well that nobody at their Lutheran church had a clue unless they realized he was one of *those* Petits.

His parsimony in his own lifestyle was a good thing for those wanting Bernard's extra resources. He and the principal spent the rest of the afternoon going over the school's books. Bernard drew more charts and graphs, trying more calculations and formulas until there was nothing more to be explored. Finally, twenty minutes before the end of the bank's business day, Bernard took his checkbook out of his pocket. He swallowed two more Tylenol pills for his back.

He didn't work here just for fun, and he didn't work here for the salary. Regardless of how imperfect Irene and Edward Petit may have been, they'd taught the young Bernard to help people and he never stopped.

He signed the check and tore it off to hand to his boss, but not without feeling the weight of it. "That's all I'll be able to do for the school year."

The principal nodded.

"Why did Paj come to me about this?" Bernard asked. It suddenly occurred to Bernard that it was unusual for the counselor to come to him regarding something about school finances. "I thought it had to have been about a student."

"She just happened to come see me in my office when I was thinking about calling you in," he said. "She updated me about a somewhat new student in the lower grades, in fact, a boy from out west of Minneapolis who lost both parents. You have a cousin named Noelle? She recommended our school to his guardian aunt."

"That's a surprise," Bernard said. He didn't know Noelle very well. Irene had kept him and Mardi sequestered in the western suburbs to keep them from seeing the St. Paul Petits too often, but then he had talked to her that one day in front of Dayton's and seen her at another cousin's house a few months after that.

"I was hoping you'd meet the kid," said the principal. "You haven't done any student advocacy for quite a while."

Although Bernard taught the high school boys, he took on a long-term "buddy" role with some kids. It was a Montessori or Waldorf type of practice. Certain boys were identified as needing an adult at the school who could follow them over the years in addition to the school psychologist and counselor, someone who could be a friend to the child and know him. The last child Bernard had done this for was the one just killed in Iraq.

"I'll take another kid soon," said Bernard, trying not to think about the soldier. "I guess I'm just not ready to buddy up again quite yet."

"Well that's too bad for this kid, but I know you'll be ready soon," said the principal. "That's why you work here, right? Always wanting to help others. And your cousin who told the boy's guardian about this school—she must be the same way."

6. The Blizzard, 1991

You could count the times Noelle Nichols had gone out of her way to help anyone on one hand and still have a couple of fingers left over for the times she'd kept her panties on during an entire first date.

One of those panties-on dates was with that boy she'd loved watching at the baseball diamond since third grade. She'd talked him into watching a movie with her in the basement of a mutual friend's house, but he stopped at second base. He didn't want to lose his virginity to her.

Maybe later, after. But, after he lost it to someone better, he stayed away.

It wasn't that Noelle didn't like helping people. She thrived on approval from people she wanted to impress. Today, her parents were not those people. They asked her to help shovel the sidewalk, "to be a contributing adult member of the household," but she was too busy working on her tan.

It was only the first of November 1991, the day after Halloween. It wasn't even winter yet, but the snow wouldn't stop. There were already fifteen inches, according to the news. Each foot in TV weather terms meant a four-foot drift across the alley where she would need to back out her car.

The forecast had gone from a potential foot of snow to meteorological terms nobody had heard before, like *bombogenesis*. There were going to be twenty-eight inches when it was done, with drifts in some places eight feet high.

So, Noelle slid into her tanning bed instead of her car.

Her father had a whole garage for his toys, but this pod-like tanning contraption took up a third of Noelle's tiny bedroom in her parents' miniature red brick Victorian. She wore her string bikini because she liked to have tan lines. Men approved of tan lines. Those swimsuit-shaped white patches made it like seeing Noelle in a bikini and naked at the same time. She knew the power of that.

After Noelle spent thirty minutes sandwiched between the ultraviolet tubes, the timer dinged like a toaster oven. One glance out her window was enough for Noelle to decide to call in sick. She picked up the phone and pressed the buttons for Fran Hart, the shoe department manager in charge of scheduling.

Nobody answered. She checked her tan lines in the mirror and set the timer for fifteen more minutes. But before she could get back into the tanning bed, the phone rang.

"Is this Noelle?" The voice sounded deep and hopeful.

"Yeah, who is this?"

"It's Dean Ohlman. I'm above you on the phone tree. I'm supposed to tell you Dayton's is closed because of the snow. Free day, I guess?"

It was Friday. She'd been out at a bar for Halloween with her friend Debra the night before.

"Do we get paid though, since it was their decision?"

"Uh...I don't know. So, what are you going to do all day?"

"Well, if Dayton's is closing it must be impossible to drive." She turned on the Zenith TV in her room and saw the news graphics flash across the thirteen-inch screen.

Even 3M was closing. Nobody could get anywhere, except for the tow trucks, which were busily towing cars because the declared snow emergency made it illegal to park on half of the streets.

Dean took a deep breath. He had practiced what exactly to say. "I have a pick-up truck. I could come get you and we could watch movies at my apartment. There's a pizza place next door—or I'll make nachos."

The other option was for Noelle to spend the day snowed in with her parents. According to the news, city workers like Carl Nichols were being told to stay home and on call. Annette didn't work at Petit's Party Central today even if it could open. Noelle gave Dean her address and directions.

"So then, with the phone tree, am I supposed to call someone next?" she asked. "I don't have the sheet."

"Uhh." He lowered his voice as he came clean with her. "I begged Kalmer to trade names so I could call you, but I don't have the sheet either and we forgot to trade info on the rest of our tree branches, I guess. I'll call Kalmer and call you back."

Noelle smiled. Dean was sweet. After she received and fulfilled her phone tree assignment, she took her time getting ready for him to pick her up.

By the time Dean pulled up to the curb in front of Noelle's family home on Butternut Avenue it was clear they would not be going back to his place. Noelle leaned out the door to yell that he had to park in the alley if he could get through it. Within seconds, her freshly curled hair was covered in snow. She'd been doing her hair and makeup and figuring out what to wear for the entire two hours it took Dean to drive from South Minneapolis through the blizzard.

A loud engine noise went silent as Carl turned off the leaf blower he'd been using on the freshly fallen snow to keep clear the path he'd already shoveled from the garage to the back door of the house.

"You're not taking my daughter anywhere in this mess," Carl said as Dean climbed the steps at the back door and walked straight into the kitchen. Carl followed him, scooping and scattering a mixture of rock salt and sand on the steps out of a big green Menard's bucket, even though they would be covered again within minutes.

"Obviously, Dad," said Noelle, holding the door open. It was times like this that it would have been so much better if Noelle would just live in the small cottage just outside of Swede Hollow on St. Paul's East Side that she had inherited from her grandmother. Her mom's mom, Greta Pettersson Petit, was the one who had taught her how to sew.

Annette Nichols took Dean's snowy coat and hat and told him where to put his wet sneakers. "No boots?" she asked.

"Please, Mom." Noelle glared at Annette. She hadn't had a boy over since college and it was horrible then. It was one of the reasons she'd gone to live on campus, and one of the reasons she hadn't wanted to move back. But that was before her dad built the garage. Maybe he would disappear into it and they could just go to her room without him roaming the hall outside her door, burping and making his presence known. But Carl stuck around, asking Dean about his schooling and future plans.

"I'm pretty good with sales," Dean said. "I keep track of my best clients on index cards in a recipe box, and I call them when we get shoes they would like. I have some other ideas, too."

Carl curled back his upper lip. "Ideas on how to sell shoes better? Recipe box? Heh, heh."

"We're going to watch TV in my room now," Noelle interrupted.

Carl laughed. "There's no space in there for two people with all the shoes Noelle's been collecting since she started working at Dayton's."

Noelle groaned.

"I saw Imelda Marcos on the news again today," he went on. "Looks like she's finally got to pay up for all those shoes she bought with the people's money. Have you seen the footage? Three thousand pairs. Of course, Noelle's not too far behind."

"Come on," said Annette. "Imelda Marcos never owned a single pair of shoes before she got married, and she only has one thousand and sixty pairs."

"In that case, I think Noelle already has her beat." Carl put on a coat to make the trek to his fort, then turned around. "She wants so badly to be the rich customer that she forgets she is only the worker."

It was true. But who did she get that from? Carl, with his city-worker pay and garage full of gadgets? Her fashion purchases didn't cost nearly as much as his power tools.

Maybe someday they would, if she didn't stop. Noelle hadn't the inspiration to sew her own clothing lately. It was easier to turn her paychecks around into the fresh and ready-to-wear outfits from Dayton's. Carl liked to complain that the thin, clear plastic sticks Noelle left around the house when she yanked the price tags off of her latest purchases looked like fish bones. After paydays, it looked like someone had left behind the bones of an entire trout.

Annette took a block of ground meat out of the freezer and changed the subject. "I assume you'll be staying for dinner, Dean. We might even need to put you up for the night in Carl's heated garage."

Noelle knew this kindness on her mother's part was fake. Annette didn't know yet if Dean had money, or potential, or maybe nothing at all, like the jackass she had married for love.

"It's as easy to marry a rich man as a poor man," Annette would no doubt remind Noelle at a later date. Annette had been so relieved when that chubby-cheeked ball boy whom

Noelle had pined for all through her school years married early and Noelle was forced to give up on him.

Another half-foot of snow had fallen in the minutes Dean stood there in the kitchen with Noelle's parents.

"Thanks, Mrs. Nichols. I guess we'll see when it stops and if the plows come through."

Up in her bedroom, Dean gawked at the tanning bed while Noelle dropped a Bryan Adams cassette tape into her tune box.

"You can try it out," she said, turning on the timer. She didn't turn away while he stripped down to his boxer shorts, but she gave him a towel to lay across himself.

He lay there, glowing under the purple lights, the tiny goggles over his eyes. "So, you really are related to that family that owns Petit's Party Central?"

"Yeah," said Noelle. "My mom's brother and his son run it and my mom works there part-time. I don't know if you've been there. It's kind of like high-pressure sales."

"And that woman who works up in advertising, with the punky haircut? I heard she's part of your family too."

"That's Mardi Wirt, my cousin. Her dad is my mom's brother, Edward Petit. Mardi didn't change her name back to Petit after she got divorced from her musician husband. Mardi's brother, Bernard, is pretty cool, but Mardi has always been a bitch."

Noelle didn't know Mardi well, but she had that on good word from her mother. Of course, Annette felt the same way about her sister-in-law, Irene—that she was a snooty bitch. Naturally, Irene's daughter would turn out the same.

"Everyone has heard of Petit's. I haven't been there, but they advertise on TV so much." Dean admitted he'd seen her in the tanning bed commercial. "I guess that's why you have your own."

"Yeah, although it's all I got for modeling." She gazed at the periwinkle paint peeling from her plaster wall.

Dean took off the little tanning goggles to look at her and his eyes followed to the peeling paint and the sewing machine sitting among piles of fabric.

"You need to wear the goggles, or your eyeballs could burn," she said. He put them back on and rested his head.

"I guess people think you must be pretty rich."

"My mom didn't get much of an inheritance from her parents. She got this house for her wedding gift though. It's an old brewery neighborhood, and a Petit distillery neighborhood before that. That's what the family did way back before it was even called St. Paul."

"The Petits had a distillery? You mean like whiskey?"

"Yep. That's pretty much how St. Paul got started. There was this guy named Pierre—or Pig's Eye—Parrant, and his success brought other French-Canadians like my ancestors who thought they could do even better making liquor for the Indians and the soldiers at Fort Snelling. Then they got into beer, then retail. By the time my grandpa, Sam Petit, took over, it was all retail—from billiards tables to beach balls."

Noelle conveniently forgot to mention the Petit family's quarter-century in prostitution. "So, they built this house in the 1880s, but it was rented out for decades before my mom got it. It's not worth a whole heap."

"Is it on that historical registry thing?" Dean asked. Noelle looked him over, knowing he couldn't see her very well as he lay under the lights. His chest was as broad as she'd imagined from how he looked in his suits, and his nipples were shades pinker than his red lips.

"It should be, but they kept it off, which is a good thing because then my dad couldn't have built his modern garage on the property. There are all these rules."

Dean nodded. "So, then, I don't mean to be nosy, but I guess I imagined you living in a mansion."

Noelle explained that her mother's brother, Tom, got the mansion on Summit Avenue when their parents died, so his son was the lucky one living there. They ran the business. Her grandparents' inheritance skipped over her mother and Edward, but Tom got the mansion.

"But they gave us other grandkids these random properties they owned," she said. "I got a tiny cottage east of here that's as old as this place, but it's in a real low-income neighborhood."

"Why don't you sell it and buy a different one?" Dean hadn't known many single women Noelle's age who owned their own house (or a tanning bed, or a sewing machine, for that matter).

Noelle picked up an old framed wedding photograph of her Petit grandparents from the late 1930s. Her grandmother, Greta Pettersson, wore a simple white gown, but no veil or jewelry. Her grandfather, Sam Petit, wore a suit that looked custom-tailored. A pocket watch peeked out of his vest pocket, secured to a vest button with a chain.

"My grandma would haunt me," Noelle said. "Her family did laundry and sewing for rich people. That's how she met my Petit grandpa, Sam. It was a big deal when her parents got enough money to move up out of Swede Hollow and buy a house on a real street above the hollow. She kept it to pass down to me and now I rent it to tenants."

"Cool," Dean remarked. "That's so impressive that you have a house, even if it's little and in the ghetto."

Noelle scowled at him, but he didn't see her through his tanning goggles. "I didn't call it a ghetto."

"Oh, sorry, I didn't mean to...I thought you said it."

"One time—by then it was already way more Italian and Mexican than Swedish—the government came and burned down all the old houses in the hollow, including their first home in America. They could feel the flames. My grandma was grateful for her family's house up on the street."

Noelle felt bad about lecturing Dean, so she reached over to caress his crotch over the towel and his boxers.

He sprang up and hit his head on the tanning bed ceiling. "Your parents!" he whispered. "Geez!"

She jumped back. "Well, what would we have been doing if we'd gone to your place?"

"Watching movies, like I said." Dean lay back down just as the timer dinged. He lifted the lid and sat up, swinging his now-pink legs over off the side of the contraption. "You shouldn't sneak up on a guy's goods like that."

She looked out her bedroom window at Dean's rusty old truck next to the big garage, then turned to notice the new uplifted form of his boxer shorts. "The goods don't seem to mind."

She pulled the knob that turned on the old TV. There were the increasingly alarming weather reports, a commercial for the Barbara Walters show that would be on in a few hours, a breaking story about a college shooting in Iowa, and more reports on Imelda Marcos. The camera panned across the rows of shoes—each pair like a different species of colorful lovebirds.

"Maybe I could go get the VCR from downstairs and hook it up to my TV. My dad has a big video collection."

"Why don't we just go downstairs and watch a movie? Your mom could sit with us."

Noelle blinked. No guy had ever said anything remotely similar to her as what had just come out of Dean's ruby red mouth. He wanted to watch a movie with her and her mom.

"Seriously?"

"Sure, and we could help her make dinner."

"She'll be shocked, but okay." Noelle didn't turn around as Dean stood up in his boxer shorts and pulled on his jeans. He had definitely gotten some color.

"You can shower if you want," she said. "You know, tanning bed smell?"

He sniffed himself. "No, that's okay, unless it grosses you out."

"No, let's just go downstairs then."

Annette busied herself cooking a casserole of egg noodles and Swedish meatballs. She'd made a salad. Dean brought the dishes to the table as Annette asked Noelle to get her father.

Carl was ravenous. "Rub-a-dub-dub, thank God for this grub," he said in prayer, so fast that Dean hadn't even realized he was supposed to bow his head as Annette and Noelle had done.

As they dished up the noodles and meatballs, Dean said, "Noelle told me your brother runs Petit's Party Central, Mrs. Nichols. That must be so cool to have a store like that."

Noelle looked up from her food, first to her dad. He finished his bite of meatball and swallowed. Then he took a big swig of beer, crunched the can with a loud noise, and set it down on the table.

Annette nodded her head up and down. "Oh yes, Tom does a wonderful job, and his boy is helping the store find new customers too."

Carl burped. "You're going to need some help shoveling out your truck."

Annette waved him off. "Oh no, there's plenty of room here. News reports say no traveling."

"I'd rather work at Dayton's than Petit's," Noelle said, returning to the previous conversation. "On my first day I got to that corner where Mary Tyler Moore threw her hat in the air and I wished I had a hat so I could toss it just like on the show. Nobody ever feels like that when they're going to work at Petit's."

"Praise God," said Carl. "My baby girl has a brain."

Annette gave Carl a dismissive look, but added, "Of course she does. Maybe Noelle didn't participate in all the right student clubs or get some fancy internship, but she's smart about work and managing her rental home. She can do whatever she puts her mind to."

Noelle agreed, appeasing both parents. "A lot of the department managers started out selling, like this manager named Fran. Then they can become floor managers or buyers, or do jobs like Mardi's."

"Is that what you plan to do, young man?" Carl asked Dean.

"I don't know yet. Like I said, I have some other ideas, but all in sales of some sort. What about you, Noelle—do you think that's what you want to do?"

It was so unusual for a boy—okay, a young man—to ask her about her career plans, and right at the dinner table with her parents. "No, maybe not. I don't know what I should do."

They finished eating, and then Dean insisted he and Noelle help Annette wash the dishes. There was no dishwasher, just a scrub brush and a yellow bottle of lemon-scented Joy.

Noelle and Dean sat down to watch Barbara Walters, and then Noelle got up to put on a *Raiders of the Lost Ark* videotape. Annette, a little deflated about Dean's drop in potential as evidenced by the dinner table conversation, decided not to bother watching the movie with them. She went up to her room when Carl went back to blasting the noisy leaf blower at the snow. As the movie ended, Annette brought clean sheets and a blanket for the couch. Carl had refused to let another man sleep in his garage.

Noelle went up to her room and took a look out the window at Dean's truck, now so buried in snow it would be hard to tell if it were a junker or a brand-new Land Rover. She put on a cotton nightgown and her robe and checked her make-up in the mirror. With a dry cotton ball, she wiped off just a little bit of it.

One more TV show wouldn't hurt.

She went back downstairs and sat next to Dean for a sitcom rerun. When the show ended, she kissed him with her mouth closed, like her first kiss in the seventh grade behind the bleachers at the baseball diamond. She lay her hand in the same spot on Dean's body as before, but more softly. This time he let it rest there but still didn't make any moves other than to stroke Noelle's hair. Then Noelle kissed Dean again and broke away, his blue eyes following her in the darkness as she climbed the creaking staircase back to the room with the peeling periwinkle paint.

7. Daisy Sale, 1992

The seasonal rhythm of Dayton's department store life went like this: White Sale in January, Anniversary Sale in February, then the Spring Flower Show. Daisy Sale in May, Warehouse Sale at the offsite industrial facility in August. The Jubilee Sale in September was most everybody's favorite, although each year the shoe dogs were punished with Gary Gorman's dull lecture about the definition of the word "jubilee."

Single sale days landed here and there between the busy Friday after Thanksgiving and the day after Christmas, giving texture to the steady six-week run of the eighth-floor holiday exhibit.

It was best not to start working there—to become a *Daytonian,* as the old-timers would say—during any of these blow-out sales.

Pierre St. Hilaire's first day as inventory coordinator (a.k.a., stock boy) for Women's Shoes happened to be the first day of the Daisy Sale in May 1992. The Caribbean immigrant had twenty minutes before the opening bell to learn the inventory and hang the last of the signs reading, "Our Daisy Sale Won't Last Forever!" Petals were shown falling off of the daisies.

Even the cleverest, most creative marketing departments in the industry had moments of desperation.

The main stock room was divided by color, then by heel height. Gary hobbled over to a corner. "The boots are kept up in the less accessible loft, and the new sandals along the wall closest to the sales floor," he said. "Come fall, you'll move the boots to that wall and put all the sandals up in the loft."

Pierre nodded, his brow lifting in agreement at such logic. As a stock room worker, he wore not a suit, but not the jeans he was allowed either. Khaki pants and a twill shirt with a box cutter, pen, pencil, and notepad in the front pocket would become his everyday uniform. "That makes perfect sense," he said in French-accented English. "The goal is to keep the in-season styles where the salespeople can reach them most quickly."

A large male shoe dog with curly hair came out of nowhere and ducked under Pierre, not seeming to know his own size, and grabbed four shoeboxes from the sandal wall to set aside for a customer who had promised to be first through the gate.

"Excusez-moi," Pierre said, looking up at the tall man with a winged female warrior tattoo sticking out from under his rolled-up shirt sleeve. Pierre was quite tall himself and not used to getting run over by pedestrians.

"Ooh, sorry! I'm an oaf. Name's Kalmer" the man said, balancing all the boxes in one hand and giving Pierre a powerful handshake with the other before he vanished. Kalmer reminded Pierre of a painting he had admired in the island of Martinique's *Sacré-Coeur de la Balata.* A giant, fast-flying angel, but with his forelocks cropped, wild copper curls falling to his shoulders.

Pierre listened to the morning pre-opening pep talk given by a floor manager. The talk jazzed him. He momentarily forgot that he hadn't imagined finding work as a stock boy after coming to the United States from Martinique. He'd taught himself English and come to Minnesota for his degree in computer science. He got the degree, but not so easily the job. His parents thought he and his fiancée, Johanne, should come home. They had a tourism business, and he could work for them. And Johanne, with her ecology degree, was wanted home to put her education to use in Martinique's rainforest.

He promised his mother, through the mail, that he would work his way up. Each week he and Johanne received a one-page letter from her in a small blue envelope with French stamps and a hint of her perfume.

Pierre thought of his mother now as the gates opened and shoeboxes piled up within minutes.

After a mad hour of returning rejected shoeboxes to their rightful spot in the back, the action hit a lull. Pierre stepped out to the sales floor. While the shoe dogs stood guard, he glanced over their badges in hopes he would memorize their names by the next day.

Dean Ohlman stood close to Noelle at the desk, sorting through an old recipe card box that appeared to store his clients' sizes and preferences, along with notes about where they were going on vacation, or whose wedding they were attending, or what job they were interviewing for. This way, Dean leaned over to explain, he could remember to ask them about it the next time they visited.

Noelle, the pretty one with the brown highlighted hair and hourglass figure, made a series of phone calls. A customer stood at the desk, looking anxious.

"Hello, St. Paul," Noelle said to the person in the Dayton's store on the other side of the river. "This is Minneapolis. Do you have a size seven narrow in the Bandolino 'Cassie' in red?"

She waited several minutes but got turned down. She made the same attempt again with the locations in the malls the Dayton family had helped develop. "Hello Southdale, this is Minneapolis. Do you have a..."

Brookdale agreed to check on the size and never came back to the phone at all. Finally, Noelle scored the seven narrow at Rosedale. Pierre casually watched as she proceeded to transmit the payment and delivery information.

"Did you get the commission for the sale or did the store at Rosedale?" he asked when the customer was gone. Noelle couldn't immediately make out the word "commission" with his accent, or even "Rosedale," even though she knew some French. She took a moment, looking up at the tall stock boy before it sunk in.

"Rosedale," she said, "but sometimes I get a sale from another store."

"All of the inventory info is in the Dayton's IBM computer system, but you cannot access it?" he asked.

Dean looked up quickly and blinked, then jotted something down on an index card. Noelle stared at Pierre blankly, taking a significant amount of time to cognitively process his long accented sentence. She said, "No, that's why we call around."

Pierre nodded. The IBM register was connected to the system well enough to accept the SKU as it was typed in or scanned and bring up a current price. But there was no computer that employees could visit to look up what inventory they had, or which other store had the shoe a customer needed. People had to search the expansive stock rooms all across the metro. And since the corporation had all the Hudson's stores too, and now even Marshall Field's, a desperate customer could have a sales consultant on the phone all day tracking down a rare shoe all across the country.

"So, you spend fifteen minutes tracking down a size, and someone else gets the commission, but you don't think that's inefficient?"

Noelle gave up on listening to whatever point he was trying to make, but she tipped her ear toward the Afro-Caribbean French spoken in his longest and most melodious sentence yet. Pierre didn't aim to excite the young woman with his accent, but he could see her lips part and hear her breath quicken as she melted into his voice. His accent was his superpower.

He loved his fiancée completely, but at moments like this, he was just as red-blooded as any man.

Dean ventured to the aisle and approached a customer. Noelle finally formulated a response to all of his questions about efficiency and innovations. "Learning a different way would probably be hard too," she said.

Pierre intended to walk away, but he couldn't help himself. He wasn't playing with her. "If a computer told you who had the size seven narrow in that style, you could call the right store first."

Some of the shoe dogs heard this and started to listen to Pierre's idea. Noelle got his point but didn't acknowledge it; however, she stood transfixed by how his "if" came out "eef," and how his voice became so insistent. Another customer began waving a shoe at her.

Gary agreed that having a handle on inventory was vital to Dayton's, especially here at the flagship store, but he seemed to be all talk.

Pierre's job was to run freight from the subterranean loading dock to the shoe stock room and put it on the shelves. Even Kalmer questioned whether a stock boy's ideas were possible. Kalmer would love it if it meant improved service. There had been times when he packed up shoes and had them delivered via taxi cab to a desperate customer. Dayton's had an account with Yellow Taxi for such rare decisions, which all were empowered to make, but which only Kalmer relished making.

Dean rang up his sale, half listening to Pierre's concept of computerized inventory. The flagship store, in truth, no longer kept up with the times. Although the marble floors still gleamed, and the crystal chandeliers still sparkled, in many ways it operated in 1992 like it had when it opened in 1902. The hold shelf circled a black hole. Mismated shoes took up a whole wall.

Gary shook his head and sighed. "Anything you don't like about Dayton's right now is the fault of the corporate powers that be," he said. "They really only care about their Target stores now anyway. We keep our ideas to ourselves."

"Pardon me?" Pierre said, sort of a *pardonnez moi* spoken in his best English.

"A real Dayton hasn't managed the business in decades. It was different when they did. They would take your idea right up to the office and do something about it. Back when..."

He started talking about a "Mr. Bruce," one of the many Dayton men called Mr. plus a first name. Gary said this Mr. Bruce had a son who was now the state auditor. Mark Dayton had plenty of Dayton-Hudson Corporation stock, but no desire to control the company. His personality leaned more public servant-like.

Gary's memory of a utopian *Daytonia* might have been a bit nostalgic, but the company had changed.

"At my orientation, they said we were all 'empowered'— that's the word they used," said Pierre. "They said we should take the attitude that Dayton's is *our company.*"

"Whose company is Dayton's?" the trainer had asked.

"It's our company!" they had all chanted in unison.

So, the old spirit's still there, Gary noted, or at least a manufactured version of it. The corporation still taught trainees that George Draper Dayton was known for being "enticed" by problems, not put off by them.

Pierre felt enticed by problems, too. Johanne called him a dog after a bone.

"Well, don't worry about solving all the inventory problems," said Gary. "They're nothing but job security for you. It's all part of the system."

"But if it's *our company,*" said Pierre, "I'd like us to build a better system."

That night in bed, after making love to her, he knew his fiancée would listen.

8. *Westwood Lane, 1992*

Mardi Wirt pulled at her chunky earring, a large gold shell with an inset trillium of purple tanzanite. She'd bought the set, applying her employee discount, as her first purchase after she decided to trade in life as a French teacher for a higher paying marketing job.

A few years later, Mardi bought herself a small share of an investor position in a tanzanite mine.

Tiffany's promoted tanzanite—previously known as blue zoisite—as early as the seventies, and the entire supply rested in one part of Tanzania, just miles from Mount Kilimanjaro. It was expected to run out in twenty years.

Mardi, who loved purple even before Prince made it popular, followed her heart. Her father, Edward, helped her complete the purchase one day as they sat shoulder to shoulder at his mahogany desk while Irene hiked five-miles with her new Nordic walking poles to pick up her prescriptions at Supplee's Community Drug in the Wayzata Bay Center. With any luck, she'd stop into The Foursome's women's shop and be gone for hours.

Irene would fall over in horror when she found out what her daughter was about to buy now. That's why Mardi wouldn't tell her until she sealed the deal.

Mardi was thirty-three. With no second marriage or even a boyfriend in sight, it was time. She sold the odd piece of Florida land she'd inherited from her Petit grandparents in 1987. It would have been cool to hang onto, but now the money went to better use as a solid down payment on a house in the preppy town on Lake Minnetonka Mardi had once termed "lame."

Now, like her mother, she couldn't think of anywhere she would rather live than the western suburbs. Although she still mocked Irene for so many things, she had to agree with her on that. And after Bernard revealed his Petit genes by moving to St. Paul, Irene would have to be thrilled with

Mardi for buying a house with a Wayzata 55391 zip code. She'd one-upped her own mother. Leapfrogged her.

That zip code punctuated the address of a murder-suicide house, but the house cost nearly forty percent below market value. So maybe Irene would require convincing, but Mardi felt certain Edward would be open-minded.

While Mardi knew that a man named Andrew Hess had shot his wife, Catherine, and himself—and that a young son had witnessed it—superstitions didn't bother her. The house had been cleaned. If her mother wanted to gripe about it, she could invite her pastor to come and bless it, not that Lutherans did such things.

It seemed unbelievable that the wood and stone house sat on the market so long that the bank took it over. It didn't have a lake or golf course view, but it wasn't far from either. Tucked into the double lot at the end of Westwood Lane, it felt peaceful and serene. As long as you didn't think a murder-suicide history disqualified it from that description.

Mardi asked her real estate agent, "Are people really that hung up on it?"

Not much commission came in through the sale of bank foreclosures for the agent. She'd be better off getting Mardi into one of her townhome listings in Plymouth.

"It's also a question of what people might think of someone who would buy a house where something so gruesome took place," the agent said. "When you buy a dress at Bank's, you don't have to tell people it's from a liquidator warehouse, but everyone in the neighborhood will know you bought a foreclosure whether you tell them or not. And they know why it sold for pennies."

"Well, not *pennies*." Mardi broke out into a small sweat at the thought of spending two hundred thousand dollars.

She had the money, as long as she kept her job. It wasn't easy to take off time for the closing and the move, especially with her project of getting computers ready for each department. The IBM rep handled the systems, and some foreign stock boy had landed a leadership role in the project.

Then Mardi had to tend to her "What does Becky want?" project, the new trend in persona marketing.

Each marketing staff member was responsible for one composite character created out of market segmentation studies. Mardi got "Becky Sharp"—every low-born social climber who came in for a party dress and, Mardi hoped, walked out with the dress, three outfits festooned with designer logos, and accessories for each.

A marketing intern with an English minor had named Mardi's assigned persona after a character in the novel *Vanity Fair.*

If the imaginary Becky Sharp holstered her Dayton's card and went seeking status at the new Mall of America instead, Mardi's paycheck would be at risk. A life-sized cardboard cut-out of this vapid customer type stood at her desk to remind her of that.

The agent took one more shot as they waited for an appraiser to show up. "What happened is just appalling. You know, I adore parquet, but I can't even look at the parquet floor in the living room where they found them."

"I don't care about status—that's my mom's thing," Mardi said. "And I love the parquet floor."

Within days, she faced the stack of closing papers. One after another she signed and initialed.

The keys were hers, keys that had once belonged to Andrew and Catherine Hess, now on a mortgage company keychain. The movers were already at her Minneapolis apartment, loading up a truck. U.S. West promised to put in the phone line the moment the papers were notarized.

Yes, the girl who had once written "Wayzata sucks" on ripped jeans now owned a home there and a shared financial position in a gemstone mine in Tanzania. Oh, and she collected pieces from some new Spanish clothing designer line she'd found in Dayton's Oval Room; the designer gave an eclectically punkish flavor to a vintage 1940s look.

How she'd grown up. Her mother should have been thrilled, but Mardi decided to tell her brother about the house first.

Bernard approved of her purchase the minute Mardi told him about it over the phone. As long as it had a good roof and solid plumbing and wiring, it sounded perfect for her. It was what he had to say next that brought a lump to her throat. "I know who the little boy is though. He goes to Twin Cities Success."

"But you teach high school. I heard the kid was just five or six when it happened two years ago."

Bernard explained that the most troubled students had a long-term advocate among the faculty, and that he had been asked to be his. He'd said no, but he still felt bad about it. "Anyway, the boy has a name. It's Owen Hess, and he has talent. He's a little artist, according to Paj Yang. He lives with an aunt."

"I didn't ask."

Mardi never wanted to hear another word about the kid or his parents who had lived and died in her house. She thanked God her family hadn't known them. She hung up, agreeing that Bernard should come over to Westwood Lane as soon as he could leave school.

Soon Mardi heard her home's musical door chimes for the first time. The zesty aroma of a Maggie's Restaurant pepperoni and sausage pizza wafted in along with her brother. After a quick tour, they sat on the floor eating on paper plates while the movers brought in the furniture and boxes. Bernard kept getting up to help them, but Mardi told him to stay put. She *paid* for their labor. Besides, the phone line had just gone live. She needed him next to her while she called their parents.

Irene answered the phone.

"Hi, Mother. I'm calling you from my new Wayzata home," Mardi announced. Bernard sunk his teeth into another square slice of Maggie's pizza as Mardi told Irene about all the heavy lifting she'd been doing with her finances and house hunting since they'd last talked.

"It's a white wood and stone house at the end of Westwood Lane, down the street from where your tennis partner used to live. Black shutters and striped awnings. Do you know which house I mean? The green and white striped awnings look like they've been here since the fifties."

It stood a couple of miles from the Petit's Plymouth house, in a neighborhood where they didn't know anyone but the tennis partner. Mardi thought she might have to explain, but then Irene's phone fell with a *clackety clack*.

Mardi accepted a saucy square of pizza from Bernard as she heard her mother come back to the phone.

"Mardi, darling," she said. "I'm sending your father over there right now. He can help you get out of it. They must not have told you, sweetheart. A terribly violent crime transpired in that house. Dreadful gossip. I think they were Unitarians."

"Mother." Mardi nodded to her brother as he held up a bottle of wine he brought and a juice glass from a moving box. He poured it, then slid into an eggplant-colored chair the movers had just set down in the living room.

"I doubt it had anything to do with being Unitarians," Mardi said. "There's a parquet floor—you will love it."

Bernard got up and spoke into the phone while Mardi held it to his mouth. "Hi, Mom. Mardi will be happy here. It's a beautiful house at thirty...no..." Mardi mouthed the correct figure to him. "*Forty* percent less than market value. You won't believe the built-in white woodwork and leaded glass. And they left the wicker patio furniture." He sat back down in front of the pizza box.

After a moment of silence, Irene yelled, "Edward!" so loudly that Mardi had to pull the receiver away from her ear. Then the siblings both heard the click.

Bernard looked up at the crown molding. "Don't worry. She's probably worried her friends from the club will know you bought it in foreclosure. You know how we're forbidden to tell anyone that she bought that Dior china set at Bank's."

"It'll be a big scandal in her world, I'm sure." Mardi downed her glass of wine. "And she was already ashamed that I'm not married with two little kids to enroll in the club's swim team."

"I'm proud of you, though," Bernard said. It was the first time he'd said something like this to her since she graduated from college with her education degree. "When I moved into my house, Mom came over to help me change the shelving paper—you know, that sticky lining that comes in rolls? Maybe she'll come do that. Or if she doesn't, I can help you with it next weekend."

"I'd like you to come down to the basement and look at some stuff in the furnace room. I'm sure Mother will come over to freshen up all the shelves and drawers once she realizes I'm staying. Besides, she's probably on her way here now."

Bernard nodded. "I bet you're right."

Bernard and Mardi were still inspecting the furnace room when chimes rang throughout the home. They both looked up, as if angels were playing harps on the ceiling, and then remembered the doorbell. Mardi opened the door to see her father caressing the place where the gray stone doorway façade met white wooden siding. He jaunted over to the vintage white wicker patio furniture set and petted all of it too.

He whistled and reached out to give her a rare hug. "Forty percent below market value!" Edward exclaimed. "It's terrible what happened, but it's in the past now."

9. *Abstraction, 1992*

A nurse at the old folks' home alongside Highway 12 out of Wayzata walked Ken Beranek into the lounge, seating him on a brocade loveseat. It was a good place, Hillcrest. Only the slightest whiff of incontinence, not nearly as stale as the other places Ralphina and Ken had visited, seeped out beneath the fragrance of fresh flowers in all the visiting areas.

Ken's old fishing buddy had been there to visit Ken in his room. He waved to them on his way out to a waiting taxi, but Ralphina didn't let him get away with that. The man was the same age as Ken, but now Ken looked so old in comparison to his friend who still looked like he could chop wood for the fires at their old fishing camp. She pulled him to her by his muscular white arms and then released him back to the outer world from which she and Owen had just come.

"I'm so glad Neal comes to see you." Ralphina crouched to embrace her father, who sat fully dressed, his hair combed.

Owen took a seat next to his grandpa on the loveseat and handed him a colorful drawing.

"It's our house on Westwood Lane," he said brightly, as if the bad thing hadn't happened. Ralphina stood nervously, looking down at her gnarled father accepting the work of art from Owen's young hand.

Ralphina had not told Owen to avoid saying "our *old* house" or anything about that. The old man sitting there in his cable-knit sweater vest was unlikely to remember. He didn't need to know the bank foreclosed on the house any more than he needed to recall his eldest daughter's death.

Ken's eyes drank in the abstraction of gray stone, white wood, exaggerated crawl spaces, and the flat section of roof that he'd shoveled winter after winter, but he didn't seem to recognize it or his grandson.

"That's quite a drawing, young man," he said. Owen put his hand in his pants pocket and felt his rock with the loon picture decoupaged onto it. It reminded him that he was still Owen, even if his grandpa couldn't see that. He'd decorated the rock with his mother.

Ralphina prepared Owen for disappointment when he'd told her about his idea to draw the house for his grandpa. She'd been so relieved that this drawing looked whimsical and bright instead of dark and macabre like his many other representations of the place. It seemed that the Cray-Pas oil pastels his teacher had bought for him at Wet Paint provided not only a new medium but also a new frame of mind.

Even though Ralphina wanted to stay away from the topic of Catherine's death, she was of two minds. Shouldn't seeing the art help her father remember his life and all the good times? Had he not had the house built for her mother, Vilda, his beautiful bride? The drawing was abstract, but an unmistakable representation of both the outside and the inside of the house in one cracked-open constellation of spaces and details. Owen even colored his Grandma Vilda's pink vintage perfume atomizer that Catherine kept on the dresser. The atomizer and the dresser had become hers when she and Andrew bought the home from the elder Beraneks.

Wood-paneled crawl spaces hid behind small, square doorways—only two feet high—and those doors flew about in the drawing, one of them opening up onto a stack of Catherine and Ralphina's vintage Archie comic books. How Owen remembered such things made Ralphina wonder what else he remembered so clearly. A squiggly line—a road—led to their church, the Unitarian Universalist church up by the Indian mounds, and Wayzata's library upon those mounds.

Ralphina sat down between the grandfather and grandson pair. "Dad, Owen is your grandson. He drew this for you. Do you know what it is?"

Ken studied the Cray-Pas drawing more. "It's a house and a church. You don't have to talk to me like I'm a baby. One of those modern drawings though. Like Pablo Picasso. I remember things, see? Pablo Picasso. Spanish gentleman."

Ralphina walked a line—wanting him to remember, but not wanting to bring him pain, nor frustration with himself and his disease.

"Yes, Dad, Owen's quite an artist." She took a risk. "He takes after Catherine, the art teacher. See, it runs in the family."

Ken looked up at Ralphina, then at Owen. His eyes grew wider. "Runs in the family," he parroted. "Can't ever get too mad about that!"

Ralphina laughed as if her father were a small child who had said his first word. "Right on, Daddy! You remember. You used to always say that. Catherine and I made big messes with our art, and you said you could never get too mad because it wasn't our fault that we were artists."

"Runs in the family," Ken repeated. Of course, it didn't run in the family, not really. Vilda had been a nurse and Ken worked in business. Neither of them could be called an artist.

"Mom's friend June Skaalen turned us on to art," said Ralphina. "She worked as an illustrator for Dayton's ads until they replaced her pen-and-ink work with photography. Remember when they did that, how indignant Mom was for her friend? They offered her another position, but she had no interest in anything there besides art."

"Vilda is always a good friend," Ken said, remembering his wife's name, if not her death. Ralphina cheered him on for his response.

"Ms. Skaalen always came over and set us up with art projects, Dad. Do you remember June? She treated us like we were her kids too."

"Vilda's friend was an artist. That reminds me of a story I'd like to tell you." Ken looked off into the distance and then into Ralphina's eyes before bobbing his head.

The Hillcrest nurse looked up from across the room and rushed in their direction. "Ken seems ready for a nap," she said.

"He's perfectly fine," Ralphina insisted.

The nurse tapped her toe. On the third beat, Ken's head fell backward with one sudden snore and Ralphina looked at the nurse sheepishly. She took her nephew's hand as the woman went to get a wheelchair.

"Can he keep my coloring on his bedside table?" asked Owen when the nurse returned. She nodded, took the piece of paper, and tucked it into a pocket on the back of the wheelchair. An aide helped her move Ken into the chair.

"We had to cut the visit short this time, but we succeeded in getting through to Grandpa, thanks to you and your art," Ralphina told Owen once they got into the car.

She started the engine. "And now you get to spend the rest of the day with our friend June."

June Skaalen lived in her family's old house on Nicollet Island. She had called here and there to check on Ralphina and Catherine after Vilda passed away, but she called Ralphina and Owen constantly after Catherine and Andrew's tragic death. June always offered to babysit.

This time Ralphina accepted.

Arthritis made it too painful to draw now. June's pencil hand could no longer finesse the curves of a figure. But she loved to watch Vilda's grandson become lost in his creations. Sometimes he would cry a little or yell as he worked at her yellow Formica kitchen table. She would give him a bowl of wild rice soup and a hug, and sometimes she would read to him. A few times he watched a bit of her soap opera with her. A world where people come back from the dead, suffer a little amnesia, and then turn back into their old selves after all—what was so dumb about that?

For the first time in a decade, the Jubilee Sale back in September had sales figures so low—and the holiday spending projection even lower—that Dayton's didn't hire Ralphina to play a role in the design and set-up of the walk-through display in the auditorium on the eighth floor, nor in the holiday window displays.

At one time, Dayton's had employed a whole team of display artists full-time, but now even the outsourcing budget was in shreds. The holiday windows this year were in the hands of someone the company brought in from Marshall Field's, a chain that the Dayton-Hudson Corporation had acquired.

She didn't mind losing the window displays, but the auditorium exhibit paid Ralphina's rent better than any project of the year. Local ingénues like Jack Barkla, Jack Edwards, and their crew of people from the Twin Cities theater world conjured the sets and costumes, and engineers rigged electric motors to drive the actions of each character.

Ralphina banked on the work each year, both financially and mentally. Last year's *Pinocchio* had been even more magical than *Peter Pan*. She belonged on that project.

Now, she felt lucky to get a few little holiday projects in the store, some only one or two hours. Hardly worth paying the parking fee. One such project was the holiday shoe display. She usually had a great deal of fun putting the party shoes—satin and rhinestones, gold ostrich skin, red grosgrain—all on one big table around a centerpiece she would create herself out of oversized Christmas tree ornaments on a short but voluptuous tree.

But this year, while some budget director in marketing had decided not to hire her for the auditorium, that MAL named Mardi Wirt had apparently insisted she should at least be hired to incorporate the year's auditorium theme in the departmental displays.

Ralphina hardly felt thankful for small favors when she saw the decorations.

"What exactly is that?" said Noelle, that same shoe dog who recommended the Twin Cities Success School for Owen two years before.

Ralphina wielded a large brown cat with a plumed turquoise hat and red boots, meant to be a prefabricated centerpiece for the shoe table. She plunked it down on the heavy glass. "It's *Puss in Boots.*"

"That's our holiday shoe display?"

Ralphina wiped the shedding fur off the table. "It's the whole eighth-floor theme."

"Good God, is that a real stuffed cat? It's too huge though."

"No, it's one that Jack Edwards made himself, and then rejected, for the auditorium. But they decided it would be great down here with the merchandise." Ralphina looked at the feline reject again and reassessed. "And it is, I guess, but not what I'd imagined with the party shoes."

"Yeah, maybe boots though. You know, since he's wearing some."

But boots weren't the assignment, and Ralphina got to work. It didn't take even the two hours Dayton's paid her for, so she used the rest of the time to wander around the store. Shopping while on the clock wasn't discouraged, but Ralphina had to be disciplined now that she had her nephew to take care of and so much less work with the recession.

It came easily enough for Ralphina to sacrifice what she wanted to buy for herself in order to take care of Owen's needs. She'd put her whole love life on hold to focus on him. Denying herself a new sweater or sunglasses meant nothing.

That MAL, though. Mardi Wirt would have been someone to pursue if things were different.

Ralphina thought of Mardi as cute in a kind of punk way—like her *The Clash* t-shirt she half-hid under a black blazer sometimes. Her purple baubles dressed it all up enough, and Ralphina liked how Mardi pushed a boundary that others didn't dare push at Dayton's. She'd even seen her in a skirt with bare legs. She remembered that day— wondering if anyone called her on it. There may not have been a specific rule against wearing a punk band t-shirt under a blazer, although it was probably implied, but the rule on some sort of sausage casings for legs stood enshrined in the dress code. Mardi usually wore pants, or black tights—never nylons.

She would have liked to have asked her out to dinner, or maybe on a Zen weekend retreat. But she had no room in her life for that now. She would have to forget about it, at least until Owen grew up and healed a little more from his loss.

Thank God Catherine and Andrew never had more kids, Ralphina thought. On the other hand, Owen was lonely. He'd made a couple of friends at the charter school. Sure, they had problems, but anyone could see they were cool.

Owen got ready for bed with no fuss that night after Ralphina brought him home from June's house. After the visit to Grandpa Ken, he had made a full day of rummaging through June's old couture drawings and asking her so many questions about each one that it wore her out.

He hadn't wanted to come home. "June's house is funner than our place," Owen said.

"More fun," Ralphina corrected.

He climbed into the bed Ralphina had moved from his old bedroom on Westwood Lane, set his loon rock on his nightstand, and fell asleep.

10. *Silent Night, 1992*

Dean knelt at a pair of small, narrow feet whose pink lacquered toenails shone through their silken hosiery. Allison from Accessories slipped one foot into the pearl leather pump Dean held open with both hands. She arched her back, her cheeks glowing with pleasure. Her thigh tilted open as she inspected the shoe from the instep, then swiveled the other way, pushing her hip toward Dean, to gaze upon the delicate heel.

"I'll take them," Allison said, slipping back into her booties. She swung her blonde hair and produced Dayton's and employee discount cards from a small pink clutch.

Dean accepted her teasing gaze with a *thump-thump* to the shiny shoebox but didn't flirt back. He never did, but especially not with Noelle standing nearby.

Hosebag, thought Noelle.

Noelle and Dean had driven in together at noon, but it was the end of his short shift while Fran had given her the long graveyard shift. Noelle's sudden jealousy over this little scene pushed her to accept Dean's wish to hang out together tonight instead of taking the bus home to sleep early. Dean kissed Noelle and left, excited about coming back for his one-and-only at closing time.

"It's an honest living, selling shoes," said Gary Gorman, twisting his silver shoe horn around and around as he stood at the edge of the jade carpet bordering the marble walkway. Noelle looked up and saw in him an older man.

Gary was thirty-four years old.

Noelle issued one of her silent prayers: *Dear God, please return me to the wealth of my ancestors so I won't be forced to work here and listen to crusty old dullards like Gary any longer.*

They both stood near the holiday party shoes, a sensible strategy two days before New Year's Eve. The Middle Eastern shoe dog held his position in walking shoes, gambling on women with New Year's resolutions. The department said their goodbyes to him earlier that day since he had landed an engineering internship. The walkers held his last chance for commissions.

Kalmer ensconced himself in the juniors section across the marble walkway, hoping only for a few low-dollar sales. Squatting down on the floor, he now served up Doc Martens combat boots to a set of teen twins with their mother.

Noelle watched from afar as the twin girls asked Kalmer if they could get a better look at the Valkyrie tattoo that extended from his forearm to his wrist—they knew their Nordic mythology—and he pushed up his suit jacket sleeve so they could see it and his Minnesota Vikings tattoo.

As polite as Noelle and Gary may have acted to one another during such lulls, if a customer were to approach, the one who saw her first would holler a greeting to mark his or her turf. Gary's previous gentlemanly behavior on the sales floor had died over the better-than-expected 1992 Christmas season. Several months of bleak sales had to be made up for once customers started showing up again. Gary had a wife who worked a part-time bakery job, and they had a daughter to keep in training designer jeans.

But once again, no customers appeared.

"Why do you have your own shoe horn?" Noelle asked.

She knew better than to get Gary going but felt too utterly bored to stop herself. She hardly ever used the plastic shoehorns in the desk drawer. Rarely would Noelle put the shoes on a customer—only when they stuck their foot out like they expected her to do it.

Gary ran his index finger over the antique silver object with *The Dayton Company* engraved on it. "My grandfather was given this silver shoe horn as a gift from his uncle, who played the Dayton's piano. It was a gift for becoming the top shoe salesman in his first year. My grandfather gave it to my father, and when my father retired, he gave it to me."

Gary was a firm believer in a good shoe horn.

"You can hold it." He handed the shoe horn to Noelle, who tried to somehow hold it without touching it.

Noelle already knew Gary was a third-generation shoe dog. His father helped open Southdale, the first enclosed mall in the nation, and then Ridgedale. At one time Gary and his father even worked at Ridgedale together. Noelle couldn't imagine being a man who worked in a shoe department his whole life. In a TV sitcom called *Married with Children,* Ed O'Neill played Al Bundy, the disgusting father-husband character with that career.

"You seem to fit right in, so maybe you'll be a lifer here," Gary said. Noelle's upper lip curled back, an unbecoming expression she'd inherited from Carl Nichols.

Gary saw before she could pull back from her ugly cringe, but continued. "Do you know that the first Dayton to arrive in America was a shoemaker and a shoe salesman?" Gary asked. "Ralph Dayton arrived in New Haven, Connecticut in 1639."

Noelle daydreamed about something else instead of listening to Gary's story about long-dead Dayton men.

"Cordwainer!" Gary said suddenly.

Noelle jumped. "Huh? Geez, Gary. You startled me."

"Cordwainer. Weren't you listening? I was trying to remember the word. It means a proper English shoemaker like Ralph Dayton. Name spelled different ways: D-E-I-G-H-T-O-N, or D-A-I-T-O-N. Went on to found East Hampton, yet he and his son kept making shoes for people. People need shoes, my friend."

"You sure know a whole heap about history," said Noelle, looking around in hopes of a customer. She had sold nothing during the whole rush that normally happened when Minneapolis office workers ended their workday, and had sold only some cheap Sam and Libby's since. Dean, of course, had done fine with only a short shift.

Finally, footsteps came clicking down the walkway from cosmetics. Noelle and Gary mobilized themselves into position, Gary nonchalantly striding a few yards in the direction of the noise while Noelle considered sprinting through the stock room to nab the customer from the other door. She felt bad though; the old hockey-injury limp in Gary's left foot put him at a disadvantage.

The woman came into view, Noelle's only successful customer of the evening. She held her shopping bag out in front of her as if it stank to high heaven. Noelle stepped forward as the woman made her intentions known. She needed to return the Sam and Libby's.

This was getting to be a bummer. They used to be busy. Customers used to be happy. Management had changed the wage-commission formula to a "draw." They earned no commission on any shoes up to the point of meeting the wage. Noelle's paychecks had dropped by ten percent.

But Gary's paychecks had dropped by almost twenty percent because the new formula was implemented across the board. Those who had worked there the longest no longer earned higher wages or commission than the newbies. The company considered it fair because the long-timers still had better benefits. And they'd been there longer; they should have their loyal base of customers to call when the perfect shoe came in.

But loyal customers were fewer. With the unsteady stock market, Minnesota's famously frugal heiresses cut back.

"This fucking sucks," Noelle said.

"Hills and valleys," replied Gary. "That's retail."

"Gary, they've changed the whole system. Even if it gets better, our pay has been cut. You get that, don't you? I'm young, but if you want to change your career you need to get working on it, like, now!"

"I'm only thirty-four."

"I know. That's what I meant. You're young enough *now.*"

"Let's not worry about me. Now you could become a buyer, you know. That's the traditional path here. Unless you have some other dream, of course, like Fran. She puts in a lot of effort here, but she also writes and sells her articles to magazines. And she's not looking to get married, but she'd like to have a baby. Is there something else you would like to do in your life?"

"Not really."

It so easily could have turned out that Noelle's mother would inherit a fortune, and then she would have been in line for some of that Petit family nest egg. That's what she grew up thinking. But however it had been decided, the whole thing had bypassed her except for Grandma Greta's East Side cottage. *It's so unfair,* she thought.

What she really needed to get working on was breaking off this relationship with Dean Ohlman and finding *a man with higher potential.* Annette's medieval words, grabbing hold. Annette's words were never about believing her daughter had her own *potential.*

It had been almost fourteen months now. Her parents had finally stopped bothering her about not coming home most nights. Still, she usually left Dean's place not entirely satisfied. He came so fast. He lasted a little longer with her on top, and fortunately, he could go again. And unfortunately, again, he came faster than a tenth-grade boy.

Noelle usually had to plan for at least two preemptive fucks before Dean could have even a chance of going the distance.

"He's seaworthy," she'd said to her friend Debra one night while drinking sidecars at The New French Café. "His ship just comes in before I set sail."

"Then I wouldn't really call him seaworthy," Debra said. "More like a Jet Ski. You're gonna need to climb up on his dashboard."

Noelle said she did that a lot. "Sorry to end the metaphor party, but to put it bluntly, is a good fuck too much to ask of my future husband, which he's been hinting that he'd like to become? Of course, some guys don't do the other thing. My future husband has to do both."

Dean did whatever Noelle wanted him to do, within his control. He couldn't control how Allison from Women's Accessories liked him, but he never returned her teases. He went to church with Noelle's family on Christmas Eve. After mass, he'd asked what kind of ring she wanted.

"A big, huge diamond, at least two carats," she'd answered.

She feared a Christmas proposal and gave a sigh of relief when it didn't happen. Dean seemed like a lifer here in Women's Shoes, with his little recipe box of client info growing all the time, and now his interest in Pierre's computerized inventory project. He was gorgeous now, yes, but how many years until he might turn into Al Bundy?

So, Dean wasn't her dream husband. And while being a shoe dog was not her dream job (she didn't have one), Noelle did like working at Dayton's. Not because she liked helping people. Not because people needed shoes. But because the shoes Dayton's carried were pretty. They were *stimulating*—the colors and textures, the designs. She liked to behold them: Stuart Weitzmans, Robert Clergeries, Joan & Davids, and even the Ferragamos, which were old lady shoes but impressively crafted nonetheless. She had her eyes on a pair of gold Walter Steiger pumps and a pair of Bally riding boots, just waiting for them to get marked down.

Those Bally boots were a work of art. Thank God her parents weren't making her pay rent.

But working there too much longer...no. It didn't run in Noelle's blood like it did in Gary's, or even as much as it did in Fran's. Noelle noticed that when Fran's customers slipped her hook after trying on many pairs of shoes, Fran somehow reeled them back in, usually for the first shoe she had recommended to them.

Such silence filled the department that Noelle decided to go walk through the *Puss in Boots* exhibit on the eighth floor before closing time. She'd never gone to the Dayton's walk-through exhibit before, not even the previous two holiday seasons she had worked there. It stayed open for two more weeks after Christmas.

No one stood in line, and Noelle entered the dark auditorium with uncertainty. That changed when she came upon the first scene. The whimsical props cast a spell on her. The cat, a horrible creature, was all that the third son of a grain miller received for his inheritance. The other sons received the mill and mules. But the trickster cat won the hand of the princess for his master. The cat turned out to bear blessings as an inheritance after all.

She reached the exit wishing the series of life-sized dioramas with moveable parts and animatronic characters would never end. A glance at her watch told her she had time to walk through it again before going back to work to close out her cash register.

How had she never been to this before? How did Dayton's manage to put it together, and something new each and every year? Santa's chair, placed strategically between the exhibit's exit and the gift shop, sat empty since Christmas had passed. She sat down on it for a moment, cradled in its velvety warmth, and remembered the empowerment speech from the employee orientation she'd gone through more than two years before.

"I'm Noelle, and this is my company," she said to nobody in particular. An elf asked her if she wanted a picture with him, and she got up quickly to leave.

Kalmer had closed out her register for her. "I thought you got lost in *Puss in Boots,*" he said, waving his brawny arm in the air for humorous effect. "I almost came up there to drag you out!"

When Dean pulled his truck up to the employee door, Noelle asked him to take her for a drive.

He kissed her. "Where are we going?"

"Take 94 all the way to St. Paul and just keep going until the exit at East Seventh." They glided along slowly on the icy highway until Dean took the left-hand exit.

"East Side, huh?" he said. They passed brightly colored gingerbread Victorian homes, more Swedish in color selection and lacy woodwork than any other Victorians in the country. They passed homes with plywood covering the windows. The neighborhood had long been poor. Even the junior Hamm's Beer tycoon had been a hold-out there until he died in 1931, well after the other tycoons had moved to Summit Avenue or the lakes. It always seemed like a rejuvenation lay just around the corner.

Noelle put her hand on Dean's thigh until she had to point out where to take a left onto the street where her cottage sat.

A large sheet of painted plywood sticking up out of the snow read "EAST SIDE PRIDE." Noelle groaned. She'd forgotten. The wife had called her to ask permission.

Noelle had wondered why they would bother to ask about sticking up a sign in the yard, and she'd said, "Sure," tuning out the words coming over the line. "Whatever."

"It's a fucking billboard!" she said now.

What she hadn't considered was that the husband worked as a concrete installer. He had secured the giant sign, as his wife had likely explained, with concrete footings. It was the largest East Side Pride sign anywhere between highways 35E and 94, the whole damned East Side.

The words were painted in kelly green on a white background, and the *i* in Pride was a paintbrush, with a splotch of paint for the dot. A flower curved around the final *e*.

"The children need to feel proud of where they live," the wife had explained to Noelle, "like they belong here."

From the street, Dean and Noelle could see the tenants sitting together in front of a TV and their decorated Christmas tree. Multicolored lights covered the cottage. A lit fake palm tree and a snowman stood by the yard sign. Moments after they pulled over to the curb, another family pulled up with pots and trays of food. They looked toward Dean's truck and waved. "Hola," shouted a little girl.

In the dark, Noelle's inherited house looked more like a joyous Christmas *casa* than a dilapidated dump.

"So, this is actually your house?" Dean asked. "Then why haven't we done it here yet? You could tell your tenants we need them out while we clean the carpets or something."

Or they could go wait outside for about thirty seconds, Noelle thought to herself.

They sat there until the father stood up and peered out the window. He waved, as if to see if they were another family wanting to join the party. When Dean started up the truck again, the man closed the curtains.

"My tenants never stay for long," Noelle said. "We can do it there when they move out."

She felt Dean harden as she touched him, and then she added, "For now, let's drive around back and down the alley."

It would be a preemptive fuck. She knew they wouldn't be together much longer, and tonight when they got back to his place she wanted him to last a good, long time.

11. Problems That Entice, 1993

By January of 1993, Pierre St. Hilaire had worked at Dayton's for eight months, longer than he'd expected. He had accomplished more than any stock boy, a.k.a. inventory coordinator, in Dayton's history.

He'd gotten computers at six cash register stations throughout the flagship store, probably two years before it would have happened otherwise. The pilot project now underway trained guest consultants on how to track down inventory for customers with a few keystrokes. Yet, he still rode the freight elevator and slashed boxes open with his X-Acto knife. He'd been recognized for his initiative with a two-dollar per hour raise, but maybe a real promotion lay in store for him later on. Johanne assured him there was no harm in asking.

He hoped it would be a promotion out of the zoo of a stock room, where he was regularly subjected to presumptuous women who thought he was flirting with them every time he opened his mouth, just because of his French accent. Then there were the shoe dogs who thought of him as their own personal minion. And finally, the cardboard cuts to his hands and wrists, so dry from Minnesota winter and forced-air heating that they sometimes drew blood.

Among the other trials and tribulations of working in the department stood Gary Gorman. Pierre grew up with Caribbean storytellers in his family, so all the talking didn't bother him. But his relatives in Martinique told much more riveting stories. Even the short letters that came in the small blue envelopes with French stamps from his mother each week contained better stories, although they sometimes made him homesick.

Gary's stories helped the shoe dogs pass time when no customers came clicking their heels down the marble walkway, but stock room work never ended.

Pierre still couldn't get away if Gary nabbed him to explain how the Dayton boys had to start out on the sales floor or in the stock room, or how the young Douglas Dayton had started right there in Women's Shoes.

"Did your father and grandfather really like working here?" Pierre asked.

"My great-grandfather, too, he worked here when it was Goodfellow's Daylight Store and George Draper Dayton was only one of the partners. Then there were decades of it being a family business. It's been going downhill ever since the family gave up control. There's just no heart in it anymore. Pretty soon they won't even have a piano player."

Another time Gary opened his mental encyclopedia to the time George Draper Dayton bought a coal mine at age seventeen, then to when he got into agriculture and banking down in Worthington before settling into retail. All that, plus marriage and children.

Gary said that the employees of old knew the founder to be more energetic—even happier—when the store lost money. It signaled an opportunity for change.

Mr. Dayton would have been happy to be there now.

Pierre got that. He felt the same way. He never felt happier than when he was trying to solve inventory problems with the IBM systems engineer and the marketing managers. It was never as easy to forget about his homesickness for Martinique as when he was immersed in the pilot project. It required system engineering work on a stock boy's wage, but that might change.

Not every problem needed a computer solution. Pierre talked to the floor managers about implementing another change, one that didn't make him any friends.

Each salesperson was made to feel personally invested in the inventory, like they owned a tiny part of the company, by spending the first thirty minutes of every shift maintaining an assigned row of shoeboxes.

Many of them saw this change as Pierre's ruse to shirk his responsibilities. It was his job to maintain the stock.

Within days, it all became more orderly. When salespeople had to keep a section of their own neat, they put the shoeboxes back in the right place every time. Soon, they began to find styles and sizes faster. They lost fewer shoes and created fewer mismate pairs. They all sold more.

Pierre spent little time analyzing this success. Johanne had moved up from washing Petri dishes to assisting in the ecology research in the lab where she worked. He had his own research to do if he hoped to become what she believed he could be.

And that was much more than a twenty-six-year-old glorified stock boy.

12. First Avenue, 1993

Dean Ohlman's father worked as a bricklayer. Nearing what should be retirement age for such a physical job, he had just learned how to apply the new brick and stone veneers that were putting his trade out of business.

Noelle's father worked on a city roads crew. Her mother married him for love, but now he did nothing but crush beer cans and watch TV in his precious garage. This lesson Annette imparted to her daughter as often as she could.

On Valentine's Day, Dean presented Noelle with a quarter-carat diamond ring and a proposal. She said, "Maybe ask again over the summer?" She planned not to last with him another week.

Soon, February neared its end. The break-up hadn't come along as planned.

Dean planned to take Noelle to a Greek restaurant near Uptown one night; he favored it for their dates because it was cheap but adequately romantic if you went late enough to miss the booster-seat crowd. But then his friend offered him two tickets to the *Red Hot Chili Peppers* concert at First Avenue, the club that Prince made famous. Neither of them knew much about alternative or punk rock, but Noelle's friend said they should go.

Debra didn't understand why Noelle stuck with Dean, though. "You work right in the middle of downtown. Can't you meet a banker?" she asked.

"Sounds boring," she responded, but neither would Noelle consider accepting a proposal from a future Al Bundy. Tonight, she decided, would finally be the last night.

She spent the afternoon getting highlights at The Hair Police, a salon where the stylists wore thick-soled combat boots and ironed Noelle's hair straight. She drove straight to Debra's apartment to finish getting ready. The night before, she had fired up her old sewing machine—the last gift she'd ever received from Grandma Greta—and made herself a black and purple rayon dress cinched at the waist with a wide elastic zipper belt. The design idea had come to her and she couldn't find anything like it at Dayton's or elsewhere.

She'd put on weight, but compensated with black high-heeled boots. She dabbed Debra's honeysuckle oil on her wrists, neck, and inner thighs.

Debra gave Noelle the key to lock up and went out. Dean came to pick her up there. He wore a new burgundy button-down shirt.

"Hi," he said. Noelle breathed in his citron cologne as he hugged her with one arm. He usually complimented her, but something in his face showed uncertainty about her new look. And yet, not total displeasure either.

Dean zipped the belt up and down a few times, like a toddler playing with a Dressy Bessy doll. She unzipped it for him, pulled the dress off over her head, and zipped the belt back onto her naked waist. She stood there against Debra's antique armoire in her bra, panties, and belt, and then a moment later she had only the belt. Dean looked at how white her cushiony bust and bottom were against her golden tan. These were the tan lines that Noelle knew drove men crazy, but Dean didn't need to see her tan lines to want her. He always wanted her. He turned off the lights.

When a woman who smells like honeysuckles and a man who smells like citrons touch and kiss each other's bodies in the dark, it holds promise.

Promises sometimes prematurely abort.

Dean came within seconds. He apologized and French kissed her hard right in the spot she'd wanted to press him into that day she stood above him on the stock room ladder, the spot she always pressed him into after each time he ejaculated too fast. She'd had enough of this routine, though, so she climbed atop his drooping shame and stayed until he rallied. Like a jockey with no option but to win, she rode until, finally, they came together. She tumbled off of him, thinking, *I have to do everything*.

They arrived at the concert late and left early, sitting in his car on the street outside of First Avenue.

"Will you please marry me?" he asked. "I want you to be my wife," he said. "I want to watch TV together in our sweatpants and eat nachos on the couch after work. I want us to travel together, maybe start our own shoe sales business and have babies."

"You do make good nachos," Noelle said. "Let me think about it. I need to sleep in my own bed tonight."

He drove her to her family home on Butternut Avenue. "Drive safely," she said as she stepped out of the truck. She ran into the house and left her painful boots by the door.

They were both supposed to work the next day, but Noelle woke up with a sore throat and called in sick. Dean tried calling her, but Annette told him she needed her sleep. Noelle slammed NyQuil for four days, then emerged from the fog with a final answer: Dean might have made a sweet

husband, but her mother was right. He didn't merit a real
St. Paul Petit like Noelle Nichols.

Before the end of March, Dean left Dayton's for a mail-
order catalog business in the IDS Center across the street.
Noelle ran into him sometimes on the outdoor Nicollet
Mall.

A bit further into the future, she would notice that where
went Dean, so went Allison from Women's Accessories—
the blonde one might envision when hearing the song
about the angel in the centerfold.

Allison, with the eyelashes that didn't need mascara.
Allison, who spoke French well enough to translate for
tourists. Allison, who wrapped each precious scarf she sold
in white tissue paper and sealed it with a gold foil Dayton's
sticker just like they taught in orientation. Allison, who was
up for a buyer position. They would probably send her to
fucking Paris to buy scarves.

Eventually, Noelle realized that she no longer saw Dean
or Allison around at all. *Pas du tout.*

13. *The Infirmary, 1993*

Noelle was blessed with a "refreshing" and "bright"
imagination as a child, one of the kindest school
nuns had once insisted at a school conference. Annette
had looked around like the nun must be speaking about a
different child. Eventually, this spark, if it ever truly existed,
faded, proving Annette and Carl right.

Perhaps too much partying in college could be blamed.
But Debra partied just the same and she seemed to get
smarter and more ambitious all of the time.

Noelle didn't possess nearly that same drive, but she
was selling more shoes. Her greatest achievement was an
award for customer service. Someone who tried on all the

Keds turned out to be a "secret shopper," a paid customer-spy reporting back to management. Noelle had been on point with her, knowing the secret shoppers were out.

Getting that award made her hold her head higher. *Shoulders back, tits out,* as her grandmother had taught her. Her name soon topped the productivity chart.

Still, she became lonely. A few men in the store grew comfortable enough with her to flirt, especially now that Dean was gone. Noelle's need for attention, now even more desperate, sometimes resulted in seemingly accidental exposures of the lacy tops of her thigh-highs. After a security guard mentioned his appreciation of her pink string bikini in the commercial, she wore it under a button-down dress one day and shared a peek of the bikini top as she walked past the security office on her way to punch her time card. Later, the guard found Noelle in the stock room and pressed against her by the sandal wall, right where anyone could have seen.

That flirtation was followed up hours later with sex on a sectional couch that took up half of the security guard's studio apartment, although his performance had not matched his confidence. He had not been seaworthy at all. She'd gone home afterward and watched *The Tonight Show* with Annette and Carl, and that had been more fun.

Perhaps the pink bikini could be put to better use with someone else.

When Pierre followed her up to the stock room's boot loft the next day to help her find the right sizes of Bandolino riding boots, she assumed he planned a seduction like the others. No matter that she had asked for his help finding the boots, knowing exactly where they were up in the loft. It was almost April, and these boots were the dregs of the seasonal clearance.

Pierre asked Noelle boring questions about the inventory, and about finding shoes for customers, and about all kinds of stuff that made no sense to her since everything seemed fine the way it was. She hoped she didn't have to start using the computers. She mistakenly, perhaps hopefully, reckoned Pierre was just using these conversations about systems as a pretense to talk to her. The way he said *Noëlle,* for example, with the French accent for her name that she had rarely heard pronounced correctly—was that his way of seducing her? Or was it just how he talked because of wherever it was he was from?

Martinique—that was it, she remembered. Noelle imagined it to be a sunny, carefree place blessed with tropical fruity versions of French pastries, and she wondered why someone from there would move to *Minne-snow-ta.*

Pierre was only doing his job in helping her, perhaps, but she flashed him a lacy thigh-high in thanks before bringing the boots out to her customer. He seemed surprised, although Noelle was uncertain whether or not she had made an actionable impression. Pierre, engaged but not yet married, wasn't as easy for her to read as the security guard with the studio apartment.

She would have to try harder.

The Louis-style heel, splayed fatter at the base, didn't appeal to Noelle, which was best for her wallet. It should never have come back in style for the '90s. *Long live narrow heels and pointy toes.* Still, when the Enzos came in, and the display consultant couldn't muster the effort Ralphina would have put forth in giving them the period ambiance they deserved, Noelle knew where to find genuine 1940s display pieces on the tenth floor.

She enlisted Pierre to go with her. They rode the freight elevator up and Noelle showed Pierre the storage area where once, long ago, Dayton's ran a nurse's station for sick or weary customers and employees. An old nurse's cap still sat on a small table next to a sickbed. Noelle pointed Pierre to the piles of vintage display gear while she perched the hat on her head and posed in a mirror. She thought she looked smashing in the white nurse's cap with the black stripe that matched nicely with her black button-down dress. Pierre stacked various vintage shoe holders and display blocks into a cardboard box.

"Let's take a break," Noelle said. She nosed through the metal cabinets, finding a bottle of Madeira wine.

"Look what the nurse has hidden away for you," she said, opening the bottle and putting it to Pierre's lips.

"We should go back," he said, but Noelle stood on her toes and pulled his head down to connect the two in a kiss. She touched the outside of his pants.

Pierre laughed. "You nearly tricked me, but I've learned about this before. Today is April Fool's Day. Thank God. I was worried there for a minute, but I see now—you are making a joke for the special holiday."

Noelle licked his ear lobe. "I like your ears," she said. "That's not a joke."

He shouldn't have come there with her. It wasn't like he hadn't heard about Noelle from the other men who talked about her tanning bed commercial. She behaved differently when Dean was her boyfriend. But Pierre had recently heard the security guard bragging that he'd gotten her onto his couch.

She kissed him on the mouth. He breathed hard but backed away. "Are you doing this because you miss Dean? You will find another boyfriend."

"Who is Dean?" Noelle said. She slowly unbuttoned her black dress, first revealing her hot pink string bikini top, then—he had now stopped turning away—her tan belly, and then her string bikini bottom. She undid two more buttons to reveal the black lacy tops of her thigh-highs and raised one high-heel shoe up onto the hospital bed.

She opened the dress and pushed her hip toward him, offering the little string bow. "How do you say 'untie' in French?" she said. She watched Pierre catch their reflection in the mirror on the cabinet door. He didn't look away. It was like watching two other people.

He saw those two bodies in the mirror, the tanned tigress swaying closer to that tall man in khakis with a box cutter in his shirt pocket.

He yielded control to this clone who walked his long fingers along the woman's hip to the little string bow.

"*Comment dit-on...*" she tried to ask him again, now in French, how to say it. "*Comment dit-on...untie?*"

He held the end of one string and saw the man in the mirror pull on it until the bow came undone.

"*Mon Dieu,*" he responded, as the front and back bikini pieces separated and fell away.

Pierre fell onto Noelle and then she crawled on top of him. The metal hospital bed began to rock, and he warned himself the rhythm was the pounding beat of his fiancée's own heart. Noelle's body like an ocean then swallowed him whole, flipped him back on top of her, and together they crashed like salty waves on the beach of the island he had left far, far behind.

14. *Bank, 1993*

The *All Dogs Go to Heaven* poster left by the previous owners came down in one piece from the wall inside Mardi's bedroom closet. Behind it, a dark hole in the plaster gaped at her like a ghoul's open mouth. She stared at it for a second then sprinted to the other bedroom. The guest room closet shared that wall with her bedroom closet. That's what this construction was about, knocking out that wall so Mardi could have one decent-sized place to hang her clothes in her own room.

A 1970s Suzi Quatro poster hung from the wall in that guest closet, and the edges crumbled in Mardi's hands when she removed the thumbtack and pulled it away. Quatro came a bit before Mardi's time as a music lover, but she set it aside to hang onto. Light shot through the hole, now that both coverings were gone. So that's why nobody had removed the posters. They hid damage.

But how did such damage occur in both closets? It was as if a miniature battering ram had been used to knock out a passage for contraband, like in some prison movie. Mardi bent at the knees and looked through the hole, seeing into her own bedroom closet. A breeze came through the open window and the poster flew to a corner across the room.

For the first week after she had moved in, Mardi tried sleeping in the home's master bedroom suite at the top of the stairs, a large room with an attached den, crawl spaces, and bathroom. It was her music room now. She loved the suite when she bought the house, but now sleeping there didn't feel right. Listening to her The Clash and Adam Ant albums there felt right. And The Suburbs, of course, her hometown band.

Mardi jumped, startled by a voice at the open window. "Yoo-hoo, darling!"

It was Irene, holding up a flat of delphinium seedlings. Irene still didn't like to come inside the house that reminded her of death. She came to help plant living things around the perimeter while Edward helped Mardi adjoin the two closets and complete the wall work needed to make it look like the guest room never had a closet. Irene would let Mardi have an old armoire of hers for that room.

"Mom, you scared me," Mardi said through the window.

"Look, your favorite colors, purple and violet." Irene held up the bedding plants. "Just like that tanzanite you invest in. Have you profited from that yet?"

"No, Mom. I thought Dad wasn't going to worry you about that. Why don't you come in for a minute?"

"Not even a necklace? They could at least send you a pretty tanzanite pendant."

"It's an investment, Mom, more like a cash crop. I'm not in it for the jewelry. I'll bring you something to drink. Where's Dad?"

The chimes rang out. Mardi grabbed her mother a can of ginger ale and went to open the front door for her father, who stood there with her old Radio Flyer wagon. Edward had pulled it along neighborhood roads in Plymouth, the hilly mile-long Ferndale Road to Wayzata, and into Mardi's neighborhood with the plants and his tools inside it, Irene Nordic-walking alongside him.

"Are you sure you want to do this?" he asked, yanking the wagon up the front step and down the hall into the guest room.

"Yeah, I don't know if it will help the value. But I'm tired of running from room to room for my clothes."

"Then sleep in the master bedroom. It has lots of space. That whole den up there could be your closet."

"I don't wanna. I think the ghosts live up there," she said. "Don't tell Mom I said that. I'm always frightened something might emerge from those creepy crawl spaces."

"Why don't you open up the crawl space walls?" Edward asked.

"Too much thick wood paneling. This closet is the only thing we can probably manage on our own right now."

Irene shouted through the window, "Maybe if Mardi had a big strong fellow, she wouldn't be scared to sleep in the master bedroom!"

Mardi leaned out the window. "And maybe Irene should come inside if she wants to provide color commentary!"

Edward surveyed the space and peered through the hole. He shrugged. "It's always something weird with these older homes. But at least the memory of the tragedy here will fade. Someday you'll make good money when you sell this place."

It was time for the fun part, the sledgehammer. They each donned a 3M face mask to keep dust out of their lungs and took turns knocking out the plaster and throwing it in a garbage bin. When they could see more wall joists than wall, they stood back.

Mardi looked down and picked up something. She shook off a layer of dust. A clear plastic cylinder, like a small bank teller tube, held a piece of paper inside.

Edward pulled down his 3M mask. "What's that?" he asked, rubbing his hands together.

Mardi pulled her mask off and cast it aside, unscrewed the cap of the tube, and pulled out the note. "It's a toy bank tube, I guess. The note says, 'Deposit slip' and 'One dollar deposited in this savings account. Name: Ralphy. Account number: 21854. Signed, Cathy, bank teller.'"

Edward looked at the bubbled handwriting. "Looks like a teenager named Cathy and her brother Ralph had these two rooms. They must have been the children of whoever owned the house before the Hess couple."

"Aww, and we knocked down their bank," Mardi said. She put the pretend deposit slip back in the dusty tube and javelined it into the garbage bin. They continued the work of removing the framing beams that separated the space into the two closets and then took a crowbar to the wood flooring in each closet. It started to look like just one adult closet now instead of two doll-house closets. They had done enough work for the afternoon. The new closet floor could wait until the next day, and Edward and Bernard would help with the sheetrock the day after that.

They cleaned up and Mardi handed her father a drink— Maker's Mark on the rocks. Father and daughter sat on the living room couch, hardly a thought about the bloody scene that once covered the parquet floor.

When Irene could hold her bladder no longer after her day of horticultural efforts, she tiptoed to the powder room closest to the entrance and then right back out again. She gladly accepted a drink on the old wicker settee that had been left on the covered patio along with two chairs. Thank God her old tennis partner moved out of the neighborhood and wouldn't spy her there. Even sitting on the Hess's old furniture, Irene looked a bit scandalized. Mardi and Edward came to join her.

After Edward pulled the red wagon behind them back to their own house, Irene again walking alongside with her Nordic poles, Mardi savored more drinks on the wicker settee until the sunlight disappeared. When she awoke the next morning on her living room couch, she didn't even remember going back inside.

15. Our Company, 1993

The day got off to a respectable start for people whose job takes place at foot level. A shoe representative came to tell them about the life and legacy of Salvatore Ferragamo. After that, even though it was still not even Halloween of 1993, the rep unveiled the spring '94 collection. The staff sat on the edges of their chairs, eager to learn more about the handmade Italian shoes.

There was beauty in this work after all. Passion, even.

But it went quickly downhill before ten-thirty when Kalmer was seen being walked out by the security guard he towered over, his penny-red curls bouncing up and down in distress. They all thought he was just on a break. The captive shoe dog trudged alongside the captor, the security guard who had disappointed Noelle in bed not even seven months before.

Kalmer so clearly could have piledriven the security guard into the marble walkway with one hand, but he never would have done any such thing.

Noelle, not normally one to risk her job for someone else, took long strides toward them in her suede Donna Karan booties. Upon catching up, she poked the security guard in his upper arm. "Excuse me, but where are you taking our friend here?"

"Noelle," Fran said haltingly. "Hush."

The security guard looked Noelle over invitingly, as if she might be asking for a second serving of himself, as if the first had been in any way satisfying. "We're taking him to the employee door. The cops will take him from there."

"No cops," Noelle said, stomping on the guard's foot. He yelped.

"Don't get yourself into trouble for me," Kalmer pleaded.

"We can't do anything about it," Fran said. "He gave a customer the sale price the night before the sale. The computer system flagged it. It's considered a form of theft."

A price adjustment could be made during a sale for a shoe bought earlier but giving the sale price prematurely was not the natural order of retail. It was seen as a cheater's way to make a sale. Still, Noelle couldn't see it as stealing, especially not for someone who had never been greedy about commissions.

The security guard continued marching Kalmer along, but Noelle re-approached and stomped on his foot again. "He was just helping the customer. I was here. She hardly spoke English and she had to catch a plane. She paid cash—maybe it was all she had."

Noelle's words got Kalmer to finally speak up for himself. "She was a few dollars short—I told them. Ha. And they say we are empowered. They said we are supposed to do what we would do if it were *our company.*"

"Yeah," agreed Noelle. "Remember the training script. Remember the slogan, 'It's my company?'"

Gary cleared his throat. "It is well known that George Draper Dayton believed those who made mistakes learned from them and became better employees afterward," he told the guard. "Kalmer is the most reliable member of our team. Nothing keeps him from showing up and doing his best work each day."

"Maybe he can get a job as a mailman," the security guard quipped.

Fran interrupted before Gary could continue arguing. "There's nothing we can do here and now. He's already been fired by Human Resources."

"Well, cops have bigger things to worry about than retail sale prices," Noelle said, her hazel eyes glaring darkly into the security guard's eyes. "And so do you. No cops."

Her menacing voice told him that she might tell someone things he wouldn't want known. "Okay, fine, no cops," he said. "I'll just walk him out."

Kalmer had never been anything but a friendly colleague to Noelle. With his tattoos on too-big muscles, and zeal for hockey hair and the Minnesota Vikings, he was definitely not her type. But she didn't like to see him go like that. He had been sweet, and different than the other men.

And now he was gone.

Fran patted Gary's arm, and Gary leaned into her for just a moment, a gesture between two people who seemed like they had worked together since the Great Depression, although they were only in their thirties.

Fran pulled her hand away and whispered, "Well, tomorrow I'm going to accidentally take a two-hour break after I clock in. I've worked off the clock plenty and I have somewhere to go. Can you live without a manager all morning?"

"Let me think about it," Gary said, trying not to sound shaken about what had happened. "What do you think, Noelle? Should we let Fran take an extra-long break from *our company* on a busy fall day?"

"Sure, and I need a break from *our company* right now," Noelle answered. She thought she'd sneak away and take a morning rest in the relics of the old infirmary, that place known only to some. That place from an era she had never known, when owners cared for sick employees. Now they were just a number that could be flagged and expunged from the system without warning.

The shoe dogs ignored Noelle. Fran had been taking off a lot of time lately, and they began to wonder where it was that she needed to go and when she would get around to posting the schedule for next week.

All of the shoe dogs but one, that is. Gary nodded. Only he knew about the effort, and the heartache, it was costing Fran to make her dream of motherhood come true.

16. Popover, 1993

Noelle and Debra lunched in the busy Dayton's Oak Grill Room on the twelfth floor, seated by a fireplace that had already seen three hundred years of history when someone brought it over from Salisbury, England. They planned to visit the holiday exhibit on this Black Friday that Noelle somehow had not been assigned to work.

"Do you have butter brickle ice cream?" Noelle asked their waiter, a finely chiseled model male specimen.

The waiter shook his head, setting a popover in front of Noelle and her friend. The rolls—burnished brown and crisp on the outside, hollow and eggy on the inside—were the classic Oak Grill Room delight.

Debra gasped. "That's a weird craving before lunch. We haven't even eaten our popovers."

"I was thinking it would taste great *with* the popover. You put butter on it, so why not butter brickle?"

"Are you sure you don't have a popover of your own baking in there?" Debra pointed at Noelle's belly.

"I'm sure. I just had my monthly curse, along with all the usual sore feet and backaches. Whew! I'm seriously considering giving up these high heels."

"Sore feet and backaches are pregnancy symptoms too. And your back has been hurting all the time."

Noelle leaned back in her seat and interlaced her fingers over her belly. "I'm not pregnant." She lowered her voice to a whisper. "Pierre was so worried, so I took a pee test. Single pink line; that's a negative. I've been pretty regular anyway—I've never been like clockwork."

Debra stared at her. "What about that Bozo before Pierre, the one with the studio apartment?"

Noelle smirked. "The security guard? He couldn't keep it up long enough to make a deposit. And there hasn't been anyone else after those two."

"It might as well be me to tell you...maybe ice cream before lunch is why you've gained so much weight. And how many trips to the Marketplace Deli do you make every time you work a shift?"

"Not all guys mind these frozen-yogurt-fed curves, you know. I've only gained ten pounds or so. I've been behaving like the nuns from our school. I might just reclaim my virginity for my future fiancé."

The waiter brought their orders to the table—wild rice soup and a Mandarin chicken salad for Debra, baked pasta with ham and béchamel sauce for Noelle. "At least I'm not anorexic like you," Noelle said, looking at Debra's salad and soup cup. She flagged down the waiter to ask for another popover.

The two young women rode the elevator to the eighth floor and entered the chute formed of red velvet ropes until they reached the end of the line. As soon as they stopped, people began piling up behind them.

Noelle's eyes rested on the brunette head in front of her. It sported a punky angular haircut with a preppy purple headband tied in a knot at the nape of the neck. Noelle poked Debra, mouthing the name *Mardi*. She grabbed Debra's elbow and turned around to push the family behind her forward to create a cushion between herself and her cousin.

Sensing something going on behind her, Mardi turned around and looked her cousin up and down.

"Noelle...you're looking great," Mardi said. "Nice stiletto pumps."

Fuck, Noelle thought, now she would be next to her cousin in line for ages and then all the way through the exhibit.

"Hi Mardi," she said. Then she turned to Debra. "This is Mardi Wirt, formerly Mardi Petit."

Debra flashed a smile. "You're Noelle's other cousin from the western suburbs? She's told me a little about Bernard. What do you do?"

Noelle responded for her cousin. "Mardi is a MAL."

Mardi pursed her lips. "Marketing-advertising liaison. I substitute teach some too—my degree is in education. And you are...?"

"Debra." She stuck her hand out to shake, but Mardi turned back around.

Noelle knew she should have just ended it there, but she didn't. "Did you come to the holiday exhibit all by yourself? Why didn't you bring Aunt Irene?"

Mardi's father, Edward, was Noelle's favorite of her mother's two brothers, but his wife had always been a nightmare. Noelle wondered what role Irene had played in the fact that her children ended up with properties that were worth much more than what Noelle inherited. Of course, neither of them had received what Uncle Tom and his son got.

"Oh, Irene is mall walking today," said Mardi.

She didn't mention which mall, but it was the "mega mall," the nickname of the Mall of America. Although Irene was a lifelong Dayton's shopper and had sworn she would never enter that ugly behemoth of a mall in Bloomington, she had succumbed to the magic of Nordstrom. Her mall walks gave her an excuse to shop there. She could get in nearly four miles at the mega mall, with full shopping bags as hand weights to boost her calorie burn.

"And how is Aunt Annette? Still living in the old brewery house? And you too, still?" Mardi asked rhetorically.

"Yes, my own house is rented out to a Mexican family in need. I give them a good rate so they can have affordable housing. And I heard you picked up a house in Wayzata for a good price?"

Noelle was proud of herself for that last line. She usually couldn't think of a good dig or a comeback until an hour after the chance had passed her by, and here she was having regular repartee with Mardi. She'd almost said "a house to die for," but that would have been over the top.

She wondered if Mardi knew Ralphina well enough to realize the display designer's nephew was the child orphaned by the murder-suicide in Wayzata, but she kept her mouth closed.

The line moved and they entered the auditorium. The *Beauty and the Beast* theme pulled Mardi and Debra into another world, but Noelle felt less enchanted by it than she had been by the *Puss in Boots* exhibit the previous year. Maybe the popovers and baked pasta had induced the indigestion she felt coming on. She yawned.

Suddenly, a terrible back spasm knocked Noelle down into a crouch-and-curl position.

"Hey yogi," said Mardi, "What the hell are you doing? Can't you just tour the exhibit without any bizarre drama?"

Noelle stood up, barely. Debra grabbed her by the arm. "Is it your back again?" She pulled her up.

"It's fine." Noelle pulled away and distracted herself from the pain by observing a life-sized diorama of Belle with a stack of books inside the library of a cozy French chateau. Another spasm roiled through her back and she tried to stay upright as she rocked back and forth.

"Oh my God, what is wrong with you?" Mardi whispered loudly. "Do we need to call Holly Bell?" Holly Bell was the all-purpose service desk reached by phones mounted throughout the store.

"No, please don't call Holly Bell. It feels like I have a broken rib, but my mom thinks maybe I've been having some pleurisy. It runs in the Nichols family."

"Or it's that second popover you ate at the Oak Grill Room," said Debra.

"Figures," said Mardi, tightening her purple headband.

They wandered ahead through the scenes of Belle, the Beast, and Belle's father. The Beast was losing his brusqueness, and Belle softened toward him as he showed her his own library. The lifelike characters made slight mechanical movements—the Beast handing Belle a book, Belle's mouth cracking open into a smile of surprise that such a hideous creature would like to read.

The three women dropped their snide comments to watch it.

"I don't know what it is. It's so simple, but I could watch the Beast hand Belle that same book, Belle smile, and the Beast pull it back over and over all night," Mardi said. "I've never missed an exhibit my entire life since I was born."

Noelle looked at her cousin and back at Belle. "It's only my second time," she said. "The St. Paul Petits didn't really do this shit."

"I know," said Mardi. "And my mother is still furious that Bernard moved to St. Paul. He might even turn Catholic. He's so depressed about the North Stars team moving to Dallas."

Noelle's back pain subsided for the moment, and she and Mardi guffawed over the absurdity of the family's divide. A family behind the three women nudged them along. The darkness gave the Minnesotans permission for their atypical aggression and time passed in silence as they moved dutifully along the pathway.

"It's my first time in the exhibit," Debra told Mardi. "Noelle dragged me here."

Debra turned to tell Noelle she was glad she had insisted on bringing her, but she didn't see her in the dark. Mardi stood ahead, gazing at the next scene.

"Where's Noelle?" Debra whisper-shouted. Mardi looked around. They headed back against the flow of the crowd and found Noelle leaning against a wall.

"Call Holly Bell and tell that bitch to do something," Noelle croaked.

"Holly Bell will call an ambulance," Mardi said.

"No, never mind. Just take me. It comes and goes. Let's just get out of here before it happens again."

Noelle, Mardi, and Debra pushed through the crowd to the end of the exhibit, past Santa and his photographer elves and through the gift shop. "Screw this," said Mardi, seeing that now there was a line to get back on the elevators. "Follow me."

She led them to a staircase and they descended. Clipping through Women's Shoes, Noelle held her high heels in one hand. Her hosiery frayed and dampened on the gritty floor covered in slush melting off of the crowd's winter boots.

"I can't drive." Noelle handed her keys to Debra. They had driven downtown together in Noelle's car.

"I'll drive," said Mardi. She pressed the level F button inside the ramp elevator.

Within two minutes, Noelle was lying down in the back seat of Mardi's compact car, her head on Debra's lap. Mardi, alone in front, accelerated into the dizzying descent of six levels of the spiral exit from the Dayton-Radisson parking ramp.

"What the hell is happening?" Mardi asked. "And is Hennepin County Medical Center okay? It's right downtown."

"I think Noelle is having a baby. I've seen women in labor when I worked at a hospital one summer," Debra said.

Noelle's body convulsed. "Breathe!" Debra yelled at her. "Breath in and then blow out in short, quick bursts."

Debra didn't know what she was doing, but Noelle seemed to calm down with any sort of instruction, so she continued coaching her while making guesses about the situation. "She may not look pregnant, but she doesn't look like her normal self either, does she? It's not an extra popover doing this, that's for damn sure."

Mardi turned around to glare at Debra while the ramp attendant took her payment. Noelle and Mardi both furrowed their brows, briefly showing a family resemblance not seen before.

"It's pleurisy, *dammit*," Noelle screamed. Then she lowered her voice. "Or like you said, I'm just too fucking fat. But would you shut the fuck up about a baby?"

"I've heard using profanity is common during labor," said Mardi.

"You must not know your cousin very well. If profanity means labor, then Noelle's been in labor since the fourth grade. She gave the nuns at our school heart attacks."

Mardi swerved around the other cars on Eighth Street, getting into the lane to turn left onto Park Avenue a block away from HCMC. Noelle sat up as the light turned red and traffic zoomed in front of them.

Noelle yelled, "You're an asswhore for not making that light!"

Mardi flinched. "Now I see why my mom didn't want me and Bernard to hang around with our vile relatives from St. Paul."

Debra shrugged.

"Don't you dare tell Aunt Irene and Uncle Edward, or my parents, or Bernard, or anyone," threatened Noelle.

"Tell them about what? Your 'pleurisy'?"

Noelle turned off the tough girl act and began bawling. Debra wiped her forehead with her scarf and promised, "Mardi and I will make sure this is our secret, at least until you figure out what's going on here. Agree, Mardi? Our secret?"

"Our secret, sure, Debbie Dumbfuck," Mardi replied, giving profanity a chance. "What are cousins for?"

One hour and forty-six minutes later, their secret—a girl just shy of five pounds who had been hiding out in Noelle's body—lay sleeping on her chest. The baby stretched long for her scant weight, a full twenty-one inches. It was as if a baby-sized Tyra Banks had been hiding along the back rim of Noelle's rib cage.

Noelle pleaded to the doctor, still trying to deny she could possibly have given birth. "But I had a negative pregnancy test and I got my period most of the months. I never felt any kicking until today. I never even puked!"

She remembered she'd vomited, but only once. And she'd had some butterfly flutters, sure, but assumed they were just gas.

Debra concurred, telling the doctor, "She gained a little weight, but there was no baby bump. I'm her best friend and it never even occurred to me until today." Then she added, "Or...not really...I mean, not lately."

The doctor spoke in a cool and strategic crisis mode. "It happens this way sometimes. About one out of every six hundred women menstruate, or seem to be menstruating, throughout their pregnancy. One out of every four hundred women gain little weight or carry the fetus in a way that doesn't show out in front like usual or allow them to feel much movement. Many women avoid morning sickness. Only a tiny percentage of women experience all of these situations, so it is rare that there are such utter surprises. But you are certainly not the first."

"But how could I not have felt her?" Noelle asked.

"It's the way she was positioned, along with other factors. She appears to be about one month early, as well. She is a long, but very thin baby. Not having that last month of growth and movement further helped her go undetected."

Noelle touched the pink and brown infant's head, running her fingers over the softest short fuzz. *I can't fall in love with her,* she thought and then said out loud, "I know I conceived her on April Fools Day, but she's the one who fooled me."

The baby looked up, giving her some side-eye, and Noelle imagined her infant mind asking, *Who the hell is this slutty loser? Surely she's not my mother.*

The new mother let out a horrible sob.

"I know your family is difficult," Debra said. "But you don't need them."

Mardi cleared her throat. "The Petits aren't all bad."

"It's not just the Petits," Noelle said. "It's this Petit. It's me, Noelle Nichols. She's gotta do better than me."

"I know we haven't been close cousins, but Bernard and I—we can help."

"No," Noelle said. She wouldn't fulfill her wish of returning to the wealth of her ancestors through single parenting. "No, you can't. I had other plans."

The doctor paused, not wanting to interrupt but he had protocols to follow. "The baby's Apgar scores are good, but she needs preemie care starting now. I suggest we let you recover for a few hours before you begin to learn about all of the possibilities and resources."

Two nurses came in, on cue, with white capsules and a paper cup of water. One lifted the baby off of Noelle's chest and set her down in a clear plastic box, swaddling her with a warm blanket.

Noelle took the pills and then looked down at her breasts.

"We will take care of her with formula until you decide about breastfeeding," one nurse said. The other took Noelle's blood pressure, then shooed Debra and Mardi into the hallway to encourage Noelle to sleep after her shocking ordeal of unexpected labor and delivery.

Noelle heard Debra ask the nurse how an adoption would happen in such a sudden situation, then heard the nurse's reply about legal requirements for the father to sign papers. If the father was known, he had to be given the opportunity to take custody of the child.

Mardi was ready to go home. She had a substitute teaching gig for Bernard the next day she'd almost forgotten about, and she definitely needed to have some drinks tonight to prepare. But she paused. The baby was her cousin.

Stepping back into the room, she asked if she could hold her.

The nurse allowed it but only for a moment.

"She looks a little like a Petit," Mardi said. "And don't take offense but I'm glad she doesn't look like your dad's side of the family. I guess I don't even know who the father could be. Who's your boyfriend?"

Noelle felt discombobulated. It only slightly registered to her what Mardi was asking.

"I don't have a boyfriend," she said, giving Debra a *don't-you-dare-tell* look when she noticed she had stepped back into the room.

Debra gazed at the infant Noelle's cousin held in her arms. "I called a cab, but I'll be back."

Mardi stroked the baby's soft belly. She responded by arching her arms as if doing the backstroke. "Looks like she's going to be a swimmer," she said.

Debra leaned down to sniff the baby's head. "Our little popover," she said. "She smells fresh out of the oven."

"Our little popover," Noelle repeated. She steeled herself against these feelings. There must be a hundred hopeful couples, just waiting to give her baby the world. She would let her go to one of them. She would trust. There was only a deep denial of her sadness as she started to drift off.

A woman with a social worker name badge entered the room, rousing her from her near-sleep.

"A French name," said Noelle to them all, as if waking from a dream. "If I have any say, I would like her to name her something pretty and French. Maybe Simone or Giselle. Or, I know, Genève. Can I name her Genève?"

17. *The Announcement, 1994*

A few weeks after Noelle returned from her time off due to "back problems," a baby announcement arrived in the department mail.

Gary had missed Fran since she'd quit, but he'd kept her secret and crossed his fingers that this time it was real. And there she was, a baby named Genève Sharon Hart, middle name in honor of Fran's mother. The announcement hung on the bulletin board for a week. Finally, Noelle, who had just been promoted to Fran's position, took it down, shoved it in her skirt pocket, and rode the escalator to buy a white chocolate macadamia nut cookie from the Marketplace Deli.

She sewed a simple cotton jumper of pink French chenille that night and sent it anonymously to the address on the envelope the announcement came in.

Annette walked in on Noelle as she wrapped the jumper with gift paper taken from Annette's closet, but she didn't say anything unusual. Noelle had spent some nights at

Debra's after the birth, purportedly because Debra needed help with something. It didn't seem like Annette or Carl knew anything, thank God. Nobody was supposed to know anything with a closed adoption. Not that everything went the way it was *supposed* to go. She wasn't *supposed* to know who got the baby. It wasn't *supposed* to be someone she knew.

It was *supposed* to be wealthy folks, like her ancestors, Genève's ancestors. At least one of them should have this prayer, this wish, come true.

She'd assumed the baby would get two parents, but she hadn't stated any preference. At least she knew Fran was responsible, unlike herself.

Noelle had surprised herself by admitting to knowing who the father was—she could have just told the social workers she didn't know. Maybe some small part of her hoped Pierre would want the baby, would maybe even break things off with his fiancée and ask her to marry him. It wasn't her plan. He wasn't the man she was waiting for, so she couldn't explain why she'd let it enter her mind. Maybe just her ego. After all, he hadn't been able to resist her the one time, up in the old store hospital.

But a life with her apparently had not entered his mind. Pierre raced to sign the papers as soon as he was notified of his legal paternal rights to the unexpected infant, so fearful was he of Johanne finding out.

A part of Noelle wanted to bring Fran's announcement up to Pierre's new office and gaze at the picture of Genève with him. He would have seen his own eyes in the baby's face. But she didn't bring it to him, and she never told him Fran had adopted their baby either.

Now that Pierre worked upstairs and Noelle didn't have to face him, she didn't have the chance to ask if he'd had any second thoughts about the adoption as she had.

Surely, he did not.

Pierre had traded in his stock room chinos for Perry Ellis suits and silk ties. His life stayed on track because he, along with the ecologist who believed in him and was now his wife, had worked too hard to let anything or anyone derail him. Certainly Noelle Nichols, disenfranchised Petit's Party Central heiress and tanning bed model in a hot-pink string bikini, was not part of the planned ecosystem.

Johanne could never know about any of it, not the bikini nor the baby. She held in her heart a desire for their own baby, now with both of their careers in America launched and everything they had struggled for having finally come to fruition.

PART II. 1997-2001

18. Genève and Fran, 1997

Fran and her baby first formed their bond on December 12, 1993, the third day of Hanukkah.

She'd had one close call before, months of hoping and taking time off work to quietly arrange all of the details of an open adoption. In the end, the teenager changed her mind. Her middle-aged parents wanted to help her raise her boy.

Fran pictured a utopian open adoption with letters and photos to and from the birth parents. They could visit. The child would never feel abandoned but only benefit from the extra love.

Of course, she could have gotten a sperm donor instead of adopting a baby. She probably could have even convinced her old shoe dog friend, Gary Gorman, and his sweet wife to let him get her pregnant. She laughed at that thought—Gary probably talked the whole time when he had sex. He probably lectured his wife about the history of sex.

She missed friends like Gary back in the Twin Cities, but she was happy here in Clayton, Missouri. Her grandmother and mother helped out, and they weren't too far from the bigger city of St. Louis.

When she'd received the call about a baby girl named Genève, Fran went from feeling nearly hopeless to being a mother in sixteen days. It would have happened even faster, but the baby was premature and needed weeks of respiratory care. The hospital and social worker gave her permission to visit by appointment.

It had become less common, but the birth parents elected a closed adoption, sealing access to identifying information. She knew the baby had spent just two days in the maternity unit with the birth mother, who appeared in court to relinquish her rights when the baby was appointed a transitional care foster mother. The only right that the birth mother had maintained was the right to name the baby on the original birth certificate.

As the adoptive mother, Fran had the right to change it. Many adoptive parents, she was told, chose a new name and kept the given one for a middle name. Fran couldn't bear to do that. It seemed important, somehow, to bond with this baby exactly as she was.

As for Genève, some difficulty bonding was to be expected. She'd been used to a different mother's voice heard after her birth as well as through the water of the womb.

Genève and Fran did bond—but in different waters. They became attached in the pool of a Jewish Community Center in Clayton, the city where Fran had requested a transfer to be a multi-department manager at one of the Dayton-Hudson Corporation's Target stores.

With their giant red bullseye signage and rows of *cheap chic* goods, Target stores had grown out of the bargain basement of Dayton's and become their own much more profitable business within the corporation.

Fran got a new employee number in her parents' hometown, working for the same shareholders. So much for shaking things up in the world.

Genève swam before she could crawl on dry land. The baby swim class was full of infants making their primitive strokes, holding their breath by instinct as they swam four feet between their parents and instructors.

Genève swam six.

Fran showered the baby in her arms in the locker room of the JCC so often that she hadn't given her a bath since her adoption ceremony.

The Networking Adoption Program's chapter of Stars of David, a national group for adoptive Jewish families, taught that the conversion ceremony could occur at any time. Her mother, Sharon, had asked Fran to arrange it right away. Genève would not remember the small, square tub in which she was immersed. She wanted to swim in it and cried out when her limbs hit the walls all around her. Sharon dropped a silver coin into the bathwater.

With a prayer, the community welcomed the baby to its midst. Adoption stories were found in Jewish text, and almost all Jews were open to the idea of conversion through adoption. Sharon Hart repeated a ceremonial prayer, along with chants of Genève's name, for eight days.

She had never been so religious.

Genève was a baby on the move, breaking free of the Cookie Monster afghan knitted by Fran's grandmother. The baby's great-grandmother's knitting was perfect, stitched meticulously to Cookie Monster's last crumb, but no swaddling could hold Genève in place.

In no time at all, Genève turned four. She still carried her baby blanket around with her, but she left it for longer and longer periods as she got busy with preschool and swim lessons.

Fran began to let go of her baggage, too. The exhaustion forced her hand.

"It's normal," her doctor told her, pushing her hair behind an ear. "You need to close the books on some other parts of your life to free up energy for Genève."

"I'm not doing much besides a little swimming," Fran responded. "Besides a retail job. I guess that keeps me moving a lot of the day."

"Keep up the swimming. I'm not only talking about physical energy but mental energy too. What things are weighing on you that you could finally let go?" the doctor asked.

The doctor wasn't a psychologist like Fran's sister, but her sister was never her confidante. Fran found herself responding. "That I didn't tell my old boyfriend the truth," she said. "It was so long ago, but I lied. I hadn't been accepted at the college we'd planned to attend together. I mean, I had been accepted at first, but then it turned out to be a mistake. I didn't want to hold him back. So instead of telling him, I just didn't show up, and then I broke up with him."

"How long has it been?"

"Twenty years or more. I'm sure if I'd gotten married by now, I would have forgotten all about him."

"It doesn't always work that way," the doctor said. "Maybe the bad feeling about the lie would have stayed with you. Maybe holding onto that lie is still taking your energy."

Fran would rather shake it off, or try to swim it off, than tell Bernard. But it could bring closure. It was the adult thing to do. As she looked back, she didn't know why she hadn't been straight-forward in the first place back when they were so young. Brains aren't fully developed until mid- to late-twenties, as her psychologist sister lectured. She would have to remember that in her role as a parent.

But for now, life was busy enough. She would not go out of her way to talk to Bernard Petit. Never take a step backward, Sharon often said.

And anyway, with a busy four-year-old like Genève to keep in swimsuits and goggles, life was definitely not going backward.

19. The Red, 1997

Bernard found himself working late quite often in the early spring days of the 1997 school year. A quick smoke break was all he needed after sending most of the boys home on their buses and some in their halfway house vans.

Tonight, he tapped away on his computer, drafting a budget request to bring students on a trip to help sandbag the rising Red River. There was no time for fundraising, and anyway, Bernard was the only member on the fundraising committee of the skeleton parent-teacher association. The budget request didn't really have a chance. Bernard would probably end up writing a check for the whole thing. Now that Paj had convinced him to take the trip, he couldn't imagine letting the opportunity slip away.

Minnesota kids rarely got a day off school for bad weather in the 1990s. Only the most extreme blizzards made the cut for a snow day. And while most kids can't believe their luck when it happens, a day at home with their parents or alone poses threats for others.

So, when Bernard's first-hour current events discussion one Monday morning revealed the kids' concern for children in the Red River Valley trapped in their houses after a succession of blizzards, he encouraged action. That his students expressed such empathy for strangers living five hours northwest of Minneapolis impressed Bernard. He couldn't just brush them off when news reports warned that, once the snow melted, a flood was going to come and take Red River Valley houses with it.

Moorhead and Fargo; East Grand Forks and Grand Forks; Breckenridge and Wahpeton; these were all "twin cities" much like Minneapolis and St. Paul, two municipalities separated by a river. The difference was that these twin communities in the Red River Valley shook hands via bridges over the river border between two states—Minnesota and North Dakota.

The university climatologist Bernard had invited to speak told them this: The soil had been charged—already full of water—during the 1996 rains. More than ninety-eight inches of snow had fallen in Fargo and one hundred and seventeen in Grand Forks. A freak blizzard and freezing rainstorm going by the name of Hannah hit on the fifth of

April, months after officials already knew things could get wet. Sandbagging started in the middle of April, but the region needed more bags, many more.

The boys checked on the situation each morning, so they were among the first to understand that the snow melting signaled when the danger really began, although the official forecast predicted that the snow melting into the river wouldn't exceed the dikes.

The climatologist showed them how predictions work, and how rivers have a way of upending them.

The Red River runs north, he explained. Snow melted in the southern part of the valley as it warmed. The water would rise, but the river was still too jammed with ice in the north where it needed to flow. Minnesota and North Dakota, and points north into Canada, were in for the worst flood in a hundred years, and all the farms, roads, and towns were at risk.

The climatologist hoped that if enough people could fill bags with sand and build walls with those sandbags along the river, the water could be contained even if the river crested a couple of feet higher than predicted. Lives and homes could be saved, and the flood of 1997 would not go down in history as one of the worst floods since the glacial Lake Agassiz receded, leaving the flat, nutrient-rich plains that attracted farmers to the land.

Bernard stood up, leaving the Excel budget spreadsheet open on his laptop. He walked down the hallway and saw Paj's door open.

"Hey," he said. "Want to walk to the vending machines in the lounge?"

"I already got my dinner," she said. She held up a bag of jalapeno-flavored kettle chips.

The sight of Paj, who always brought the herby soups and papaya salads her mother made, eating out of the machine tonight proved how overworked she was.

"Walk with me anyway?" he asked. She stood.

Paj was now the lead counselor in the school. In fact, she was the only one. Budget cuts had led to the loss of the school psychologist, which could have been an impossible loss at a school like Twin Cities Success. But the psychologist hadn't ever helped the boys anyway—at least not directly. She had been more interested in mining the data about them for her academic journal articles so that she could complete this "real world" stage of her career and get a tenure-track faculty position teaching the nation's future school psychologists.

The situation under Paj, while still inadequate, was just about as good as before.

"I needed to talk to you, but I was going to do it tomorrow," Paj said. "I have a hundred and fifteen old case files to package and hand over to families for kids who graduated years ago. I'm not sure how our old psychologist got so far behind. Some kids who graduated in 1990 don't have their own file yet. I'm going to get them all caught up so kids can get their file the same year they graduate."

"As they should," Bernard said. "What did you need to talk to me about?"

"Do you know your students have been coming to me, feeling worried about the kids in the Red River Valley?"

"Yes, I'm working on the budget request now. I'm going to do whatever I can to take them on the trip so they can volunteer."

"Good. I mean, you've instilled in them your values and empathy and now you need to allow them the opportunity to help those people you've been worrying them about. Most of these kids have never had the chance to see that selfless work could mean something."

"I agree. These boys needed to know how it feels to be the do-gooder."

"Some of them have parents or grandparents who raised them to volunteer at their house of worship. But most have never had to do anything for anyone, other than at home, where they take on too much burden."

"Got it. I'm working on it."

"So, what I wanted to say is..." Paj waited while Bernard slid several quarters into the machine and his Pearson's Salted Nut Roll fell to the bin below. "I think you should bring Owen Hess along too."

They took a seat in the lounge and Bernard noticed that Paj held a fat folder in her arms. She set it down on the chipped Formica table.

"Isn't he only about ten or eleven?" Bernard had never officially met the kid. He remembered that he had turned down the principal's plea for Bernard to mentor him back when he first came to the school.

"He's twelve now," Paj said. "I've been looking for an opportunity to give him more purpose. He struggles to understand why he survived his parents' murder-suicide. His real interest is art, but he wants to help people too."

"Having a twelve-year-old would change things for the older kids. Can't you find him some service-learning opportunity closer to home?"

"Well," Paj said, thumbing the corner of her folder. "He's been working on a paper about some artist who painted murals a long time ago. One mural is up there where you are going. I thought it would be neat if he could see it."

"I know he has an aunt. My cousin is the one who told her about this school. Can't the aunt take him?"

Paj pulled out her secret weapon: guilt. "I know you didn't want to mentor Owen, but I'd really like you to give him just a bit of your time. Would you like to hear about my current research on the benefits of service-learning projects for children with trauma?"

Bernard knew it would only be a few more years until he would have Owen Hess as a student in his classroom. He tried to imagine. He would never be able to get Mardi to substitute for him if she had to meet the kid. Mardi preferred to pretend no murder-suicide ever happened in her house, or that at least there were no living victims.

"No, you've told me about your research. I just don't think the boy would do so great away from his guardian. I'd worry about that at his age."

"He's doing pretty well," Paj retorted. "That's thanks to his aunt and this school. His teacher this year really encourages him with his art."

Bernard knew Paj had played a role too. She always did. There were hundreds of kids who were in a better place thanks to her counseling. He saw the folder creep closer to him on the table. "So that's his file there, isn't it?"

Paj nodded and stood up. "I'm going back to my office to try to get through this backlog. Come see me when you're done reading it."

Bernard opened the folder that had "Owen Hess" printed on a white filing tab. He tore open the red wrapper of his Salted Nut Roll. The top page was Paj's file log. It listed the materials in there: the meetings with Owen, his guardian, and an elderly family friend, as well as copies of police and psychology reports. Under the log sheet was a long, double-spaced report, dated just the day before, and signed by Paj.

The report summarized his situation at the top: twelve years old, gifted in drawing and painting, a sweet and loving boy who liked to help younger kids and seemed comfortable with older kids and adults. Ongoing sensitivity, like crying over small problems, but no self-harm for the past six months.

Under that, Paj had pulled together a single narrative of Owen's tragic loss. It read:

Owen loved his mother, with her wavy "peanut-butter-colored hair" that he remembers always brushed against him so softly. Catherine Hess was in tune with art and nature, her curious eyes always searching for the beauty in the world to point out to Owen.

His father Andrew's temper scared him, especially after he had gambled away all of their money and taken out loans using the equity of Catherine's childhood home. But he could also be a loving and generous father between tantrums. Andrew tried to get Owen into T-ball, which he didn't want to play. Owen took after Catherine, an art teacher who liked to make her own paper on which to paint birds and other wildlife. She'd once been a runner-up in the selection of artwork to appear on a special commemorative stamp featuring Minnesota's state bird, and Owen's favorite, too, the loon.

On that cool October day in 1990, Catherine had asked family friend June Skaalen to watch Owen. June told him stories about his Grandma Vilda. There was always something new that Vilda's daughters and Owen had never known before, like about Vilda placing second in a 1948 Lake Minnetonka waterskiing competition, just a year after giving birth to Catherine. June had gone with Vilda's husband, Ken, to cheer her on, Ken holding baby Catherine upon his shoulders.

Owen wanted more stories about his Grandma Vilda, but Catherine had returned to pick him up too quickly.

Catherine had gone to the bank and withdrawn eight hundred dollars in order to leave Andrew. She confided in June Skaalen that Andrew threatened her and that she was going to move out of the house in Wayzata and into a building in Minneapolis with a security door. Getting Owen into and out of school each day without his father taking him back would be a challenge, but she would figure it out or they would move further away.

Catherine would take the first step the next day when Andrew was supposed to travel.

Even with all these gears in motion, she tried to be calm for Owen and to make Andrew think she'd had a normal day. She'd brought Owen back home and they made decoupage rocks. She set her purse on the kitchen counter near the table where Owen cut a picture of a loon from a *Minnesota Monthly* magazine. The money and bank receipt were in the purse, along with the brochure about the apartment.

She didn't expect Andrew to be home until five-thirty.

He came home early. He'd done that other times out of paranoia. He would show up at her art classroom door to check on her. One time, she forgot to tell him she was substituting at a different school while her usual class went out for their spring track and field day. He'd gone that day to find she wasn't there and raged all evening, believing she was out cheating on him.

He came in through the family room sliding door just after they'd set the rock aside for the second coat of shellac to dry. Catherine and Owen picked out a Berenstain Bears book for her to read with him in his room before his afternoon nap.

The police evidence suggested that Andrew was sitting there with a tall glass of gin and her open purse when she went back out to the living room. He probably threatened to kill himself if she left him, according to June Skaalen. He had done that before.

Owen awakened and listened quietly. Catherine begged Andrew to put his gun down and lower his voice. Owen was sleeping, she told him. She insisted she wasn't leaving him, that she'd opened an account to save for a surprise trip for their anniversary and that she wanted them to talk about it that night. He pulled out the apartment brochure. She said that was something the bank was handing out, helping to promote it. He didn't believe her. He reminded her they'd been so happy the weekend before at a gala event for the arts, that he did all that stuff for her even though he didn't care about art. He reminded her how excited Owen had been to see them so dressed up.

"And now you dare to turn him against me?" Andrew shouted.

"Don't point that gun at me," Catherine begged. "Or at yourself. Please put it down."

Andrew growled, "Go get that thing that you've been hiding from me. I need it now."

"I don't know what you are talking about," she said.

"I heard Vilda telling you before she died that she had some important stuff to give you. I don't know what it is, but you do and you'd better give it to me now."

"She never gave it to me, whatever it was. My mother and father never owned anything valuable besides this house. There's nothing. It must have been something important to her but not worth anything to you."

"I'll let you leave if you give it to me, but you're not taking Owen. Give it to me now!" he yelled. He'd already stuffed her roll of cash into his pants pocket.

Owen tiptoed into the hallway. Catherine heard his little feet. "Owen, run outside!" she yelled. "Go next door and call 911!"

Andrew lurched into the hallway with the gun still pointed toward Catherine. "You stay here." He picked up Owen, ran him down the hallway, and dropped him back onto his bed. Catherine slipped into the kitchen to pick up her longest, sharpest knife to defend herself, but Andrew reappeared in seconds, wrestling it from her and tearing at her dress at the same time. She tried to stab him, but only drew a scratch before he turned it on her and slashed her throat.

Evidence suggests she died immediately of blood loss. Andrew had dropped the gun, so he went back to the hall to get it and stick it in his pants. He then dragged Catherine from the tiled kitchen floor to the living room.

Owen tiptoed back out, scared and brave at the same time. "Daddy, fix Mommy's neck," Owen recalls pleading.

Andrew prepared to roll Catherine's now pale, bloody body into the Persian carpet covering the parquet floor.

Owen held his rock. It was dark and gray, he says, like Lake Minnetonka at night. He wanted to throw it at his dad, but it wasn't a very big rock, and his mother had told him he was a nice boy. His true nature would not be to throw rocks.

Seeing Owen with his rock brought Andrew back to reality and he looked at Catherine's body, recoiling in horror. He began to wail apologies, begging Owen to help him, to stay with him. "I accidentally cut Mommy," Andrew told his son.

"Why?" Owen asked.

Andrew took a deep breath, a strange calm coming over him. "What a nice rock you made," he said. He held the rock and ran his finger over the still tacky shellac that sealed the cut-out image of a loon. He pressed his forehead to Catherine's and cried.

Owen recalls taking the rock and setting it far away so his father wouldn't ruin it. His mother wouldn't like that.

"Owen," Andrew said, clenching his jaw. "Do you know where Mommy might have kept some jewelry we've never seen her wear? Or a bank certificate or anything like that? If you do, we can sell it and go live far away. Someplace really nice."

"I don't know what you mean," Owen said. "I just know you cut Mommy. Is she dead? Can you make her wake up now?"

Andrew stared at Catherine's body, no longer able to look Owen in the face. "It might be some gold or more money. Anything like that?"

Owen shook his head and tears flew from his face.

"Okay, Owen, don't cry," Andrew said. "You can always remember Mommy. I need to go be in heaven with her now. I promise we will all see each other there someday."

Andrew kissed Owen, put his finger on the trigger, and shot himself in the head, splashing his brains all over Catherine's body. Owen attempted to clean up the scene before getting a neighbor, reporting that his grandmother always told him the house couldn't be a mess for guests.

This report includes the self-reported memories of a very young boy and elderly family friend. Its use pertains to making decisions about the considerable needs of a special student, and not for any other purposes, legal or otherwise.

Paj had jotted two notes in the margins. One concerned the decoupaged rock with the loon on it, which Owen was still allowed to keep in his pocket as an exception to school rules about potential weapons. The other was about Owen's guardianship under Catherine's sister, named Ralphina Beranek. Bernard had never known her name and didn't imagine Mardi would want to know it either. The poor woman, whoever she was.

Bernard put the report back in the folder and wiped a tear from his eye. He folded the wrapper over the end of his unfinished Salted Nut Roll and shoved it in his jacket pocket.

Back at Paj's office, he told her, "You can call the kid's aunt and tell her Owen is invited to come on the trip."

"You changed your mind?"

"I don't know if I've told you this, but my sister Mardi lives in the house in Wayzata where this all happened. She bought it years ago from the bank after they foreclosed. The Hess couple had it mortgaged to the hilt, I guess."

"That's a weird coincidence," she said. "It must feel strange to read the story of what happened there. I don't think I need to remind you that the report is confidential."

Bernard handed Paj the folder. "Yeah, I won't be sharing the details with my sister, but I see the light."

"You had to see the dark to see the light," Paj said.

Bernard nodded. "I'll get a packet of info for his teacher to send home with him tomorrow."

20. Aunt Ralphy's Worries, 1997

Ralphina's unpolished nail traced across the pages of the Twin Cities Success School directory.

The 1997 flooding of the Red River Valley would go down in history, and her nephew had been filling bags with sand in East Grand Forks when the dike broke and the city flooded. They followed the evacuation orders but hadn't found a safe passage out of the city when the buildings near their lodging caught fire. Ralphina saw an apocalyptic view of flames reflected in floodwaters on the news an hour before she got a call from the school counselor. Paj Yang and the teacher leading the trip had been calling to assure parents. It rated as the second most horrible hour of Ralphina's life, not knowing if Owen was safe. The counselor said they'd gotten out and would spend the night in the White Earth Nation, where the teacher knew a tribal leader who'd offered the use of an old dormitory-style cabin.

Someone would call the next day with the expected bus arrival time, the counselor told her, but the next day had arrived hours ago and no meditation could calm Ralphina's fearful mind. They should have called by now.

The school's office phone went to voicemail. Owen's homeroom teacher's voicemail greeting said she only responded to calls after school and during her 11:05 to 11:20 prep "hour." It was already past noon.

Her fingernail went down the list. Bernard Petit. That was the name of the teacher leading the trip. Ralphina remembered he was the cousin of that shoe dog named Noelle who first told her about the school. He must have a sub for all the kids who didn't go on the trip. She picked up the phone and began to dial. After only two rings with no answer, she could stand it no more. Owen must be almost back at the school from that Godforsaken disaster zone by now.

Ralphina hung up. Curried lentil soup from the night before burned in the pit of her stomach, undigested.

What had caring for Owen done to her? She had never been like those mother hens. It wasn't the Zen way. She wasn't even going to let him go on the trip, but an artist he wrote a paper about painted the side of a building in East Grand Forks in the late 1930s. He wanted to see the faded mural before time took it away.

When would she ever take him there? Never.

She didn't blame him for wanting to see the mural. She'd become interested in Henry Camlo, too, after spending hours at the library with Owen. One of his paintings, *Wild Ride,* depicted a woman who looked so much like Ralphina's mother—Owen's grandmother—they had to look at it over and over, tracing those candlelight-colored ringlets with their fingers. If not for the caption explaining that it had been painted at a train station in Chicago, and if not for the creases across the woman's blue dress, it most certainly would have been Vilda Livdahl Beranek.

Vilda had never mentioned Chicago, and she never would have worn a wrinkled dress. Nonetheless, the painting made them feel something for Henry Camlo, and they both hung their heads when they read that the artist died in a flood.

In August of 1955, the double whammy of Hurricane Connie and Hurricane Diane hit the East Coast. The Naugatuck River flooded in Waterbury, Connecticut, "the Brass City," where Camlo had been commissioned to paint a mural of brass clock manufacturing.

Clocks! Such an ordinary thing, and yet it employed so many. The public funding of arts in the WPA era was over, but factory owners commissioned WPA artists to capture the significance of their businesses. Murals persisted as the art of the people, by the people, for the people, even when they were commissioned by wealthy magnates.

The factory owner's limo driver had picked up Camlo from the train, they learned. Both men got carried away by the burgeoning river, their bodies found weeks later.

Knowing that sad story didn't exactly motivate Ralphina to send her nephew into a flood zone, but she marveled at Owen's passion for art.

He tried many styles and forms, including murals, right on the wall in his own bedroom. Ralphina designed eclectic displays, but Catherine earned the title of artist. Nature art, with a touch of whimsy, of movement—that was her style that she liked to teach to others. Owen was picking up where his mother had left off.

A deep breath welled up inside her and she held it, imagining air and light clear her monkey mind. Owen had survived his parents' violent deaths. He'd survived the flood and the fire. He'd survived having her as his guardian.

Why did she worry? Did she think seeing drowned cows and a couple of buildings on fire was going to traumatize him? Hell, he was probably drawing the whole scene with his Cray-Pas oil pastels.

Ralphina put on her lightweight sweater and a red scarf from the Faribault Woolen Mills. She ran out to her car and felt that spring in the sun's warmth, so she took off the scarf and set it on her passenger seat. The chill returned and she picked it up again and twirled it around her neck. She would get Owen off the bus the second it arrived and take him straight to that Wet Paint art supply store his teacher liked. He could pick out whatever he wanted.

❀ ❀ ❀

Mardi Wirt had not craved a drink this badly since her first week at the Hazelden Addiction Treatment Center in 1995. She'd been sober for two years now and told herself she would make it one day at a time. Or one class period at a time anyway.

She was proving her masochistic tendencies by taking vacation time from Dayton's to substitute teach at the Twin Cities Success School.

Not like she had anyone to take a real vacation with anyway.

At least the first-hour class was gone up north on that trip. She'd slept in until past seven each day, but that had been the only good thing about the whole week.

She'd said no to the substitute job at first. Bernard asked, "Then could you come up and help sandbag instead?"

Mardi agreed to step in if she could get the vacation time approved.

Bernard's friends hadn't wanted to fill sandbags with a bunch of troubled teenagers either. Nobody wanted to visit the icy climate of the Red River Valley in the spring, especially not with those weather reports. Bernard asked a woman he'd started seeing, having recently broken up with one he'd been seeing off and on for five years. He needed more help. The new girlfriend said she had been up in the northwest corner of Minnesota before and hated it even in summer, and that the volunteer lodging sounded like a good place to get lice.

That was the end of that relationship.

Nobody except Bernard's students wanted to sandbag, these kids who were supposedly such monsters.

Only one parent and one grandparent volunteered. Paj, also, had walked right into this one by goading Bernard into including Owen.

Some parents nearly refused the trip for their kids, while others looked forward to the very moment that the bus would leave and give them five days of peace. In the end, the entire first-hour class was able to go. Bernard paid for a bus and a driver, lodging, and everything else not covered by the one hundred and sixty-five dollars he squeezed out of the principal.

There had been points of brightness in the otherwise thankless week of being Ms. Wirt instead of plain old Mardi—a boy smiling and raising his hand, another one bringing a plate of warm cinnamon churros from his mother. Otherwise, she couldn't wait to get back to her much easier job and wondered why on earth she had bothered to maintain her teaching licensure. It was an impossible job.

Never before had she respected her brother so much.

Mardi picked up the folder Bernard had prepared for her. She needed to use her fifteen-minute prep time to call the families to tell them the bus would get in at around one-thirty. During the one year that she'd taught French right after college, there were phone trees for things like this, but Bernard had given her very specific instructions about making sure that each family knew when the bus would return. He'd been through too many miscommunications about kids and transportation before.

Mardi started calling numbers from the top of the roster. As her finger ran down to the last line, she came to the youngest student's name:

Owen Hess.

Bernard had told her that the murder-suicide survivor of Westwood Lane was going on the trip, but now she would have to call the guardian of this child.

They wouldn't know she lived in the house, but it was better to remain strangers. She would give the school secretary that job. She peeled a Post-It Note off a pad and affixed it to the desk.

She traced her finger across the row to find the name and number of the guardian. Her fingernail stopped, then fell away, then flew back and dug into the page, making a half-moon-shaped impression under the name:

Ralphina Beranek.

Mardi's eyes blinked and raked across the name again. Ralphina Beranek.

No person in the world could have that name other than that goddess of display design. But hadn't she worked with her enough that she should know if Ralphina had anything to do with Owen Hess? She didn't gush about her private life. And Bernard had never mentioned Owen's guardian's name. Why should he? Even if he knew her, he didn't know Mardi knew Ralphina—that Mardi *thought* about Ralphina.

But who was Ralphina Beranek to Owen Hess?

Mardi chewed on a finger. Maybe Ralphina was a volunteer foster parent, and maybe she'd even adopted the child through the county system. Or maybe she was a friend—or the sister—of Catherine Hess, the murder victim? Or the sister of Andrew Hess? Now she recalled, perhaps Bernard had mentioned a guardian aunt.

She wished now that she'd responded in a more receptive manner to the nosy neighbors who tried to gossip with her about the history of her house and the family who lived there. But why learn more about them? She had profited off of the tragedy already and had no right to muse about the victims too.

If there was no running allowed in the halls of the Twin Cities Success School, it wasn't like that rule hadn't been broken by every single teacher in some sort of panic. So Mardi ran. When she got to the secretary's desk, she tried to act calm, as if she were only there to make a request in the typical manner. She held out the yellow Post-It loosely stuck to her pointer finger. "Please call this guardian. She'll need to pick up the child when the bus arrives at one-thirty or tell you if he will require a ride home."

It was already one o'clock.

Mardi paused as the secretary peeled the Post-It off her finger, then casually asked, "Have you met her?"

"She's Owen's aunt. Poor kid. It's a good thing his mother had a sister to take him after she died."

The memory of Bernard telling her that the boy lived with an aunt came back stronger. It was the night he'd first seen her house.

As the secretary picked up the phone, a door flew open behind Mardi. A warm breeze settled over her.

"When will the bus arrive?" she heard a voice call out. The secretary set the receiver back on its base.

Mardi stood perfectly still and kept her gaze on the secretary as the woman approached from behind. Slowly, as the woman now standing next to her discussed the situation with the secretary, Mardi could feel eyes catching on her purple bouclé sweater, then raking across the nape of her neck. Mardi tried to look in the other direction, but she couldn't resist the pull.

She lifted her head and turned to see her, Ralphina the Ballerina, the most exquisite human being alive, in a white sweater topped off by the reddest wool scarf.

Ralphina parted her lips as if she were about to say something. Mardi did the same, but both remained silent.

The guardian of Owen Hess and the object of Mardi's perfectly normal, only-a-little-bit-gay dreams were one and the same. Mardi felt two simultaneous urges that contradicted each other:

One, she wanted to flee the office and make sure this woman never saw her again and never found out that she bought the house where her sister, Catherine Hess, had been murdered.

And two, she wanted to kiss her.

❁ ❁ ❁

The screech of brakes reached the front office as the yellow school bus pulled up ahead of schedule. Ralphina rushed out to the curb, while Mardi rooted to the office floor for a moment before trotting out behind her. Mardi saw the first student off the bus step out and look around.

The kid waved a Cray-Pas drawing of flood and fire as he shouted, "Ralphy! We got thanked in person by the president of the United States. And I saw the Henry Camlo mural of the farm workers harvesting wheat."

Mardi knew this had to be Owen. But, *Ralphy*...why did that sound so familiar? He was calling to his guardian, who had never been known at Dayton's as anything but Ralphina, with or without "the Ballerina" as a suffix.

Ralphina ran to hug him and look at his Cray-Pas artwork. "The way you colored the fire reflecting in the water is incredible. And I can't wait to hear about the Camlo mural. I'm so glad you are back here safely with Aunt Ralphy now."

The memory came back to Mardi. That toy bank tube she'd found in the wall of her house with the deposit slip for Ralphy signed by Cathy. She'd assumed it was a boy—a Ralph. But was it Ralphina and her big sister Catherine? Had they grown up in that house, and "Cathy" was the Catherine Hess who lived there later with her husband?

Mardi had been living in Ralphina's house all of this time. The room with the Suzi Quatro poster—that had to be her bedroom.

The urge to flee grew stronger, and a drink or four would be needed, too, unless she could quickly bow down to say her serenity prayers ten times over. After this week, she also needed one really long nap.

But seeing the way this "Aunt Ralphy" looked at Owen with so much love, Mardi couldn't help but wonder: Could anyone ever be so lucky as a person for whom Ralphina's face lit up like that?

21. The Infirmary, 1998

Dayton's had been changing almost unnoticed for decades. Little things, like how the annual bonus, replete with a whole turkey for each employee and a big holiday party in the auditorium—even a handshake from a real live Dayton brother—transformed incrementally over the years into a voucher for a free slice of compressed turkey loaf in the employee cafeteria. The last year had been so glum they didn't even get that.

Retail predictions grew stronger for the 1998 holidays. The auditorium show was decided: It would be *How the Grinch Stole Christmas.* Even on a budget, the locally famous art producer Jack Barkla had gone all out on the previous year's *Nutcracker,* designed in the style of the Maurice Sendak version. It was going to be hard to beat, but this one was going to be the most jaw-dropping exhibit in a decade. Dayton's could afford to do more this year. This time they would do up all the windows on Nicollet Mall, just like in the old days. A special menu was created for the Oak Grill Room. Whole families would come and spend the day, leaving with shopping bag handles circling both arms like bangles on a Maasai bride.

For all of these plans, Barkla would need his best crew. And his best crew would need Ralphina Beranek.

Ralphina had been in such high demand at the Mall of America lately that she'd even declined work from some of her regular customers in Uptown. The mall paid more. Now the priorities were aligned with bills—the heat, the electricity, and the list went on.

And there would be college someday, she hoped. Owen still had anxiety, but something had changed in him after the sandbagging in the Red River Valley. He'd turned his focus from his own trauma outward. He'd taken an interest in other people. He'd even begun to mow lawns for the busy families in Kenwood. He did it at no charge for the elderly residents, although some paid him anyway. The extra cash for Owen took a little bit of the burden off Ralphina.

Household finances had been okay, but an eighth-floor auditorium gig was impossible to decline. When she'd done them in the past, the feeling she got was like she'd become a part of living history. When Jack called her to say they were going to take it over the top for the Grinch, she nearly screamed with excitement before calming down into a Zen prayer of thanks and a Vinyasa flow yoga session at the new studio in Kenwood. She would need to conserve her energy for this project.

Ralphina's thoughts about Mardi ran the gamut in the past year and several months since she'd been surprised by running into her at Owen's school. She had even left her a voicemail once at her Dayton's office shortly after Owen returned from the flood field trip, asking if she wanted to meet for lunch at the Lions Tap. It had been a dumb move to make a call like that without any good pretense. She hadn't received a response. She felt stupid for having called her, and at the same time hoped to see her at Dayton's when she showed up for the job.

As a freelancer, and one seen by many as aloof, Ralphina didn't trade much in company gossip, but she did know Mardi had once been married to a man—a local musician— but they'd divorced. She could have called her to come work on an advertising set. But she hadn't responded to the voicemail message or done anything to get in touch. She probably wasn't interested.

Mardi needed a nap. She hadn't any Madeira wine or liquor in the old infirmary cabinets anymore, but at least there was that bed. Occasionally, she found evidence that others came: a pair of glasses, a pack of rolling papers, an empty Doritos bag. But most employees didn't realize there was a tenth floor. Once, Mardi felt tempted to tell an exhausted pregnant deli worker about this place of rest and peace. But the store infirmary was her secret hideout. If anyone got caught using it, management would probably fence off the whole floor.

God forbid anyone rests for more than five minutes at work anymore.

Next to the infirmary on the vast tenth floor was a corner full of vintage bolts of fabric. Ralphina Beranek plucked one of them from obscurity as she set the Christmas table for the Whos of Whoville.

Asleep in the bed, Mardi lay unnoticed as Ralphina browsed the old fabric collection. But then she rolled from her side onto her back, making the metal bed creak. Ralphina came banging into the dark relics of a nurse's station with a bolt of fabric at least six feet long.

"Who's there?" Ralphina called.

Ralphina entered with the long fabric bolt held out in front of her. Mardi awoke.

"Put down your weapon," she said, her voice hoarse from sleep. "It's me, Mardi Wirt."

Ralphina lowered the fabric. "Ah yes, Mardi Wirt. Sleeping on the job?"

"Just a healthy little nap," Mardi said. "Napping at work is going to be the wave of the future."

"Not for freelancers," Ralphina said. "But I could rest for a minute." She dropped the giant fabric bolt at her side and sat down. Mardi sat up. They shuffled their feet on the floor until Ralphina spoke.

"I'm just wondering about that day I saw you at my nephew's school...I hadn't known that you were a teacher too. How do you fit it all in?"

Mardi shrugged. She waited, still groggy. Ralphina finally asked, "Do you know Owen?"

"My brother told me about him."

"Your brother?"

"Bernard Petit is my brother. And Noelle—in Women's Shoes—is our cousin. Of course you don't know about our family. Petit's Party Central doesn't hire freelancers.

"Okay..."

"But I didn't know Owen was your nephew until that day when you came in to get him after the flood trip."

That seemed to be the right answer.

"I've been thinking about you," Ralphina uttered.

Mardi acted as if Ralphina meant it in a congenial way, not that Ralphina was that congenial. "I've been thinking about you too," she said, letting it hang there.

Ralphina touched Mardi's shoulder. Then she made herself stop. "I'm sorry. Anyway, I have a lot to do on this Grinch exhibit."

"And I have to get back to work, after about five more minutes of rest." Mardi lay back down but fixed her gaze on Ralphina. For a moment, she forgot about her secret that she lived in the murder-suicide house Ralphina grew up in.

She didn't know if she even knew how to do it, but she made an attempt: She gave her a sultry smile.

Ralphina lay down beside her. It was a tiny bed and Ralphina was tall. She lay at the edge of the mattress and put her arm around Mardi's waist while Mardi stayed flat on her back.

"I'm really not gay," Mardi said. "I'm like ninety-nine percent straight."

"I imagine you are," Ralphina said. She propped herself up so she could lean over Mardi's face. Then she kissed her. "That was for your one percent."

They kissed again. A lingering kiss. Not too hungry. Giving, yet demanding nothing. Ralphina's upper body hovered over Mardi's, then she lowered herself on top of her and they kissed once more.

"You never called me back about going to Lions Tap," Ralphina said.

"Maybe I don't like burgers."

"I should have suggested Sri Lanka Curry House."

"It closed." They both furrowed their brows.

Then Mardi sat up, shaking off the feelings of seduction. "It's not that I'm afraid of...being with you. But because there's something you don't know that will make you hate me."

Ralphina picked up the bolt of fabric. "Why would I hate you? We hardly even know each other. I only know that I want you...to come over. Tonight. Straight from work."

Mardi looked down, weighing how much it would hurt if Ralphina knocked her over with an ancient bolt of fabric. She just wanted it over, wanted it out, to stop hoping she wouldn't find out.

"I bought the house."

Ralphina stood still for a moment, hugging the fabric. She understood, and Mardi could tell that she understood, but Ralphina asked anyway. "What house?"

"I didn't know it had anything to do with you. I didn't know you were the kid's aunt or anything until that day I saw you at the school. I swear."

"You bought my childhood house from the bank? The white house on Westwood Lane in Wayzata?"

"I didn't know. The puzzle pieces started coming together on the last day I subbed for Bernard. Your name was on the phone tree with a dotted line to Owen Hess. But I still didn't know yet it was your house."

"I tried to sell that house for two years. The bank finally took it over, sold it to some bottom-feeder. That was you? You were the bottom-feeder?"

"*I didn't know*. And I couldn't afford more—I was lucky to find such a beautiful place for that price."

"It was our house: My mom and dad, and me and Catherine. Then Andrew and Catherine bought it from our dad after our mom died because she wanted to raise Owen there. But Andrew gambled away all the equity. It was like losing that house again and again."

"I didn't know that you were even the kid's relative at all. The whole family was unknown to me except that Bernard told me that the child was at his school."

"Your cousin Noelle told me about that school. Didn't she tell you that he was my nephew?"

"No, we weren't always close, and she never said anything about you to me. And honestly, neither of us would have figured you as a Wayzata kid."

"Well, I was. We went to the private school for free because our mother worked there," Ralphina said, her voice becoming corrosive. "I didn't think anyone I knew would buy our haunted freakshow house. God knows nobody in the neighborhood wanted anything to do with it."

Mardi stood now, edging toward the freight elevator. "I apologize. I'm really sorry."

"How much has the value gone up now that it's been nine years since the event?" Ralphina slammed the fabric bolt down to the floor. "Gonna flip it soon?"

Mardi's eyes filled with tears. "As you said, we hardly know each other. I didn't know. And I love the house. I've owned it for years now, all by myself. It wasn't a flip."

"Not a lot of people can stomach buying a murder-suicide home. The bank must have let you have it for really cheap, and I guess you didn't mind the history. It didn't mean anything to you. Or maybe you thought it was cool."

Mardi thought back to that first night, sitting on the floor with Bernard eating a pepperoni pizza right where it had happened. Ralphina was right—she hadn't cared about those strangers.

Both of them gulped. Whatever had almost happened between them, it couldn't happen now.

But Mardi felt the need to clarify one thing. "That day, even after I saw your name on the flood trip roster, I still didn't know how you fit in. And then I didn't even imagine it was your childhood home until I heard Owen call you Ralphy."

Ralphina jutted her chin in the air. "Ralphy? Why? That's just what my family calls me."

"When I was remodeling the closets, I found something with that name on it. It was a toy bank tube in the wall between two bedroom closets. You know, the kind of tube you send up at the bank drive-through."

Ralphina sat back down on the bed. Her acorn skin turned a pasty shade of green.

Mardi continued, "It had a pretend deposit receipt in there for one dollar for the account of a Ralphy. And it was signed by a Cathy. I didn't think of you, or even of your sister, although I'd heard her name was Catherine Hess. I just thought it was from some previous owner's kids—a brother named Ralph, and his sister Cathy."

Ralphina stopped listening after Mardi mentioned the bank drive-through game.

"We had so many games when I was little. Cathy was a lot older, but she would play with me. She would be the bank teller or the teacher or the nurse. The only bad thing Cathy ever did, besides make her messes with art, was knock that hole in the wall between our two closets so she could play bank with me. Our parents didn't even get mad at her. 'Can't get too mad about that!' our dad always said about whatever creative thing she did."

"I'm so sorry," Mardi said. "It's terrible what happened."

"But now there you are, living in the house where my sister was killed. Sleeping in her bedroom, I guess. Spending evenings in the living room where Owen watched his father shoot himself in the head."

Mardi didn't know what else to say. It was mostly true. "I'm taking good care of the place. It's just me, but I try. I sleep in one of the downstairs bedrooms. My dad has helped a little. My mom planted flowers."

Ralphina stared, her eyes the color of tiger's eye stones and as hard and lustrous. "Okay, yeah, and knocking down closet walls. I have to get back to the auditorium." She walked out, heading toward the freight elevator with her fabric dragging behind her.

"I still have your Suzi Quatro poster, if you want it!" Mardi shouted, but Ralphina was gone.

It felt more real when you knew a victim than when they were strangers. When Mardi went home that night, everything would appear a little different to her about the house and she felt like a jerk for not having seen it that way before.

But maybe it was for the best not to start something. Maybe it was better to be alone. And yet, that night when she slid into her bed, she most definitely did not want to forget it. The part she most wanted to remember was Ralphina's lingering kiss, her pressing against her, and how she told her she wanted her to come over straight from work.

If only she hadn't told her the damned truth.

22. Wade, 1998-2000

Wade Sorenson wasn't just any math teacher.

"I'd rather hold out even longer than thirty-two than marry a regular arithmetic asshole," she told Debra.

"You've *wade-ed* through too many Mr. Almost Rights just to end up with an underpaid math teacher," Debra concurred.

So many bad puns with the name Wade.

Her bedroom in the old brick family home on Butternut Avenue seemed to be shrinking, even though Noelle took up less space now (thanks to fen-phen) to don a string bikini once again for a new series of Petit's Party Central commercials. This time it was turquoise blue, sewn using the same old brown tissue pattern pieces from which she had sewn the pink one almost ten years before.

She allowed more fabric outside of the edges, and was more generous with the string to stretch the suit across her ass.

She didn't look bad. Nobody changed the channel. Uncle Tom put her in a hot tub commercial too. She looked best above the bubbles.

She even spoke in these latest commercials, and viewers believed her to be not just any tanning bed and hot tub model but a fully enfranchised Petit family heir.

Some—like Wade Sorenson—inquired within.

He found out that she worked in Women's Shoes at Dayton's in Minneapolis, so he brought his mother (of all people) with him late one cold and sleety evening, under the pretense of taking her to see the *How the Grinch Stole Christmas* exhibit in the auditorium on the eighth floor.

Noelle staked a position by the holiday party shoes where she had just repeated one of her regular prayers, *Dear God, please return me to the wealth of my ancestors so I don't have to work when the roads are icy.*

Her strategy soon paid off. Strolling along the walkway, a woman picked up the Evan Piccone black satin pumps.

"Wade, honey," she called to a young man sauntering ever so casually behind her. "Would these look nice with my windowpane velvet dress?"

"The one with all the colors?" he asked. She nodded. He shrugged but lasered in on Noelle.

Once Noelle had made the sale, he playfully grabbed her business card meant for his mother. "I confess—I've been hoping to meet you."

"You came here to meet me?"

She gawked at him. A mother shopping for Stuart Weitzman or Ferragamo shoes would have made for a more auspicious sign. *Ugh,* she thought, although at least he wasn't old like some of the vendors that Uncle Tom had tried to marry her off to as if she were a pawn in his business games.

"I like your dress," he said. Noelle looked down at the seafoam green dress and shell-pink pearls she'd bought on clearance. She wore pale pink self-adhering thigh-highs to match the pearls. It made for too much of an Easter look for November, but she'd felt like wearing pastels that day.

"So you really came with your mother to meet me?"

"Yes, I usually shop at the Mall of America, where I recently opened the Mathy Taffy Tutoring Center."

Noelle noticed the brag, but he was nice looking. He went on to explain that parents dropped off their kids for some lively fun with fractions, algorithms, and taffy pulling. The taffy pulling was the gimmick that brought shoppers in to discover the center in the first place. Taffy sales supplemented the tutoring income and provided a marketing giveaway when Wade appeared as a sponsoring vendor at various events in the Twin Cities. The kids would improve their math skills while their emancipated guardians shopped for resort wear and Franklin Covey leather planners, or (*Hallelujah!*) dined without children.

Plenty of customers showed up for this deal, which included a Camp Snoopy amusement park wristband with each eight-week tutoring session. Mathy Taffy centers at two of the Dales—Ridgedale and Southdale, probably— were in the works for the following year.

"Enough about me," Wade said. "Let's talk about you over dinner."

❀ ❀ ❀

Wade was also Catholic, French, Swedish, and whatnot like Noelle, a pleasing match for the Petits.

For the cons, from Annette's perspective, he expected more from her daughter than beauty and a business connection. He pushed Noelle to move up from department manager, perhaps to floor manager, and someday even manager of a whole department store location.

Annette lacked the confidence in Noelle to picture this.

If she could be that successful, why did she need Wade in the first place? Surely a pointless question. Her daughter's newest pair of heels was higher than her IQ.

Noelle thought Wade seemed pompous. But she followed his advice and learned how to use the inventory system and the other new systems that followed as Pierre St. Hilaire rose higher in the administration.

It was only a few weeks into her relationship with Wade when she'd learned the system well enough to train others and she became one of the managers of the first floor.

Despite Wade finding her through the Petit's Party Central commercials, he never asked her to put on the bikini for him.

He was lustful, but conventional (oddly conventional, considering he'd come up with such a whacky business idea as Mathy Taffy, suggesting to Noelle that perhaps he'd gotten the idea from somewhere else and researched the hell out of its viability before implementing his plan).

He was looking for a well-connected wife.

Noelle wasn't as connected with the Petits as he imagined, but Annette suggested she let him think so.

Wade said he didn't mind if Noelle had a bit of a past, but he had no idea, really. He liked taking her out to places she'd never gone before, like the Guthrie Theater. Fundraisers for education-related nonprofits fit especially well with Wade's giving portfolio, and he made sure Mathy Taffy achieved visibility by sponsoring several events each year.

Noelle presented nicely at the first such event, and their photo and names appeared in the who's-who features in *Minnesota Monthly* and *Mpls.St.Paul* magazines.

This publicity pleased Noelle because she got to brag about it to Debra, who retorted with a double cliché, "It might be smarter to fly under the radar when you have a skeleton in your closet."

Wade considered these outings with Noelle in the public eye as a trial run, and she passed the test. He looked for a ring and called Noelle's family's church in St. Paul to inquire about the soonest date available for a wedding. It was New Year's Eve, he was told, and he put a hold on it.

She nearly broke it off one weekend when she was feeling a little queasy about him. But they went to a party that night and she noticed a business lawyer there who took such an interest in his Mall of America business that it seemed she might snatch him up and take him home with her.

Noelle's mother didn't think Wade counted as catch-of-the-year, but then again, the prayers to be returned to the wealth of her ancestors had gone unanswered.

Noelle could do far worse—she could fall in love with and marry someone like Carl. Or another lifelong retail salesman like Dean.

The morning that Wade asked Noelle to marry him, they made love under the covers. At eleven-thirty they entered the golden gates of the J.B. Hudson Jewelers located inside Dayton's, sizing Noelle's diamond solitaire that Wade had already selected by himself.

This acceptable fiancé's attributes included a home across the road from Bush Lake in prestigious West Bloomington—rented at the time she met him, but he bought it before they got engaged—and a less nightmarish mother than the mothers of other boyfriends she had trialed.

Wade's mother never even made any negative comments about St. Paul—only saying things like, "It's so far east!" and, "Such nice Catholic churches!"

The lot across the street from the swimmable Bush Lake was worth more than the house, but Wade had always liked the idea of a lake home. Well, *practically* a lake home. They could walk to the beach. Noelle, having grown up across the street from a not-so-swimmable part of the Mississippi River, felt thrilled to move into the house. Bush Lake was perfectly clear out to a few feet and surrounded by more parkland than private homes.

Bush Lake didn't fill up with boaters pulling up to get dinner dockside, like at Lord Fletcher's on the large multi-bay Lake Minnetonka, which her Petit cousins grew up a few miles away from, and it wasn't as known as the Minneapolis lakes. But, it was a house in the western suburbs, and her future children could play in the sand while Noelle worked on her tan and then went shopping at the fancy Lund's grocery store. Wade could fry up fresh sunfish over a fire and Noelle could serve arugula salads.

It wasn't some bullhead pond. There could be ice skating. And hot cocoa.

So, Noelle felt ready to join Wade in this life of math and the mall and a suburban Minnesota almost-lakehome.

They married a year later at St. Thomas More church in St. Paul. The bridesmaids were Debra, of course, and Mardi, with whom Noelle had become closer after their odyssey through the *Belle and the Beast* exhibit and the Hennepin County Medical Center.

Close enough to treat like a cousin who was not entirely estranged, anyway.

They wore cornflower blue and freshwater pearls. They wore extra-dark tans; Noelle insisted they use her tanning bed.

Everyone came. Carl Nichols's parents and siblings and their families showed up, bringing their cheap gifts instead of having them shipped to the house from the bridal registry as everyone else knew was the mannerly thing to do.

Uncle Tom, his wife, and Noelle's cocktail-pounding older cousin and his date all came. Even Uncle Edward and Irene crossed the river into St. Paul, as did both sides of Wade's family. Noelle and Annette Nichols both felt the absence of Grandma Greta Pettersson Petit, even though she had been gone for twelve years. They'd missed her the most when they picked out Noelle's bridal gown and the bridesmaid dresses at David's Bridal, knowing that Grandma Greta would have loved sewing them all with Noelle.

Nobody made much mention of Grandpa Sam Petit.

Uncle Tom's son made a ten-minute drunken toast in Greta's honor before getting in his car and driving home without his date. Bernard Petit gave the jilted young woman a ride.

Back when Noelle and Debra had danced to Prince's song *1999* in their Catholic high school, it seemed 1999 was far in the future. But now Noelle danced to the song on the verge of 2000, already with the tiniest embryo growing underneath her wedding dress.

In time, Noelle settled into Wade's house and made it her own, replacing almond-colored appliances with stainless steel, and bisque Formica countertops with granite from the quarries in Cold Spring.

But to Wade's annoyance, Noelle wouldn't sell her grandma's hovel on the edge of Swede Hollow. He went once, lured by promises of nearby Swedish pastries. A drunkard lay passed out in a buckthorn hedge across the street, his whiskey bottle on the grass.

"A come-back of this neighborhood is just around the corner," Noelle told him. "We'll regret it if I sell."

"Why did your grandma even keep this place after she married Sam Petit?" Wade asked.

Noelle shrugged. She knew why; her grandma had once told her. The Petit bride kept the cottage for days when she tired of being Mrs. Sam Petit and wanted to go where she had belonged as the hardworking laundress and talented seamstress, Greta Pettersson.

Plus, Sam Petit may have been a total fucking dick.

"Well, don't expect me to help you maintain this dump," Wade said. He didn't like St. Paul, and he certainly wouldn't venture over to the East Side again. Not for all the cinnamon rolls at the Swede Hollow Café.

23. *What Becky Wants, 2001*

Noelle dragged ass every time Mardi saw her, pissed about first-floor sales figures and pregnant with her and Wade's second child.

But they hadn't held a real conversation since Noelle's wedding until one Tuesday when they both found themselves at the funeral luncheon for Grandma Greta's sister in the musty basement of the St. Thomas More church.

The cousins had become a bit friendlier over the past eight years since fate had inserted Mardi into the secret of a baby and a closed adoption. They made small talk in the frozen yogurt line, but it was hard to know what to say besides, *Hey.*

Mardi couldn't exactly ask, *Hey...wondering if you've heard anything about your little popover because I heard that your old boss Fran Hart, AKA my brother Bernard's high school girlfriend, adopted a baby with the same uncommon French name as your baby.*

Or, *Hey...suffered from any more pleurisy lately?*

Other than the anomaly of Mardi's stint as a bridesmaid, their relationship barely doddered along until the great aunt's funeral.

Irene returned from the buffet set up by the church ladies. "Did you see how your slatternly cousin's lace camisole shows above her low-cut satin blouse?" she whispered into Mardi's ear as she began to nibble at her hamburger hotdish with distaste.

She'd grown up on hotdish but somehow remembered the Lutheran church ladies' version more fondly.

"Mom," said Mardi. "You never hit it off with your sister-in-law. Fine. I don't care for Annette either. But cut my cousin some slack."

She stood up and glided over to a seat by Noelle and her parents, leaving Irene to fume.

Other than hearing some stories that included Grandma Greta, it was a boring affair. Talking with Noelle got Mardi through it better than mingling in the family circles.

"Have you seen Ralphina Beranek lately?" Mardi asked as casually as she could, making sure Annette and Carl weren't listening.

"She's around but not as much. Why?"

Mardi spoke as quietly as she could in the noisy room. "I found out that she—and this is so sad—is the aunt of the kid whose parents were the murder-suicide pair. I think they haunt my driveway. I slip and fall every time I have to shovel."

"Icy driveways can be murderous in our great state," Noelle intoned.

Mardi ignored the comment. "Ralphina told me that it was her childhood home. Her sister Catherine was the wife killed. The couple had bought the house from their parents."

"I didn't know Ralphina grew up in your house, or that it happened there. But I knew she was his aunt," Noelle said.

Mardi's jaw dropped. "Well, doesn't anyone fucking gossip around here anymore? You could have said something."

"Yes, I could've helped you piece it together if you'd talked to me more," Noelle said. "And if I had a brother who taught at the kid's school, I probably would have been able to fucking figure it out, too."

"Gee, thanks," Mardi said, not taking the insult too personally. She knew Noelle liked her well enough since she'd included her in her wedding party. Of course, she didn't seem to have many other friends.

She considered telling Noelle about the kiss but decided against it. It was hard enough to put it all into words for herself.

"You're right, I had all the dots and didn't connect them," Mardi said instead. "I lost the picture before Ralphina's image took shape."

She remembered back to the day that Ralphina asked for a backdrop for the Neverland exhibit from the tenth floor. When Mardi returned with the fabric, Ralphina was gone. Someone told her it had been an emergency, but Mardi never asked about it. She'd stayed away for weeks.

That must have been when the murder-suicide happened.

How nobody gossiped about it was odd, but Ralphina wasn't staff. She didn't have to put in for family leave with HR. She didn't share the same last name as her sister.

"That's okay," said Noelle, standing up to go back to the buffet. "Maybe being sober now is robbing you of your creative thinking."

Mardi had quit drinking, had entered *recovery*. Noelle, when not pregnant, had taken up Mardi's former love of Madeira and other fortified wines. The more fortified the better.

When Noelle returned from the buffet with Jello bars topped with Cool Whip the talk turned to her pregnancy, not a favorite topic for Mardi. The bikini-bodied bitch already had a daughter with Wade. The girl was born in an early autumn. But Avril sounded like a pretty French name, didn't it?

Noelle spooned rainbow Jello into her mouth. "I want to pass on the full richness of the *Pe-tee* family heritage to my children."

The family never pronounced it that way. They said Pet-it. Even though Noelle was a Nichols, the bullies knew she came from Petits and called her *Noelle Letsya Pet Tit.*

"I can help you learn more French," Mardi suggested. She spoke and had briefly taught the language, but she didn't care so much about being French. They were so far removed from France and the Canadian voyageurs.

"Cool," Noelle replied, then lowered her voice to a whisper. "Her French name was the only thing I was able to pass onto, you know...Genève."

She burped and changed the subject again. Mardi listened with interest.

Noelle had somehow landed on her feet, now feathering her West Bloomington nest with many discounted purchases from the store's Home department.

After the September 11 terror attack in New York, staying in became more tempting, but Noelle explained that Wade took it to an extreme. He worried the malls were bomb targets, and he showed up to work less and less. He hired employees to do the tutoring anyway, and he managed the business more from home. A few families, especially from the Mall of America, dropped out, but the business was now in three locations.

"Business is still strong enough to allow stingy-ass Wade to install an in-home theater," she said. "Avril and our next kid can watch Blue's Clues on a screen as big as the backside of Grandma Greta's house."

❀ ❀ ❀

Back at her Wayzata home on Westwood Lane after the great-aunt's funeral, Mardi decided her life wasn't half as nice as her cousin's.

The windows leaked. The bills came in too high for a single person on a middle-manager salary and occasional substitute teaching jobs.

Even her "fun" investment in a tanzanite mine went awry. An investigative story hit in November, two months after the terror attack. A national newspaper reported that tanzanite was an Al Qaeda business—that profits went straight to terrorist activities. Wearing a tanzanite necklace was like having Osama bin Laden's face ironed onto your chest. It didn't matter if the story turned out to be wrong.

She'd put retirement savings into the mine, too. All that was worth pennies now. Mardi never wanted to wear her favorite color again, although she'd live with the violet linen curtains she splurged on just the year before.

She'd wanted so badly to be brilliant, like Bernard with his microwave popcorn investment. Or to have gotten Dayton's to move into the Mall of America in the nineties and to have received all the glory for the success.

Or to fall in love, be happy. Maybe try teaching French again—become Madame Wirt. Or to change her last name back for once and for all and become Madame Petit. She hadn't forgotten that dream of teaching a class how to sing *Sur le Pont d'Avignon*.

Instead, Mardi held on and performed her job of trying to lure customers back into the stores with desperate ads threatening that whichever sale they were on in the rotation was ending soon.

A former intern with an English degree had once named a marketing persona after a social-climbing character named Becky Sharp in the William Makepeace Thackeray novel *Vanity Fair*. That intern now worked levels above Mardi in the department and had revived the persona projects. She believed that understanding what Becky wanted held the key to the company's marketing success.

Unfortunately, the Becky Sharps of the world didn't seem to enjoy going out shopping anymore. Department stores exhausted them. Survey data indicated that today's social climber was overscheduled. She wanted a quick pick-me-up from her purchases, not to spend a day hunting in a multi-level building for them.

The cardboard cutout of the fictional Becky appeared tired. "Leave me alone," she seemed to say to Mardi, or sometimes, "Take me to Tar-zhay," what everyone like her called the corporation's Target stores.

Somehow, Mardi survived—barely, and without so much as a salary adjustment for inflation—a major shake-up within the larger business. The Dayton-Hudson Corporation had renamed itself Target Corporation in 2000. And now, toward the end of 2001, the Dayton's and Hudson's department stores rebranded to become Marshall Field's. Meanwhile, the citizens of Minnesota elected the founder's great-grandson Mark Dayton as U.S. senator.

Things were changing but not in a way that helped Mardi pay her bills. The corporate office handed out copies of a book titled, *Who Moved My Cheese: An Amazing Way to Deal with Change in Your Work and in Your Life.*

The parables in the book insulted Mardi's intelligence. She threw the paperback across her living room.

24. Marshall Field's, 2001

Noelle jabbed a red-for-Christmas fingernail through the plastic shrink-wrap and peeled it away. She opened the box of Frango mint chocolates and shoved two pieces into her mouth, one for her and one for her plus-one. Hidden under her loose and breezy dress from Target, which sold surprisingly cute maternity clothes, kicked the baby due soon after the holidays.

The Frangos were an old company tradition. Not a Dayton's tradition, though.

Minnesotans still felt dismayed that the store now bore the name of Marshall Field's instead of Dayton's. It wouldn't change much, Target Corporation promised. The Frango mints had been sold at Dayton's ever since the corporation acquired Marshall Field's during Noelle's first year on the job. Since the name change, the green boxes spilled even more bountifully across all surfaces. They tumbled onto the floor, to Noelle's annoyance, every time she slammed a register drawer.

The Frangos were made famous in Chicago by Marshall Field's but originated with a Seattle store Marshall Field's had once acquired. Maybe control over the Frangos was the secret reason for all department store takeovers and intrigue, Gary Gorman conjectured.

Noelle looked at a new shoe dog slipping navy pumps onto a Northwest Airlines flight attendant. They used to buy maroon; there must have been a flight attendant uniform update. Noelle's nose dripped. Would she still be here when the next generation of flight attendants came in for the next Northwest color scheme?

Would she still be here when the flight attendants could start wearing flats?

Covering Women's Accessories, Handbags, and Juniors as a floor manager while pregnant convinced Noelle to ditch her heels for Aerosoles, waffle-patterned, soft rubber-soled shoes.

Noelle envisioned Dean Ohlman's new life. She dug her fingernails into her inner wrist until half-moon-shaped red marks appeared. The pain helped her forget what she had heard about him.

It did not make her happy, this news. It was easier to distract herself with chocolate and the employees fretting about the public's reaction to the store's rebranding.

Noelle, who gobbled up the assigned readings from *Who Moved My Cheese,* asked, "If sports fans coped with losing the Met Stadium to build the Mall of America, shouldn't shoppers be able to deal with change? To find *new cheese?*"

"I don't care about the name either," said the new shoe dog. "But the new look makes me gag."

"What, you don't like the stripes?"

"A thousand people just got killed by terrorists in New York City," said a college girl selling shoes weekends and evenings. "There's anthrax in the mail. The polar ice caps are melting."

"Well, we do work *here,*" Noelle replied. "Not at Santa's workshop in the North Pole."

Noelle worried little about the polar ice caps in 2001.

For days after the attacks of September 11, however, Noelle had hidden away in the first floor's many stock rooms. Noelle noted the terrorists liked skyscrapers. She thought of the IDS Tower, with its Crystal Court, right across the street. If it came down, Marshall Field's would be buried in glass.

"You should come over and have dinner with me and my wife and daughter," Gary said. "We have a collection of Dayton's memorabilia"

She tried not to wrinkle her nose at the dinner invitation, but at least talking about the stupid branding got her mind off of pregnancy heartburn, Dean Ohlman, and terrorists.

Noelle's cousin had been in on the decisions, she told the college student. "Mardi said the stripes have been market tested."

The entire cast of cardboard characters had stood before Noelle one day when she'd popped into the marketing office for a department managers meeting. She learned that the market persona project was really about survey and sales data, not Mardi reading a cardboard character's mind.

Becky Sharp adored stripes, surveys showed.

Gary stood up straight. "Change is part of the game, and it's how Dayton's took over many other department stores over the decades—Schuneman's in St. Paul, Fantles in Sioux Falls..."

Noelle wiped her nose and touched her belly. The sugar from the chocolate made the baby fidgety in there.

"It was Goodfellow's Daylight Store when this building opened," Gary said. "George Draper Dayton had bought his way in as a new partner in the existing business when he hired architect Charles Sedgwick to reimagine this building."

Noelle burped quietly and swayed in her Aerosoles.

"Think of it this way," said Gary. "Dayton was a plant guy. He grew up working in a nursery, grafting and budding. He could do a hundred trees a day when he was only fourteen. When he moved from New York to Worthington, Minnesota to be a banker, he still grew trees. Sometimes he helped farmers, and sometimes he took over distressed properties and brought them into bud and bloom. Later, with Goodfellow's, he bought the business outright and grafted Dayton's right onto it. Then he..."

"Brought it into bud and bloom," Noelle said, finishing his sentence. She'd worked with Gary long enough to do that.

"This is the history of the state. Our cities are grafted onto Indian villages. Nobody thinks about Goodfellow's anymore, and nobody thinks about those Indian villages. Little Crow's Kaposia is just South St. Paul to you and me."

Noelle said, "I know. My little house by Swede Hollow Park that I rent out to tenants—same thing."

"Swede Hollow, exactly. That neighborhood grafted itself onto a previous neighborhood a dozen times over, maybe a hundred times over going back twelve thousand years to the Clovis people."

Noelle's knees ached. She'd been budding and blooming enough on her own for the second time in two years.

Her second child (third, she always noted mentally) appeared, according to the ultrasound, to be a boy. She planned to name him Nicollet after a French geographer, Joseph Nicollet, as Mardi had suggested. Wade suggested Joseph, worried that bullies might call him Nicole. Noelle begged him never to say that again.

Just as regarding the current life of Dean Ohlman, and just as regarding Noelle's first pregnancy, Noelle hoped some things would always remain unspoken.

PART III. 2005-2007

25. Funeral, 2005

A grandfather's funeral wasn't the kind of a place to bring a date, but Ralphina smiled upon seeing that Owen brought one to Ken's. At least there was live music, if you counted the bugle playing taps in the driving snow at Wayzata's Groveland Cemetery.

The David Lee Funeral Home had coordinated with the military vets bureau, Ken and Vilda's old church, and the cemetery. All Ralphina had to do was grieve. Owen was now a college kid at the Minneapolis College of Art and Design with a sincere young woman at his side to hand him tissues. Ralphina had nothing to stop her from her own lamentation.

But again, as with Vilda's death and then Catherine's murder, her eyes remained painfully dry. She hated herself for that. Didn't she love them enough to cry?

Ralphina realized she wasn't the only one with dry eyes at the reception in the Wayzata Unitarian Universalist church on Rice Street. General Mills retirees, vets, old friends like June Skaalen, and even the pastor, whooped it up. Ken's buddy Neal told stories about the war and their fishing trips up to Neal's cabin on the Poplar River in Lutsen. Neal confessed that they rarely went fishing on their trips up there. It had really been about getting away and being men, eating with their hands and splitting enough logs for a thousand fires.

"So that's why we never got to eat the catch," Ralphina said. "My mom never caught on to the ruse?"

"Ha!" Neal responded. "Vilda was just grateful to me for getting Ken out of her hair."

June slapped Neal on the back. "Well, ain't that the truth."

Neal broke from the circle and approached the large photo of Ken on the standing easel. His shoulders went from shaking with laughter to quivering with grief. June glided over and put an arm around him. Why, Ralphina asked herself, couldn't she spring a single tear for her father if a World War II soldier could cry like that?

Neal faced the others and told of that last trip to Lutsen when Ken wandered off after going outside for firewood. Neal drove around and found him in the Lutsen Lodge gift shop asking for a postcard to mail to his folks on Nicollet Island. Ken's parents had been dead for twenty years and hadn't lived on that urban island for forty.

"You dears haven't had your real Ken for so many years," an old neighbor said. "Owen, do you have any memory of what he was like before?"

Owen smiled, and his date touched his elbow. "I was maybe three when I watched Grandpa Ken help Ralphy build a backdrop for a display. My mom was into her painting, but Ralphy liked the complicated projects with all the moving parts. I remember my grandpa getting really excited about her ideas."

"That's a good memory," Ralphina said. "Dad helped me with set designs ever since my days with the high school plays. Thank goodness I've had those theater design skills to fall back on. As little as the theater pays, retail display work just isn't steady enough."

"Aren't you working on the Dayton's displays anymore, dear?" asked June.

"Oh no, not much. You know, it's been called Marshall Field's for more than three years now."

June waved her away. "I'll always call it Dayton's!"

Ralphina looked around. An old neighbor reintroduced herself to Owen while ladling punch for herself. Neal sat in quiet conversation with another veteran.

"Speaking of Daytons," Ralphina said, seizing the opportunity, "the last time I saw Dad before he died, he said something about Mom being a nurse at Dayton's. I thought he was confused with how I often freelanced there, or how you illustrated ads there. But he quite clearly said my mother worked at Dayton's as a nurse."

"What specifically are you asking me?"

Ralphina gathered her patience. June could be so evasive. "Did my mom work as a nurse at Dayton's, in the infirmary—what they used to call the store hospital—on the tenth floor?"

"Why of course she worked at Dayton's, dear! Vilda and I both worked on the tenth floor. That's where I did my illustrations."

Again, so vague. Ralphina targeted the question further. "But did she work there as a nurse?"

June stuck her chin in the air. A quick nod followed.

So, it was true. The same abandoned infirmary where Mardi had lain in the old metal bed and Ralphina had kissed her—she never imagined her mother had once been a store nurse.

"Why didn't I know that?"

"No reason, I'm sure." June waved her hand with a flourish as if shooing away any more such pointless questions.

"It's strange because I thought I knew my mother pretty well."

"She only worked there for a year or two before she got married and became a part-time nurse at the Highcroft school. Taking care of kids was where her heart was."

"Sure, I get that. But our parents brought us to the downtown Dayton's holiday exhibit in the eighth-floor auditorium every year. Never once did Mom say, 'And I used to work just two floors up!' Nor did she mention it when I started getting lots of work there."

"Those Dayton boys employed almost everybody we knew at some point, Ralphy. It would be more remarkable if Vilda had never worked a single day there."

As the church ladies began covering the leftover food and hoisting chairs up on tables, the funeral-goers took the hint and donned their coats and hats. Ralphina hugged Owen and thanked everyone for coming. Hoping to learn more from June, she offered her a ride home.

"Neal's daughter will drive me," June said. "I'll call you soon, dear."

Now it was just Ralphina, staring at the photo easel and willing a tear to come. She leaked exactly two of them before giving up and heading to her car.

It hardly made sense to leave Wayzata without driving by the old house, *but only for the good memories, nothing to do with Mardi Wirt living there,* she promised herself.

Ferndale Road led to an intersection, where just beyond, another road turned onto Westwood Lane. Two old neighboring houses Ralphina once loved were now gone, replaced by architectural edifices twice their size. The house at the end of the lane looked dark as the sun melted behind it. Just as she reached closer, a light came on in the kitchen window.

Ralphina turned around as fast as she could and drove away.

26. *Paint, 2005*

Owen swirled the dot of blue into the jar of yellow paint. It was a mini jam jar, like the kind hotels give with room service. Owen had collected them during the road trip Ralphina took him on after the class of 2003 Twin Cities Success School graduation.

Finally, almost two years later, he had the perfect use for them. It was the first day of his field-teaching credit course for art college. He would lead Bernard Petit's class in three painting sessions and had already primed the canvases for them. The blue dot blended in, transforming the bright yellow to an eye-popping chartreuse. Owen demonstrated how he tested the paint.

"See how it's too thick?" He made eye contact with several students. "We'll need to add a touch of solvent."

The students followed suit, mixing in blue paint with a small but sturdy paintbrush. How much blue depended on what shade they preferred. They could mix in red instead of blue if they liked orange. They each had their own mini jam jar of yellow. Tubes of the other colors sat in the middle of each group of desks. At ages fifteen and sixteen, all the boys had mixed paint colors before. But Owen introduced them to oil paints, not baby stuff.

Brushes mixed, then glided paint over canvases to saturate them with color. Eyes took in the intensity of the colors, no student's shade the same as another's.

Owen's first student-teaching experience got off to a satisfying start the moment he saw a boy's face turn from anxious to calm. Art held power in that way. Teaching was not Owen's program track at the Minneapolis College of Art and Design, but the school required one semester of it. Owen's mother had loved teaching art. Now Owen seemed to be thinking maybe he could love it too. Sometimes he lay in bed late at night talking to Catherine about it, hoping she could hear him from the spirit realm, wishing she could tell him what to do.

When a student gawked and cawed at the variety of peacock shades striating across his canvas, Owen said, "Now I see why Mr. Petit likes you guys."

A boy named Shaun made a guttural noise. "You're not our teacher and this is stupid," he muttered. "I hate painting."

Owen flinched, then froze for a moment. Bernard looked up from the schoolwork he'd been grading at his desk. He shouldn't micromanage. He stayed in his seat, keeping his eye on the situation. Owen relaxed again and walked over to check out Shaun's paint, a dark urine-colored concoction.

The canvas displayed a mess of murky clumps and soggy spots.

"The beauty of painting on canvas," Owen said to the students, "is that anything can be fixed. It might turn out differently than you planned, but that can be a good thing."

Bernard beamed. The Twin Cities Success School alumnus had grown so mature and confident. Shaun, however, twisted his face in displeasure. His paint refused to extend beyond one unspreadable dollop. He pushed his brush furiously in all directions on the canvas, but the color wouldn't budge.

"This part is just the background. No big deal," Owen said. "Let me help you."

Shaun surveyed the room. He saw twenty-four nearly completed backgrounds. For all the boys but him, the color magically spread over the canvas in smooth but richly varied textures. His face fell, but his eyes seemed to look up and ask for help.

Bernard saw how his former student responded so capably to the tough kid.

But it was too soon to feel secure.

Before Owen could react, Shaun sat up straight again, picked up his canvas, and flung it at Owen. Owen cried out, and the corner of the canvas frame slammed into his cheekbone, just an inch from his eye. His whole body clenched to resist the urge to whip it back at the kid. Even after fifteen years of therapy, it wasn't easy.

Bernard leaped toward them.

"Should I go get the security guy?" asked one boy.

Shaun's chest puffed out. "No, you fucking narc!" he yelled to the boy, a target for the glass jar he held in a pitching position.

Owen's urge to slug the kid grew stronger, but then he felt the weight of the decoupaged loon rock he still kept with him at all times. He slid his hand into his pocket to hold the millions-of-years-old stone.

Shaun's eyes flew to Owen's hand going into his pocket. He had seen that same move before when a drug deal went wrong for his mom's boyfriend.

The boy charged toward Owen with the full force of his sixteen-year-old body, but Bernard stepped in his way. Shaun bowled him over an empty chair. One hip hit the ground first, then both knees. Bernard's right arm and shoulder tore as they caught on the overturned chair.

At the same time, Bernard, being Bernard, looked around from his heap-like position on the floor and noted that this had all been his fault. He thanked God that the school year was almost over. And he reminded himself that, should he need to head to the hospital, he would need someone to care for his new puppy.

Dino—named after the Minnesota North Stars hockey player Dino Ciccarelli—needed food and crate cleaning, as well as some scratches behind the ears.

In hindsight, he knew he'd seen stress and exhaustion in Shaun's eyes when he raced into the classroom ten minutes after the bell. Who knew what happened at home this time? But he'd ignored it in hope that his students would be perfect today for his former student to teach them something special.

Shaun knelt to the floor and looked up in fear. Owen held the rock in his open palm for Shaun to see and caught his own reflection in Shaun's wet eyes. "It's just my favorite rock," he said. "I made it when I was a kid."

"Dumbass," Shaun said. "I thought you had a gun."

Bernard lifted his head from the ground. "You can get the resource officer now," he said. The student who had offered took off down the hall.

"And Paj Yang! Don't come back without Ms. Yang," Bernard yelled after him.

The injured teacher put his head back down, saw swirls of blue, yellow, and red paint all around above him, and passed out.

27. Bernard's Convalescence, 2005

Sprawled on his sister's couch lay Bernard, knocked out on OxyContin again. He felt no pain. Mardi and Noelle sat on the loveseat across from him. Avril and Nicollet lay on the floor in front of Mardi's TV in the upstairs room, the former master bedroom. Noelle had brought a French-learning DVD, but Avril begged for the Blue's Clue's video she knew her mom had in her tote.

On top of his other injuries, the doctor discovered that Bernard had crushed a vertebra in the classroom incident. He spent two weeks in transitional care after the first two surgeries. It was either Mardi's or their mother's house after the third, and Mardi won hands-down because of the main level extra bedroom and Irene's *I-told-you-so* attitude.

His black lab puppy, Dino, was already there destroying everything, and now his parents, friends, and colleagues stopped by often. Paj brought Hmong cuisine from her mother's growing catering business. The brothy dishes, her mother said, would heal his bones.

Mardi's place had become the liveliest little murder-suicide house in the Midwest.

On Noelle's Saturday off, however, a lull set in regarding Bernard's visitors, and she took advantage of it. She needed to talk to Mardi.

"I think Wade is in love with the woman who is managing the Ridgedale Mathy Taffy Tutoring Center," Noelle said. "Mathy Kathy, they call her. They stood so close behind the counter when I went over there this morning. The body language. I think their genitals were communicating."

A snore rose up from the couch and Bernard shoved his pillow away from his face. He said a choice word or two about the Minnesota Wild hockey team.

"The name Mathy Kathy, oh my God," Mardi said, ignoring her brother. "But I'm surprised you go to the malls to check up. I didn't think you liked to *wade* into his territory."

"Very funny. I was shopping. And I don't care about that prick, but I've never cheated on him."

Mardi looked surprised. "You haven't? Never?"

"No, I wouldn't, and I'm too tired for that anyway. After I collapse from work every day, I have to do almost all the housework and all of the running around with kids."

"I'm sorry," said Mardi, jumping up to move the pillow that had fallen across her brother's face again. "His business is doing so well, and you are rising in the ranks at work. Maybe you need to hire more help around the house. Then you could have more fun."

"I'm done with fun. If only I could do things over."

"Like what?"

"I would marry Dean Ohlman." Her voice squeaked, pain emanating from her wrist as her nails dug into it.

"Knowing who he is now, anybody would marry Dean Ohlman," Mardi said.

Noelle hadn't been close with Mardi when she was seeing Dean. Everyone knew about the former shoe dog now. The internet had confirmed the rumors about his success.

"Then why didn't you accept his proposal?" Mardi said, raising her hands in bafflement before answering her own question. "I know. You thought he would never make more than thirty-five thousand dollars a year. And now he makes money off of so many shoppers today who can't get their ass to an actual store, which turns out to be pretty much everybody."

"My regrets have nothing to do with Dean being a dot-com multi-millionaire," Noelle insisted. She glanced at Bernard and only slightly lowered her voice to say, "He was a premature ejaculator. In hindsight, though, who cares? I liked him. I could have been happy, even if we had to live in my East Side hovel. Even if we had to live in a tent at the bottom of Swede Hollow."

Mardi twisted her nose when Noelle said 'premature ejaculator' and Noelle remembered she had only told Debra about that part. She waved it off. "And now he's living with a Golden Gate Bridge view in San Francisco, married to Princess Allison of Women's Accessories."

Her fingernails plowed into her wrist again. She had been doing so well with not hurting herself about all of her mistakes lately.

"I heard Allison came in one day when she was back in town and she bought Revo sunglasses at full price," she murmured. "Dean's bricklayer father convinced them to invest in the new brick and stone veneers. Another fucking bonanza!"

Mardi winced for her cousin. She knew that Aunt Annette, if she knew, must also be dying with regret. Noelle heard things here and there from Gary Gorman, that guy in Women's Shoes who never shut his trap.

"They are all the richer since the veneer masonry market took off, and Allison lost all the weight after having the twins and working with a personal trainer. Meanwhile, I'm living with a big asshole I can't stand to sleep with. In fact, it would be a blessing if Wade were a premature ejaculator. Instead, he goes on and on like a feral boar."

Mardi threw Noelle a Frango mint chocolate from a green box. "Have you ever really been in love? Don't count Dean, whether you were or not. Did you ever love any other guy?"

Noelle told Mardi about her two long-term boyfriends, and then she answered the question. There was the boy from her neighborhood, the baseball player. She thought she'd come close to making him love her. At least enough for him to put his hands up her shirt a few times before he decided not to go further.

"So what happened?" Mardi asked. "How did it end?"

"We went for a walk one day in the rain. I thought we'd sneak under some bleachers, but before we reached the baseball diamond he stuck his hand out for me to shake."

She'd never forgotten the rejection she'd felt when he'd said, "Friends?"

"Maybe he didn't know how much you liked him since, I mean, *if* you were fooling around with other guys."

"Oh yeah, Roger that. I'm sure he thought I was a slut. But to say, *'Friends?'* like that is the worst, especially in the pouring rain and when it's the only person you ever wanted that bad."

Mardi tossed another Frango to her cousin. She looked at Bernard to make sure he was asleep, then asked, "Do you ever regret giving up Genève for adoption?"

"Yeah. Sometimes." She paused and nodded toward the green Frango box. Mardi threw her another one.

Chocolate on her top lip, Noelle added, "But then I wouldn't have Avril and Nicollet, so...no. But you shouldn't ask such hard questions."

Remembering the kids in the upstairs room, Noelle stood to go check on them and their DVDs. She came right back.

"Do you think Fran has any idea Genève is yours?" Mardi asked.

"I don't know how she would. If Wade were a better person, I could try to open the adoption. Then I wouldn't have to find out things here and there on the internet. She swims, did I tell you? She's only eleven but her name comes up in all these swim meet results online. Butterfly is her best stroke."

"Butterfly is the hardest!"

"*Unh huh,* it is!" Noelle brightened with pride.

"Could you tell Fran and make it open now? At least open for you if not Pierre?"

"Not unless Wade and I get divorced. He never would have married me in the first place if he'd known I'd had a baby."

"Especially a black baby..."

"No baby. But oh my God, yeah, a black baby. And by a man who was already engaged. I was a big, fat slut."

"Don't beat yourself up," said Mardi. "Anyway, I have something to share with you too."

Bernard now faced the back of the couch but still seemed fast asleep. "I'm gay. I mean, I'm a lesbian or something. I think I've known for years now. It's probably pretty clear to you that I'm not looking for another husband."

"Duh," said Noelle. "I think I guessed that shortly after you divorced the one you had."

Mardi took the box and plucked a mint chocolate from its white ruffled cup. "Well then, there you go. I'm a lesbian and you gave up a baby for adoption. Where'd you get the name Genève anyway?"

"You will recall that I was delirious. But I wanted something French, ya know. A little Petit. A little Pierre."

The Frango parchment cups littered the coffee table in front of them. Noelle picked up several and stacked them one inside of another. She tore a hole through the middle with her finger and formed them into a ruffled skirt worthy of wear by one of Avril's Polly Pocket dolls.

Bernard turned himself around on the couch and blinked. He reached for his water to take a sip.

"Can you feed Dino?" he asked, "and please don't let him get into your chocolate. It's toxic for dogs." He turned around and fell back to sleep.

Noelle and Mardi looked wide-eyed at each other and tried not to gasp.

"There's no way he heard us," Mardi whispered. "But he sounded so lucid."

Noelle shook her head. "No way. Or no way he'll remember."

28. Oxy Dreams, 2005

When the doors to Twin Cities Success School swung open in the fall, there was no longer the same Mr. Petit in the classroom.

The painkillers, at least, helped him sleep. He was smoking again, and more than once Dino barked at him as he drifted off to sleep in a chair with a lit Merit Light, having now stepped down the nicotine on the way to quitting again. He didn't really care about his own health now. He just felt bad smoking around the dog.

With the loss of activity, Bernard began to fade in color and spirit. He was aging before his time.

On one of his mother's rare visits to his house in St. Paul's Irvine Park over the Labor Day weekend, a new neighbor asked—not out of flattery—if she was Bernard's sister. It was Bernard's age that the neighbor misestimated rather than Irene's, but Irene took it as a compliment.

Like most school teachers and administrators, Bernard felt almost useless by the end of the first day of school but still had to prepare lesson plans until at least nine. On this night, for the first time, he could not fall asleep even with the pain pills.

Possibly, his diet contributed to his exhaustion. Or so said his girlfriend. It was not full of the "power foods" this newest woman sort of halfway in his life insisted he needed.

The week went by unremarkably. No boys' lives were changed by having Mr. Petit as their teacher. He read the season's hockey outlook, one thing to look forward to after the NHL lockout the season before. He skipped his Saturday volunteering gig at the Little Sisters of the Poor nursing home in his neighborhood.

A grayish cast appeared on Bernard's face, two ashen ovals replacing the pink camellias that had once been his cheeks.

Mardi substituted for him twice in his second week of the school year, calling in sick at Marshall Field's, when he couldn't get out of bed. She offered to bring her brother to Hazelden Addiction Treatment Center for an evaluation. He declined.

Bernard skipped the fall dinner event with teaching colleagues during the third weekend after school started and got takeout, beer-battered walleye from one of St. Paul's many Irish pubs. He ate it straight out of a Styrofoam box and smoked and drank while grading homework assignments and mustering the strength to work on a plan to get Twin Cities Success School out of debt before its authorizer pulled the plug.

The only other thing he really cared to do for himself anymore was to drive down to the St. Paul Yacht Club and sit on his houseboat, which he had rechristened as Pepperdine.

Although Bernard had not had an excessive amount of school spirit for his alma mater, he had his own reason for renaming the ramshackle houseboat after Pepperdine. The college founder, George Pepperdine, had believed it was wrong to amass a fortune to use for worldly goods. He warned of the danger selfishness posed to the soul. At Pepperdine, he benefitted from the gift of another. He would take that gift and pay it back in service of education. Seeing Pepperdine painted onto the back of his beat-up boat reminded him to give little to himself and a lot to others.

From his highest window at home, Bernard could see the river. He knew the riverbanks were being developed along the Warner and Shepard roads, and that soon he would look at rows of condos instead of the Mississippi. He would never lose his view from his grandfather's houseboat. Sometimes, he could even fall asleep upon the softly rolling river without his medicine. He always kept it on him though. He always had the option.

He would never bring his new girlfriend to the boat. The Pepperdine was his place alone, and anyway, it was Fran who popped into his mind as he drifted to sleep on the boat one evening with the help of his OxyContin.

Two secrets now entered Bernard's mind. He seemed only to remember them when he was on the same drug he had taken when he had first heard these secrets at Mardi's house.

First, Fran's adopted child was his own cousin Noelle's baby, somehow born without the rest of the Petit and Nichols families finding out.

And second, his sister Mardi was gay.

He'd been lying there in a drug-induced fog when he heard Mardi and Noelle talking. Lying down now in his own boat in the same kind of a fog, the words came back:

"Well then, there you go. I'm a lesbian and you gave up a baby for adoption. Where'd you get the name Genève anyway?"

The words would be forgotten by morning when the medication had run its course, as if a wormhole had opened and closed.

Genève. Such an unusual name, the kind that really only comes to one in a dream anyway.

Fran had adopted a baby named Genève.

Bernard knew that much about Fran because the talkative man, Gary at Dayton's, told him so years before.

He never could help himself. Fran never wanted to talk, but he'd tried enough times that her closest colleagues knew who he was. He had stopped by Women's Shoes on his way to have lunch at the Oak Grill Room with Mardi and their mother. He would never forget that day because it was when he'd learned that she moved to Missouri, where her parents were from. She'd fulfilled a dream of adopting, Gary said, and left. It seemed like an ending to him.

What he didn't remember in the morning after his night of drug-fueled dreams on the houseboat was that Fran's baby had anything to do with his cousin or his sister.

He lay in his boat with the morning sun shining through the window and thought of Fran with her black hair—shiny, smooth, and bouncy. As he stripped off his clothes to get into the boat's small bathroom shower, he turned to the mirror hanging on the wall and noticed his hair. He imagined what Fran looked like if she had started to gray, too. Standing under the low-pressure stream of water, he remembered her as his teenage lover, then as the woman he'd seen through the window of the bus near Dayton's in 1990.

It didn't occur to Bernard to look for her on the internet to see how Fran looked now. Seeing just a picture of her was unthinkable.

It would have to be the real woman, live in the flesh, or nothing at all.

29. *Taking Inventory,* 2006

Fran used to go to the Clayton library once every week to explore the internet. But when her psychologist sister received a large advance for her book on the teenage brain and gave Fran five hundred dollars for her birthday, Fran added to that her own savings from her Target paychecks and splurged.

She brought home the Hewlett-Packard desktop computer, preloaded with all the software.

Genève could use it for schoolwork, too, she reasoned.

"Create user profile," the startup menu instructed her, asking for a user name and password.

Fran chose her own name, then looked around her apartment. She let her eyes settle on the ancient melon-colored Diane von Furstenberg dress that Bernard's mother had given her eons ago to try to get her to dress nicer for the country club. Irene Petit had to have bought it at the Wayzata Crazy Days sale.

She typed "MelonDVF" into the password field.

The names she searched belonged to people she thought might be perplexed at her curiosity about their lives, but she knew she couldn't be the only one using her new internet account for such voyeurism.

One former cheerleader from Fran's school in Minnesota held patents in superabsorbent polymers. Money went this cheerleader's way every time Fran stuck a Kotex pad onto her underwear or diapered Genève. A kid who shoved sand down her shirt on the playground was the 2005 Builder of the Year. A Hebrew school classmate turned out a best-selling comic book series.

Fran searched for some of her old colleagues too, including Noelle Nichols, who didn't have any online results other than a marriage record and a couple of old chatroom comments from men about those Petit's Party Central commercials with her wearing a bikini.

A Middle Eastern shoe dog-turned-engineer invented a new kind of highway guardrail, and a Bahamian shoe dog started his own haberdashery. The Amish woman was back in the good graces of her Harmony community, at least enough to be allowed to advertise van tours of Amish country. The theater student shoe dog came up on the Guthrie Theater website, unfortunately as box office staff.

Dean Ohlman founded a website selling shoes and purses, which was now the third-largest such website in the world. The business used data from previous purchases and searches and sent special deals for pretty, shiny things that its algorithms determined would tempt customers.

The high-tech version of the client file he once kept in an old recipe card box even conferred VIP status and rewards.

"Wow," Fran said out loud. She whistled. "Wow." She and Gary Gorman had written a few letters a year, so she already knew Dean had done something with shoes in the early dot-com days but didn't realize he was that big of a deal. Noelle Nichols must be kicking herself for breaking up with him, Fran imagined.

She kept searching names. Browser results named Pierre St. Hilaire as the senior vice president for inventory strategy at Target Corporation. Fran knew about Pierre's big job already, thanks to Gary. She scrolled through all the results on his name, just to see what else there was to know.

Every once in a while—she tried to keep this one down to only once every week or two—Fran paid a virtual visit to the publicly discoverable life of the one male she ever loved who really loved her back.

What she learned now about Bernard Petit's life was that he'd agreed to be featured on an Irvine Park neighborhood website, he had a new puppy he'd named Dino, after Minnesota North Star Dino Ciccarelli, of course, and he liked relaxing on his houseboat and teaching economics and life skills at an all-boys charter school in St. Paul.

She saw nothing about sailing. Nothing about a wife or children.

She saw nothing about his life falling apart, either.

He wasn't married when Gary wrote to her with a mention of Bernard stopping by Women's Shoes soon after she moved. But by now, it was surprising. He was forty-seven.

Fran's internet connection didn't do well with photos. Bernard's image loaded line by line—his silvering hair, creased forehead, his benevolent smile. He looked older to Fran, naturally, than the last time she'd seen him looking for her while visiting his sister at Dayton's. But it wasn't just age in those hazel eyes. It was something else.

Pain?

Thirty years had passed since she rested in his arms, so carefree aboard his sailboat on Lake Minnetonka.

And now she saw him on her screen, his image right there in her own home, looking like a probable disappointment to Irene. A teacher of children who were so challenged that they couldn't handle a regular school, helping people as he'd always wanted to do.

But succeeding at it? His eyes said, *not really.*

She felt relief that she never needed to be so good. It turned out it was a lucky gift that her acceptance to Pepperdine University had been rescinded.

Who cared anymore why the admissions office rejected her while she was in the middle of working with the scholarship office to understand their generous offer? It still baffled her, but if anything in her life had gone differently, she wouldn't have Genève.

So, no regrets.

Fran bookmarked the *St. Louis Post-Dispatch,* the *New York Times,* two social justice websites, the new website that her Humanistic Jewish group had built, and of course, she bestowed a bookmark on *Ms.* magazine. She bookmarked *Adoption Resources* and another website about adopted adolescents' needs.

The other adoptive parents she met had open arrangements. They sent photos and letters to birth mothers and one even had visits from the birth father. Although she envied those arrangements, nowadays Fran only wondered from time to time about Genève's birth mother and father.

One evening, Fran took the bus home from work. It had been a frustrating day, with mounds of clothes piling up in Target dressing rooms and nobody bothering to put them away. She leaned her head against the bus window.

Pierre St. Hilaire, Target's senior vice president for inventory strategy, entered her mind.

She had the urge to talk to Pierre about the problem, but she dismissed it. He was too high up now—she would have to ask her store manager for help. Still, she remembered Pierre fondly, his downturned eyes and long eyelids, how his brow would rise and fall when he thought through inventory problems at Dayton's. She remembered when, as a stock boy, he'd created a three-tactic system to keep the stock room neat and orderly.

It was funny, the similarity.

Genève's face, especially how her downturned eyes expressed her thoughts and her brow had risen so high and fallen so low the night before. She had been working on a system to reorganize their kitchen pantry.

Pierre's and Genève's faces melded and merged for a moment in Fran's mind. Like father and daughter.

The bus lurched forward and jolted Fran out of her absurd vision.

Pierre was most certainly not Genève's father. He was engaged to Johanne in 1993, not fathering children with someone else. He was a nerd. He could be unintentionally charming, with that French Islander accent, but if he ever slept with another woman, it would be one who liked a challenge.

She fell further into thought and missed her bus stop.

When Fran got home, Sharon showed her all the amazing things Genève had done that day. She didn't really need her grandma to babysit her anymore. Genève practically ran the household, with a home for every object and every object in its home.

What other twelve-year-old created systems for the laundry, systems for the pantry, and systems for grocery lists?

She kept inventory.

Fran set cookies on the counter. Keebler, as she was no baker. Sharon promised she'd fed Genève a proper dinner.

"I met a kid today who was adopted and he and his birth parents exchange pictures and letters a bunch of times every year. Didn't you want to let my birth parents do that?"

Genève ate a cookie while she packed her Clayton-Wydown Middle School Swim Team duffle, for night practice.

"I would have let them, but they had to make a hard decision and apparently they thought it would be best for you if you didn't know them."

"Best for me or best for them?"

"We don't really know, sweetheart. That's why I said, 'apparently.' We only know they chose it; we don't know what happened. I have to trust that they chose it for you. And I also trust that you know we'd better get going or you'll be late for your night practice."

"But don't you know anything about them?"

Fran set down her purse. The swim coach was never happy when they were late, but these conversations didn't happen at convenient times. "I know your mother was white and your father was black," she answered. "I realize that leaves a lot of room for your imagination."

"And you said they gave me my French name. Or should we say German or Swiss?"

"Good point. Maybe you're named after the capital of Switzerland."

Genève pulled at the drawstring of her blue hooded Clayton-Wydown Middle School sweatshirt. "Then my name would be Bern. Everyone would call me Bernie."

Fran laughed. "Right, I forgot. Geneva isn't the capital."

"It also means juniper," Genève said. "It comes from German. It's a very uncommon name that makes me easily findable, you know."

Fran knew that. For Genève, being found could end badly or it could end well. "I could have changed it or made it your middle name, but it was so pretty," she said. "Now, aybe if your name was Bern...well, we could have gone with Bernadette."

Genève searched Fran's eyes. There had to be more. She waited, then said, "One of them must be tall. That's why people usually think I'm your *bio-kid,* you know. Because we're both giant Amazon women."

"*Bio-kid,* hmm," Fran said. She ran her fingers through her daughter's curls, then playfully pulled Genève's sweatshirt hood over her head. "Hadn't heard that term, but yeah, one of them must be tall like us. Probably likes cookies."

Tall and French-speaking and black, Fran thought. And living in Minnesota and perhaps good at systems engineering. And those eyes.

The combined characteristics could possibly define hundreds of people, yet only one person came to Fran's mind again and again:

Pierre St. Hilaire. He was not possibly Genève's father. But they would like each other, Fran mused. Perhaps someday they would meet.

30. *Macy's, 2006*

By September 2006, the red star of Macy's claimed all of the former Dayton's, Hudson's, and Marshall Field's stores.

"The logo is said to have come from a tattoo that Mr. Macy got on a whaling ship off of Nantucket," explained Gary Gorman.

Had the whales he hunted taught him how to open his mouth and eat all the smaller stores like so many bream? Did those who came after him develop an appetite for big fish, and even other whales? Dayton's had long kept busy acquiring little fish here before merging with Hudson's and buying Marshall Field's. But the current corporate parent of Macy's, Federated Department Stores, had swum in bigger waters with its mouth agape for even longer.

One of the biggest whales Federated had gobbled was May Department Stores, which bought Marshall Field's from Target Corporation in 2004 without changing its name.

Target Corporation was now completely divested of its department stores, of its own roots. Federated did the natural thing in an era of efficiencies and consolidation. It turned all the Marshall Field's stores into Macy's, including of course what used to be the Dayton's flagship store at 700 Nicollet Mall.

The Marshall Field's name had been slowly floated around Dayton's for years before that name change, via the Frango chocolate boxes. But the Macy's red star marched in with less familiarity to Minnesotans who had not lived in New York City or other Macy's towns. Having a Macy's store at the Mall of America didn't make it feel as familiar to downtown and Dales shoppers as the corporate bosses had hoped.

It made sense now, how Target Corporation had brought Dayton's, Hudson's, and Marshall Field's all under the Marshall Field's name. That name was best known nationally and worth the most on the market. Selling off a collection of varied store brands would have been so much messier.

Marshall Field's in Minnesota had been, at least until Target Corporation sold it, just a new nameplate on a store that would always be Dayton's to many. The stores still had the same Mandarin chicken pasta salad in the Marketplace Deli. The restaurant on the twelfth floor was still the Oak Grill Room. The stores at the Dales didn't change a lot either.

Macy's hired back Noelle's old colleague, Kalmer, who pushed up a pant leg to show her a new Viking ship tattoo on his calf above a Vikings football helmet tattoo. It wasn't only for his sake that she vouched for him. Noelle's departments needed dependability right now.

She remembered the security guard's joke the day Kalmer had been fired for giving an out-of-town customer the sale price the night before a sale—he said that if he was as dependable as Gary insisted he was then he could get a job as a mailman.

It was apt. *Neither snow, nor rain, nor heat, nor gloom of night stays these couriers from the swift completion of their appointed rounds.* That was Kalmer, all right, on time and unshakeable. Hardly anyone knew he developed his traits growing up on a farm north of the cities. Cows, farm parents, and his small-town football team required him to do more than show up.

Noelle just hoped her new corporate employer would not discover that the person she vouched for had once been escorted out of the building by security.

Macy's extended to Kalmer no Daytonian promises of empowerment. They gave him a nametag, a line on the now computerized schedule, and a lower wage than that of the thousands of workers they'd just laid off.

Noelle stayed. She hadn't thought she would still be working six-plus years into her marriage and after the birth of two children. Wade encouraged her to climb the ladder. Even if he would never return her to the wealth of her ancestors (and even if he was a cheater) there was one good thing about Wade: he believed she could do it.

Strangely, he even believed she was smart.

Turnover, previously something Noelle had thought of as a crispy pastry with an apple filling, became a destabilizing and unwelcome force, but one that Macy's was unwilling to stem. Turnover was just one more of many reasons Noelle showed no interest in going for a higher-level manager position. It seemed safest to hold her floor manager post.

"Maybe some of the younger Dayton kids will come buy this building and bring back Dayton's here," said Noelle one night when she was hanging out in her old department to check out what kind of shoes the Macy's buyers were bringing in.

"They won't buy it. They'll do something new and different. This place is Macy's now, and someday it won't even..."

Gary suddenly peered at Noelle's face and said the only concise words she had ever heard come out of his mouth: "You should get that spot checked."

Nobody who already had way too much sun in her teens and twenties should clock more tanning bed time in her late thirties. The trade-off of that glow from her new Aztec 3000 tanning bed was loss of elasticity and a small but growing splotch on Noelle's cheek that her mother and Wade, and even Wade's mother, asked her to get checked.

The dermatologist biopsied the suspicious spot with a punching tool. It was only precancerous. The doctor said she was lucky. He took pictures of a dozen other spots to monitor.

She still spent her days off work in the summer on their neighborhood beach, slathering cocoa oil, SPF of four, on her sagging body. She just looked better with a tan, especially where the stretch marks she had avoided when pregnant with Genève and Avril appeared in triplicate during her third pregnancy with ten-pound Nicollet.

There were moments when Genève's birth came back to her, but she replaced those with memories of Avril and Nicollet's babyhoods. She had *les enfants adorable* with Wade. There was no need to have regrets, she told herself. She spent her spare time in the winter scrapbooking for these two children, thinking they would be so grateful for these heirlooms someday. Noelle briefly fantasized that she'd made it an open adoption and could receive photos to scrapbook for Genève, but only the photo on the adoption announcement that Fran had sent to Dayton's sat at the bottom of one of her scrapbooking bins.

As Wade's business grew, the St. Paul Petits took more interest in Noelle again. Not for modeling tanning beds though; she didn't even look good enough for the pool table ads anymore. She counted now as a bonafide business connection, with her husband being featured in Twin Cities Business Journal.

Noelle enrolled her kids at a private French immersion school and daycare, where parents tried to outdo each other with volunteer work, spring breaks on the Cote d'Azur, and fromage sandwiches in children's lunch boxes.

She tried to speak to the staff in French, even though they could not understand her. It wasn't long before Avril said, "Mommy, please don't speak French. You don't know how to say the words right."

That did not stop Noelle from her French craze for her children. Avril and Nicollet listened to the Putumayo CD of French Caribbean music until they could sing all ten songs by heart. They became regulars at the Alliance Française for Cinema-kids Sundays.

Wade didn't understand the whole French immersion thing when it was time to select a daycare or school and asked why they didn't choose a more important language, like Spanish or Chinese. Noelle offered him the school's brochure titled Why Learn French? which named forty-three countries where the language was spoken.

"Maybe three of which we'd ever want to visit," Wade said, pulling at his strawberry-blond whiskers as he glanced at the brochure.

Noelle's throat tightening, she pulled out her research folder and handed it to Wade.

"Learning a second language helps kids learn math more easily," she said. "It's the neural pathways. It doesn't matter which language."

Wade reviewed the research and relented.

Noelle hoped her undeclared firstborn child was taking French in middle school. Sometimes, she imagined that she would take all three of her children to France, or to Martinique, and they would all speak French together.

It could never happen as long as she remained married to Wade. But how long would she remain married to the cheater, now that was another question.

31. BonneReve, 2006

The pie-shaped wedges of a pain pill Bernard quartered with a paring knife weren't perfectly even.

Which one is the biggest? he asked himself.

He selected that one and swallowed it with a sip of the acai-berry and flax-seed smoothie Tanya had brought over. He took a BonneReve sleeping pill too.

Tanya wasn't exactly a new girlfriend, but an old one he let back into his life at a time when they both needed someone and neither had the energy to try to impress someone new.

Soon, he would be weaned off of the pain pills and on only two prescription medications: a stimulant for day and a BonneReve at night. His new doctor expressed confidence that, eventually, he could manage his pain with Advil and exercise. It was Friday evening, and he hoped this weekend would get him on track so he could cope with his classroom and other faculty-level challenges come Monday.

BonneReve had been working for thousands of people. Most of those people didn't drink and take prescription opioids along with it.

At least Tanya was someone to talk to before the combination of alcohol and pills knocked him out. Not that he should have been talking to her about things he wasn't even supposed to know himself. But the meds effaced his discernment between the thoughts in his head and the thoughts he would say out loud. She ignored his ramblings and went to go pee.

"Your faucet is dripping," Tanya said when she got back from the bathroom. "Maybe now would be the time to get out that one-hundred-piece toolset I bought for you?"

It was definitely not the time for that.

"Did you ever learn the economic theory of comparative advantage?" he asked. "I'll call a plumber in the morning."

Ten minutes later, his eyes blinked open and Tanya peered into them. "Are you asleep or awake?" she said. The BonneReve seemed to bring on a third state of being some nights.

"Where is Genève?" he asked.

"*Giselle,* you mean?" Tanya answered. "The ballet? Your mom said it's coming to the State Theater."

Bernard's eyes closed.

A minute later, they opened and he slurred, "Did you ever see my cousin, Noelle, when she was pregnant?"

"Yes. I saw her and Wade at their Christmas Eve party before she had Nicollet. God, she was huge."

"No. Before Wade."

"I didn't know you before she was married to Wade," Tanya answered with a dismissive wave of her hand. "You need to go to bed."

"Genève," Bernard said.

Tanya looked up from her laptop. Bernard's eyes were wide open, more the grayish color of green bentonite clay tonight than hazel. Tanya suddenly became curious. "Why did you ask if I saw Noelle pregnant before she met Wade?" she asked.

"Noelle likes French names. Avril, Nicollet...Genève." He wasn't even slurring his words anymore; nobody would have known he was talking in his sleep.

Tanya got up and sat at the edge of the couch where Bernard lay. "Who said? Did someone say Noelle had a baby named Genève?"

"Mardi said it. Or Noelle. They both talked about her."

"Geez, Bernard. Any other beans you want to spill before morning?"

Bernard dreamed of dark red kidney beans spilling from his mouth all over the tiled floor of the Victorian parlor. He remembered something about Mardi being gay.

"Beans," he said. "Mardi has more beans."

Tanya tried to ask Bernard more questions, but he was done talking.

"Don't take that medicine tomorrow," she said. "I don't want you to forget about getting that bathroom faucet fixed."

Pulling on his arm, Tanya made Bernard get up to use the bathroom and walk up the creaky old stairs to his bedroom. She showed herself out the door but came back in a minute when she remembered something.

Bernard's girlfriend could never go anywhere without her laptop, especially when she had new information to look into.

32. Community Cable, 2006

Fran forgot all about the day when her daydream merged the face of Pierre St. Hilaire and her own daughter together into one. Then, two months into the seventh grade, the school called about Genève's "impulsive behavior."

"She just stood up, stormed up and down the aisles, and took every student's pencil!" the teacher complained into the phone. "Then, again without my permission, she distributed pencils she had sharpened herself."

Fran found herself in the bathroom doorway as Genève applied Chapstick and hair balm. The dropping November temperatures and the apartment's forced heat took their toll. "Why did you take everybody's pencils today?"

"It distracts me when people randomly get up to sharpen their pencils during class. It bothers other kids too."

"The teacher says you often act on impulse and wonders if I should bring you in for some sort of an evaluation."

Genève balked at the suggestion. "It's a predictable routine I'm trying to create, a daily exchange of dull pencils for pencils that I have sharpened by the batch. It's the exact opposite of impulsive."

Fran took a deep breath. "Maybe she meant compulsive. Or obsessive-compulsive."

"Or *she's* obsessed with control." Genève, point made, flew out the door to visit her friend Zoe.

Fran remembered when Pierre removed all the chairs from the stock room, forcing predictable break schedules in sanctioned lounge areas.

Order. Process. Systems.

Once Fran began to see the resemblance again, there was no unseeing it. She tried to let it go. It wasn't her mystery to solve. Genève was her daughter, and that was that.

Fran hopped down a couple more internet rabbit holes about Pierre's career and Johanne's ecology research, but then shut down the computer.

She and Genève had their lives to live.

If it had been up to Sharon, Fran's life would have included a nice husband by now. Never mind that Sharon's own husband was a sedentary blob. Sharon wasn't such a feminist anymore in her personal life.

"I know you sleep in that ratty old Women Unite to Take Back the Night t-shirt," Sharon had complained one day. "Don't you want to have something a little nicer for bed?"

"It's vintage now," Fran said. "I could get a lot of money for that shirt."

"Please do," Sharon retorted.

Fran dated. She had not been totally celibate. Still, there was nobody.

The darkening fall month of November was no time for someone who tended to get the winter blues to read Sylvia Plath's *The Bell Jar*. Fran made that mistake. She lay in bed every non-working hour for weeks, with her blue paisley comforter over her head, feeling hopeless.

She had all but forgotten Genève's thirteenth birthday.

A man tapped Fran on the shoulder. "Could you help me roll these electrical cables so I can reposition this camera at the far end of the pool? I don't have any help today."

Fran looked around. Of all the spectators, why was he asking her? But her bad winter mood lifted a little when his clean-shaven face broke into a winsome smile, so she let him show her how to crank the handle on the cable roller. He signaled his approval at her attempt.

Fran twirled the handle with a little sway to her hips, against her better judgment.

Genève was reaching the end of the school trimester when she rose as a top competitor for the Clayton-Wydown Middle School Greyhounds. Fran could lie in bed no longer.

It was at this high school where Genève wanted to learn by watching the older kids. The cameraman for Clayton public access cable filmed their meets.

"I'm Jim," he said upon his return from repositioning the camera. "Thanks for helping me get ready to film the second half. Do you have a swimmer in the meet?"

"No, my daughter's in middle school," Fran answered. "She likes to analyze the high school swimmers."

The break ended and Genève returned from the concession stand with chocolate chip cookies. Fran nodded goodbye to Jim, who grabbed her hand in a quick shake as she and Genève climbed up into the bleachers.

Did this man just see Genève and not even make a funny face or look away?

It seemed so, or else he was just good at hiding it. Often, men who flirted with Fran frowned when they saw that her daughter was mixed-race, and some had the gall to ask whether or not Fran was Genève's 'actual' mother. Jim saw her but turned his smile right back to Fran.

The smooth-faced cameraman appeared at the next Clayton-Wydown Middle School swim meet, even though one had never been covered on television before. This time, he needed help in the truck, where he had a mobile studio of camera monitors and software to create the on-screen graphics.

He confessed that he just wanted to see her, that he hoped they could get together.

Jim showed Fran how to make the digital banners show up on the live-to-tape show, with each swimmer's name and cable channel sponsor acknowledgments. The truck was warm and she took off her coat. He showed her how to put up the Clayton-TV logo for a station-identification break.

During this break, he kissed her.

After the meet, Fran dropped Genève off directly at her mother's house and told Sharon that, yes, this one might amount to something.

For the next two weeks, Fran and Jim dated as if they'd been together for years. She cooked. He had her over to his apartment for take-out stir-fry and wontons. Fran took Jim to meet her parents, and Jim flattered Sharon about her Hanukkah meal, even though everybody knew that Sharon's challah was too heavy and her greasy latkes had been the source of many jokes.

Maybe they would even take a trip to Chicago with Genève and stay at a hotel with an indoor water park.

Why not? Everything was going so well.

33. *Mary Poppins*, 2006

"I've been to every Dayton's eighth-floor exhibit at Christmastime since 1964," bragged Wade's mother. "*The Land of Trolls* was the first, you know. Thank goodness Macy's didn't put an end to it."

She sat in the passenger seat of her son's Chevy Suburban, shivering under her black fur hat. The children wiggled, dressed in their stiff Christmas best, in the second-row captain seats. In the SUV's third row sat Noelle, making faces no one could see at her mother-in-law.

Avril and Nicollet were six and four, the perfect age for it this year. After the *Mary Poppins* exhibit, they would stand along Nicollet Avenue for the annual Holidazzle parade, another Dayton's tradition now sponsored by Macy's.

A storm coming up from Oklahoma had brushed the Twin Cities on its northeastern path to Lake Michigan. Fine snow on the ground caught the wind upward from its blanket on the ground and danced like wisps in the wind.

Noelle watched out her window, heading back to Macy's after putting in a full day there because Wade's mother thought it was important they go as a family. They parked in the ramp and entered the store through Women's Shoes.

Kalmer, who had sheared off his long mullet curls before being hired back by Macy's, held the title of department manager and reported to Noelle. He looked up from his task of helping a new shoe dog with the cash register. He strode over to the aisle to meet Noelle's family and crouched down to introduce himself to the children face to face.

Wade tried to hurry them along after having his fingers nearly crushed by Kalmer's football player handshake, but then Gary stepped across the aisle from Junior Shoes. "I guess tonight's the night," he said cheerfully. "We just saw Pierre and his family come through not ten minutes ago."

Wade nodded at Gary but kept them moving. "You're not their friend. You're their boss," he whispered harshly.

Stalling in hope of missing a run-in with Pierre, Noelle sampled a smear of lip color at the Lancôme counter. She pulled her mother-in-law over to ask what looked better, shimmery or matte. Wade caught his mother's arm and pulled her toward the bank of elevators.

Avril was allowed to press the button inside the elevator. "Eight, nine...eleven...Mommy, why is there only a circle where there should be a ten?" She tried to press the blank button, but it was only a slug.

"Because there is no tenth floor," Noelle answered.

"There has to be. Or else the eleventh floor would have to be called the tenth floor."

"Our little mathematician!" her grandmother chirped."Just like your daddy!"

Noelle hung back as the elevator full of people emptied out onto the eighth floor. She breathed more easily, not seeing Pierre and Johanne in the line. Wade's mother kept the children busy reading the posters along the hallway walls.

They reached the mouth of the exhibit, where the magic would begin. The kids grew even more excited for the promised visit with Santa Claus at the end. They wanted to ask him for a parakeet.

"Santa doesn't bring parakeets, or any other birds," Noelle told them.

She sure as hell hoped Santa wouldn't bring a bird, her sideways warning glance at Wade seemed to say. He shrugged.

Avril recalled the previous year's exhibit, *Cinderella,* but Nicollet was too young to remember. "I didn't think *Mary Poppins* could be as good as *Cinderella,*" Avril said, as if she were a six-year-old entertainment reviewer. "The one the year before that was too scary."

The 2004 exhibit had been an *avant-garde* interpretation of *Snow White.* Wade's mother had remarked that the starring character looked like a heroin addict and she hadn't exactly been wrong.

Avril's eyes took in the moving dolls. She laughed with delight when the governess and her umbrella flew up into the sky.

Nicollet ran ahead and Noelle had to keep her eyes on him until the end. She had nearly forgotten that Gary mentioned the St. Hilaire family until they exited the display and she saw Pierre, alone in the distance, looking at ornaments in the gift shop. Where were his wife and kids?

"Time for Santa pictures!" Wade's mother shrilled.

Noelle hoped she blended into the Christmas crowd with her red and green rayon blouse.

Her children's heads perked up and they craned their necks forward. "Mommy, that boy up there is speaking French!" Avril exclaimed.

Noelle stood still, holding her own coat and the coats of both children over her arms. Like half the women there, she was really just a coat rack.

Wade tapped his toe, waiting for their turn, and didn't seem to mind when his own kids pulled the rest of them ahead in the line. He gave a *what-can-I-do* kind of smile to those he passed in line and none of them did anything more than look at one another with disapproval for the line-cutters.

"*Bonjour!* I'm Avril and this is Nicollet," Avril said to the boy. He and his mother appeared to be of African descent, like a few of her classmates and their parents who were from French-speaking countries. "Do you go to my school?"

The three children began speaking in French about school, then about what to ask Santa to bring them.

Noelle came face-to-face with Johanne St. Hilaire, who wore large glasses and resembled a coat rack like the other women in line. She carried not only her own gray wool coat, her son's coat, and a tote bag full of hats and mittens, but snow pants folded over her arm, too.

Noelle had met her once before at a Women's Shoes picnic but had avoided talking with her. Johanne was small and her glowing face was smooth all the way to her hairline, where a thick French braid encircled her head. Noelle could not tell where the braid started and where it ended.

"Hello," she said to Johanne, only because the children looked like they were gearing up to force the two women into a conversation.

"Hello," Johanne said. "We have met once, at the Women's Shoes family picnic. I'm Johanne. My husband, Pierre, was your department's inventory specialist. He works at Target now."

She pointed toward Pierre, who stood at the edge of the boutique.

"Of course," Noelle said. "I can't believe you remember me."

She wondered, *Why does she remember me?*

Wade scanned the room, his eyes landing on Pierre sifting through *Mary Poppins* merchandise.

Johanne's son looked up at his mother and asked if it was okay that the two new friends stay in line by them. She looked apologetically at the people behind them. It wasn't her decision on who could cut the line. She told him, *"Tu peut parler avec eux."*

Avril introduced herself and asked her in French what her son's name was. The boy answered her directly. His name was Paul. Nicollet piped up with his own introduction too.

"How do they know how to speak such proper French?" Johanne asked Noelle. "And they have French names too. We named our son Paul because it's a known name here."

Noelle's smile glittered with pride. "They speak French because I am French. Petit is my mother's maiden name."

"No, Mommy," Avril spoke up. "We speak French because we go to French immersion school." Wade's mother patted her granddaughter's shoulder.

"I send you there because you are French like me," Noelle explained to Avril for Johanne's benefit, untying and retying the bow on her holiday blouse.

The children continued their conversation, which sounded so lovely to Noelle, who adored hearing her children speaking French with such ease. Paul told them about a planned trip to Martinique after Christmas. *Chaque année, au moins,* Noelle heard him say; they went at least once every year.

Noelle exhaled when the St. Hilaires made their Santa visit and moved on. Her kids climbed up onto Santa's lap. They did not forget to ask for a parakeet. Wade laughed when the terrible Santa went too far in agreeing about the bird. The satisfied children hopped off Santa's lap and Noelle quickly made her photo purchase.

Meanwhile, Pierre joined Johanne and their son to enjoy every last moment in the auditorium—or perhaps to stall them there while Noelle's family made their exit. It was an unspoken collaboration of avoidance.

"So, you worked with that guy, huh?" Wade said as the elves herded the departing crowd back to the elevators. "That lady's husband?"

"Yes, he was our stock boy, but he's at Target now."

"A French-speaking stock boy from the islands! Well, why didn't you say hello?" Wade's mother asked.

Noelle pretended not to hear.

Wade snickered and kept walking. "I need new shoes. Something with a thick sole. Think our old shoe sales gal can help pick out some good ones?"

Nicollet pushed all the wrong buttons on the elevator. "The kids are tired, and we don't want to wear them out before the parade," said Noelle. "Why don't you get your shoes and then meet us down on the street?"

She wanted to get as far down the street as possible so they wouldn't run into the St. Hilaires again. But Wade got his shoes with his family by his side. They rode the escalator down to the first floor and bundled up for the cold before exiting to Nicollet Avenue.

Noelle walked them down only a couple of blocks before the children saw a chef making *crêpes* at the open window of a French restaurant called *Vincent*. The building boasted intricate carvings in stone above the entryway and windows. It was a sight and an aroma impossible to resist.

"Daddy, we want *crêpes!*" the kids cried.

Wade took out his wallet and paid as the chef ladled batter onto a hot cast iron galettoire, sprinkled it with sugar, and folded it onto a paper plate. A sous-chef dolloped whipped cream and pistachios onto the plates for each child and one for Wade's mother as well.

Wade looked at Noelle as if to offer, but she knew it was a set-up. He'd always told her she "didn't need" any dessert. She shook her head.

"Look at the pretty Holidazzle floats lining up," Noelle said, pointing down Nicollet Avenue. "I think I see Frosty the Snowman! Let's go further that way so we can be the first to see him."

"But it's warm right here," Wade's mother said. The hot *crêpe* iron warmed the space around it and the family refused to budge from their toasty microclimate.

"We can see the parade right here, can't we?" said Wade. His mother removed her large woolen scarf and folded it up on the curb as a seat for Avril and Nicollet.

The adults stood and looked on, and a moment later Noelle heard a voice. *"L'arôme! On y va!"*

As she feared, little Paul St. Hilaire had sniffed out the crêpes. *Mon Dieu,* she said to herself. *The fucking crêpes.* Naturally, Paul spotted Avril and Nicollet.

"Encore, quelle surprise," Johanne said to Noelle. She wore a violet mohair hat, a pop of color against her gray coat. "Pierre, you know Noelle."

Wade's mother turned to meet Pierre. "How fun for my grandchildren to have another little one to watch the parade with them."

Wade finally stuck his hand out. "Wade Sorenson."

"I am Pierre St. Hilaire."

"So I hear. And you work in the stock room at Target now?"

Pierre nodded halfway. "I am still in inventory."

Johanne adjusted her hat to cover her ears and reached down to do the same for her son. "He's Target's senior VP for inventory strategy now," she said.

Wade stroked the reddish-blond whiskers that had become a goatee on his chin. "I see," he said. "Quite a promotion."

"And what do you do?" Pierre asked, looking down at Wade, who was at least five inches shorter.

"I own an education business with multiple mall locations. Our main one is at the Mall of America."

Pierre nodded. "Education is so important."

The children were chatting away in a mix of French and English now. "You must have liked giving Pierre orders in French when he was a stock boy," Wade said to Noelle, seeming to challenge her. "Why don't you say something in French now, babe?"

"My French is not very good," Noelle said in English to Pierre. "But indeed, I've always liked the language, so I do remember that about you."

He nodded.

Johanne, looking at her husband, said, "Noelle and Wade even gave their children French names, Avril and Nicollet." She pointed to the children sitting on the curb. "Nicollet is sitting right there on the curb of his own avenue!"

Johanne was a full foot shorter than her husband, and she lifted her head up toward him as if looking for a reaction. As a senior member of the Target leadership team, he was used to talking with all sorts of people, even feigning interest when necessary. Tonight, he was different.

"We named him Nicollet for the explorer who mapped the Upper Mississippi River," said Noelle. "I assume Nicollet Avenue is named after the same man."

"You named him that," said Wade. "I call him Nick."

"Your children are very cute," Pierre said. Nicollet wiped his snotty nose on the sleeves of his winter jacket.

Avril surprised Pierre by answering in French, *"Merci, monsieur, mais mon frere n'est pas mignon."*

"They go to the private French immersion pre-school and elementary," Johanne conveyed to Pierre. Wade, not excusing himself or offering one to anyone else, walked up the street for a hot dog from another vendor. He ate most of it before he returned, then stood with his arms folded in front of him.

Illuminated Nutcracker Fantasy characters floated up the avenue and the dull sound of nylon mittens clapping arose from the sidewalk crowds. Noelle watched Wade out of the corner of her eye. He held Nicollet up for a better view of the bedazzled floats and dancing characters.

Johanne also became less talkative, watching the parade with her own child except during one moment in between floats when Noelle caught Johanne studying her from behind those bicycle-wheel eyeglasses. Finally, the parade ended and they said goodbye, relieved to escape the cold.

The children fell asleep in the Suburban on the way home. Wade and his mother talked softly about a business trip he planned to take and how Noelle would need extra help with the children. Noelle hadn't heard anything from him about this trip to Kansas City. He had not asked her to go with him.

They dropped off his mother and in another ten minutes pulled into the garage. Wade and Noelle carried the sleeping children to their rooms.

Within moments of climbing into bed, Wade rolled on top of Noelle and took possession of what was his. And although Noelle enjoyed it no more than she ever did these days, she felt a certain satisfaction. Maybe she was wrong to think he was having an affair with the Ridgedale location manager. Certainly he hadn't suspected her and Pierre.

Things couldn't be that bad. At least they had not run into Fran and Genève.

34. Bat Mitzvah, 2007

While the synagogue Fran's parents took the Hart family to in the 1960s and '70s was a real hippy joint, Fran and Genève belonged to a congregation (if you could call it that) that didn't even have a space. Fran dropped Genève off for Jewish Sunday School at a large table in the middle of Protzel's Deli just outside of downtown Clayton.

Sharon thought Fran should hold a morning service for Genève's *bat mitzvah* celebration the first *Shabbat* after her thirteenth birthday. But that had long passed.

With her November blues, Hanukkah, and Jim's family Christmas in the way, Fran wasn't on the ball.

The rabbi, a red-haired bohemian-looking woman who wore a "Free Palestine" t-shirt, taught a half-dozen or so children Hebrew and Arabic so they could be future peacemakers. The adult and family meetings were on Friday nights at her mid-century house on the Old Bonhomme Road. Since three of the six kids in the current group were twelve or thirteen, or going on thirteen sometime in the coming year, she thought it would be fun to celebrate together with a vegetarian feast and a special *Birkat-Hamazon*—an after-dinner grace. Torah readings would be optional.

Presentations on the creative or scholarly project of each kid's choosing would follow the meal and any Torah readings that may or may not happen.

"Anything that expresses your inner Jewish self," Rabbi Rachel said. "However the spirit moves you."

Genève's friend Zoe's project—conjured during brainstorming sessions with the rabbi—was a dance, interpretive of surviving a desert sand storm and gathering manna from heaven.

Genève's project idea hadn't exactly made itself known. "I'm not sure about my inner Jewish self," she said.

"Then do it about that," the rabbi answered, as she set a bagel with cream cheese in front of the girl.

Rabbi Rachel didn't distinguish Genève from the other children. Adopted children were no less Jewish than those born to Jews. Questioning one's identity was a rite of passage for everyone. It was just a little harder because Genève's Humanistic Jewish identity was not so much a faith. If there was no creed, and if it wasn't an inherited ancestral ethnicity for Genève either, then what was it? What was her inner Jewish self, exactly?

"Then don't sweat the Jewish part," said Rabbi Rachel, her long skirt billowing. "You can't go wrong if you just write about *who you are.*"

The exhortation to write about *who you are* was how Genève would soon end up delivering a presentation on swimming in Rabbi Rachel's living room on the day of her *bat mitzvah* celebration.

But first, the search for a topic had brought Genève to the Clayton Library. Other interests being economics and how she came to be adopted, some keyword searches led to a theory on the economics of adoption. Genève crinkled her brow as she came upon economist Gary Becker's point of view that children available for adoption comprised a market. People adopting children were shopping. People giving up their children for adoption were making economic decisions, and they weighed the expectations of the child's performance in these decisions.

Genève printed the article and showed it to her grandmother, whose rambler she was staying at—in Fran's old room—while Fran and Jim went away.

"These are only theories," said Sharon.

Genève took the paper back, straightening its edges. She slid it neatly into an orange folder inside her checkered backpack.

"Grandma," she said. "Theories aren't just guesses like some people think. A theory is a hypothesis that has held up to rigorous scientific testing."

"If there's any truth to it, it's probably not much different than it is for parents who decide to have their own children. Your mother didn't shop for you, and if you present about this it will hurt her feelings."

"It's *supposed* to be about me. Do we have any cookies here?"

"I like your swimming idea much better. It fits you."

"I haven't decided against that idea, but I'm not letting go of this one yet. And—bonus—the economist is Jewish."

Sharon pulled the Keebler Sandies out of the drawer and set two on a plate. "So is Mark Spitz."

Genève presented after a boy's hip-hop remix of seven Shel Silverstein poems and before Zoe's interpretive dance. She wore her Clayton-Wydown swim team warm-up suit and a gold sailboat necklace, having asked her mother's permission after discovering it while reorganizing her jewelry box.

Fran and her parents cried as they listened to Genève's poetic comparison between the butterfly stroke and the metamorphosis now underway as she took on the responsibility of "adult" Jewish life. Free of the requirement to make it about being Jewish, she'd happened upon the story of Judith Deutsch-Haspel, a top Austrian athlete stripped of all her titles after she refused to swim in the 1936 Olympics in Berlin in protest of Adolf Hitler.

Genève would do the same if she were ever put in that situation, she explained. It would be her responsibility to refuse. In this realization, Genève began to discover her true inner self.

Still, she wanted to know, what was the reason, the story, and *the system* behind how she came to be Fran's daughter?

She went back to the library and came home with a book of Gary Becker's economic theories.

Fran heard the thud as Genève plopped *Treatise on the Family* on the kitchen counter and walked over to see what it was. The cover read, *By Gary Becker, Winner of the 1992 Nobel Prize in Economics.*

"Another economist caught your fancy?" she asked.

Genève opened to a bookmarked page and read a paragraph about how birth parents decide to let their children be adopted and how adoptive parents try to determine "quality." She set the book down and pulled her soft brown curls into a terrycloth band.

"What were *you* looking for? Didn't you want someone who looked like you?"

Fran ran a finger over the book cover. "*Hmm.* Fifteen years out of date, this book." She looked her daughter in the eyes. "I could have gotten pregnant if that mattered to me."

"But you wanted a *baby,* right? What if it would have been me, but older. Then what? You wanted me as a brand-new baby, but you wouldn't want me—the same person—if it was later and I was, like, eight years old."

"Then I would have made the biggest mistake of my life. I don't want to think about it." Fran pulled Genève onto the couch with her. She was glad Jim was out late filming a volleyball meet.

She continued, "When I got the phone call, before I even saw you, I knew. Your birth mother could still have changed her mind at that point; that had happened to me once before. But once I got to hold you, I wasn't scared of that anymore. I can't explain how I knew, but I felt this strange connection to her even though I had no clue who she was. It seemed like...like she had given you to me with her blessing. I felt a *chorus* of blessings, almost. I knew that this time was for real."

Genève asked Fran if they told her on the phone that she was black or mixed.

"I'd already documented that I didn't have a preference on that. They said, 'We have a baby who would like to meet you,' and I ran out the door in an ice storm without a jacket. I couldn't take you home right away because you were premature."

"I know. Being premature is why I have to train hard to have strong breathing power when I swim. But I thought you couldn't take me home right away because of the legal process."

"That too. But they let me come. They let me hold you."

"It was in Minnesota, right?"

"It's right there on your birth certificate. Minneapolis, Minnesota."

They didn't talk about what else it said on there. Genève already knew that her birth mother had named her but that her mother's name wasn't printed on there, nor her father's. Only the sealed original that Genève would probably never see listed them. Genève's birth certificate was only a replacement record, issued after the adoption decree.

"I'm going to take a bath now," Genève said. She went to start the water.

"Don't take that library book in there," Fran shouted down the hall. "Becker's theories are already all wet."

Genève returned. "He's a good economist, Mom. And anyway, he's giving me some ideas."

"What ideas?" Fran asked the only 13-year-old she knew who read economics texts.

"Older children don't get adopted, but maybe you could show people pictures of them when they were cute little babies next to pictures of them now. Then grown-ups would see that it's really a person they would have loved as a baby, so why not love them now?"

"You're onto something, I think," Fran said.

Genève amazed her like this all of the time. It could not be easy to be a mixed-race kid living in a working-class apartment building with a single adoptive Jewish mother in a mostly rich, white, and Catholic town like Clayton.

But Genève seemed well adjusted, despite the occasional phone calls from the school.

Fran leaned toward the remote control, about to turn on the TV as Genève headed toward the bath.

Her daughter turned around. "It's the system that isn't working well enough yet. We just have to learn about all the things that make up the system. And then we have to get good, nice people to fix it."

Genève left the book on the counter and closed the bathroom door behind her. Fran stared at the closed door and heard Genève turn off the bathwater and climb into the tub.

On the other side of the door, Genève lay back into her lavender-scented white bubbles. Lavender, she knew, was supposed to relax her, but she couldn't lie still. Something in her felt unsatisfied.

In truth, Fran would have understood if Genève had pushed harder for information about her birth parents. But Genève didn't want to risk hurting her feelings any more than she feared she already had. Her mom seemed so much happier lately. She didn't want her to hide under her comforter all the time like before, forgetting to do much of anything for her birthday and acting like she didn't even like their life together.

She just wasn't sure she could wait much longer.

35. Camlo, 2007

Demolition was going to be one-fifth of the cost of Mardi's flooring project, to begin as soon as the contractors could get to it during this busy Minnesota April.

Homeowners got ants in their pants about getting indoor projects done before summer. If summer ever came, that is. Temperatures rose to fifty degrees two days before, yet fell to seventeen—with snow to boot—today. Mardi set the heat low to keep the bill down and kept warm in a Norwegian Christmas sweater, compliments of Irene. Unlike Noelle, Mardi had no Florida Keys spring break vacation to warm her bones.

Mardi's new realtor suggested she replace the parquet floor, the house's spookiest reminder of the murder-suicide. The house had already sat on the market for months one time before. Mardi took it off the market for the slow winter months, but she faced pressure to sell it now before the spring real estate season ended. The writing was on the wall for more layoffs at Macy's, and Mardi still hadn't recovered from her botched investment in tanzanite.

A pre-finished maple floor would cleanse away that gruesome, haunted vibe some would-be buyers described. It wouldn't even cost that much if she could clear away the old floor herself.

Wrecking things, Mardi knew, was where she excelled.

But who could help? Edward gave her his tools but said his knees were getting too cranky for that kind of thing. Bernard, almost two years after the student's attack, still suffered from back pain. Mardi had the day off of work and, unless some magic genie were to show up, she had to do it.

Today was the day, if only Mardi had a helper.

The door chimes rang.

"Guess where Wade and the kids are?" Noelle shook the snow off her satiny white parka on the front porch before stepping into the house. She held a noisy birdcage in one hand and pulled a blanket off of it with the other.

"I wasn't expecting you," Mardi said, watching Noelle let snow melt off her boots onto the foyer floor. "Or the bird. Leave your boots on the mat please."

"They're in Montreal!" Noelle pulled her boots off and her Smartwool socks came off with them, leaving her barefoot. She looked at Mardi's red and green sweater. "Geez, Mardi. It isn't Christmas and I can't say that's your style. It's like forty degrees in this house."

"Someone always forgets to tell Minnesota when it's spring and it's the warmest thing I own. What's going on with you?"

"Wade ran off to Canada with his Ridgedale Mathy Taffy manager."

"Mathy Kathy?" Mardi stifled a giggle. "And she's there with Avril and Nicollet?"

The blue parakeet double-chirped, as if to say, *Yes ma'am.*

"Yes, while I take care of the filthy fucking bird. It won't even use the bird bathtub I bought for it."

"I didn't know birds had bathtubs."

"Well, they do. Just like wild birds have public birdbaths, or at least they bathe in a puddle. They are supposed to know by instinct how to wash themselves, but not this idiot."

"It's cute—what's its name?" Mardi asked.

"Dakota," Noelle said, unhappily. "The kids were supposed to give it a French name—that was the condition."

"But it's impressive that they want to honor the American Indians whose land we live on," Mardi said with optimism.

"Dakota Fanning," Noelle clarified.

Mardi looked at her blankly.

"Dakota Fanning, kiddie actress. Will probably overdose and die before she turns eighteen. Wade's mom took the kids to see *Charlotte's Web* right before Christmas."

Noelle took off her parka and stuffed it into a closet cubbyhole, too tired to put it on a hanger.

"Wade says he and Kathy are presenting together about opening a new tutoring center in some mall there," Noelle said, switching the subject, her voice heavy with rue. "I used all my vacation hours for Florida, and he says his mom can't help this week with getting the kids to school and back. So the kids will do the hotel's kid program while they present together, and then Kathy is watching *my* kids the other days while Wade is in meetings. He basically said they are doing me a favor by taking them on their 'business trip.' As if."

"Isn't it bad for the kids to miss school?"

"That's what I argued. But he literally said, 'Let's not drag school into this conversation!'"

"A guy who works in the field of education says that?"

"He said the trip will be educational and that I should be happy he's taking them to a French-speaking city."

"And he didn't even ask you to beg for a vacation-hours advance to go to this city in the province of our ancestors?"

"He's sleeping with Kathy, obviously. I want to kill him. And I think I will kill him."

"Noelle, it's not good to say things like that while standing inside this particular house."

"You could ask me to sit down." Noelle walked barefoot down the hallway and teetered over onto a living room chair, her legs resting atop the cushioned arm. "You know I thought we had a good time in Florida, like everything was okay. Then he just packed up and off they went."

"I know how you can get rid of some of that anger," Mardi said. "We're going to rip apart this floor. I have guys coming to put in a new one, and they'll charge four hundred more if they have to demolish this one first."

"You mean you need me for free labor?" Noelle pulled her bare feet up under herself and shivered. "That's not why I came over. Can I have some socks? Mine are wet."

Mardi went away and came back with socks and an extra pair of old athletic shoes. "Here you go. I'll take you out for a drink at Blue Point when we're done."

"One drink. Really?" She flung her arm at the parquet floor. "This would take all day. I know you're desperate to sell, but changing the floor seems unnecessary. Seller's market. Just put up a sign. It will sell fast this time, probably for a shitload of cash."

"I need to make sure. You never know when the market is going to turn."

"That's true. I'm thinking of putting Grandma Greta's cottage up for sale too if my current tenants don't renew.

It's become so easy for people to qualify for a loan. I think they're looking to buy."

"You should sell that old dump to them."

"Yeah. If they want it. I've gotten past the nostalgia. But you shouldn't sell this one. And why replace the floor?"

"It's the right thing to do. I've told you it was Ralphina Beranek's sister who was killed here."

Noelle didn't know what went down between Mardi and Ralphina. Two years had passed since Mardi told Noelle she was gay or at least trying to figure out what she was, but that's all she gave away. Not a word about anyone in particular.

"I can't remember though if Ralphina knows you live here."

"Yeah, she knows. I thought I told you," Mardi said. She took the last sip from her morning coffee. "So, I'll show you what to do and we'll be done in no time. And then we'll go to Blue Point, okay?"

"I thought you were too broke to go out in Wayzata these days. Of course, there's always the Muni." Even the Muni, the municipal liquor lounge, had raised prices.

"Blue Point has a happy hour, and sober drivers drink free pop and Perrier."

"Sober drivers? Why would we drive? It's a ten-minute walk." Noelle was trying to walk more to lose weight, at least enough to compensate for all the animal crackers and fruit roll-ups she'd consumed in between having children and discovering diet pills.

"For the free pop and Perrier, obviously," Mardi answered. "Have I not mentioned that I am broke?"

"You really are desperate." Noelle turned her nose up as Mardi handed her a long-handled crowbar from a set of her father's tools on a mat in the corner.

Mardi ignored the comment and waved her arm toward the floor. "Here, I'll show you what we're going to do."

They changed into old clothes and for the next four hours, they swung, pulled, and pried their way across the living room floor with Dakota the parakeet tweeting along to the alternative rock public radio station called *The Current.*

Finally, the chevron-patterned floor lay in pieces. Underneath lay one stained section of wooden subfloor, the piece onto which the blood from two bodies once seeped through a Persian carpet and between cracks of old parquet.

"I guess I always knew they couldn't have gotten it all clean," Mardi said.

Noelle drew her lips back into a cringe but didn't say anything. Mardi turned away from the blackened blood of Ralphina's sister and her husband. How had she lived here all these years and never really allowed herself to acknowledge it? Seeing the stain made it undeniable.

She forced herself to stop those gears from turning. Thinking about death wasn't going to get the house sold.

To get the parquet out of the house they threw pieces into a big Macy's cardboard box, dumping them load by load onto a tarp in Mardi's side yard. She hoped the installation crew would haul it away without charging her.

Back inside, Mardi said, "Most of the subfloor can stay. The boards look good enough for them to nail the new floor into. Can you unscrew the...dirty...piece?"

Noelle sat down on an unstained section. "I think I'd like that drink right here and right now. You can unscrew it."

"Sorry. Sober house, no alcohol. We'll leave right after we get that piece out. You can unscrew the board while I go get something to hold us over." Mardi pushed the button on the power screwdriver that put it in reverse, hoping the decades-old screws attaching the board to the joists would ease right out.

Noelle took over the power tool and got started while Mardi went to pour orange juice. It was afternoon, not morning, but the Tropicana was all she had. She fixed a plate of cheese and crackers and grabbed the Gedney pickles. Maybe this would fill Noelle's belly so she wouldn't order pricey scallops and crabcakes at Blue Point.

When Mardi returned, Noelle had lifted and moved the plywood subfloor section up and off to the side. Mardi looked at her with new eyes. Noelle wasn't all cheesecake. She had some grit. Body odor too, mixed with the scent of sawdust.

Noelle leaned in between the joists. She pulled out the longest packing tube either of them had seen since Mike Brady brought home architectural plans on *The Brady Bunch*.

"What's this?" Noelle pushed her hair out of the way.

"Did you just pull that out of my floor?" Mardi set the plate down. "Maybe it's the blueprints for the house."

"It looks about that old."

Noelle found a cap at the end of the cardboard tube and popped it off. She pulled and pulled until a rolled-up canvas about five feet long came out. She unrolled it and lay it on the floor seven feet across. The cousins stared at it and then at each other as it rolled itself back up.

They'd only caught a glimpse, but it was enough to guess it was a stunning rendition of a place they both knew all too well—the building at 700 Nicollet Mall.

Mardi sprung up to get four heavy books so she could set one on each corner of the canvas to hold it down flat. Noelle smiled for the first time that day. "That's no finger painting. Now you can afford to buy me *two* drinks and the brown-butter scallops."

They kneeled to examine the canvas. Mardi ran her finger over the signature in the lower right corner. "Henry Camlo," she whispered. "It must have been put into the floor from the drop-tile ceiling in the basement."

Nothing was the color it should have been. The building screamed lime green instead of its true sandstone color, and the street was hot white. The sky glowed orange with streaks of yellow. A truck drove away from the building. A window dresser changed the displays.

"Henry Camlo," Noelle repeated after Mardi. "Is that somebody famous?"

"Maybe 'important' is a better word. I think that's what Bruce Dayton called him when he advised my mom and dad to buy a small Camlo painting. It's hanging in their living room, above my dad's wingback chair."

"I've never even been to your parents' house," Noelle said as she touched the part of the painting where the hands of the delivery truck driver could be seen on the steering wheel.

Noelle had been there as a baby, but Irene hadn't allowed Edward to invite Annette and her family over in all the years Noelle could remember, even though Annette was Edward's sister and Noelle his niece. Family gatherings took place at the big house on Summit Avenue, now owned by the other Petit brother. Mardi had only been to Noelle's parents' home since reconnecting as adults.

"Do *not* touch this Minnesota masterpiece with your pickle-y fingers," Mardi said.

"But *'Gedney, it's the Minnesota state pickle.'*"

Mardi rolled her eyes at the commercial jingle.

"You know, I've been praying forever for God to return me to the wealth of our ancestors," Noelle said. "Maybe he answered it for you instead of me by mistake."

"Yeah, I vaguely recall that my parents paid six thousand dollars for their small and less interesting painting."

They forgot about going to Blue Point and spent the evening eating more cheese and crackers, washing it down with the whole carton of orange juice.

"It's funny how there's no Dayton's sign in the painting and yet we both recognized it right away," Noelle said. "He really captured it. I've worked in that building for seventeen years and I barely noticed those big round windows with all the frou-frou around them. It's like I've never looked up at the building. Look at the rosettes—they match the brass rosettes along the rim of the display windows."

"I've worked there even longer and I never noticed that the top floors aren't part of the original building. Look how you can see it's an addition. And look at the—oh my God—*the infirmary*. That's a nurse in the window."

Noelle leaned forward again. "She's holding a hot water bottle. And look, behind her, at the orange cabinets. They're green, but he's painted everything in all the wrong colors. It's all still there, and that hot water bottle with the plaid cover—it's right there on the tenth floor to this day."

Mardi stared at her. "I know. I've been up there. You have, too?"

Noelle looked at the nurse in the window again. "I don't go up there too much," She lowered her voice and it cracked. "Genève was conceived on that creaky little bed."

Mardi's jaw dropped. "Wow. What would Nurse Moholt say?"

Noelle grimaced. "Who's that?"

"The person whose signature is on thirty years worth of patient logs that are still sitting there."

Noelle looked down. "I'd like to believe such an experienced nurse wouldn't judge."

"I'm sorry. I didn't mean it that way, really," Mardi pleaded.

Noelle ignored her. "Maybe that's Nurse Moholt, then."

"Too young, I think," Mardi said. "This says 1946 by the signature, and the nurse looks like she's in her twenties. I found Thora Moholt's signature on paperwork from the late twenties to 1957. She was probably this nurse's boss."

The sun went down. For a long time, the two sat on the floor with the lights off, not talking at all. Mardi wanted to confess that Ralphina had kissed her there on that infirmary bed, but she realized the import of Noelle's liaison there was much bigger than her own. Out of their base act came the only newborn baby Mardi had ever held in her arms. Mardi had never forgotten Genève, so how could Noelle?

Noelle stood to turn on the ceiling light and a floor lamp. Another hour went by with them looking at the painting, Mardi's mind drifting back to the day of the kiss. She remembered Ralphina on top of her, so firm and so light against her at the same time.

It was now ten at night. They had hardly left the room in over twelve hours.

"What should I do with it when I'm sleeping?" Mardi asked.

"What do you mean? It's not like someone is going to suddenly know you found a valuable painting and break in here in the middle of the night," Noelle said. "Do you want to roll it back up?"

"I don't know."

Mardi didn't know anything. She didn't know if she would call Ralphina or not. It had to have belonged to her family somehow. She didn't know if she would give it to her, or keep it for herself, or sell it privately to put an end to her money problems.

Or maybe she would call her parents and ask them to call someone. The Dayton elder and his art-loving wife, Ruth, would be intrigued. It was Bruce Dayton's grandfather's building, after all, in a painting by an artist he considered important.

"Nobody would ever want to paint Petit's Party Central," Mardi said out of the blue, half to herself.

"But can you imagine if they did?" Noelle asked. "*Butt-ugly!*"

It started as a laugh, then a hoot, then they howled so hard as they tried to picture it that the noise ceased and they just held their stomachs.

When they finally settled down, Noelle asked, "If you don't mind—I mean, I could go home—but maybe I could sleep in your music room upstairs?"

Mardi shrugged. "Just stay with me. It's been a long time since I've had a sleepover. I hope that bird doesn't chirp all night though. I can't call in sick tomorrow. They're looking for any reason to let people go and there aren't a lot of job openings in department store administration right now."

She lifted the books off the corners and the canvas began to roll itself up again. As they each picked up an end of the massive painting, Mardi noticed the writing on the back.

It was a title and inscription:

"Our Company"
For my nurse, Vilda. I will never forget you.
My love forever, Henry

Mardi gasped. Dakota the parakeet cooed. "I can't believe we looked at this thing all day and night and never turned it over. Vilda was Ralphina and Catherine's mother."

"Who was their dad?" Noelle asked.

"I just found out his name was Ken," Mardi said. "But, clearly, Vilda had a romance on the side, or maybe it was before she married Ken."

They were too exhausted to consider this ancient affair of the former lady of the house for very long. Noelle put the blanket over the birdcage to quiet Dakota for the night. Together, they carried the painting into Mardi's room and fell into bed. Noelle was asleep in seconds.

Our Company rolled itself more loosely than before against the wall on Mardi's side of the bed. She closed her eyes with the odd colors of it still in her mind, and with a moral certitude that accompanied the decision that she reached in the minute before she fell asleep.

It would be wonderful to get a windfall like that, of course. But right was right. The windfall wasn't meant for Mardi.

She'd jotted down Ralphina's number the day in 1997 when she'd left the voicemail invitation to lunch at the Lions Tap. Surely, she still had that little piece of paper in her desk. Mardi fell asleep, half savoring the anticipation of calling Ralphina Beranek and half worrying that this news would change everything Ralphina had probably known about her mother.

36. Sorry, Becky, 2007

The piece of paper Mardi expected to find in her desk was not there. She was certain she had seen it two hundred times over the past ten years.

The marketing assistant had Ralphina's number in the vendor files and Mardi dialed, her stomach tightening with every ring that went unanswered.

"This is Mardi Petit; I need to talk to you," she said after the beep. "It's not personal or anything...it's about something in the house. Please call."

As soon as she hung up, her phone rang and an HR specialist called her into an unscheduled meeting.

Within four minutes, Mardi had been fired from Macy's, not even by the HR manager she knew well, but by some underling in a Chanel suit. The woman promised a good reference as she handed her a folder titled, *Resource Information for Separated Employees*. The cover of this folder displayed the Macy's logo and font, but without the triumphant red star. They knew the full brand identity treatment looked too garish for layoff materials.

An HR assistant escorted her back to the lobby, handing her tissue after tissue, then brought her back to her desk to pack her belongings. The assistant doubled as a security guard in these moments to prevent disgruntlement from leading to sabotage. But she was hardly cut out for it. She held her face in her hands the whole time, bellowing, "This is awful! I'm so sorry!"

As Mardi dumped her things into a box, the missing shred of paper slipped out from between two vintage inter-office envelopes, and Mardi saw the stem of forget-me-nots she'd drawn in blue ink next to the name *Ralphina* and her phone number. She secured it to a folder with a paper clip.

As she turned to vacate her office, the human-shaped cutout of Becky Sharp, the status-obsessed marketing persona based on the character in the novel *Vanity Fair,* stared at her. She didn't have the heart to put Becky in the recycling bin after the project leader left the company. Now, she fell flat on her cardboard face.

Becky had become real to her. Even when the company abandoned the persona trend for the last time, Mardi never stopped caring about that two-dimensional fraud. Mardi was the only one in the upstairs offices, she was sure, who understood her.

After all, Becky Sharp was not so different from her cousin, Noelle. Or from most of the Petits, really, male or female, or from Mardi's mother, Irene.

The HR assistant tried to help Mardi pick her up. Mardi waved her away. Bending over, she considered taking Becky Sharp home with her. Instead, she wiped her tears away with her bare hand and left her there on the floor.

"I'm sorry, Becky," Mardi whispered. "I hope you find what you're looking for."

The truck was parked out in front of her house when Mardi got home five hours earlier than usual. A sudden opening in the schedule meant the wood floor was being done today. There was no choice in the matter, now that the old parquet sat in a heap in her yard.

She would disappear and let them work, but would have to return and write out a check. It would be one of many checks she'd need to write, but now the only money coming in to cover them would be a few weeks of severance pay and unemployment.

With its prefinished stain lighter than the old parquet, the new floor brightened and opened up the room. Somehow, though, it saddened Mardi. As if the murder of Catherine Beranek could just be planked over like that. Mardi called her realtor and asked her to start showing the house right away.

By the next morning, Mardi started to back off her certainty about handing the art back to Ralphina. It was legally hers. What if she sold it to a museum where everyone could enjoy it? That would be legal and ethical, she told herself.

Only...would it be in the news? That wouldn't be good. Would a reporter question why she didn't give it back? Surely, Ralphina and Owen would hear about it instantly. It became not a question of right and wrong anymore, but a weighing of financial survival with other costs.

So she went to see her mother.

Irene, Mardi knew, would say that absolutely she had every right to the painting after spending years living in that frightful house.

Or, Mardi imagined, maybe Irene would tell her she should donate it to a museum in her own name. *Imagine being associated with the art world like that,* her mother might say. *Picture your own name etched on one of those bronze donor plaques right alongside plaques with Dayton and Whitney and Pohlad names on them.*

Mardi nearly dropped her teacup when Irene said, "You already know in your heart what is the right thing to do."

Irene didn't even ask to come over and see the painting or ask if it was similar to her own Henry Camlo. She just remarked that it might be a wonderful discovery for the rightful owner.

"As you get older, you want to look back and feel you did right by people," Irene said. "And when you don't feel that way, it's something that you wake up regretting every day."

Mardi stared at her mother, mouth agape.

Edward walked in and listened as Irene relayed the story. "A Henry Camlo painting of Dayton's flagship store?" he said. "I should contact Bruce Dayton right away. It would mean a lot to him to be able to get a look at it sooner rather than later."

"Not yet," Mardi answered. "I need to wait to hear back from someone else first. She might be in for a shock."

37. *Missing Child, 2007*

The desktop computer chirped to announce an incoming email. Fran hoped it wasn't the Target store manager. She'd called in sick already. They should leave her alone.

It wouldn't be Jim, not after what had happened over the weekend.

Fran lifted herself out from under her blue paisley comforter. She then yanked it back up to her chin for a minute, only to push it down again. Genève would be home after swim practice and she would have to pull herself together and explain things.

But how?

Genève had been dying to go to her friend Zoe's dance recital. At the last minute, Fran shelled out thirty-two dollars for two tickets and didn't regret it after Zoe's show-stopping dance to *The Trolley Song* from Judy Garland's 1944 movie, *Meet Me in St. Louis*.

She put on her tightest jeans and a low-cut lacy top. At the last minute, she reclaimed the gold necklace with the sailboat pendant Bernard have given her so long ago from her daughter's dresser and clasped it around her neck. She no longer had to think about its provenance, just how the nautical charm drew the eye to her cleavage.

It was only natural that she would go surprise Jim in his Clayton Public TV truck during the intermission.

It was not natural, however, to open the TV truck door and find Zoe's mom straddling and bouncing up and down on him in his producer's chair. Fran fell down the three-step block under the truck door, picked herself up, and ran inside to pull Genève out of the snack line.

Fran forbade Genève from seeing Zoe ever again. She'd come to her senses today though, after having all day to think about it. It wasn't Zoe's fault her mom was a skank. It wasn't even her fault. Jim had done this. *Cheater.*

Genève didn't know a thing about the scene in the TV truck—she wasn't old enough to know such things. She only knew that getting grounded from her best friend was totally unfair.

The computer chirped again.

Fran dragged herself out of bed to the freezer and took out a block of frozen chicken. She opened a cabinet and pulled out a packet of processed Teriyaki sauce, then sat down at the computer table.

The email was from the Clayton library. Books Genève had put on hold were now available. They were novels in Spanish. Fran smiled, remembering how the week before Genève and Zoe had learned to roll their "R"s and tried to teach Fran. They'd all ended up on the floor, laughing at how Fran's tongue stalled out mid-*Dorito.*

As she was about to turn off the computer, she noticed another tab open in the browser. One click led to Pierre's Target leadership team portrait, his eyes staring at her.

She was sure she hadn't left that website open. She hadn't even looked at it lately. Her daughter was the only person who used the computer over the weekend. Frantically moving her cursor around the screen to see what else was open, she came upon the browser history page. Fran hadn't realized her web surfing left a trail.

Bus brakes squeaked in front of the apartment building and she quickly shut down the computer.

Fran waited. She set the chicken to thaw in warm water and imagined her daughter chatting with the neighbor boy who also rode the after-school activity bus.

But she never came up. Fran called the boy's apartment only to hear that Genève wasn't on the bus. She called the school, but the office was closed.

As she searched the school directory for the swim coach's number, her phone rang.

"This is Genève's swim coach," said the voice at the other end of the line. "I was wondering if she's feeling better and if she's still planning to swim in the meet on Saturday. If she is, she can't miss practice tomorrow."

Fran managed only to say, "My daughter would never miss a meet."

Then she dropped the phone, her head clanging like that damned trolley song from the recital. That's when she'd picked up the phone again and called her mother.

38. Sleep Driving, 2007

Bernard Petit didn't even go to Paj Yang's goodbye party.

So much of the staff had left since the school's finances crumbled, but this last departure hurt the most. He should have been happy about Paj's new juvenile social services job in Minneapolis. He told her he'd take her out for lunch on her last day, but he backed out at the last minute.

He smoked two packs of cigarettes that day. It was a new record. And he was back on the full-strength Merits.

Drinking scotch became a nightly routine. The booze facilitated his denial.

He had his parents and Mardi. He had some friends. His black lab, Dino, never left his side. He was as loyal as the hockey legend himself, and Bernard would never trade him as the North Stars had eventually traded Ciccarelli.

He had Tanya, too, he guessed.

That evening, a Thursday, Tanya brought over a Cossetta's pizza for Bernard and an oversized salad and chia seed smoothie for herself. Bernard wanted to sleep, but she helped him stay awake until he was done grading student papers. She sat with her laptop, surfing her new Facebook account and the gossip web boards Bernard knew she liked to follow. He teased her about it some, but not too harshly. Gossip and true crime were Tanya's guilty pleasures, just like smoking and eating artery-clogging food were his.

When she left at ten o'clock, Bernard packed up his satchel and put it by the door for the morning. It was time to swallow his BonneReve capsule.

News reports stated that the medication might soon be banned. Cautious doctors had stopped prescribing it. Bernard's doctor saw BonneReve as nothing short of a miracle. It helped Bernard sleep so soundly, in fact, that at one o'clock in the morning he slept right through his own visit to the kitchen for a leftover slice of pizza.

At two o'clock in the morning, Bernard slept through getting into his own car and driving it to Harriet Island. Dino jumped in for the ride. Bernard, in his dream, wanted to catch the moonlight from his houseboat. The dog whimpered in the passenger seat as his master traveled the route he'd driven a thousand times.

39. Currents, 2007

"**H**ello Minneapolis!" a passenger shouted, awakening Genève as the bus pulled into the station.

Her original idea was to become a stowaway on a towboat up the Mississippi, but the more Genève looked into traveling to the Seacore barge terminal across the state line into Illinois, the better a Greyhound bus sounded. Pricier, and not as cool as being a stowaway, but less complicated. She'd put on make-up, and at her height, the cashier didn't ask for ID when she purchased a ticket with her savings.

It was all pretty easy. Except that this wasn't Minneapolis. It was St. Paul, the sign notified her once she disembarked and the bus pulled away. She didn't mean to get off here.

She walked a couple of blocks and peered across the Mississippi River. It wasn't Minneapolis on the other side of this part of the river. That divide she'd read about was further west; here the river divided St. Paul between the downtown business district and a recreation area.

Genève didn't know that. Thinking it must be Minneapolis over there, she found a bridge to cross. A variety of houseboats bobbed up and down and she made her way toward them.

The marina boardwalk was quiet. *Pepperdine* was stenciled in cursive on the stern of one of the older boats. Her mother said that word to her once, something about a place she'd wanted to go to college, and it had stuck to her like a piece of peppermint gum.

She took it as a sign that this was her safe place for the night and climbed aboard.

The cabin door was locked, but Genève climbed the short ladder to the open upper deck. A bald eagle dove straight into the river, then swooped back up with a fish in its mouth. Never had she seen that before. Never had she sat on the deck of a houseboat either. Merit cigarettes and a lighter sat in a clear plastic box under the deck chair. She picked up the pack, smelling the tobacco. Sparks flew as she flicked the metal wheel of the lighter. She jumped back when a flame shot up. Inside the box with the cigarettes was a key on a whistle keychain.

Maybe it was the key to the cabin. She would try it and see. But first, Geneve wanted to explore the rest of the boat. She put the plastic box back under the chair and backed down the ladder to the main deck.

The urge to swim was a powerful one, even though the night air chilled her. Only the blackness of the water at night stopped her from jumping in. The Mississippi River, she noted, was no middle school swimming pool.

The Clayton-Wydown Middle School swimming pool!

The big swim meet—she'd miss it and let her team down. And her mom and grandma. She had never hurt her mom like she must be hurting now. But why should she care? Hadn't her mother been mean, forbidding her from seeing her best friend for no good reason? And keeping secrets from her about her father.

She'd told her she didn't know anything. She lied! At least that's how Geneve felt at first when she found the man in the computer browser history. Now she worried. She would have to let her know she was safe.

Just not yet.

Geneve reached the main level railing. She pulled off her Target sneakers and felt the May night air on her feet. Lying on her stomach, she reached down to shake hands with the river. She sat back up and hung her long legs through the railing to feel the cool water whooshing through her toes. With the stars in the sky and the water on her feet, Geneve breathed a sigh of relief.

It was good to be somewhere close to where she might find her father—maybe even tomorrow. Now, she just needed some food. And sleep. She went back to the upper deck and took the key out of the box, then climbed back down to the cabin door.

As she was about to open it, a man lumbered, zombie-like, up the walkway and headed straight to the dock for the *Pepperdine*. A black dog trailed behind him. Genève crossed her fingers, hoping he was going to another boat. She tiptoed around the cabin to the other side.

The man turned toward the *Pepperdine* and put a leg up on the lower deck. Had he followed her there? The dog sat down on the dock, standing guard, then jumped onto the boat. Genève sidled back around the cabin, hoping for a chance to disembark. The dog sniffed the air. He turned his head toward her, woofed once, then trotted her way. She came to terms with the fact that she was about to be discovered, but the dog only whimpered and shoved his nose into her hand. He wanted her to do something, but she didn't know what.

Appeasing the dog with ear-scratching, she peered over at the man.

He didn't seem aware of her, or even of his dog's whimpering. He climbed under the railing and stood almost off the side of the boat, hanging on with one hand. There was something not right about him, but he didn't scare her. He seemed to be more of a danger to himself.

The dog whined again, turned toward the man, then trotted back to Genève. He whined louder and circled her, trying to herd her in the direction of his master. He woofed. The man swayed over the water.

The dog barked loudly, and the man let go.

Genève yelled, "Hey!" A loud splash joined with her voice and the dog's barking to disrupt the quiet night air.

The dog leaped in as the man sank under the black water. Genève darted to the other side and climbed under the railing to where she saw the ripples of water and the desperate dog. She scanned the surface, but he was gone.

She dove.

What seemed like almost a minute later, she surfaced with him in a vice hold around his shoulders so he couldn't pull her back down with him, as she'd learned in water safety class. She scissor kicked toward the dock, the dog paddling along behind them. As she came closer to the dock, she yelled, "Can you breathe?"

The current grabbed their legs from underneath and dragged them out again. The stars in the sky seemed to go dark as the dog circled them in the river. Awakened from his trance, the man strove to break free from the current. Genève put her strongest strokes into motion, pulling him back.

The man took hold of the dock's edge and coughed, sputtering out only a few drops of water. They pulled themselves and the dog up onto the wooden structure. The dog shook himself off, water droplets flying off his jet black coat in every direction. For some reason, this made Genève laugh. She'd never known dogs were so funny, or so brave.

The man gave her one grateful yet baffled look, which quickly turned into a scolding.

"You should never swim in this river," he said, sounding like one of her teachers. "What were you thinking?"

Then he lost consciousness. The dog licked Genève's hand and recommenced barking.

Genève's aunt conducted research about the adolescent brain, so the girl knew teenagers didn't always think before they took risks. But Genève had never been thinking so clearly, so logically, as in that moment when she dove into the river. In that split second, she'd inventoried risks and calculated consequences. She believed she could help.

But now, with him lying there passed out on the dock, she hadn't a clue what to do next. There was the whistle on the keychain. She could use it to call for help.

The dog's Labrador retriever ears stiffened, then swung forward. Genève's ear, too, caught the siren in the distance. It got louder, then blared. It stopped, and Genève heard the sound of running. Two EMTs pounded down the wooden walkway from the parking lot. She ducked back onto the boat, hiding near the railing on the far side of the cabin.

"Male, unconscious, but breathing," one of the men said into his handheld radio. "Bring a stretcher."

A yacht club member in a dark wind suit stood at the end of the dock. One of the EMTs went to the woman. She knew only the man's first name, that he taught, and that the dog was his. "I only heard splashing and the dog barking like crazy. Guy must've fallen in and then got himself back outta the river," she said.

A minute later, a male police officer and a female EMT arrived at the dock. The police took over talking to the club member while the EMT brought over a stretcher and a board. They woke the man enough to assess him for any spinal injuries or broken bones. He wouldn't move, so they maneuvered the board under him, lifted him onto the stretcher, and made their way back to the waiting ambulance.

Genève peeked around the corner. The police officer glanced back at the boat, but then the EMT asked if he would help with the dog.

Once they all left the marina, Genève went back to where she had left the key and slowly turned it in the cabin door lock. Inside the dim room, she found a small shower with a bladder-like tank. With her clothes still on, she stood inside and turned it on. There wasn't much pressure. Only the marina's lights through the cabin's windows allowed her to see at all, but she could feel the sediment wash away from her clothes and down the drain. She peeled away her clothes and turned off the shower, squeezing shampoo from a tube and lathering the outfit and her hair. Turning the water back on, she rinsed clean. The water turned to a trickle, the bladder tank empty.

One clean towel sat on a shelf. Genève used it to dry off, wrapped it around herself, and went quietly to hang her clothes to dry on the deck railing.

Back in the cabin, Genève found a large can of Planters mixed nuts. In a small refrigerator sat an orange drink and a piece of sponge cake layered with chocolate and whipped cream cheese inside a plastic container. She broke the seal. The cake smelled like her mother's coffee, but with a note of her grandparents' drinks.

Genève had not been raised to take what wasn't hers, but hunger overpowered her. She ate the rest of the cake with one hand and put the nuts in her backpack for tomorrow. The shower, snacks, and bed for the night would have to be her reward for pulling the man out of the water. She fell asleep under a St. Paul Saints baseball blanket to the gently rocking motion of the boat named *Pepperdine*.

40. *Irene's Confession, 2007*

"I wish they could have brought him to the hospital in Edina," Irene whispered. "The one next to Southdale."

Edward murmured back, "Surely you would not go to the mall at a time like this. Stores won't be open this early, anyway."

"Of course not. It just would've been nicer to have him closer to home." This hospital stood so close to the state capitol they could see the chariot, horses, and human figures at the base of its dome from Bernard's window.

The gleaming gold quadriga did not impress Irene. "But you're right," she said. "We can spend a day in St. Paul every once in a while. I suppose they had to bring him to whichever hospital was closer to where he had the... accident."

Bernard promised he had not tried to kill himself. It was a side effect of BonneReve, this business of driving and eating in the middle of the night. Irene and Edward hoped they had reason to believe him.

As it wasn't his first back injury, the surgeon would have to insert morsels of bone into the disc space to fuse the spine. She suggested the Petits go do something and come back later. She could reach them if need be; this is what cell phones were for.

"I must admit I've been intrigued by Forepaugh's," Irene said, a guilty look on her face. Forepaugh's was a restaurant in a mansion down the street from Bernard's place. One of her friends from the club said it was excellent. A testimonial from the socialite had to mean something.

"We could visit Tom or Annette," Edward put his hand on Irene's elbow.

"I don't feel like explaining about Bernard to your family, honey," Irene said. "Not yet. I hope you don't mind."

Bernard stirred in his bed.

"Lunch at Forepaugh's it is, and let's just hope Bernard's accident doesn't make today's news. It's only seven-thirty."

"*Ahem.* I'm so happy you two have your entertainment plan worked out." Mardi made her entrance, dressed in rumpled clothing, with her hair a mess. She wore no hairstyle these days. Her mother looked her up and down. Irene and Edward were always impeccable by six-thirty in the morning, even though neither had to go anywhere except by choice anymore.

Bernard turned his head slowly to her and smiled. "Thanks for coming. I'm sorry about all of this. Dumb stuff."

"What can I do for you?" Mardi asked him.

"How does your schedule look today?"

"Jobless. Soon homeless." Her house had sold.

"Mom and Dad will pick up my car and Dino. Mom called the school. The security officer will spend the first hour with my class. The secretary was going to call around for a sub too, unless..."

"I can do it. A hundred bucks a day is a hundred bucks a day. Or is it ten bucks a day at Twin Cities Success now, on a post-dated check? I can't remember."

She looked at her outfit and ran her fingers through her hair. "I'll have to wear this. Can I run over to your house on my way and take a shower?"

"Yeah, use the key under the blue flower pot. Grab my satchel. It's full of graded papers you can hand back. The kids did a good job—I hate to make them wait to see their grades."

Irene raised her eyebrows. "You remember grading papers, but you don't remember how you fell into the river or got out or even remember driving to the marina?"

"Sorry, Mom. I don't remember much after taking my sleeping pill."

Mardi looked at her phone. "I want to let Paj know you are here if that's okay. I know she doesn't work there anymore, but she'd want to know."

Bernard nodded. "She shouldn't worry. She must be so busy with her new job. Can you call Tanya?"

Mardi didn't commit to that last request.

"So, the security guy takes first hour and then I have prep time, and then it's economics and life skills for the rest of the periods, right?"

"Yes. Thanks." Bernard gave her a flat smile. "It's a good thing it's almost the weekend. And that I won't be teaching life skills class today. I wouldn't be too credible."

The whole family glanced up as the medical team arrived to take Bernard into surgery. Mardi kissed her brother on the forehead and whispered in his ear, "None of the Petits are credible in life skills."

❀ ❀ ❀

Bernard awoke. The familiar comfort of pain medication rose euphorically in him and transformed his pillow into a fluffy cloud. He nestled in, relishing the buoyancy. He would try to find a way back to this feeling without the drugs. He didn't have a choice, not if he wanted to live. But first, he needed his spine to heal.

Paj sat by his side in a comfortable visitor chair where her feet didn't touch the ground. He started to say something, but she put her finger in front of her mouth. "Later. I have things to tell you, too. I will call you soon. Rest."

When he looked again, she was gone. He must have drifted. On his tray sat a lidded white bowl of broth, clear but fragrant with the essence of Thai basil. He didn't have the strength to reach for it, but the next time he awoke a nurse helped him sip.

He drifted off again, and this time when he awoke it was Irene who sat in the chair. Her foot tapped the floor.

"Hi Mom," he croaked.

"Your father is out walking Dino. They treated him like a hero at the police station. Those St. Paul officers sure loved how he's named after one of their own."

"Dino Ciccarelli is from Canada, not St. Paul."

"I mean one of their own Italian folks, you know, those St. Paul police are all Italians and Irish."

"Ah, got it."

"I just hope Dino'll be happy at our place until you can go home. I'm going to stay with you as long as you need me."

"That means you would need to sleep in St. Paul."

She grumbled at him for teasing her, but it was a good sign he was doing well. "We had a lovely day in St. Paul, I have to admit, although the story of the Forepaugh mansion is ghastly. This city has a terribly seedy history."

Bernard asked the nurse for coffee when she came in to check his vital signs. It had been decades since he missed his morning cup. And he wanted his Merits.

When she left, Irene said, "I wanted to talk to you about something. Edward thought it would be best if I came back alone."

Her voice trembled as she moved from the comfortable chair and pulled a wooden one next to his bed. Bernard wondered. It could be so many things. Maybe his surgery had been botched. Maybe someone died. He knew it was not that his parents were divorcing. Years ago, that could have been it. Now they were glued at the hip.

Irene bit her pinkie finger, then put her hands back in her lap. "It's a confession. I don't want you to think I'm telling you now just because you're in this vulnerable state, but...well, it's just that I should have told you long ago."

Bernard looked toward the door. It was probably some apology about how she hadn't encouraged him to be a teacher or to move into the house in St. Paul. He wished someone would bring coffee.

"It's about that girlfriend of yours." Irene paused. Her tongue was stuck.

"Tanya," he said.

Irene shook her head. "Fran."

Bernard waited. Maybe this was some drug-induced dream. He never imagined he would hear Irene mention Fran Hart's name again.

She continued. "I know you always wondered why she didn't show up for college at Pepperdine. It hurt you terribly when that relationship ended."

"I never understood. She just didn't come. And she wouldn't talk to me. You know, she ended up going to college in Missouri, and then she came back to Minnesota and got a job at Dayton's. It didn't make sense."

"That's what I need to tell you. I need to tell you why. At least why she didn't show up at Pepperdine. I don't know if it will help you understand the rest of it or not."

"You know why?"

An aide came in and set a paper cup of coffee on the tray, along with a box of Nicorette gum. Bernard hardly noticed it. "Please tell me."

Irene took a breath. There was no going back now. "It was something I did. I didn't think she was right for you then. Mothers have dreams for their kids, and you were so..."

Bernard's eyes remained wide open now. Fran. He remembered their plans. They were going to sail on the Pacific together. To make love out there on the ocean. Fran was going to shake things up on the conservative campus in the Malibu Hills with her 1970s women's lib.

What had his mother done? He put his face in his hands.

"I know you might never forgive me, but I can't keep it from you any longer. You have to know your father had nothing to do with it. I told him and our pastor several years ago, but now I have to tell you."

Bernard forced himself to give her permission to continue. "Then tell me."

She started. "I had an old high school friend whose sister-in-law worked there, in the admissions office. I said some things. And then, it surprised me, I have to say, how quickly it happened. Her acceptance was rescinded."

Bernard's mouth opened, but no words came.

Irene talked through her tears. "I guess she just let you think she had decided not to go instead of telling you that she didn't get in after all."

It all made sense now, even in Bernard's post-surgery fog. Things had never been clearer, except for why she later moved back to Minnesota. But people do that. Minnesota pulls people back. But the rest was so obvious. Why hadn't he thought of it?

Fran thought she had been legitimately rejected and she didn't want to drag Bernard down with her. Bernard let his head drop into his hands again. "I should have figured it out then."

Irene's face drained of color. "Oh, no, you cannot blame yourself. I deserve every bit of your anger. I'll never know how your life might have been different."

"Oh, I am not blaming myself." He glared at her. "Was it because she was Jewish? Or working class? Too liberal? Did she threaten you in some way?"

Irene gave Bernard a solemn nod. Her answer was unspeakable. It was all of the above.

As exhausted as he was, he couldn't stop. "After all of those years thinking she must have fallen in love with someone else, or that she hated me, or thought I was disgusting, it was your fault all along. And I stayed at Pepperdine, living the Malibu dream that you stole from her. Did you know they were going to give her a scholarship? Huh? Did you know that?"

"I'm sorry, I'm so sorry. It was a big mistake. I have felt guilty about it for thirty years."

"She worked hard in high school. She was so smart. It must have felt like getting pushed down the stairs. And she already struggled, not thinking she was as smart as her sister. She must have been so ashamed after telling everyone she was accepted. My God. Do you have any idea what that must have done to her?"

Bernard knew Irene had wanted so much for him. Her father had grown up on a failing farm before he went into finance. Irene grew up with the idea that you had to keep climbing. She somehow hadn't been able to see that Fran had so much to give. She only saw trouble. Even if Fran had nothing, at least they had love. Bernard had never found that again.

The nurse came in to check Bernard's vital signs again and Bernard resisted complaining. She did her business quietly, aware that she was interrupting. Often in such situations, a family member would be in tears over their loved one's close call with death. But such dramatics couldn't be allowed to give her patients more stress. This man exhibited raised blood pressure and reddening in the face. It was a good thing she had checked on him. The mother would have to leave.

"Ma'am, I think it's best if we let Mr. Petit take a little snooze."

Sobbing, Irene took a tissue from the box on Bernard's tray and stood up.

"I'll leave you two for just a minute, and then I'll be right back to get him all tucked in." The nurse pivoted on one foot and departed.

"Mom," Bernard said.

"Yes, sweetheart?"

"I don't need to hear any more about this. But there is someone else who does. I don't know when or how we'll meet up with her, but I want Fran to know she was accepted to Pepperdine without question—without any legitimate question, that is."

Irene nodded. "If I ever have the chance, I will tell her what I did."

She took her things and left the room, gratefully believing that she would never have the chance. She'd gotten it off her chest, and that would be that. Sleep would come easier now.

Bernard took a long sip of the lukewarm coffee. The nurse came back in and showed him how he could press a button on the IV line to deliver a dose of pain medication straight into his circulatory system. As she fluffed his pillow and pulled his blanket up to his neck, she promised it would only dispense what he could handle.

Bernard pushed the IV button again and again. If only it could always be as easy as a button. His pain washed away and he drifted off into that in-between world he had known before.

A face formed in his mind. A girl. She looked sixteen or seventeen, but something in her manner told him she was younger. Her skin was pure warmth, glowing in the night's darkness, her eyes more familiar, serious. There was something else familiar about her, but what?

The image dissipated, then came into focus again. Her head was framed in wet curls, and now he could see water. Water flowed all around.

He struggled to bridge memory and wakefulness. These memories only came with pain medication or BonneReve. They would be lost if he couldn't write them down. But he couldn't wake to write without breaking the dream-state connection to that night.

"CODE BLUE. CODE BLUE. ALL DOCTORS PLEASE PROCEED TO THE SIXTH FLOOR."

The floor-wide speaker blasted Bernard's awake. He gulped air like someone who'd been suffocating.

And then he remembered. The girl had pulled him up from the depths of the marina. Somehow, she had been there at his boat.

Who was she?

He took a pen from the tray, but the only paper was the menu he was supposed to mark to choose his breakfast for the next morning. It would be Saturday and the menu offered extra weekend choices. Next to where he should select an omelet or French toast, he wrote: *Girl saved my life. Who?*

And then he remembered her face again.

Now another memory came. It was when he was recovering from the school incident. He lay on the couch at Mardi's house, drifting in and out of consciousness. Mardi had said it: Fran's adopted baby, Genève, was Noelle's baby at birth, but Fran didn't know. Nobody could find out.

It sounded like just the kind of soapy stuff Tanya followed and conjectured about in her online chatrooms, thinking she was some kind of sleuth.

Bernard picked up the pen again, and where he was supposed to mark whether he wanted a biscuit or toast, he wrote: *Noelle/Fran/same daughter.*

It was a breakthrough, documenting memories from his black-out. It was like he'd accomplished time travel. Now he could go to sleep.

41. Remembering, 2007

The hospital orderly squinted at Bernard's menu. "This says somethin' about a girl saving your life and two women being the mama of one girl. Nothin' about what you'd like for breakfast?"

He held it up so Bernard could see. It was his writing, and he tried to remember scribbling the words.

Mardi appeared in the doorway.

"He'll have an omelet and a biscuit, please," she said. "Strawberry jelly for the biscuit, and orange juice."

She handed her brother a take-out coffee cup emblazoned with a flying caribou. "I brought you the good stuff."

The orderly checked the boxes while Mardi peeked over her shoulder at her brother's writing on the menu.

"So exactly what do you know, and how do you know it?" she asked.

Bernard shook his head.

Mardi had not followed Genève's upbringing, even though holding the premature infant in her arms had been one of her life's most pure experiences of love. She never would have known the girl existed if she hadn't lined up in front of Noelle and her friend that day for the holiday exhibit. Bernard was the only person she'd ever been tempted to tell, since the adoptive mother was his old girlfriend, but she had stayed firm in her resolve not to disrupt Genève's life, nor Noelle's.

Bernard rubbed his eyebrows, but couldn't answer Mardi's question.

"I'm a different person when I take the medicine. There was something I was remembering last night when I was on the pain meds—something that I knew or something that happened the other times I was medicated. What I wrote on the menu...you will have to help me figure out what it means."

It came back to Mardi, Bernard knocked out cold on her couch as he recovered from being injured by the student two years earlier. That was the night she and Noelle stayed up late talking about the birth, about what Noelle thought about the coincidence of Fran being the adoptive mother.

And, Mardi wondered, hadn't she told Noelle that night that she thought she was gay? Perhaps Bernard had heard that too.

She stood next to his bed. "You're going to need help with your addiction to pills," she said, "As a recovering alcoholic myself I promise I will be there for you." Then she put her finger on the button of his IV's pain medication delivery system. "But do you mind? I mean, if you are hurting now, just a touch of the juice?"

Bernard nodded. "Of course I'm hurting. I had pieces of cadaver bone packed into my spine yesterday. Push the darned button."

A minute later, Bernard's face lit up for a moment and his mouth moved, but then it went slack again. He seemed to doze off. Mardi pressed a button on his bed to raise him just enough to tip the Caribou Coffee toward his mouth. He sipped.

"I remember you and Noelle talking about Fran's daughter, Genève," he said, now partially awake in both worlds. "Noelle said she gave birth to her."

"*Shhh*. Okay, that's a secret you gotta keep. And what else do you remember?"

"I don't know for sure what else from that night. But I remembered that the other night there was a girl on my boat and she jumped into the river to save me."

Mardi threw her head back and laughed. "You really were wasted! No way. A girl on your boat? It was an angel I suppose?"

"I can't explain how she got there. It sounds bad. I could get in trouble. But she's too young to be out there alone."

"Well, I don't believe it, but we have to tell the police in case it's some runaway," Mardi said, seeing how lucid Bernard seemed now with his memory. As she reached for the phone, she said, "But back to Noelle. I tried to call her first thing this morning because it's her birthday. Wade answered and said she wasn't there, and then she didn't answer her cell."

Bernard nodded, then savored more sips of the coffee.

As Mardi was about to pick up the hospital room phone to dial the police, her own cellphone rang. She answered, "Grand Central Station."

It was Gary Gorman, of all people, that fixture of Women's Shoes. "I'm sorry to bother you, Mardi. I need to reach your cousin, Noelle, and she's not answering at any of the phone numbers I have for her. I was lucky to find your number. I was hoping you could help me track her down."

"I'm trying to reach Noelle, too," she said into the phone, aware that Bernard could hear Gary's loud voice even though her cell phone speaker wasn't on. "What's going on that's so urgent with you?"

"My wife and I have Fran Hart and her mother at our house. You know Fran, right? She dated your brother many years back and worked with me at Dayton's until she moved to Missouri."

"I know who Fran is," Mardi said. This couldn't be good. "*Why?*"

"Her daughter is missing," Gary said, cutting to the chase at Mardi's command.

Bernard pushed a button to adjust his bed and set his takeout coffee cup down on the side table. Feebly, he took the cell phone from Mardi's hand. "We are about to call the police. I think I saw her."

Mardi gawked at him. "You think that girl was Genève?"

"Okay, good," Gary said. "But I gotta tell you something else. My wife saw some rumors on one of those local gossip websites about your cousin, Noelle, being the biological mother of Fran's missing daughter. The police won't tell Fran if it's true. They probably don't even know."

"Which site?" Bernard asked. "Those websites aren't very well vetted."

Mardi was shaking her head furiously at Bernard and making the cut sign across her throat.

Gary said, "Well, that's true, but the thing is, the person who posted it—my wife says that woman said she heard it from one of Noelle's cousins, a Petit family member. I thought maybe..."

Bernard set the receiver into his armpit and whispered to Mardi. "They know. I must have told Tanya when I was blacked out. She posted it on one of her sleuthing groups."

"Bernard!" Gary yelled into the phone. Bernard put it back to his ear. "Is it true? This is an emergency. If Genève is looking for her biological parents, knowing who they are helps us know where to look for her."

Mardi balled one fist and hit herself in the forehead.

Bernard could hear Fran's desperate voice in the background. He said, "It may be true."

"I need Gary's address," Mardi said. "I'll meet them and help find the girl. I have to find Noelle, too."

After Bernard hung up the phone, Mardi made the call to the police. Afterward, she opened her laptop. "I just want to see what she looks like first," she said, searching and clicking on a story about the missing teenager.

"That's her," Bernard said. "She risked her life to save mine."

"I wonder if Wade has already heard about Noelle," Mardi said. "And crap, I bet Aunt Annette and Carl know."

"Why don't you try to call Annette and Carl and see if she's there?" Bernard suggested. "Or try Macy's again?"

Mardi shoved her laptop back in the bag without answering and headed toward the door, running smack into the orderly carrying Bernard's breakfast. The orderly held fast onto the food, but Mardi dropped her things and had to stop to pick them up.

"By the way," Bernard said as he lifted the metal cover off the plate, "I did remember one other thing you and Noelle were talking about that night. And I want you to know that I think anyone would be lucky to have you in her life."

Mardi turned back and hugged her brother gently. She had to go. There was even more she needed to talk to him about, but not now. It was all too much right now.

Tomorrow, she told herself.

42. *The Infirmary, 2007*

Noelle woke up in her childhood bedroom at her parents' house on her fortieth birthday. Her cell phone sat dark and lifeless, probably because the only charger cord at her parents' house was a frayed relic of the time Carl briefly owned a cell phone before declaring them the end of civilization. Noelle's choices were buying a new cord or going back to the house across the street from Bush Lake.

Noelle had gone home the day before to find her belongings on the front porch. Wade's mother charged out with Dakota in its cage, the tiny green bathtub it never used, and a box of birdseed.

"What's going on?" Noelle had yelled. "Why is my stuff out here?"

"We older people can read the internet too, you know," she said. "News about a missing biracial kid from Missouri is getting around. My sister read some very interesting things online, and guess whose name came up as the kid's birth mother?"

Noelle stared, her face frozen.

"You should know!" Wade's mother shouted. "Turns out you had an affair with a black man!"

"So, it all comes down to that he was black," said Noelle.

"Our family is *not racist,* I will have you know." Wade's mother wagged her finger at Noelle. "We just don't like liars. Remember, *I* even invited that black family to sit next to us at the Holidazzle parade last year."

The woman wedged the birdcage into Noelle's back seat. "*Hmm,* come to think of it you did act funny around that stock boy."

"*Former* stock boy, you vile shrew! At least you could put out my shoe collection."

She took the birdcage out of her car and set it back by the front door as her mother-in-law stomped back into the house. "The fucking bird is the last thing I need," she grumbled to herself.

Seconds later, a box of shoes came flying out the door.

"Oh, that's not even a fraction..." Noelle took advantage of the open door and forced her way in to get more of her belongings, like the sewing machine from Grandma Greta that was pretty old now but she didn't want any other woman to touch. She loaded it all into her front seat, got back into her car and took off.

She would need a lawyer to get the rest, but Noelle told herself all that mattered was that her kids were safe, and she would see them soon. She swung the steering wheel hard to the right. She would go to her parents' house, hoping they didn't know everything.

At least I didn't let her foist that fucking bird on me, Noelle thought.

As soon as she'd turned onto Bush Lake Road, she heard a noise. *Peep peep.* Then again. *Raaaalk!*

Her mother-in-law must have put the parakeet in the hatchback trunk when Noelle went into the house.

"God fucking damn!" she screamed.

She arrived at the silent, empty house on Butternut Avenue. Her parents weren't home and she realized she hadn't spoken to them in weeks. She fed the bird and slept for nine hours, never once missing Wade by her side.

As baffled as she felt about how her secret ended up on the internet, and as sour of a taste she had in her mouth about being separated from Nicollet and Avril, Noelle had to go to work the next day. Nobody could miss work now. A day off in the current Macy's environment equaled career suicide. It was the last thing anyone wanted to do, apart from waking up in their parents' house on their fortieth birthday.

Noelle's last birthday had been acknowledged at work with pink-frosted cupcakes in the stock room of her old department. As a manager of a whole floor now, it wasn't the same. She missed being part of a team, a department. As a floor manager, employees tended to avoid her.

It wasn't like Wade planned to celebrate her. His early present to her was that he'd stopped hiding his hunger for Kathy and then let his mother kick her out of the house. He probably wouldn't even have the kids call to wish her a happy birthday.

Annette made her an omelet stuffed with bacon in exchange for Noelle's unwelcome explanation that she and Wade were separating. She gave her the usual birthday gift: a Target gift card.

Although Noelle hadn't figured out exactly how Wade and his family seemed to have read online about her true first child, she didn't think her parents knew yet. Carl wasn't home and Annette bought that they'd just had too many fights. Then, thinking the better of it over a large bite of smoky bacon, she told Annette about Wade's affair to garner some sympathy she figured it wouldn't hurt to have in the bank. It worked. Her mother dipped the tongs into the pile of bacon and set another extra crispy piece onto Noelle's plate.

She couldn't imagine how her Catholic father would react to her separation, much less to the rest of the truth.

The bullseye on the Target gift card seemed to stare up at her, wanting her to fall into its crimson, round center, its promise of fulfillment. Noelle felt happier looking at it, anyway. It would come in handy as she started over. She just didn't know where or how.

Once she got to work, it appeared some coworkers had planned to do something nice for her birthday after all. A Post-It Note stuck to her timecard read: *Please come up to the manager's office before you punch in.*

Would there be cake? God, how she wanted cake with frosting and confetti sprinkles. Fuck the diet. Noelle craved sugary comfort; she needed somebody to care enough to give her that.

She put her timecard back into the slot and rode the escalator down to the basement to check her hair and makeup in the ladies' room. The florescent lights did nothing for the new age spots and under-eye circles, nor for the little scars from her skin biopsies, all benign. At least her hair still looked good, rolling out in caramel-fudge-colored barrel curls across her shoulders.

She walked past her usual basement coffee counter and to the elevator, pressing the "11" button and noting—as always—the round stainless steel slug that sat in the cavity where the "10" button should have been. She hoped they would serve coffee with the birthday cake.

The manager's secretary greeted her, but the office seemed too quiet for a party. Maybe it was a surprise.

"I got a note to come up here?" Noelle said, her sentence rising into a question.

"Oh yes. Noelle. Actually, you are to be seen in the HR office, not in here."

The bouncy birthday balloons in Noelle's mind deflated. She felt the walls pressing into her as the secretary walked her down a narrow hallway to the office of a woman sitting at a desk, gripping a white folder.

"Please sit down," the woman said.

Mardi had described this exact scene from her fateful last day, right down to the HR specialist's suit. Macy's had kept the Oval Room name up on the third-floor designer enclave, and this suit clearly came from that toniest section of the store. At least someone at this store had stable and lucrative employment. She knew people joked that HR's motto was, "Here to the bitter end—we'll turn off the lights."

Noelle refused to sit.

"I want to thank you for your nearly, uh, two years of service at Macy's—and previously those years at Dayton's and Marshall Field's."

"I've worked in this building since 1990," Noelle asserted.

"You are aware, of course, that retail department stores are fighting for survival and that we have to realign positions to the current budget capacity," the HR specialist continued, smooth as her candied apple nail polish. "I'm sorry. Your position has been eliminated."

Noelle glanced down at her own unpainted nails. She hoped that next the woman would offer a different position, even something for less pay.

The HR specialist offered only a practiced look of empathy, along with the glossy folder. "I have some resources to share."

Noelle grabbed the folder and let herself out of the office.

The secretary, who had been standing outside the office door, stopped Noelle before she could take off in a sprint. "I need your signature here and will accompany you on your way out," she said. "I'll be happy to help you get anything you need from your office."

"You have to babysit me?" Noelle said, but she noticed the secretary's red face and shaky voice. This probably wasn't in her job description. One of those *other duties as assigned.* The poor thing followed Noelle to the doorway of her office tucked away in the stock room behind the juniors clothing and stood watch while Noelle put her belongings into a large Macy's shopping bag the secretary brought along for her.

There were only three things in there Noelle cared about: a framed photo of Avril and Nicollet, a desk lamp shaped like the Eiffel Tower, and a newish pair of sheepskin winter boots she'd worn to work through the end of March and hadn't gotten around to bringing home.

"We have to make one more stop," Noelle told the secretary. She led her through the back rooms of three departments until they reached the freight elevator that went to the tenth floor.

"But I don't know if I'm supposed to...what's up here?" the secretary asked. She was a nervous kitten, hunching up her shoulders. "I didn't even realize there was a tenth floor."

"Just what *does* anyone think is between the ninth and eleventh floors?" Noelle said. "Dark matter? *Narnia?* Wait here."

Noelle turned into the old infirmary just as two men, a waiter from the Oak Grill Room and a manager from Linens and Bedding, walked out. The linens manager held his head high. The waiter blushed.

"Don't mind me, guys," Noelle said. "Just picking up a souvenir."

She opened the green metal infirmary cabinet and pulled out the old plaid hot water bottle.

She didn't know why she took it, maybe just because it didn't seem like it should end up in a dumpster if Macy's ever decided to clean up the place. She ran her finger over two dust-free liquor bottles in the cabinet, then ran the back of her hand over a brand new Raymond Waites flat sheet that neatly covered the narrow bed.

The infirmary, Noelle saw, had its regulars now. A small and disparate crew of lost souls somehow found a floor otherwise lost to history, lost to a time when business owners hired nurses and devoted space to care for sick staff and customers.

Noelle opened the drawer and took one last peek at the yellowed patient log. Nurse Moholt's last patient signed out in 1957.

She walked back to the elevator and showed the secretary what was in her bag. "See, I'm not stealing anything. It's just my hot water bottle from when I wasn't feeling good."

The secretary craned toward the old nurse's station but didn't take a step. A secret place in the building to go when you aren't feeling good, or when you need some privacy, or for a drink to calm your nerves?

Noelle could see it in her eyes. She would be back.

They rode the elevator down to the first-floor stock room. Noelle walked ahead of the secretary and out the chute-like vestibule onto the shoe sales floor and straight to the employee exit. As security searched her bags at the employee exit for the last time, the tears began to flow past Noelle's crow's feet and down her sun-splotched cheeks.

She went out the heavy glass door and straight ahead rather than toward the parking ramp.

It was her birthday, *dammit*.

She threw her purse over her right shoulder, adjusted the Macy's bag into the crook of her left elbow, and set her feet southwest down Nicollet Avenue. She hadn't forgotten she had that gift card.

There was only one thing to do at a time like this anyway, when you get fired on your fortieth birthday while bunking with your parents after your husband replaces you with his employee, and people are posting your biggest secret on the internet, and that secret is your missing child who doesn't know you and you can't do anything about it.

You go pile a bunch of wonderful odds and ends you don't need but can't resist in a cherry red plastic cart.

At Target, of course.

43. *Two-Level Target, 2007*

"I'm sorry sweetheart, but the vice presidents don't work here in the store," said the woman in a red polo and khaki pants just like Genève's mom wore to her job. "They work in the corporate office down the street, or you can go up one level and through the skyway."

Her name badge sported a red Target bullseye and read *Sylvia Ramirez, Guest Service Manager*. Although she had to look up to respond to the girl looking for Pierre St. Hilaire, the girl appeared to be younger than her height conveyed. Sylvia had her own children. She eyed the girl's Clayton-Wydown Middle School Swim Team duffle, checkered backpack, and tangled hair.

"Oh, of course," Genève said. "Which direction?"

Things happened in downtown Minneapolis. It just usually wasn't a kid looking for a company exec. "If you can tell me who you are, I can call over there and see if I can reach his office staff," Sylvia offered.

"He's my dad, but he might not be expecting me."

"Well, let's give it a try." Sylvia dialed the corporate office and an operator connected her to the vice president's secretary. She explained, and moments later Genève heard her say, "That would be wonderful. Thank you."

"He's coming?"

"His secretary seemed a bit confused, but she said he'll be on his way. Please have a seat."

Genève would have curled up right there on the red bench and taken a nap, but her heart raced. After catching her breath, she saw something she had been too excited to notice at first.

This Target featured two special tracks sandwiched between the up and down escalators. Five red shopping carts traveled up. Three descended. When a cart reached its destination, it thrust its way through a tiny swing door and rolled out so its owner could reclaim it for another floor of shopping. The Target where her mom worked didn't have shopping carts riding escalators next to their owners. Like pets. Like something out of a sci-fi movie.

She looked away to see what else was different about this two-level Target, but her attention swung back to the escalators. A loud curse came from a white woman with long brown curls. She had a large shopping bag in the cart with what appeared to be an Eiffel Tower sticking out of it.

"*Goddammit!* I forgot the charger," the woman yelled. She got her cart, affixed it to the other track, and rode back up.

Crazy people, Genève thought. Of course, this was downtown. People were weird in downtown St. Louis, too.

Sylvia returned, now with a man wearing dress shoes and a gray suit. When his nervous eyes landed on the girl, he loosened the knot of his burgundy silk tie as if he would otherwise begin to choke. Sylvia led him to her but kept one eye on him while she hurried back around the counter where a line of customers had formed. She would not let him take the girl anywhere without verification, vice president or not.

"Are you Pierre St. Hilaire?" Genève pronounced the name with an American accent, but something other than Minnesotan to Pierre's ear. She hoped he found it acceptable.

The man dropped to sit on the red bench. She looked into his eyes, which turned down on the outsides like hers. His eyelids trembled now, and so did hers. "I am. And what is your name?"

He knew her name, unless it had been changed. He had seen her given name the day he signed his own to the paperwork. He said it now. "Is your name Genève?"

She nodded. "You know who I am?"

Sylvia came from around the counter. "I thought you said he was your father, honey. I'm afraid I don't understand what is going on here."

Genève and Pierre held their gaze with those same-shaped eyes, in which anyone could see that they were father and daughter. She answered. "He is my biological father."

Sylvia moved back behind the counter and picked up the phone, speaking quietly into it while the long-lost pair struggled for words. The manager had dealt with enough bizarre activity in her downtown store to know when something was fishy. The VP could have Sylvia fired, but she had to watch out for young innocents.

"Where do you live? Where are your mother and father?" Pierre asked.

"My mother is in Clayton. That's a suburb of St. Louis. She almost got a husband, but they broke up. You're my only father. I wanted to travel on a towboat, but that would have taken too long, so I rode the bus."

Pierre stood up, then sat down again.

"Oh, *ma chérie*. Your mother must be so worried."

Genève pulled away, but he grasped the tips of her fingers. "Don't bolt from me now. You came all the way here to find me, right? Don't go. Let's talk."

It was such a gentle hold he had on her. No man besides her grandpa had ever held her hand. She looked at his long, dark fingers. It was time to call her mother, but she didn't want him to let go.

Sylvia eyed the VP's hand and talked faster into the phone. She hung up, then walked rapidly, trying to look casual, over to a short cooler by the nearest register. She grabbed two Cokes. "Here, please have a drink on me while you two reconnect. Take your time and let me know if you need anything. I am here to help."

Clearly, the police were on their way.

Genève looked off into the distance. Someone else had caught her attention. It was the offbeat woman with the long hair who'd just gone back up the escalator before Pierre arrived. She'd returned to the first floor, her shopping cart stuck in the wheel slot of the store's futuristic escalator. Genève watched as the escalator's emergency auto shut-off activated. Three other customers stood with their own pet carts heeling next to them.

"I think that's the woman you should be helping," Genève said to the manager. "Something is wrong with her cart. And maybe with her."

The perturbed woman climbed over the gate and pulled upward on the handle of her cart, trying to disengage the wheels from the track. She howled, "Some fucking birthday. Help!"

Pierre looked up, prayed a *mon dieu,* and then fixed his gaze back on Genève. He paused. "And did you say you were looking for only me? Or were you also hoping to find your, uh..."

But Genève looked past Pierre. Noelle stared at her now, letting go of her cart. She glanced at Pierre, then back to the girl. Sylvia kept her eye on all of them while calling for escalator assistance over the store's speaker system.

Noelle abandoned her shopping cart and walked slowly toward the father-daughter pair. Genève stood.

"Genève," Noelle said to the girl. She had to look up at her, yet those limbs were so thin and childlike. She flashed back to when she held that small but long warm body that she hardly believed had grown inside her.

"How do you know my name?" Genève asked. She looked at Pierre, who stood. "Who is *she?*"

Noelle thought she'd cried enough tears after being fired, but as her eyes filled with more, she reached out to touch her. "My little popover."

Genève flinched and turned her head toward Pierre's chest, touching her forehead lightly against his tie. He closed his eyes with paternal pleasure. *"Who is that lady?"* she asked him.

Pierre put his arm around her shoulder. "She's the one who gave you your name. She likes the French ones."

So, the nut job with all the escalator drama was her birth mother. "It actually comes from German," the girl said. "And my mother is named Fran Hart," she said.

"Fran Hart from Dayton's?" Pierre looked to Noelle for an answer. She nodded.

"I don't need another mother," Genève said. "I just wanted to find my father."

"You're right. Fran is your mother. I found that out. We knew each other, but she didn't know I gave birth to you."

Noelle, like Pierre, saw she had nothing to fear now. Wade had not been worth having to keep Genève a secret anyway—except that he had given her Avril and Nicollet.

"I'm so sorry," she said. She dropped to the girl's feet. "But this is the best birthday I could ever have."

Sylvia stood with her mouth open, her hands pulling on the collar of her red polo shirt, when the police arrived. Out in front of two officers walked the child advocate, dressed in plain clothes—a white cotton t-shirt and a flouncy green skirt.

She reached out. "Hello, Genève. My name is Paj Yang. I'm happy that you are safe. We have some things to sort out somewhere close to here. I'm going to stay right with you the whole time. Okay?"

"But this is our daughter, our biological daughter, I mean. She came all the way from Missouri to find me," said Pierre. "Can I come along? Please?"

Noelle stood next to him and nodded. She wanted to go too.

A police officer took a step forward. "He might've lured her here."

Pierre took a step back.

"I came here all on my own, sir," Genève insisted. "I found an article about him on my mom's internet history and I knew he had to be my dad."

Paj took another step out in front, standing between the officers and the others. "Everything will work out," she said. She reached out with one hand each to touch Pierre and Noelle on their elbows. "It does not look like you have any parental rights, and she is a minor. So, we're going to work through the system here. Noelle Nichols Sorenson, correct?"

Noelle nodded.

"I worked with your cousin, Bernard, for many years. And I know Mardi too. I'm going to do what's in the best interest of this young woman here, and right now she has been missing for five days. She needs care and we need to let everyone know she is safe. We can get in touch soon."

Genève touched her head to Pierre's silk tie again, whispering something so inaudible she wasn't sure what she'd said herself. It didn't matter.

She turned to Noelle and pointed to an employee wheeling a cart toward her. "It looks like they got you unstuck."

After Paj walked Genève to the car outside and the officers took down some information, Noelle took her purse and her giant Macy's bag with her belongings out of the cart.

She pulled the phone charger cord out from among the other merchandise.

"This is the only thing I really needed," she said. "It's just so hard to come in here and not spend two hundred dollars."

Pierre smiled at her. "We plan it that way."

Noelle fumbled with the charger as she studied Pierre's face. His brow was furrowed, but she wasn't sure if it was in anger or something else.

"I'm sorry," she said.

"Why are you sorry?" He didn't sound angry.

"Johanne—she was so nice to me that night we saw you at the eighth-floor exhibit and Holidazzle parade."

"Johanne is my life," he said. "I didn't see any other way back then. Maybe if the baby hadn't been a complete surprise, I would have had time to think about how to handle it all better."

Noelle wiped her eyes. "You know, that day in the old store hospital section of the tenth floor, I just wanted someone to want me. And now you are going to have to tell Johanne everything."

"I already have," he said.

Noelle didn't understand. "When?"

"That night, after Holidazzle. She just knew, and I had to let it out. I told her everything about you and the surprise birth, and about signing away my rights so you could give our baby to a waiting family."

Noelle was surprised Johanne had caught on that night. Wade had acted rudely but had not accused her then, maybe because he was already having his own affair.

"What did she do?" she asked.

"She took Paul and went to stay with her parents in Martinique for two weeks. I almost couldn't go on, but she came back to me. We tried to put things back together for a year, but she and our son are back in Martinique now.

She studies ecology and pesticides, and she landed a grant-funded project there."

"I'm so sorry," Noelle said. "I hope she comes back."

"It's strange," Pierre replied. "She called me last night and said I should come to visit my parents and our son. She had a dream about Genève. She said she didn't know why she cared, but she felt worried for her."

"She even knows her name?"

"Yes, she knows everything now. I hoped she could forgive me."

"It's taking her a long time, but maybe she will. Wade and his family just found out and it didn't go well."

"I'm sorry for you too," Pierre said.

Noelle's face brightened. "But our girl! She's so amazing."

"And Fran is the one who adopted her. That turned out all right." Pierre handed Noelle a cotton handkerchief from his breast pocket for the mascara staining her cheeks. "I have to go now if you are okay. I would like to place a call to Johanne and Paul."

"I have to go home too." Noelle touched Pierre lightly on the arm and walked to the red Formica lanes leading to cash registers. As he took off through the revolving door to Nicollet Avenue, she set the Macy's bag on the floor and the phone charger cord on the counter for the cashier to charge to her Target gift card.

Noelle gathered her belongings and pushed herself into the revolving door. As she circled, she heard pounding on the glass from another compartment. It was Gary, and in the next compartment came Fran, who smashed her face up against the glass. The door ejected Noelle out onto the sidewalk in time for her to see Pierre disappear into the Target corporate office. Gary, Fran, and an older woman circled back out and piled up behind her.

Mardi caught up to all of them and reached out to grab Noelle. "Have you seen Genève?" she asked. "She ran away and is here in town. And they know! They all know."

A cell phone rang and Fran pulled it out of her pocket. She talked for a minute while Noelle told the others that the police had taken her, probably to the police station or the social services center several blocks away.

"They wouldn't let me go along with her," she said.

Fran closed her flip phone and clasped onto Noelle's arm. "They'll let you come along if you're with me."

Noelle nodded toward the Target Corporation building, "Pierre was there too."

"We'll catch up with him soon, but now we just need to go see Genève," Gary said. "Back to the car!" They all followed him down the street to the ramp by Macy's, where they had first gone looking for Noelle.

Gary drove with Fran in the front passenger seat. Mardi sat in the middle of the back seat between Fran's mother and Noelle.

"I don't know where you've been, but you're sleeping at my house tonight," Mardi said. "Everyone will probably have heard about this by the end of the day."

"Wade kicked me out and I got fired. But you have enough going on with your move. I thought I'd go to Debra's place."

"Come to mine instead," Mardi insisted. "You can help me pack boxes."

Noelle agreed. She wondered if now was a good time to say something more to Fran. But it wasn't. Fran's shock at discovering Noelle was Genève's birth mother, and that she might not have dreamt up the idea that Pierre was possibly her father, was eclipsed by the only thing that mattered to her now—getting Gary to drive faster.

"By the way, *Joyeux anniversaire, ma cousine,*" said Mardi, putting her arm around Noelle. She squeezed her tightly. "How fabulous does it feel to be forty?"

44. Wheeling

"Tanya is on the phone," Irene said, holding Bernard's cordless receiver to her chest. "She wants to check on you."

Bernard maneuvered the wheelchair toward his front door. "I can't take the call. I have to go somewhere."

Irene talked into the phone and put it back on its base. "I never liked Tanya," she said, but then caught herself.

Mind. Own. Business.

Irene had only one purpose there: to help Bernard settle in after being discharged. It was Monday morning. She checked the dog's water dish and tried to pull her nose out of her son's affairs.

"I don't mean to nag, but did you take your nicotine?" she asked. "You told me to remind you."

"Yep," he said. "Chewed, not smoked."

"I hope the gum helps you really quit this time," she said. Then she couldn't resist asking, "Where are you going?"

"I'll tell you when I get back."

He got himself through the front door and headed down the temporary plywood ramp off his front porch. Dino followed him to the edge of the yard, and Irene stood there for a minute, her posture stiff, before she called the lab back to the porch.

Gary had offered to pick him up, but Bernard wanted to roll. He wouldn't be in the electric wheelchair for too long. The yacht club was only thirty minutes away, he guessed, although he'd never traveled there by chair. He rolled out of Irvine Park, crossed Eagle Parkway, then took a shortcut through the Science Museum of Minnesota to take the elevator that would bring him up a few stories so he could roll out onto Kellogg Boulevard. He wheeled along Kellogg, then turned right onto the Wabasha Bridge.

The Mississippi River often went unnoticed by people driving around in service of their busy lives. On foot (or on chair, as it were), and no car roof over him, Bernard saw a bald eagle circle and dive for its prey. Trees leafed out everywhere, outlining the riverbank in green. He looked down from the bridge and saw one small, uprooted tree traveling toward the bridge on its way downstream.

He watched for a moment, thinking about what Mardi had told him that morning on the phone. The school was closing. She had his classroom under control, but he would have to go in and say goodbye to his students.

If he hadn't been on a mission, he would have watched the tree until it floated under the bridge and beyond sight. Maybe such a morning meditation would have untangled one of the many knots in his head.

If nature provided meditation, industry gave St. Paul vibration. A train's whistle blew and its engine hummed as it chugged around the bend. A small plane flew over Bernard, preparing to land at Holman Field. The train crossed the trestle bridge. A towboat pushed a triple-barge load up the river.

Bernard stopped again midway across the bridge to look at Raspberry Island below. A rowing team set out for practice.

When the sidewalk ended on the other side of the Wabasha Bridge, Bernard kept rolling on Water Street. It was a good day for a spin, a good day to be out of the hospital.

It was a good day for anything and everything. Gary and his wife were bringing Fran.

Fran wanted to see where it happened. She wanted to be able to picture it, to face her fears of what could have happened and to see exactly how Genève made it out of the river's current alive. Gary begged Fran to hear the story from Bernard. It didn't have to lead to anything, but now they had Genève to connect them.

Her daughter had saved Bernard's life. Fran could at least be civil. She could at least say hello.

As he navigated the last section of the pathway between Water Street and the yacht club, Bernard saw her. Her melon-colored dress flapped open and exposed one thigh when she stepped out of Gary's car. It couldn't be the dress Irene had given her in 1976—the one Fran had joked made her look like an upscale Hare Krishna.

They walked toward the marina. Fran looked over her shoulder and saw Bernard wheeling up behind them on the dock. She froze for just a second, then she waved but only slightly, her fingertips touching Harriet Island air.

What did he expect? That she would run into his arms? That she would climb onto his lap and they would roll off into the sunset?

Gary walked over. He had that slight limp from his hockey days, made worse by too many years of working the sales floor. Bernard would need help getting his chair onto the dock. He felt self-conscious now, one crippled man needing aid from another one.

Fran didn't come toward him. She stood there, looking out at the water until Bernard reached her.

His hazel eyes brightened. "Hi," he said.

Fran smoothed her dress and ran her hands over the bow of its wrap-around sash.

Gary's wife caught up to them and took his arm. The couple walked back to the riverbank.

There were no other words at first. Bernard forgot about what Fran was wearing and just saw her. The same girl, now nearly fifty like him. They both had strands of silver in their hair. They both had creases around their eyes, but they were the same two people who had made love out on his family's sailboat on Lake Minnetonka.

There was still time.

Fran averted her eyes first. She pointed at the name *Pepperdine* painted in blue on the stern of the boat.

"I told you I would meet you at Pepperdine," she said. "Here I am."

It was only a nervous joke, but it cut him. It was more than thirty years ago that he thought she stood him up. Now he knew the truth, and she would soon know too. He pushed up off the armrests and stood.

"Should you do that?" Fran asked.

"A bit more each day. It's my second major back injury, third one altogether. I'm an expert at recovering."

She came one step closer to him. It did look like that dress. She had never been a clothes horse. Or one to buy a lot of jewelry either. He stared at the sailboat pendant on the chain around her neck.

Fran put her hand up to the charm. "I don't know why I wore it. Genève pulled it out of my jewelry box to borrow and I took it back just the other day. I hadn't worn it in years. Decades."

"But you still have it. You kept it."

Fran seemed reserved, so he willed himself not to touch her. She had not made a move to hug him either. He decided he could ask her about Genève.

Fran nodded. "She's okay. Paj—I hear you know her—she is supervising a lunch today for Genève and her newly discovered biological parents. It's good. I'm happy, but I wish she had gone about a safer way of finding them than running away."

"She's safe though. You must be so relieved," Bernard said.

"Yes. I hope everything is going to be okay for Noelle and her husband. Pierre and Johanne, too. Genève is only thirteen. She didn't stop to think about how her actions could affect their lives."

Bernard nodded and took both of Fran's hands. "Her actions saved my life."

They looked out at where it had happened. "She dove right in and pulled me up. I can't remember everything—mainly just the determination in those eyes, and in those strong limbs."

"She dove?" Fran said in horror. "She could have been paralyzed. It's as if I never made her watch *Joni*."

"I don't know, maybe she jumped. I was down below."

Fran squeezed back on his hands. "It's not as bad as I had pictured it here though. I'm glad to see it's more of a marina than a raging river."

"It's smooth on the surface and it's not too deep, but the undercurrent had a will of its own that night. Genève's will was stronger, luckily for me."

Bernard and Fran loosened their grip. She dropped her hands to her sides. "I can't stay long. Paj recommended a family mediator. Noelle and Pierre and I are going to talk about opening up some ways for Genève to get to know them. And for them to know her."

Bernard nodded. "I hope I will get a chance to thank your daughter for saving my life," he said. "And I want to see you again."

"There's just a lot of things that I need to deal with," said Fran, but she didn't back away.

Bernard listened as Fran explained how Paj was helping her through the system. He was selfish to think he could spend time with Fran now. His back ached, but he stood straight. "You've been through so much."

"It was hard. I've had some trouble pulling myself together lately, too, like you. I couldn't sleep for days, not even Saturday night—the day we found her—because I was so wound up. Last night was a little better. Of course, Genève has slept well at Gary's. And on your houseboat that night. She thanks you for the snacks and the shower."

Bernard beamed. The girl had slept there and eaten his food. He hadn't known.

"I'm glad the *Pepperdine* was there for her." He scratched the bridge of his nose. "You and Genève could sleep at my house tonight. I have lots of bedrooms."

He had blurted it out too abruptly.

There he was, thinking of himself again. He wished he hadn't said it, and he sat back down in his wheelchair. "I guess I stood up too fast. I'm sorry. Of course, you don't want to do that. The Gormans are great hosts."

"They are, they are." Fran lowered her voice. "But did you know they don't drink coffee? They don't even own a coffee pot. They gave me tea this morning."

Bernard pushed up on the armrests and stood again. "I have coffee."

Fran pulled on the bow loops of her sash as if to tighten it. "I do need my coffee when I wake up."

"And," Bernard said, encouraged to push it a bit further. "Technically, if you are opening the adoption, Genève is my cousin's biological daughter, so..."

Fran completed his sentence. "She is family. She's your second cousin, once removed. Or something like that."

"So, you'll stay? You can go to sleep at eight o'clock if you want. Seven o'clock! I won't keep you up, and in the morning, we'll have coffee."

Fran took a step closer to him again. Her sailboat pendant caught the sun between her breasts. The light shone in Bernard's eyes.

"Your mom can stay at my house too," he said, squinting. His own mother could go home, right after she made the confession she needed to make to Fran. He hoped Fran would still want to stay with him after that.

"My mom likes tea though, remember?" Fran said. "She's very content at the Gormans. I'll just need to go back there and pick up my things later. I have a load of laundry in their washer. Maybe you recognize this dress your mom gave me years ago. It was the last clean thing I had to wear."

"Speaking of my mother," Bernard said, "I think she owes you a new dress."

And then he did the unthinkable. He put his hand to Fran's chest, his fingers grazing her skin as he lifted the sailboat charm toward him and then dropped it back between her swells.

45. Tear Down

After all the work Mardi had done on her beautiful house, the buyers planned to tear it down.

"This is the new Wayzata," the realtor said, smiling into Mardi's glaring eyes.

So many people had discovered the ancient sacred place on Lake Minnetonka. Beyond the librarians who sat in the Wayzata Public Library atop the burial mounds overlooking the lake, few people had more than a clue about how sacred it was. The builders for the tear-down replacements knew. They crossed their fingers their mansion projects wouldn't run into Dakota Indian remains or artifacts that would cost them a year in delays.

The house that Mardi hadn't been able to sell before sold in two days at the asking price. She'd assumed the buyers were impressed by the 1940s woodwork, the stone around the entryway, the plaster walls.

But what really impressed them was the large lot at the end of Westwood Lane, close enough to walk into the town and to the lake, yet tucked away for privacy. They already had an architect.

Mardi leaned her forehead against the fireplace mantel and closed her eyes. This was the house where Ralphina had played with her sister, where secrets were kept, where art had lived, and where she had gutted the last traces of domestic violence. A teardown? She wished she could undo the deal and somehow pay her bills. She wished she had the Petit fortune, or at least that she could get her tanzanite investment back. Or her job.

The best she could imagine now was to buy a condo, or maybe move into an apartment with a roommate. Noelle wouldn't go to her parents now, not after how they had reacted. Carl wouldn't even come out of his garage.

Mardi's phone rang after the realtor left. "Speak of the devil. I was just thinking about you," she said before launching into the hideous plans the new owners had of taking a wrecking ball to the house and building a gauche new mansion in its place. Mardi held the phone close to her ear and let her cousin try to convince her that it didn't matter.

"I found out my tenants aren't renewing the lease," Noelle said, turning the conversation back to herself. "Anyway, I called to see what was going on with the painting we found. Did you ever reach *la ballerina?*"

"No luck with Ralphina," she said. "And what does your tenants moving out matter? You always get new ones. Surely you are not going to move into Grandma Greta's old shack."

"Yep. I'm returning to the wealth of our ancestors. God listens. Never forget that."

"Wrong ancestors!" Mardi shouted into the phone, laughing. "It's the Petits we mean when we pray for that— the French ones, remember? Not the launderers of Swede Hollow. Not the Petterssons."

"God listens, but he's old. Doesn't hear so great. Petit, Pettersson, you know. Practically the same name."

Mardi bit her lip, but God, how she had needed that laugh. "I'm sorry. I thought maybe we would get a crappy apartment and try to be roommates for a year."

Noelle was firm on her decision. "Maybe your brother can help me dig the East Side Pride billboard out of the front yard. Damn tenants cemented it in."

"His back is still no good. Plus, you probably can't pry him away from Fran before they head to Missouri. I can help you do the kitchen shelving paper though."

"Debra already called the shelving paper. But let's get together before that. We can job search. Or, hey, we could just sell that Henry Camlo painting and go to Marseille for a few weeks."

"You're supposed to stay out of the sun."

Mardi said goodbye and set down the phone. She rested her head against the fireplace mantel again for a long time.

The mantel surely made a dent in her forehead, which she went to inspect in her powder room mirror. She would have to explain it to the young man coming up to her door, the one she could see through the window as he stopped to touch her wicker settee.

Ralphina was the second person in ten minutes to have pushed the glowing circle next to the stone-framed door and heard the chimes coming from inside the house. She remembered when her dad had installed them in the sixties.

She would not be pushing that button if her nephew hadn't called, if Owen's car were not at this moment out on the curb in front of the house. His message sounded so insistent.

Mardi's messages she had ignored, not that it hadn't been tempting to call her back, but who knew what she was trying to pull.

Owen, on the other hand, was Owen. He never lied and would never make her go to any trouble if it wasn't important. He said he got some files from his old school counselor; reading what he had told the counselor made him remember something important that might still be in the house. And he thought he knew where.

Owen had known for some time that Mr. Petit's sister lived there, but he couldn't reach him. So he called her. She'd told him she was closing on the house the next day.

It seemed unlikely to Ralphina. Owen had met with a psychologist several times before he'd ever talked to Paj Yang. How would she have gotten new information from him? And what would be important enough to make him go back to that house, to Mardi Wirt's house? It wasn't like Vilda and Ken were rich, and certainly not Catherine and Andrew. There would be no hidden family jewels.

"Hi, Ralphina. Nice of you to come," Mardi said as she opened the door. If she meant it sarcastically, it didn't come out that way.

Ralphina wore a long shirt dress she'd thrifted. The top three buttons were undone, showing her smooth chest, upon which she wore no necklace.

She saw that Mardi wasn't so spritely now. Her eyes had circles underneath them and she didn't have that preppy-punk look today. Her angular haircut had grown out, and not in the intentional beach-blown style that was popular now. The angles were still there, but not the precise edge.

Ralphina's bitterness fell away when she saw her. "You look tired," she said. "And a little frumpy."

"You forgot 'unemployed.'"

"So that's why no Horst Rechelbacher hair cut."

"He doesn't practice anymore, so I'm waiting for a coupon deal at Fantastic Sam's."

Ralphina took a few more steps into the house and turned to the right to peek into the living room. She took note of the new floor and looked up in bleak acceptance of the change at the scene of the crime.

A loud creaking noise from above made Ralphina jump. "So, what is my nephew doing here? Does he seem okay?"

"He's agitated. He's looking for something. I assume it's the same thing I've been trying to reach you about, so I wanted to wait until you got here to show you both at the same time. He ran straight up to my music room and hasn't come down. I tried to tell him it's not up there."

"What's not there?"

Mardi headed up the stairs, but Ralphina moved ahead of her, veering toward the room that was supposed to be the master bedroom.

The short, square door to the dormer crawl space stood open.

"Owen?"

Ralphina heard no reply, only the quick and shallow breathing of a young man, and then a little cry. She ducked down and crawled through the door. Mardi came up behind her and got on her hands and knees.

In the crawl space, Owen sat under a bare pull-chain light bulb. In his lap, he stretched out an unframed canvas about two feet by sixteen inches. Ralphina walked to him, bending at the waist to avoid hitting her head on the sloped ceiling. She leaned over his shaking shoulders.

It was Catherine at maybe eight or nine. She wore a yellow cotton dress with white lace trim on a rounded collar.

"Ralphy. It's my mom. It's her. Look."

Ralphina put her hand on Owen's shoulder to steady herself, then knelt, her hair brushing the canvas.

She heard Mardi say, "There's another painting?"

The face on the canvas in Owen's lap looked back at Ralphina through time, through pain, through death.

So many times, Ralphina had pulled out old photographs, tried to connect with her, tried to cry. She'd felt almost nothing. It was as if she lost the memory of Catherine when she died and Owen became her own to raise.

Everything else in front of her disappeared, even Owen, and Mardi behind her. It was only Cathy and Ralphy now, in the crawl space where they had played, even though Catherine was so much older. More like a playful aunt than a big sister, really. The painting showed Catherine at the age she would have been soon before Ralphina came along.

Two tears fell from her eyes onto the painting. Owen brushed them away from the canvas.

"Hey, Cathy," Ralphina said. She rubbed her wet eyes against the back of Owen's shirt. "How did you know this was here?"

"I read the school counselor's old report, and then I just remembered the rest." His fingers traced the signature on the canvas. "Henry Camlo. Why...how?"

Ralphina peered closer. "The artist you wrote a paper about in middle school. You went on Mr. Petit's flood trip so you could see that harvest mural Camlo painted in the Red River Valley. You went in 1997, I think."

"We laid down thousands of sandbags. I'll never forget that trip or the mural. But I don't understand. I know Camlo did other work besides the WPA-style stuff, but did my mom ever tell you he painted her?"

"No, I don't think so. Nobody told me about it."

They looked again at the signature. Owen turned around and remembered Mardi was there, squinting under the bare light bulb. But this moment was between him and his aunt.

"Thanks, Ralphy, for taking care of me all those years," Owen told her. "I know you didn't get to have much of a life besides me."

"You were everything I needed then. You took care of me too."

Owen looked back toward Mardi. She asked, "Are you ready to see the other one?"

"There's another one?" Ralphina said. "A painting?"

"Oh boy, is there ever. I tried to reach you. I didn't know about this one. It's lucky Owen remembered when he did. My cousin Noelle found the first painting under the floorboards in the living room, but I wouldn't have found the portrait of Catherine. I'm turning the keys over to the new owners in the morning. They're tearing the place down."

Mardi looked like she regretted her last sentence, but neither became upset.

Ralphina said, "After all the work you've done to this place—that's too bad."

Owen rolled the canvas of his mother with care. They pulled themselves out of the cramped storage space and out the crawl door, one at a time, and descended the staircase into the hallway in front of the living room.

"I'm glad you two came," Mardi said. "You can help me say goodbye to the place after I show you the other painting. It's bigger."

"You know, there are plenty of good memories here." Ralphina pointed down the hall and turned to Owen. "Your Grandma Vilda's parents lived here with us in that bedroom for a while when I was little, after their tenement on Nicollet Island was torn down. That was your bedroom later on, Owen. Do you remember?"

Owen's eyes wandered down the hall, then toward the all-white kitchen. They all stepped into the living room and Owen's eyes drifted to the new floor. He handed Catherine's portrait to Ralphina. She saw his right hand slide into his pocket.

The loon rock—he always liked to hold it when he needed to steady himself. "They were right here," he said, standing next to the spot where Mardi had excised the stained piece of the subfloor. They stood in silence for a moment.

Just feet away from where the dead bodies had once lain, Mardi pointed. "Under the floor right here is where this Henry Camlo painting was hiding."

She reached over to a tube, pried off the lid, and pulled out the massive canvas. The three of them unrolled it. Ralphina propped the portrait of Catherine against a chair leg, as if to allow her dead sister to witness the moment.

It seemed so big, the size of a small mural. It took a moment for Ralphina to realize it was Dayton's. And then when her eye caught the nurse in the tenth-floor window, she sucked in a breath. Her eyes traveled to the lower right corner to see the name.

"Again, Henry Camlo," she said. "Henry Camlo painted my mother and my sister. Maybe we'll find a portrait of me next."

"I don't think so, Ralphy," Owen said. "Remember, he died in that flood in Waterbury, Connecticut, in 1955. The brass clock factory owner there wanted a mural in his old WPA style. You weren't born until three months later."

"My parents have a small Camlo," Mardi said. "Complete coincidence. I can show you that one if you want me to."

Owen hadn't stopped inspecting every square inch of the painting. Now he studied the nurse.

"Remember that Camlo painting we saw in the book at the library that looked just like Grandma?" he asked Ralphina. "I never told you that I saw it in college when a group of us took the train to Chicago. It's hanging there in the Art Institute of Chicago. I stood in front of it for so long, just feeling her presence. I figured it couldn't really be Grandma, but I loved the painting anyway because the woman looked so much like her. Maybe we can find a picture of it online. I think it's called *Wild Ride*."

"I remember," Ralphina said. "The woman in the blue wrinkled dress. And I just thought of something."

"What is it?"

"Vilda— her name is Swedish," Ralphina said. "Vilda means 'wild.' We have to go to Chicago."

Owen laughed. "I can't believe my grandma was friends with Henry Camlo. So, these are the valuable treasures my father wanted to find and sell so he could pay off his gambling debts. I told Paj Yang that my dad had heard Grandma say there was something she had to give my mom. I don't know if Grandma ever told her more before she died."

"But you knew somehow."

"I had this flash of a memory of a box between two beams. I don't remember seeing the portrait, but I feel like I've seen it."

"You were so little."

Mardi flashed a meek smile toward the big painting again. "Are you sure they were only friends?"

Vilda was a small presence within the large Dayton's building and the street scene with a delivery driver and window dressers. But there was something steamy in her manner, in how she reached out to an unseen patient with that hot water bottle. And then there was the inscription on the back.

Ralphina studied it all. "The store hospital," she said.

"A store with a hospital?" Owen asked.

Mardi nodded. "Just a couple of rooms, a small infirmary. More like the nurse's office at school."

Owen looked at the two of them curiously. "You've both been there? Did you get sick at work?"

"No, it shut down decades ago," Ralphina said. "I only recently learned Mom was a nurse at Dayton's before she got married. I thought she was always a school nurse."

"Somehow, Henry Camlo knew she worked there," Owen said. "Let's show June. Maybe she knows."

Owen explained to Mardi that June Skaalen was his grandma's friend who illustrated ads for Dayton's in the forties before they completed the switch to photography. Mardi started to tell him that she'd seen an illustration area near the infirmary.

Just then, Noelle let herself into Mardi's house. She shuffled into the living room, looking as exhausted as Mardi. "I see you have found the owner of the painting."

"Yes, and Ralphina's nephew here found a second painting upstairs."

"How lucky, and just in time," Noelle said to Owen. "I'm Mardi and Bernard's cousin, Noelle."

"It was Noelle who first recommended the Twin Cities Success School for you," Ralphina told him. "I didn't know back then that Bernard Petit was Mardi's brother, or that she and Noelle were related."

Noelle excused herself to go to the kitchen. She came back with a plum in her hand.

"Ralphy, how about if Mardi goes with us to talk to June?" Owen asked. "And her cousin too?"

Noelle's cell phone vibrated and she went back into the kitchen to take the call.

"Mardi has to get ready for the closing. She probably doesn't want to get caught up in our family mysteries any more than she already has."

"But Mardi took care of this place all these years, and she's Mr. Petit's sister."

Mardi couldn't help siding with Owen, if only to tease Ralphina. "Yeah, Ralphy. Let me come with you."

Ralphina gave Mardi a wry smile. They toured the house together, but Ralphina and Owen didn't dwell. They were ready to say goodbye to the place.

"Maybe Mardi can come to Chicago if we go to look at the other painting," Owen said. "And she can help us figure out what we're going to do about these. It's gonna take some work to conserve them. They look good, but the attic and inside a tube in a floor were not ideal conditions."

"My mom thinks I should tell you to talk to Bruce Dayton," Mardi said.

"Or the museum, to start," said Owen. "And an insurance company. The sooner the better."

Mardi ran her hand through her messy hair. "And call me. Let's talk as soon as I'm done with the closing."

Ralphina stepped toward her and gave her a light and unexpected hug. "Okay," she said. "If you really want to."

Mardi smiled. She didn't look so tired anymore. "I really want to," she pleaded. "And I also want to hear what this June lady has to say."

46. Specific Questions

With artwork of unknown value in her backseat, Ralphina took off for home. She wanted to sit with the art—with the brush strokes that formed her mom and her sister—before deciding whether to call a museum, or a private connoisseur, or maybe the university's art history department.

She thought she must be some sort of psychopath for how she had never grieved for Catherine in all these years. *Sure,* she thought, *while I'm driving down Highway 394, now I flood myself with tears.* She drove slowly, barely getting herself and the art home without causing an accident.

It had been so long since Catherine's death, but the grief was fresh. Ralphina unbuttoned her shirt dress, lifted it over her head, and slipped on a white nightgown. Sitting on her small Himalayan carpet, she straightened her posture, took a deep breath through her nose, and lifted her small Tibetan singing bowl in her left hand.

With her right hand, she picked up the wooden mallet. In a clockwise stirring motion, she pushed along the outer rim of the metal bowl. At first, the bell sang in too high of a pitch, reflecting her anxiety, so she slowed her motion and breathed more deeply. The tone deepened and began to soothe her heart. The heart was the chakra this particular type of bowl was meant to balance. She intensified the pressure of the wooden mallet against the metal and rounded the outside of the bowl again and again.

The bowl sang to Ralphina, calming her heart. With one ringing tap, she stopped and set it down.

She cried for Catherine. She had never cried properly for Vilda either. Her grief for that loss joined together with her sadness over her father's death. She rang the singing bowl again, and the resentments directed at Mardi unjammed and cleared away. Mardi could have sold the painting she and Noelle had found. Nobody had forced her to let Owen in at all.

She rang the bell with a tap for forgiveness.

And now the house on Westwood Lane was just a house. The house was not Catherine, nor Vilda, nor Ken, nor her childhood. It would soon be replaced with another house.

She rang the bell for letting go. She put it in a balloon and let it float away.

Something unexpected opened up in the space formerly occupied by grief. The tears falling on the curves of her body unblocked a different chakra, *svadhisthana*. The seat of creativity, yes. But also, lust.

She tried to continue her meditation, but she'd lost focus. Mardi wanted to see her again as soon as she was done with the closing and the move. That could be within a couple of days.

Ralphina hadn't felt so ardent about anyone in years, perhaps not since the day she kissed Mardi in the infirmary, back before she knew that Vilda had once worked there. She cupped her hand between her legs as she tried to continue her straight-backed pose. Monkey mind again. She saw orange, its glow vibrating. *Svadhisthana* was a terrible interrupter unless you were trained to harness its energy. She wasn't trained, but she didn't care. It felt good to recline back onto the carpet and let lust back into her life.

At four o'clock the next afternoon, Owen made his way from his apartment so they could drive together to Nicollet Island. It still wasn't time to decide about the paintings. Today, Ralphina wanted to unfurl them in front of June and watch her reaction. If anyone alive would understand why two Henry Camlo paintings were hidden in Vilda and Ken's old house, it had to be June.

June answered the door dressed and made up, her white hair elegantly coiffed, even though they had only called her one hour earlier. At eighty-six, she still had it. Her gold house slippers sported a kitten heel. Her black silk pants and tunic shone.

"My dears," June said. "Thank you for coming to visit."

"We brought things to show you."

Without giving her any more warning than that, Ralphina uncapped the tube inside the long muslin bag Noelle had sewn for it. As she pulled out the painting titled *Our Company* and rolled it across June's carpet, Owen pulled out the portrait of Catherine. They watched June's body language.

June's eyes went back and forth, then finally landed on the portrait of Catherine. "Oh my, what a doll she was, but I have never seen that portrait," she declared. "It breaks my heart. She was such a happy little girl."

Ralphina thought she'd moved on from weeping to seeking answers. But as June slumped, Ralphina's grief returned.

This time it was Owen who brought them back to the goal at hand. This wasn't a milk-and-cookies visit, nor another funeral. Owen had cried plenty over the years.

"Henry Camlo. You know who he was, right?" he asked pointedly. "I showed you the paper I wrote about him. But I didn't think you knew about him then."

"Oh sure, I did. He was famous for capturing the soul of the American worker during the Federal Art Project of the WPA, and for many years afterward."

"Yes," said Owen. "But not famous for capturing the souls of children. And the larger painting—that's Grandma Vilda, your friend, in the window of the tenth floor of the old Dayton's building. I've seen the same figure in another Camlo painting in Chicago."

"Owen, dear, I'm not sure what you hope I can tell you. What are you asking?"

"You are all we have now," said Ralphina. "Vilda and Ken are gone. Catherine is gone, and Owen's father is gone, too. There can't be any reason left not to tell the secret that kept these paintings hidden in the floor and rafters of the house."

"I'm making tea." June stood up and went to the kitchen. While she was gone, Owen pulled out a photocopy of Camlo himself and another of the *Wild Ride* painting that he'd seen in the Chicago museum and set them on the coffee table.

When June returned with the tray, they let her sit down and pour. She lowered her eyes to the photo of the painting outside of the train station. Vilda held an orange suitcase in one hand, golden hair mussed, and wearing a blue dress that had lost its properly ironed creases and just looked wrinkled.

June's hands wobbled, but she poured without spilling. *"Wild Ride,"* June read from the caption.

"Hmm, quite a title, June, don't you think?" Ralphina studied the photo of the painting. She'd never seen her mother looking so sedate and so happy at the same time. She'd never seen her mother unconcerned about a wrinkled dress. Vilda always put herself together seamlessly. In *Wild Ride*, one of the suitcase buckles was undone as if the clothes might spill out at any second.

"Lemon and honey," June said. She stood to return to the kitchen.

"Please," said Ralphina.

June sat back down. She kicked off her golden slippers and pulled her legs up on the sofa in the way a young woman might do, knees together off to one side and feet tucked behind her. *"Vilda* means 'wild' in Swedish. I guess the artist was making a playful pun."

Owen and Ralphina waited to hear more. They dared not push too hard.

"I don't know everything. Those were different times. People didn't need to blast it all about town."

"But you were my mom's best friend. Did Dad know Henry Camlo too? I wondered if he commissioned the pieces."

"I only know about the larger painting, and the Chicago one. We were so young then. Of course, she told me all about the train ride to Chicago. It was so exciting for her." June paused. "Not that she was looking out the window at the bucolic landscape."

June's hand flew to her mouth when she giggled. She didn't sound 86.

Ralphina emitted a yawp, knowing that some friends might look at *Wild Ride* and say Vilda looked like she just got laid.

But if she wanted answers, she couldn't act shocked.

"I don't know anything about the painting of Catherine. That's a bit mysterious. I didn't think Vilda ever saw Henry again after he brought her that huge canvas. As I said, we didn't talk about everything. We were always best friends, but maybe we stopped sharing so much as we matured."

June poured more tea. She gazed at Vilda in the window of Dayton's. "Oh, but she was beautiful, wasn't she? I was surprised when you told me you hadn't known she worked there until Ken mentioned it during one of his episodes. I worked right across from the nurse's station. They let me set up my own little illustration corner on the tenth floor, where my models could escape interest from the ad men."

Owen nodded. "What do you see in the painting?"

"See how he painted Vilda's hair here?" June pointed. "A tendril was always escaping from under her cap. Nurse Moholt was always after her to pin it back. See how the steam from the hot water bottle reddens her neck? Her skin was very sensitive."

"What else do you see?" Ralphina asked.

"See how she is handing the hot water bottle to someone in the shadows?"

They saw.

"That patient, you don't see who it is, do you?" June said.

"No," answered Owen. "The patient isn't in view."

"He painted as if from outside of the building, maybe as if he were a bird looking in."

"Looking in at what?" Owen asked.

"Why, looking in at this caring nurse, your grandmother... and trying to look in at himself."

"Himself?"

"The patient. The patient is the artist." June set her feet back down on the floor and into the slippers. "I shouldn't sit that way. I never learn! My legs have fallen asleep again. I have no blood circulation anymore." She rubbed her legs to bring them back to life.

Owen asked her if she needed help, but June recovered. "There is a story in the painting, isn't there?" Ralphina asked. "What happened in between Vilda taking care of Henry Camlo and him painting her in Chicago? Even if you don't know about the portrait of Catherine, you must know this."

June sunk her golden kitten heels into the carpet and sipped her tea, holding her head high. They were right. There was no need for secrecy now.

"Vilda was supposed to send patients home or to the regular hospital at the close of the day, but Henry was delirious. As she spent the night at his side, she fell deeply under his spell. My, but he was captivating. He wasn't so mysterious to me—he was one of the most well-known alumni of the Minneapolis College of Art and Design. He'd come back here after the Federal Arts Project ended to talk to some gallery owners about selling his work. But Vilda didn't know who he was. She just saw this sick, vulnerable laborer."

"So you're saying that, while engaged to Dad, Mom ran away and boogied down on the train with her sick but brawny patient? Am I catching on yet?"

Owen shot his aunt a look. June clicked her tongue to the back of her teeth. "*Tsk tsk.* Vilda and Ken loved each other truly. With Henry, perhaps it wasn't as you so bluntly put it. She had cured him of his illness overnight."

"I never saw her look at Dad like that, but she had Catherine and me to keep her busy. Plus, nobody wants to think about their parents' love life. Now, you're saying my Mom had a torrid affair with Henry Camlo."

"Yes, in fact, I am." June lifted her chin with impudence. "And I'm the one who drove them to the train station."

June stood, the tingling in her legs still bothering her. "It was all very sudden, and her mother—your Grandma Livdahl—nearly slashed the tires of my Dodge Coupe to stop us. Vilda's father was out of town. Vilda and Henry just walked from the store right over to the tenement here on this river island in the morning and started packing her suitcase. There was no way Mrs. Livdahl was able to hold Vilda back while this irresistible man was imploring her to come with him to Chicago."

"But what about Dad?" Ralphina whispered.

June put her head down and pursed her lips. "I don't think we need to continue. Of course, you are right. She made a mistake and then she returned home and that was that."

Ralphina quickly apologized. "No, don't stop. Please. I'm just surprised. I want to understand."

"Of course, my dear." June looked tired now, but she took a deep breath. "You know that Ken wasn't Vilda's first fiancé. They had been best friends in school. Some assumed they would marry. But after Ken shipped out to war, Vilda announced her engagement to this other man, Rodney. Within months, his plane crashed. It just failed, right over the Marshall Islands. The survivors witnessed him drowning. They couldn't save him. Vilda was heartbroken."

"I've heard a little about Rodney," Ralphina said. "He wasn't a secret."

"When Ken returned from the war, he got a great job at General Mills in the cereal marketing division. Vilda's parents were so happy when she started spending time with him again. They were pleased she had earned her nursing degree; losing Rodney was such a setback for her. They thought she may never marry. By then she was nearly twenty-six."

"A regular old hag." Ralphina scratched her neck.

"It was old then not to be married. Of course, I didn't marry until later either, but my parents had oodles of money and my mother perfectly adored how I'd become an illustrator. There was no such pressure from my modern family, not even when I divorced."

Ralphina made a mental note to ask June more about her family later, but she stuck to her inquiry. "And Dad's parents, they were happy? They always loved my mother."

"Oh my, yes," June replied. "They were relieved."

"Relieved?" Ralphina cocked her head. It was an odd word choice.

"I meant to say they were happy. Everyone, Ken's parents, his bosses at General Mills, his friends. They all just rallied around them. Before they knew it, they had a date for a church ceremony and veterans hall reception. But they set the date out a little further than was the norm then."

"Why was that?" Owen asked.

"Ken and Vilda were crazy about each other, but they weren't exactly possessive. They weren't in a hurry to commit for life. Vilda still wasn't really over Rodney, and Ken, well, Ken still had some growing up to do."

"And how did he react then when his fiancée boarded a train for Chicago with the famous artist?" Ralphina asked.

"Oh, he was fine," June said, Ralphina staring at her like she was a creature from another galaxy. "I should know. I'm the one who gave him the note from her."

Owen grinded his jaw. "He wasn't mad? Or jealous? I would go ballistic if my girlfriend did that."

"No, no. Now the parents were another matter. It was horrifying how they all behaved. Vilda's mother wanted to die. Her father returned from his trip and left again just to avoid the shame on the family. Ken's parents were nervous, but they tried to pretend they didn't know. Ken, however— when I told him—he was just sort of in awe of Vilda. He found a photo of Henry Camlo. I remember him showing it to me and saying, 'Well, you can't get too mad about that!'"

Ralphina looked like she'd failed a quiz. "I know Mom and Dad always tried to respect each other, to give each other so much space. But this is going too far, June."

"And then what did he do after you gave him the note and he said that?" asked Owen.

"I think he and his friend Neal just went up to Lutsen and went fishing or hunting or something for a couple of weeks. They came back at about the time Vilda returned, and then they went forward with planning the wedding."

"Neal Arvidson?" Ralphina said. "The same Neal who was Dad's best buddy their whole lives?"

"I'm surprised I need to spell it out for *you,* Ralphy. Things were the same in many ways back then, but we just didn't need to *say* everything. And we don't need to say it now either, although we should check in on poor Neal."

"Didn't need to say everything then or *couldn't* say it?" she asked.

How could she not have seen it?

"Point taken, my dear. It would have been very bad for his career and his family for him to have anything different than a traditional marriage. And Henry—well, he wasn't looking to marry. He had several more years as a bachelor.

He finally married right before he drowned in the flood out east in 1955."

"And marrying my grandpa worked for Grandma Vilda, too, because she had lost a fiancé and was getting too old to be unmarried," Owen said.

"And they were best friends," June added. "She never regretted it. Not at all, and of course she'd had an affair to remember with Henry. For a poor Swede from Minneapolis to spend weeks in Chicago with an artist as her lover—let's just say it was enough to last. After that, she and Ken had the time of their lives raising you girls, and with you, Owen."

Ralphina sat upright and scratched her neck again. Owen and June looked at her.

"We've always joked. Catherine was born just seven and a half months after they got married. Premature, supposedly, but a solid six and a half pounds."

June refilled Ralphina's tea. "That, dear Ralphy, is another one of those things that nobody needed to discuss. And Ken was the happiest man in the world to become Catherine's daddy."

"But Henry Camlo. Then he was her father," Ralphina said. "And Owen's grandfather!"

June simply nodded and put her feet back up behind her again, the habit that would cause her to complain again about her circulation in just a few more minutes. Owen sat in shock. He could barely breathe.

"Oh, but Owen! Ken loved you so much," Ralphina said, realizing it wasn't her news to yell out as she had. "And he was still *my* father."

Of course Ken was her father. She had been born in 1956, more than eight years after Catherine.

They all sat silently for a moment. "But we still haven't discussed the portrait of my mom," Owen said. They gazed at Catherine's dancing eyes in the painting. She looked at least seven if not eight or nine.

"You said you didn't know about it," Owen added.

"I didn't," said June. "She was a busy mother and continued to work part-time as a nurse in the school. That was considered quite a load back then. It wasn't even always allowed, but the school needed her."

June continued. "I stayed busy in my artwork up until photography took over ad illustrations completely. After that, my parents died and left me this." She looked around the Nicollet Island mansion. "I made other friends, and Vilda became involved with that Universalist church. Don't imagine she didn't make a friend or two there. Perhaps we both kept a few secrets after that."

June probably had a thousand stories, having been a working artist in the 1940s in downtown Minneapolis. Ralphina would definitely have to visit her more often.

"What secrets?" Owen asked. "Do you think Henry knew Catherine was his? And if he did, why did he let Grandpa Ken raise her?"

"Why of course he knew. He visited once that I knew of when he brought Vilda that larger painting. Ken saw it too. They showed it to me. Vilda wasn't ashamed about it then, but she obviously didn't have it framed either. She probably didn't want Ken's parents or her parents asking nosy questions when they came over, or to have to explain it to you kids when you got too smart. And as for Henry not being involved in Catherine's life, you can imagine he knew Ken loved her enough for the both of them."

"And didn't he love my mom?" Owen asked.

"There is something you must understand if you want to know the full truth," June said to him. "You are the grandson of an American artist. It is from him and from his daughter, Catherine, that you inherited your gift. But Henry loved people by painting them. His father was taken from him early to be put in prison and then killed in the Holocaust many years later. Henry didn't grow up with a father. He probably showed his love the best he could the day he painted Catherine."

Owen knew from his research in middle school, and from art history classes later, that Henry Camlo did not have his father in his life. His family had been Romani people, those that were called Gypsies by others. Henry's father was in prison for some supposed theft when Henry and his mother came to America in the 1920s. She'd hoped he would be freed and join them. But when they finally let him out, Henry was already grown up. They learned much later from an aunt that Henry's father had been imprisoned again, this time by the Nazis, for his ethnicity.

"I guess that Henry came back to Minnesota at some time to paint Catherine as his way of creating something for her to know him by. You can see his love in the brush strokes. I don't know why Vilda never shared it with her."

Owen shook his head. "She was going to though. Grandma told my mom about something she had to give her. And then my father wanted to get his hands on it. Remembering that is why I went back to the house."

June leaned over to Owen and caressed his shoulder. She was getting tired. "I can see Henry in your face," she said. "I always have."

"But June," Ralphina said, sitting straight up again. "Catherine and I, we look almost exactly alike—the golden-brown hair, the brown eyes, tawny skin. People always said we looked like our mother, but then they'd ask where we got such coloring. I never even thought twice about it. But I don't look any more like Ken than Catherine did."

"I don't know what to say," June whispered, her aged voice fading from overuse. "I mean, the next time Vilda talked to me about Henry was after he died. She and I watched the news together on TV. NBC did a retrospective on his work. And she didn't say anything. As I explained, people's right to know things now has become more important than people's right to privacy. It used to be the opposite."

"But knowing who gave you your genetic material is not just 'things.' You have a right to know, in my opinion," Ralphina said. She knew they had worn June out and would have to leave shortly.

"Maybe so," June said.

"I saw that NBC retrospective," Owen said. "We watched it at the Minneapolis library when I wrote my paper. I never imagined he could be my grandfather. Grandma Vilda must have been so sad when he died in the flood."

"She wanted to know more before she would even believe it," June said. "I went to the library with her and we ordered copies of the *Waterbury Republican* and the *Waterbury American* newspapers. I remember how upset she was. And how she also had such terrible morning sickness because she was pregnant with you then, Ralphy. She was sick through that entire pregnancy."

They all sat back in their seats for a moment.

"So that was in 1955," Ralphina said. "And then I was born early the next year."

"And, Henry had just visited Grandma recently," Owen said. "We know that because he painted my mom, and she looks like she's about eight...as she would have been in 1955."

"Yes, maybe just at about the same time, and maybe Ken was on one of his fishing trips up at Lutsen with Neal." June said.

"Henry Camlo is my father too then," Ralphina said.

June rested her elbows on her knees and stared across the table as if trying to will a genie to pop out of the teapot and explain everything.

"Dad must have had a sense of humor about us being the children of a famous artist," Ralphina added. "Whenever Catherine and I would make a mess with our art supplies, he would just throw up his arms and exclaim, 'Can't get too mad about that!' Just like you recalled him saying about Henry Camlo's photo."

June laughed. "I always thought it wasn't my story to tell, but I do feel lighter now. Vilda and Ken are smiling down on us all. And Henry too."

"And my mom, she's at peace," said Owen, beaming at the painting of his mother in her yellow dress. He took the decoupaged loon rock out of his pocket and ran his thumb over its surface. "Maybe my father is too."

47. All Aboard

From the parkside approach, the neoclassical columns of the Minneapolis Institute of Art shone in contrast to the South Minneapolis neighborhood kept dark by residents who feared their electric bill.

The priceless art in this respected museum didn't stretch out across Uptown or downtown. It didn't preen from some Linden Hills lookout over the city's lakes. This museum stayed anchored right where it had risen in 1915, in the Whittier neighborhood. Now, it sat within blocks of the housing projects at Little Earth of the United Tribes, within smelling distance of the nation's first Somali restaurants, and within earshot of Karaoke night at the Little Tijuana Bar & Restaurant.

Perhaps its convenient location next to the Minneapolis College of Art and Design kept the museum in place when poverty and crime caused turnover of the nearby Victorian mansions.

That and the millions of tons of marble. It wasn't going anywhere. With Target Corporation as the lead funder, the museum built on a massive new wing.

On a June evening, the second level of the museum hummed in anticipation. Henry Camlo was their own man. Members of the press from Chicago, Los Angeles, and New York City murmured their amazement that a Camlo painting from the 1940s would be unveiled in 2007. Art lovers flocked to see it before busloads of school kids, couples on dates, and people without homes coming in from the winter cold would see it too.

The subject of the painting was a secret, but it was rumored that the acquisition came as a gift from someone unknown, and that it was the larger and more important of two paintings that had been uncovered at an older home in Wayzata.

A white cloth hung over the painting. Red velvet ropes surrounded a portable dais underneath it.

To the side of the dais, a ninety-year-old man stood next to an elegant woman dressed in blue silk. Bruce Dayton was not bent over, as one might imagine for someone living in such an old body. Ruth Stricker Dayton, his wife and partner in philanthropy, was a health and wellness trailblazer. His fine posture aspired to match hers.

A willowy woman on the dais furtively tickled the inner forearm of a woman whose hair had been shaped into new angles at an Aveda salon that morning.

These two women, Mr. Dayton knew, were Mardi Wirt, daughter of local financial advisor Edward Petit, and Ralphina Beranek, whom he had just met in these strange circumstances. He would not have known about the tanzanite earrings Mardi wore for the first time in years. The mine she'd invested in was running again, she learned that morning.

Dayton had also just met Ralphina's nephew, Owen Hess, and the white-haired woman in a Nehru jacket. June Skaalen, he knew, worked as an ad illustrator in his family's business long ago and he invited her over to stand with Ruth. June slipped under the ropes to adjust Owen's tie. She stepped back down and nudged Owen's girlfriend, Lisa, up onto the dais.

Standing behind some other museum donors were Bernard Petit and Fran Hart. Despite Bernard's cane and

Fran's recent days of desperation as the mother of a missing child, the two glowed. Genève Hart stood a foot away from her mother, her eyes taking in the beauty of the place. And there was Pierre St. Hilaire, whose hand Genève held, and Noelle, whose hand held hers.

Paj, newly married, came with her husband. Her four-month pregnant belly popped up under a fitted red dress.

Fran wore a Diane von Furstenberg wrap dress similar to the original 1976 one she owned in melon, only in the red-plum color of a Dr. Pepper can, which Fran chose herself. Irene Petit bought it for her at Nordstrom that morning—at the full price of four hundred and twenty-eight dollars. Not bad, considering she would probably wear it for thirty years or more. Accepting the dress, along with brunch at the Mall of America's Nordstrom store, signaled her acceptance, too, of the apology Irene offered.

A sailboat pendant swayed and rolled between Fran's breasts, stunningly accentuated by the wrap dress.

Next to Irene stood Edward Petit. When they noticed Ralphina running her finger along the inside of Mardi's wrist, Edward glanced at his wife. It was a look that, after fifty years of marriage, Irene knew meant: *Have you learned not to interfere, or will we need to leave?*

Irene had learned, and anyway, she wasn't going to miss the art event of the year.

Everyone old enough to be trusted with a drink so close to the art held a champagne flute. Most flutes held Prosecco. Some held Pepin Heights sparkling apple cider, which effervesced the same.

The curator for American art approached the dais. A few notes sounded from the grand piano, and the noise level dropped. She took the mic.

"We have an unusual unveiling tonight. It's a painting by Henry Camlo with a story behind it that can't yet be fully told. As lovers of art, I think we can all appreciate that this mystery is part of the gift. Now, we will each decide the meaning of the art with our own ways of seeing. This is what an artist for the people would have wanted."

She continued, "There is a special young man who has made tonight possible. Our friend, Mr. Bruce Dayton, will introduce him."

The elderly man stepped onto the dais. He put a hand on Owen's shoulder. "Owen Hess is a young artist and future art teacher who shares a special connection with Henry Camlo. Those of you who know about the business started by my grandfather will see why I wanted to be here tonight, but the evening belongs to Mr. Hess."

The pianist played to a quick crescendo. Owen motioned to Ralphina to share in the honor. She stepped up to the painting and they each grasped one side of the white cloth.

They raised it aloft, then dropped it to the floor.

"It's Dayton's," the people murmured. "Dayton's on Nicollet Mall!"

Ralphina and Owen stood to the sides so they could all examine the painting. They could hear people comment as they discovered the nurse among the other workers. One connoisseur said, "The nurse resembles the female subject of Camlo's *Wild Ride*."

The curator again stepped up to read the plaque:

Our Company, by Henry Camlo, American, born in
Hungary. 1915-1955

Oil on canvas

This painting depicts a scene of and around the building at 700 Nicollet Mall in Minneapolis, architect Charles S. Sedgwick, for George Draper Dayton. The store, first Goodfellow's, soon became The Dayton Dry Goods Company and eventually Dayton's.

Camlo, known for painting the American worker, included in this work not the glamour of the store nor its well-heeled customers, but those who kept the operation running day in and day out: A delivery truck driver, seen only as his hands upon the wheel, and a window display designer are seen at street level. Camlo placed a nurse in the window of the tenth floor, where Dayton's employed staff to care for those who had fallen ill, customers and employees alike.

She stepped down from the stage. The crowd clapped again.

The pianist played a few notes and an assistant to his side handed Mr. Dayton a velvet pouch. Mr. Dayton pulled a small bronze rectangle out from the pouch and held it out. The assistant applied a beaded line of glue to the back and Mr. Dayton pressed it into the spot outlined for it at the bottom of the larger placard. He read aloud.

Donated by Owen Hess, in honor of his grandparents, Vilda Livdahl Beranek and Ken Beranek, and their daughters, Catherine and Ralphina. The family also honors Mardi Wirt for her integrity in returning the art discovered on her property to the family, and thus to you, their community. The Minneapolis Institute of Art dedicates the installation of "Our Company" to every person who ever worked at Dayton's.

Mr. Dayton shook Owen's hand. Owen leaned in and thanked him.

The crowd began to mill toward Owen and Ralphina, preparing to ask questions they would not answer until after the *Star Tribune* reporter had completed the exclusive story the family promised to him.

Genève pulled her hands back from Noelle and Pierre and leaned into her mom.

She knew that Bernard was coming back with them. She hadn't figured out her mother's exact future with Bernard yet, but she knew he was taking Fran to see *The Police Reunion Tour* in St. Louis in July. She knew Pierre had asked permission to take her—Genève—on a vacation at that same time.

They hadn't told her what would happen after that. She tried not to ask about things that maybe they didn't even know.

So she asked, "Don't we all have to get up early to drive home tomorrow?"

"We're getting up early to have breakfast with Mr. Gorman and his wife, and to pick up Grandma from their house," said Fran. "You and Grandma will take our car, and Bernard and I will drive with his dog. We'll spend an evening in Kansas City on the way."

"I wish Dino could ride with me," Genève said. "When we get home, can I please be allowed to see Zoe?"

"Oh my goodness. That's what I've been meaning to tell you. I'm sorry I said you couldn't see her. I was overreacting about something else, and I never should have taken it out on your friendship."

"Good, then let's have her over right away," Genève said. She paused. "Does our hotel in Kansas City have a pool?"

"You want to swim?"

"I need to get in a practice if I'm going to ask the coach about staying on the swim team."

Fran kissed Genève on the side of her head.

Bernard squeezed her hand. "Knowing how you swam in the river current, I can't wait to see you compete in a pool," he said.

Genève wished a good night to all the other people she had met. It wasn't over, all the questioning about who she was and how she would relate to all of them in the future. But she was ready to go home.

Irene couldn't believe that after she'd finally let St. Paul grow on her, dear Bernard was moving all the way to a suburb in Missouri. The Twin Cities Success School had been shuttered.

Her daughter was heading east too, but just for a long weekend. She approached Mardi and Ralphina.

"I hope you enjoy Chicago," Irene said. "Just don't forget to come home. We'd like to take the two of you to dinner. Do you prefer the club or Blue Point?"

"Either one would be wonderful," Ralphina answered.

"Mom, why don't we all make dinner at your house?" Mardi asked. "Then we can show Ralphina your own Henry Camlo piece."

Looking around in hopes that anyone else had heard that she owned a Camlo, Irene said a little loudly, "What a good idea! I don't know why *I* didn't think of showing her our own modest little Camlo."

Owen heard this from behind them and smiled. He had not been invited, and that was okay. He would want to see it eventually, but he was old enough now to have other plans. He kissed Lisa on the cheek. They looked back up at Owen's grandmother, painted in the window of the tenth floor of Dayton's.

Lisa shook her head. "My boyfriend, famous patron of the arts."

"It was really Mrs. and Mr. Dayton, you know," Owen said. "They knew we would have sold it to private collectors because that's a lot of money to us. We wouldn't have had anywhere safe to put it, anyway. They bought it from us and then turned around and donated it in my name."

Owen kept the small childhood portrait of his mother, and that was enough. Catherine, newly framed, graced the wall above the wicker chair Mardi gave him from the house on Westwood Avenue. The decoupaged loon rock he once made with Catherine rested on a side table. He decided to no longer carry it in his pocket.

"It was beautiful of them to do that," said Lisa, setting her cider flute on a tray. "It's for everyone to enjoy now."

Owen and Lisa's suitcases sat packed and ready in the car, where Ralphina and Mardi also headed. They got in, and Ralphina drove them away from the bright museum into the darkness of the neighborhood, finally pulling into the parking lot of the Amtrak station. They would make it into the city by morning, and to the Art Institute of Chicago by noon. And then when the early evening light would be just right, Owen said, he would like to paint Lisa out on Navy Pier.

The conductor welcomed them aboard. Exhausted, Mardi and Ralphina said goodnight to Owen and Lisa, and Ralphina resisted hugging him. It was hard now that he was a man, but she had chanced upon someone else to hold onto.

Owen hugged her anyway. "That unveiling was the most fun thing I've done since I went on the Red River Valley flood trip when I was a kid. No! It was even funner."

Ralphina nodded. Owen was too old to correct now. "It was funner than anything I've ever done, too."

"Good night, Ralphy."

The two couples slid the doors to their sleeper cars closed. The train glided slowly out of the station. The track below them clicked into place, and the train surged ahead, rounded a curve, and picked up speed to race into the wild night.

48. Martinique

Pierre St. Hilaire's parents lived in a blue and chartreuse chateau with white trim, at the edge of northern Martinique's interior rain forest.

It would have been enough if this whole trip consisted only of the red-eye flight with Pierre and breakfast with Genève's biological grandparents, followed by a nap infused with the fragrance of the local sweet banana trees surrounding the chateau. But there was more: a long drive down the mountain into the region of rum distilleries and pineapple, where they picked up Pierre's wife and son at the gate of her parents' red-roofed white villa.

Genève greeted Paul as he climbed into the back seat, but he looked straight ahead at the seat in front of him. Johanne handed him a box and he presented it, as instructed, to Genève. She opened it to find light, airy cookies.

"*Macrons.* My mother sent more of these for our dessert," Johanne said of the supplement to the large picnic lunch Pierre's mother had packed for their day at the beach. "But these are yours and you may try one now."

Paul gently kicked the back of his mother's seat, but she didn't turn around. He finally turned his head toward his new sister, who handed him a cookie.

With no further introductions planned—no need to push things—they drove on.

Genève looked out her window. "Is that Mount Pelée?" she asked. She'd done her research, so she already knew it was and what Pierre would likely say next.

"The volcano killed thirty-thousand people in 1902 when this village was the capital of Martinique," he said.

The son of tourism entrepreneurs, he delivered his lecture on island history until they reached *La Plage de la Batelière.* The beach spread out behind the hotel where Pierre and Johanne once honeymooned, but he insisted he chose it because it was the safest for swimming on the whole island.

Genève ate just a morsel of most of the delicacies her new grandmother packed, but more than her share of the salt cod fritters, soaking them in the peppery dipping sauce. She regretted it when the adults made her wait thirty minutes after eating to swim. Making sandcastles with Paul filled the time and helped them find their words.

The only blue water she'd seen before was in the chlorinated pools at her swim meets. This blue water here in the Caribbean Sea was home to little violet and yellow fish. Genève and Paul donned swim masks and watched them flit in and out among the coral.

Johanne watched, Pierre at her side, and she swatted at his hand that kept coming back to caress her. "*Merci,*" he whispered. He kissed her ear, and she swatted his hand again but let it rest on the outside of her sarong.

Pierre's hand slid regretfully off of her leg as Johanne stood to walk toward a vendor who strolled along the beach with a Polaroid camera around her neck. The vendor's eyes were trained on the tall girl who now ventured out of the shallows. Genève jumped as a clear wave billowed toward her, and the woman snapped a single shot. Johanne approached the woman as she pulled out the film and watched the picture appear.

Johanne looked, and said, "*Je la prend.*"

The photographer aimed her camera and captured another photo of Genève jumping over a wave just before she twisted around and backstroked over to Paul. Johanne nodded and held up two fingers and was given two more instant photos, these of the children floating on their backs, side by side, on a bed of turquoise sea.

She reached into the fanny pack she had slung around her sarong and handed the photographer some euro coins. The color deepened in the photos she would give to Paul and Genève, one for each. The Polaroids of Genève jumping the waves would go in tomorrow's mail, one for Fran, and one for Noelle if she could find an address.

Johanne walked back to their spot on the sand and lay prone with one cheek to the beach blanket and an eye toward the children. With an exhale but not a word nor swat of the hand, she let Pierre rub sunscreen lotion onto her back.

49. The Wealth of Her Ancestors

The tenants vacated Noelle's house on the street above Swede Hollow. She and Dakota the parakeet had been living in Gary Gorman's basement for weeks. For the first time in her life, her own place awaited.

Gary and his wife helped her, and Gary also recruited Kalmer. Fired from the department store for his second time, Kalmer was newly minted as a proud and reliable mail carrier for the United States Postal Service.

Gary knew the whole history of the area, of course. After they finished moving, he, his wife, Noelle, and Kalmer sat down at a local *taqueria* and he told them about the Indian village of Kaposia. It had been right there on the East Side, just below the river bluffs. For once, Noelle didn't roll her eyes at Gary's history lecture. She saw herself and her family now as inlays to this rich brocade he wove. Not perfect inlays, but shapes that contributed to the whole, even if bubbled and frayed.

Kalmer downed seven tacos as Noelle wondered what new texture, what unexpected thread would next hop onto Gary's loom. Noelle paid the bill.

The next day, she found herself all alone in front of the seasonal Dari-Ette drive-in, owned by St. Paul Italians and open for its fifty-sixth season. The sun glared through the humid July air, and her t-shirt stuck to her skin. A vanilla sundae with strawberry and pineapple topping cooled her down at an outdoor table.

Noelle's dad had taken her there once, ages ago it seemed. Lunch didn't appeal to her now, but she ordered a pizza burger with a side of spaghetti to eat later. She'd come this way to fill out an address change form at the post office across from the Dari-Ette.

Children played at the playground next to the post office as Noelle drove up the street to what she knew as Parkway Elementary School. She wondered where Avril and Nicollet would go to school now. The divorce would cost her and Wade, and the private French School had not been cheap.

Wade's math tutoring centers had begun to falter. The economy shook. Families who could afford tutoring found that strip mall centers were more convenient than malls. Nobody cared about the taffy anymore. Sugar was suddenly *toxic,* and so was food coloring. Wade and Kathy spent months preparing for an expensive rebranding effort.

Parkway Elementary might be it if the kids were to live with her during the school week.

Except it wasn't Parkway Elementary.

According to the sign above the entryway, Parkway Elementary was now called *L'Etoile du Nord* French Immersion School. A French Immersion school on St. Paul's East Side?

Noelle pulled over next to the curb and read the sign again. Underneath the brushed stainless steel letters was a smaller placard that read "St. Paul Public Schools." A strange mirage, to be sure.

She opened her car door and walked up to the door. It was locked but taped to the door was a sign. It read, *Job openings for Fall, 2007: 1.) Office manager, full-time, some French required 2.) Fifth-grade teacher, advanced near-native French fluency required. Apply on the district website.*

She imagined herself trying to speak French with the teachers and principal. The principal, a round-faced woman with regal African braids, was pictured on another sign taped from inside the glass door. She studied the job sign again. At least she could tell Mardi about the teaching position. Mardi had gotten into the groove of things while subbing for Bernard during the last weeks of school, and now that the school was belly-up, she would be looking for something. Maybe teaching. Mardi and Ralphina wanted to travel in the summers.

Noelle climbed back into her car and drove down Johnson Parkway. The parkway turned left onto East Seventh Street and she drove past a taco truck, a *panaderia,* and a dozen signs in Spanish and Hmong until she was home.

She stepped into the house, leaving the pizza burger and spaghetti on a shelf next to the vintage plaid hot water bottle she'd taken from the old infirmary. She'd meant to give the medical antique to Ralphina and Mardi, but now she wasn't sure. Maybe she would hold onto it for now.

The bird chirped, bobbing its head toward the fruit basket also sitting on the shelf. The former renter had left the fruit, maybe feeling sorry for her, Noelle imagined. Next to the fruit was the framed wedding photo of her Petit grandparents. Grandma Greta's blue eyes shone lactescent in the colorized old photo. If for just one moment Noelle could have her here, her grandmother could take her by the hand and show her around the home that had been her own for so long.

Not that there was much to see, and not that Noelle would stay, not for sure anyway. She promised herself to stay only if it felt right for her future.

Not for wallowing in the past of dead ancestors, wealthy or poor.

The tiny place would have to be kept neat. The dining alcove off of the kitchen would serve as her room so Avril and Nicollet could each have one of the two small bedrooms. Genève planned to visit her for Thanksgiving and then she would put her two children in one room and give the teenager the other. One of the families she'd rented to over the years roomed five kids in the home. She would manage.

She peered through the lace curtains at the East Side Pride sign in the front yard. She could start digging that thing up and getting it out of there.

The ones who erected the sign had been three tenant families ago. But to Noelle, there wasn't much difference.

All three families had been Mexican, and they all kept the sign up. They all planted flowers around it. All the husbands worked construction. All the wives ran their own various businesses from the home—the most recent one being a drapery shop, which was why a new set of custom lace curtains now framed the windows instead of the JC Penny drapes Noelle had provided. The tenant left the new ones behind for Noelle, insisting they were meant to go with the house.

Noelle looked closer at the lacy white curtains. Seed pearls covered the tiebacks and valance. Grandma Greta would have been amazed that anyone would put that kind of work—that pride—into sewing the same grand curtains for her own house as for a paying client. And then to *give* them away.

It was even hotter inside the house than outside, so Noelle opened the back door to catch a breeze. A shovel leaned against the house. She laced up her tennis shoes and went out to get it. It might not be easy to dig up the concrete footings for the yard sign, but she could try.

As she walked around to the front, a feminine figure came up the street, a black-haired woman wearing a knee-length skirt with tall red socks and carrying a flat of bedding plants.

"Hello! Hello!" the woman cried.

Noelle had usually only spoken to her tenants over the phone or email, and she hadn't seen the curtain maker since the day the couple signed the lease.

Noelle leaned on the shovel as the woman strode up onto the lawn.

"I usually plant flowers around the sign at the beginning of every summer, but we got so busy when we bought our house."

So, it was her. Her Spanish accent was strong.

The woman had already moved into her new house. *Why did she bring the flowers here,* Noelle wondered.

The former tenant looked at the shovel in Noelle's hands then at the sign. She knit her eyebrows together. Twelve begonias, three rows of four plants each, sat in the short box. They were red, pink, and orange, all riotously ruffled, like the skirts of the Venezuelan dancers Noelle had once seen performing at St. Paul's Festival of Nations.

"I was just going to come out and do some yardwork." Noelle fluttered her eyelashes, not knowing why she lied.

It was her house and she could take down the East Side Pride sign if she wanted to. Instead, she looked around for something to shovel. She found a small pile of last year's mulch around one of the posts and began to redistribute it toward the middle.

"See?" she said a little too loudly with great enunciation. "Yard. Work."

This woman wasn't her tenant anymore. She was her neighbor. Noelle had rarely talked to neighbors at Bush Lake. She picked up a begonia in a peat moss container. The neighbor showed her how to open the bottom of the peat so the roots could grow more easily into the earth, and then she shoveled a hole.

Noelle planted a pink begonia first, then an orange, then a red. Her knees sunk into the rocky soil, sweat pooling behind them and dripping down her calves. When they'd planted all the flowers in the ground surrounding the sign, the two women stood back by the curb to see how it looked.

"You need something by the steps." The neighbor pointed. "My kids always planted tomatoes and peppers there for salsa, but it's late in the season to start those."

Noelle turned her head to the wide front steps. She had hardly noticed them before. They were old, lustered stone, not concrete like at the modern house near Bush Lake.

The neighbor touched her arm. "You come to see our new house now." They walked silently up the street and around the corner, and there it was, another house that couldn't have had more than two bedrooms. Yellow paint peeled away from the wood and a crabgrass lawn sprouted in patches and tufts.

"I'm sure you'll make it look nice," Noelle said.

The neighbor pulled up her red socks.

"It just needs new paint and a garden," she said. "Maybe a white clover lawn, good for hungry bees. We will build a deck for barbecue. You come join the party. *The more the merrier*—it is the right way to say in English, no?"

"We don't say that as much around here," Noelle said.

All of the stress of the past weeks—no, not just stress—all of the *fear* she had carried for the past thirteen years, or maybe even for her whole life, it all came up, wanting to escape, and yet it lodged itself in her sinus cavities.

As she walked home, she realized she had not thanked the woman for the fruit, begonias, or curtains. She would buy her a housewarming gift soon.

Without changing out of the dirty clothes she'd worn digging in the yard and sweating all day, she crept onto her bed and slept. When Noelle awoke at noon the next day, her sinuses had cleared. She undressed before she even rose from her bed.

Naked, she walked to the bathroom. It needed remodeling, but the tub worked and the water felt cool. Dirt dissolved off her hands and knees with the new bar of lavender soap Gary's wife had given her.

A single peach towel was all she had to dry off with, and she remembered that her bathrobe lay folded in one of the boxes in the living room.

She looked in the mirror. Her body was untanned now, and more supple. The stretch marks stood out, but she felt young again, her body her own.

She wrapped the towel around her body and went to check on the parakeet's food and water. When she saw the perch beneath the mirror was empty, she expected to see a stiff feathered carcass on the floor of the cage. Had she forgotten to feed the damn thing?

Dakota wasn't dead. It was sitting in its dry, green, plastic bathtub. It chirped.

Noelle slid the cage door up and scooted the bird out of the dry tub. She took the tiny tub to the kitchen sink and ran an inch of warm water into it, walked back, and set it in the cage.

The bird stepped back from the water and turned one black eye toward Noelle. It climbed up the series of sandpaper-covered perches, sidled over to a plastic perch in front of the mirror, and stared at its reflection for a moment.

Then—*flap, flap, flap*—small feathers rose up in the air and the bird glided off the perch for a splash-landing.

"Fucking bird," Noelle muttered, waving the airborne feathers from her face.

She grinned, though. Avril and Nicollet would like to watch it frolic in its tub.

"*L'oiseau, il fait son bain,*" she practiced saying.

A sudden thud outside her door startled Noelle.

She remembered that her mailbox was affixed to her house, unlike at Bush Lake where it stuck out from the end of the long driveway as if the mail wanted to stay as far away from her family as possible.

Securing the tail end of her towel tightly under her armpit, she opened the front door in time to see curls hanging down from the back of a mailman's cap. His hair was growing back from his short Macy's haircut, but he'd lost the mullet. It had long faded from new penny to old penny, as red hair will do, and a few white strands.

The bloom was off the rose of Generation X, perhaps, but they didn't feel that way yet. They felt more alive than ever.

"Hey!" Noelle said. "You can't say hello? You didn't tell me they gave you my route."

Kalmer turned around and put his right hand over his heart.

"It's going to be hard to keep my mind on it now," he said, looking away from her towel-covered body as best he could. "I'll come back. Soon!"

Noelle watched his shoulders rise and roll underneath his summer uniform shirt as he adjusted his mailbag and ambled down her walkway, past her East Side Pride sign. The way he held his bag flexed the arm muscles under his Vikings football tattoo.

A quickening in his step sent waves under the Viking ship on the back of his burly calf. She still didn't care for tattoos, or for football, but she tilted her head and watched the Viking ship sail toward the road. She ran her fingers through her wet hair and considered Kalmer's gait.

Seaworthy, I bet.

Leaning out just enough to reach the mail without anyone seeing her barely covered body, Noelle stuck her hand into the metal box and pulled out a local directory. She felt around to all four corners of the bottom but found only one more piece. Her fingers latched on, pulling it out of the box and into the house in one motion.

Her eyes settled over the small blue envelope, stamped with French postage and an invitation to *Découvrez la Martinique!*

Whatever it was, she didn't deserve it, not by far, she believed. She'd already been given far more than she was entitled to.

But there it was, her old address crossed out and her new address on the wide label affixed.

Printed in a typed line all the way across the envelope she read:

Please forward Please forward Please forward

Noelle slid her fingernail under the flap.

The End

Acknowledgments

This story exists because I worked at Dayton's. Maybe you worked there too; maybe you helped make it the kind of place I couldn't get out of my head thirty years later even though I only worked there for three years. If you worked on the sales floor or in the sub-basement, at one of the malls known as "the Dales," or you drove the delivery trucks, or cleaned the bathrooms, or if you worked in the offices, or wrapped gifts with both whimsy and precision, or if you worked in credit and helped me apply my paycheck directly to my Dayton's card bill, or served the popovers and wild rice soup at the Oak Grill Room—I know you have your own stories, many of them.

I can't do your stories any justice at all. I can only acknowledge them and write this one.

I would also like to thank everyone who put work into helping me improve *Daisy Sale Forever,* especially: Pauline Chandra Graf, Kathleen Cleberg, Anne Gillespie Lewis, Elliott Foster, Dede Hirt, Maia Homstad, Patrice Johnson, Matt Leach, Nancy Marshall, Laura Miller, Allison Sandve, Kristen Swanson, Victoria Tirrel, and my wonderful daughter Zari Dehdashti. A Wayzata book club and St. Paul's St. Anthony Park Wednesday Study Club (founded in 1927!) also provided beta reading and corrected my poor French.

On the topic of adoption, I was fortunate to have readers and editors, especially Sarah Hannah Gómez, who helped me understand adoptee perspectives and enlightened me on numerous literary and cultural issues as well. All mistakes and transgressions are my own.

Printed in the USA
CPSIA information can be obtained
at www.ICGtesting.com
LVHW051216300924
792480LV00003B/11